# Death in Zooville

Carla Damron's
Caleb Knowles Mysteries

KEEPING SILENT

SPIDER BLUE

DEATH IN ZOOVILLE

# Death in Zooville

## A Caleb Knowles Mystery

# Carla Damron

BellaRosaBooks

BellaRosaBooks

DEATH IN ZOOVILLE
ISBN 978-1-933523-89-7

First Printed: April 2010

Library of Congress Control Number: 2010926793

Printed in the United States of America on acid-free paper.

Cover photograph by Jim Hussey

Book design by Bella Rosa Books

BellaRosaBooks and logo are trademarks of Bella Rosa Books

10      9      8      7      6      5      4      3      2      1

In Memory of Leona Lavallee,
A caring friend and advocate for "the least of these."

## Acknowledgments

I wish to thank Ed Damron, Jim Hussey, Anne Creed, Pam Knight, Stephanie Thompson, and the Inkplots Writers Group for helping me keep this book on the right path. Cyndy Storm, Gary Geer, Tom Hurley and Emily Boothe also assisted me on this project.

Special thanks to the clients and volunteers at the Columbia Winter Shelter who taught me so much about perseverance and human kindness.

A portion of the author's royalties will be used to help house the homeless.

# Death
## in
# Zooville

Enjoy Tanya —

Carl Dann

# Chapter One

Social worker Caleb Knowles handed a paper bag that contained soap, a toothbrush, toothpaste, and a razor to the man on the other side of the reception desk. Pete (just Pete, since he'd never admit to a last name) had scraggly sideburns and a birthmark like a map of Italy on his forehead. He crumpled the sack in his raw-knuckled hand.

"You'll be in bed one-twenty-seven." Caleb recorded the name in the log. It looked like both the men's and women's dorms would fill up by sundown, a sign of the unseasonably cold November hitting South Carolina. Behind Pete, the rows of plastic chairs in the waiting room sat empty at last. Four hours earlier, every seat had held some restless soul seeking food or a warm bed.

"Glad y'all got room for me," Pete said. "I was under the Gervais Street bridge last night. Dang, it got cold. Know how cold it was?"

"Well, the temps—"

"No, wait! Let me tell you." Pete splayed his fingers and bounced up on his toes, excited. "It was so cold that when I coughed up some spit, and it landed right on my boot, well, after about ten minutes, I could flick it off with my finger." Pete mimed shooting a marble across the floor. "That's cold, ain't it?"

Henry Rudd, Safe Harbor's recovery director, looked up from the sock donation he was sorting. "Yep, that's cold."

"At least you won't have to do any spit-flicking tonight." Caleb suppressed a smile. "So, anything you need to leave at the desk?"

Pete wedged a hand into a pocket of his jeans and pulled out a knife. All guests staying in one of the dorm buildings had to clear a metal detector. Caleb slid the weapon into an envelope which he marked with Pete's name. As Pete made his way outside to the line of clients ready for a bed, Henry said to Caleb, "We bought him those boots he's spitting on."

"Good multi-tasking boots." Caleb pressed a hand against his back, feeling bone-weary. A half-day shift at the homeless center, which was a combination food bank, shelter, and counseling program, proved more exhausting than a week at the private practice—Caleb's other job. His real job.

"What the—" Henry's dark eyes widened. Caleb turned to see a man carrying a gasoline can charging through the front door.

"Hey!" The man moved fast. Caleb could hear something slosh inside the can.

"Know him?" Caleb whispered.

"'Fraid so. Crazy idiot."

The man wore a hunter's vest, pockets bulging. His ratty beard held specks of lint, like he'd been sleeping in a dryer.

"Can I help you?" Caleb met the man's gaze, assessing the paranoid glint, the twitchy left eyebrow. Was he strung out needing a fix? Or psychotic?

"I came here for some help! That's all I ask, just give me a little help here!" He held out his left hand in a beseeching gesture but his right still gripped the gas can.

"Okay. How can we help you?" Caleb came around the counter but halted when the guy tilted the container like he planned to torch the place. "Is there gasoline in that thing?"

"Where's Esther? Where is she?"

"Why do you want Esther?" Caleb thought Esther was in the food pantry with Gina, his intern. He hoped they didn't venture to the lobby.

"All I wanted was something to eat. I was hungry, just wanted some crackers and peanut butter. But Esther kicked me out of here! Y'all supposed to be a charity. What kind of charity is that?" When he shook the can, gas trickled from the spout.

"We'll be glad to get you some food. Henry, why don't you—"

It happened so fast. The guy flicked the top off the nozzle. Lifted the can over his head, gasoline blurping out all over him, seeping into the bulging pockets of his vest, splashing over his faded camouflage pants. A pinkish puddle spreading beyond at his feet.

Henry slammed a hand against the intercom button and said "Code Red, reception," just as the man screamed "Shut up, shut up, shut up!"

Dizzying fumes filled the room.

"Hey, easy." Caleb's eyes stung. "What's your name?"

The guy didn't answer. "It's Wyman," Henry whispered.

"Wyman." Caleb did his best to keep his voice calm. "Let's talk this thing through. You don't want to hurt anyone. You came here for help so let us help you."

Wyman dropped the can and groped the pockets of his vest. When he pulled out a lighter, Henry muttered, "Crap."

"Building clear?" Caleb asked.

"Should be," Henry whispered. "And they should have called 911, so we can expect the police in an hour or two."

Caleb frowned at the ugly truth in those words. The police never rushed to respond to shelter calls. Which left Caleb and Henry to deal with Wyman, the human torch.

The man's hand trembled as it gripped the lighter. If he ignited it, there would be a fireball. If he ignited it, they could die.

"Easy, Wyman. Tell me what happened. What upset you earlier?" Caleb slowed his speech. Stalling, of course. Red streaks appeared on Wyman's face. Gas dripped from his sodden hair.

"Wipe your eyes," Henry said. "I got a towel here. You want to wipe your eyes so that stuff don't make you blind."

Wyman held out a hand for the towel Henry tossed to him. "You're a good man," Wyman said, his voice sluggish. "Not like Esther. She treats me like . . . like I'm a worm."

"You didn't deserve to be turned away, Wyman." Caleb made a point of repeating the name, an old social work trick, hoping to make some kind of connection. "We're not turning you away now. What do you want? Food? How about some—"

"Too late . . . Can't help." Wyman pointed the lighter at him, his thumb poised, ready to strike.

Message received. Caleb looked at Henry, who braved a step in Wyman's direction.

"No! Nobody . . . moves." He shook the lighter and said, "Boom."

Caleb blinked to clear his eyes of the tears building. His head felt hazy. Would he pass out? What else could happen from breathing gas fumes? Hallucinations. Destroyed brain cells, like he had any of those to spare.

His mind flashed on staccato images of Shannon and his daughter Julia and his brother Sam. People who need him to stay alive. He looked at Henry, unsure what to try next.

Wyman's mouth twisted, like the fumes were getting him high. He swayed, moving a foot to keep from falling. Henry stepped a little closer, but Wyman didn't seem to notice. Henry kept moving, easing around the waiting area like a wolf circling prey.

Wyman tilted to the right, sliding as he tried to catch himself, his eyes springing open.

"You don't look so good," Caleb said to get his attention. "Want to sit down?"

"Huh?"

Henry slipped behind the vinyl sofa, rounding the small end table near the entrance.

"I . . ." Wyman lifted the lighter. Henry lunged, grabbing him. Caleb skidded in the gasoline as he snared the lighter from Wyman's hand. Wyman's head rolled back, his knees buckled, and he passed out at Henry's feet.

"Damn," Henry said.

Sirens sounded. Caleb exhaled. "Guess the cavalry came after all."


A half hour later, Caleb and Henry sat in folding chairs in the Safe Harbor parking lot as the fire department took over the task of cleaning up the gas spill. A giant fan at the front door sucked the remaining fumes from the building. Caleb drew a long, deep inhalation of cold night air, savoring the delicious, sweet oxygen, inflating his lungs like giant red balloons. Out came another flurry of coughs. "Damn," he muttered.

He hated the smell of gasoline that wafted from his clothes, hair, and skin. The EMT said it might take days for him to stop smelling it. It would take a lot longer than that to forget what could have happened.

Henry lit a cigarette.

Caleb scooted his chair away from him. "You blow up, you're on your own."

Henry smiled and took a great big puff.

At the Safe Harbor entrance, Esther Lowell had a lot to say to the police officers who had arrived ten minutes after the fire truck. Esther was a round-bodied woman in gray polyester pants, her hair pulled into a frayed bun high on her head. She had a finger in one officer's face to punctuate her lecture.

Caleb wondered what had her so ticked, but for Esther, finger-wagging was an hourly event. Gina, the social work intern, stood beside her, looking like she'd rather be having a colonoscopy. He motioned her over.

"You okay?" she asked, bending over him. "You sure you don't need to go to the hospital?"

"I was just rescuing you from the Esther tirade."

Gina wrinkled her nose. Brown curls framing a pale, cherubic face, she looked so very, very young.

"How are you doing, Gina? Kind of scary tonight, huh?" Caleb couldn't help feeling protective of his intern and somehow responsible for this. Having her work at the private practice was one thing, but dragging her to Safe Harbor was something else entirely.

"It was exciting," she said, her eyes wide. "I was helping in the kitchen so I didn't know what was going on till Henry called the code. Then we had to go outside and wait. I sure didn't know you were in danger!"

Caleb studied her, trying to gauge how upset she was from the experience. "Social work isn't usually like this," he said. "I mean, I've been in this business for fifteen years and this is the first time someone's tried to ignite himself."

"First time?" Henry leaned back in his chair and puffed out smoke. "But you're new to this shelter work. Some of our clientele can be a bit, well, volatile."

Gina's eyes grew even wider. Behind her, Esther's voice rose, shrill as a kettle whistle.

"Some of the staff's a bit volatile, too," Henry added.

Another car pulled into the gravel lot and Henry rose from his chair. Bill Evers looked like a spider as he unfolded himself from his silver Mini Cooper. He was over six feet, lean, always well-dressed, hair as perfect as an anchorman. Bill was the executive director of Safe Harbor and a good friend of Dr. Matthew

Rhyker, Caleb's longtime boss.

"Everyone okay?" Bill asked.

"I smell like the Exxon Valdez," Caleb answered.

"That was oil," Henry said, then turned to Bill. "Any word on Wyman?"

"Still at the hospital. Having some respiratory problems and they're running some cardiac tests. But they told me he was conscious."

"I can't believe he would do something like this," Gina said.

Caleb and Henry exchanged surprised looks. "How do you know Wyman?" Caleb asked.

"I was helping Esther when he came this afternoon. And he came one other time. I think it was my first day working here."

"What happened with Esther?" Caleb glanced over at the bunned wonder, who had the fire chief on the receiving end of her tirade now.

"Wyman asked for some food," Gina said. "He said he was hungry. That he hadn't had a decent meal in three days. Esther said he had a home where they'd feed him but he wouldn't go there. She said he'd gotten stuff from us just a week ago and it was too soon to be back asking for more."

"You're damn right, that's what I said." Esther marched over, scowling. "I want Wyman locked up. I mean it, Bill. The man came here to kill me and I want him in jail."

"I've talked with law enforcement," Bill said. "They're questioning him now."

"What is there to question him about? He came here to burn the place down."

"What's Wyman's history?" Caleb asked. "Is he usually violent?"

"Not that I've ever seen," Henry said. "He comes and goes. Something ain't right upstairs—" Henry tapped his forehead, "but Wyman won't see the psychiatrist. We've tried to get him in a dozen times or more."

"He's a drug addict," Esther said. "I didn't give him anything because he'd just sell it on the streets. We're running low on supplies as it is."

They watched as the firefighters loaded their equipment back on their truck. With the fan gone, and the lights winking out, Safe

Harbor put itself to bed as though nothing had happened. Caleb heard light laughter from the dorm behind the building, where homeless men found a warm bed for the night.

"Hope this doesn't make the papers," Bill said. He turned to Caleb. "Did you call Dr. Rhyker?"

"No. I'll tell him in the morning." Caleb knew his boss wouldn't welcome the news.

The fire chief ambled over. "Keep the doors and windows open tomorrow, you'll want the ventilation. Other than that, we're done." He motioned his crew to the truck.

"Go home, get some rest," Bill said to Caleb and Henry. "You both stink, you know."

# Chapter Two

Caleb awoke to a cold nose pressed into his ribs. He scrambled to the other side of the bed—Shannon's side, but Shannon was in Maine—as Cleo, his sheepdog, romped around to give his face a lick. Caleb begrudgingly opened his eyes. The clock told him he'd overslept by twenty minutes, so he needed to get up, but someone had attached pliers to his cerebellum. Was he hung-over? No. Wyman. The gasoline. He could still smell it, as if his pores had absorbed the fumes. He untangled himself from the sheets and dragged his six-foot frame into the bathroom, trying to coax as much hot water as he could from the ancient faucet. There was no washing away the odor. Gasoline marinade.

Downstairs, Caleb poured a tall cup of coffee and drank half of it while he stood at the sink. He should hire a plumber to fix that dripping faucet, but Shannon would be home soon and she had exceptional handy-woman skills. He would add this to the list of repairs awaiting her return.

The call that told them that Shannon's father had fallen came two months before. Luke McPherson, a dairy farmer who at age eighty still worked seven days a week, lost his footing while fixing the barn roof. The broken hip required surgery, followed by intense and painful rehab. Shannon took a leave of absence from work so she could run the dairy business until Luke recovered, but Caleb hadn't expected it to take months. He tried his best not to complain. Shannon had enough on her plate up in that frozen tundra known as Maine, but he missed her. He missed having her in his home and in his bed and in his life. Besides, he had leaky pipes that needed fixing.

Cleo leaned against him, herding him to her empty food dish. He filled the bowl and set it on the back stoop. After three

Frisbee tosses, Caleb left her in the yard, refilled his cup, and headed to the car.


Fifteen minutes later, Caleb opened the heavy oak door of the restored Victorian home which housed the private counseling center. He marveled at the contrast between this office, where he worked mornings, and Safe Harbor, his afternoon and evening gig. The shelter's floors were scarred linoleum while the center had heart-pine planks, polished to a mirror shine. The office at Safe Harbor had no windows, smelled like mildew, and was furnished with creaky wicker rejects. Here at the center, his second-story office had floor-to-ceiling windows, leather chairs, and carpeting as soft as a comforter.

He grabbed his third cup of coffee from the break room— Costa Rican with frothed cream, not instant with powdered milk—before heading into the staff meeting. As he sat in the chair, he noticed Matthew's pointed look at his watch.

Dr. Matthew Rhyker was never late for anything. The man was fifty years old, yet he began every day with a two mile run and a healthy wheat-germ-tofu-pine-bark breakfast. If he didn't have rounds at the hospital, he made it to the practice a half hour before the first client, arriving freshly pressed, every silver hair in place.

"Hey, I meant to be on time," Caleb said, feeling a need to defend himself. "But I couldn't drag myself out of the shower." He could still smell the gasoline. Caleb Knowles, walking BP station. "Do I still stink? Be honest. I'm having olfactory hallucinations at this point."

Gina, in the chair beside him, scooted closer to sniff. "I don't smell anything."

"You're sure?"

Matthew cleared his throat.

"Sorry, boss," Caleb said.

Gina said, "You made the news."

"Crap." He looked over at Matthew. "Not by name. Tell me my name wasn't mentioned."

"Bill's decision. Gave the press your names to spin the story. Made you and Henry out to be heroes."

"Double crap."

"Better call your brother. If he doesn't know yet, he will soon."

Caleb stepped out of the conference room and slid his cell phone out of its holster. Talking to Sam required the QWERTY keyboard. He typed the text message: **If you saw the news, I'm fine. FINE. I'll stop by later.** Maybe Sam hadn't seen the news. He was probably at his workshop getting his sculpture exhibit ready for the opening next month. Sam had made quite a name for himself as an artist and did his damnedest to meet the demand for his work. Lucky bastard.

Caleb often wondered how poor his typing skills would be if he didn't have a deaf brother. Sam lost his hearing when he was sixteen in a motorcycle accident, so they stayed connected through text messaging and sign language. Caleb had become quite proficient in both.

He returned to the meeting where Gina was presenting a case from the shelter: Cindy Lowman, a young mother who'd lost her husband, her job, and most recently, custody of her two kids because of crack addiction. She had stayed in Safe Harbor's women's dorm for four weeks. So far, all urine screens had come back negative for drugs.

"She's been clean for a month," Gina said with a wide smile. "So she gets to see her kids at Social Services."

"Is she dual?" Matthew asked.

Confused, Gina looked over at Caleb. "Dual means having both an addiction and a mental illness. Dual disorders," Caleb said.

"I'm . . . not sure," Gina stuttered. "I mean, she doesn't see the psychiatrist or anything."

"What does her treatment plan say? Is there an Axis One diagnosis?" Matthew pushed.

"Uhmm. I'm not sure I did one," she said.

"You wouldn't," Caleb interrupted. "It should have been done before they gave you her case. Barb should have done it, or Esther. And Dr. McAbee would have signed off."

"Yeah, I guess," she stumbled again. "I should have brought the chart. It must be in there somewhere."

"Good idea," Matthew said, patience clearly strained. "You

shouldn't present a case if you don't have the salient information. If I don't at least have a diagnosis, I have no way to give you guidance about what you should do next."

Caleb arched his brows at Matthew's pedantic tone. Gina was a student, doing her best. "We'll bring it next time," Caleb said. "But Gina, it's great that Cindy isn't using. You're doing good work with her."

Matthew looked down at his appointment book. "I've got a client coming in. We'll finish this up tomorrow."

Gina shot out of her chair like it had been set afire. Caleb started after her but Matthew stopped him.

"I know you think I'm hard on her, but she's a bright kid. This is how she's going to learn."

Caleb thought about arguing, but the little vein bulging on Matthew's jaw changed his mind. "What else is bothering you?"

"Just worried about the media coverage after last night. Couldn't be worse timing." As chair of Safe Harbor's board of directors, Matthew had a lot to worry about. The shelter lost a major funding source when a federal grant ran out. Local business leaders, eager to develop this neglected area of downtown—and eager to do away with the growing number of street people in Westville—wanted the shelter closed. When Safe Harbor's counseling and outreach program lost its director two months ago, Matthew had volunteered Caleb to work part-time at the shelter to help it get back on its feet. So far, it was resting too comfortably on its backside.

"Check in with me this afternoon," Matthew said, before disappearing into his office.

Gina sat in the small office beside Janice's, fingers clicking in a frenzy on the computer. "Careful, I see smoke coming from that thing," Caleb said.

She closed the file on her monitor.

"Chatting with someone?"

She blushed. "Just a friend. Hope that's okay. I mean, nobody mentioned an email policy."

"I don't think we have an email policy." When had they needed one? Their office manager Janice tried to communicate with it but had little success. She'd email Caleb a question and he'd yell the answer out his door. Matthew printed his emails and hand-wrote his response. "It's hopeless," Janice often said. "You're both utterly hopeless."

Caleb took a seat in the tiny office. They had used the room for storage before. When a colleague from the university approached Caleb about taking on an intern, they'd cleaned it out, wired it for phone and data, and bought a few pieces of furniture. Janice added the area rug, the two framed prints, the table lamp, and curtains. Gina seemed to like it, bringing one of those Zen sand thingies with a tiny rake for the table. A litter box in miniature.

"So Matthew was a little hard on you this morning," Caleb said.

Her smile capsized on her face.

"It gets like that sometimes," Caleb said. "He's a very patient man but he's under a lot of pressure right now."

"He does so much," she said, mouth still taut. "His work here. Rounds at the hospital. The shelter."

"Yeah. And he's worried about Safe Harbor. There are some bad financial problems and they're down on staff. Hiring hasn't been easy. Matthew's the board chair so he has to worry about that stuff."

"I guess everybody has a bad mood now and then."

"And next time, we'll have the file for the client so we can answer whatever he asks." He stood. "You okay?"

"Yeah, but speaking of clients, I have a question. What if one turns out to be someone you knew before? What do you do then?"

"Has that happened?"

"I think I recognized a guy from my high school. Just wasn't sure if I should say anything to him. What should I do?"

"You have to let the client take the lead. Sometimes they'll walk right up to you and start chatting. But often they're embarrassed and won't want you to acknowledge you know them. They need to feel the counseling center—or Safe Harbor—is a place where their privacy is protected. Do you understand?"

"I think so."

"The same holds true if you run into a client out in the community." It had happened a hundred times, the impromptu client contact in the grocery store or gas station or library. He'd never forget bumping into a client when buying emergency sanitary products for Shannon. Talk about awkward.

"So unless you're doing a home visit, you need to let the client take the lead."

She nodded thoughtfully. "Got it."

Caleb checked his watch as he headed back to his office. Not quite ten, so he had a few minutes before his first client. He could get a few progress notes done, which would please both Janice and his cranky boss.

Or not. Sitting in his office was a tall, muscular man, looking right at home, playing with Caleb's favorite Slinky.

Caleb tapped on his shoulder and signed: "Who let you in here?"

"Janice. She said you didn't have a client. She's getting me coffee." Janice never got coffee for Caleb. Ever. Caleb scowled when she came back to the office and handed the cup to Sam. She actually blushed when Sam thanked her.

"What is it with you and women?" Caleb signed as she left.

"What are you implying?" Sam said over the cup.

"Nothing." Caleb slapped the back of his hand against the fingertips of the other. "So what's up?"

"Just checking on you. Got your text. Saw the news." Because Sam hadn't become deaf until he was a teenager, he spoke articulately, except when he was upset or rushed. And his lip reading skills carried him in most social situations. But sometimes hearing people forgot he was deaf. If they turned away from him, or several people spoke at once, he lost track of conversation, a source of endless frustration. An interpreter was always a good idea, and Caleb prided himself for being one of the best.

"So they say you're a hero?" Sam said, smirking.

Caleb flexed his biceps like a strong man contestant and Sam laughed. Caleb liked hearing it. After weathering a few difficult years, including the murder of his fiancée and almost losing Caleb himself last spring, Sam had changed. He was more relaxed, even confident. Over the past few months, he'd agreed to give art lectures and managed to drag Caleb out to eat at least once a week. It was good to see Sam doing well, even happy.

"You are okay, though, right?" Sam suddenly turned serious. "You were breathing that stuff for a while."

"I'm fine!" Caleb said, splaying his fingers and tapping his thumb against his chest. "No destroyed brain cells. Well, no more than usual. You don't need to worry about me."

Sam lowered the coffee. "I promised Shannon to check in on you and she's definitely going to want a full report."

"No. Don't tell her. No reason in the world for her to know." Caleb could imagine how he'd feel if it was her, if she'd been in danger and he was half a country away.

Sam took another sip. "Have you heard from her lately?"

"I called her the other night. She sounded exhausted," Caleb signed. Shannon worked long, strange hours. At the barn by four A.M., home for a few hours midday then back for another milking later in the afternoon. No days off because the cows needed milking seven days a week. There was no such thing as a bovine Sabbath.

"How's her dad doing?" Sam asked.

"Still struggling. Rehab's been a struggle."

"Got to be cold up in Maine."

"She said they had six inches of snow." Caleb tried to be supportive. Shannon was making a huge sacrifice to help her dad, but her absence changed things. They'd lived together for three years and he wanted her home, selfish jerk that he was.

"She misses you," Sam said.

"I miss her too." Caleb's office phone buzzed, signaling his appointment had arrived. He pointed to it to let Sam know. "My appointment's here."

Sam stood, stretching. He was just a few inches taller than Caleb, though more broad and muscular from his years as a carpenter and sculptor. Had the chiseled features and thick blondish hair, too. Disgusting older sibling. "Guess I'll be going, then," Sam said. He handed Caleb the coffee cup. "Finish this. You look like you need it."

Wyman Carter shivered against the air blowing down on him. Not cold air like outside, but cool air breathing on his face. Through slitted eyes he could see a white ceiling, a silver vent, and a small window. His mouth was dry as fireplace ash.

The place had a nasty-clean smell: a hospital. A sheet covered most of him. His right arm lay bare beside him, attached to the bedrail by a metal cuff. Someone had taped a needle to the inside of his elbow, pinching his skin. What were they pumping into him? Some kind of poison that made his mind all blurry.

A pony-tailed man opened the door, carrying a tray. He elbowed the wall switch. Fluorescent lights blinked on.

"Mr. Carter?" The guy put the tray on a little table beside him. "Time for lunch. Wake up, Mr. Carter."

Lunch. Food. Damn, wasn't that that what got him into this mess? He went to Safe Harbor and the squinchy-faced Esther wouldn't give him a thing to eat. Not a cracker. Not an apple or can of juice. Turned him away like he was nothing better than a stray dog. He'd left Safe Harbor twitching with rage, his hunger gnawing inside him.

The man lifted a brown cover from the food and shifted the table so that it swung over Wyman. Peaches. Some kind of sandwich. A milk carton with a tiny straw attached. The guy pried off the straw and poked it through the top of the carton before replacing it on the tray.

He smelled like cigarette smoke. Wyman breathed in the scent, savoring it. Though it wasn't a cigarette he wanted, but something better. Sometimes he wanted it so bad it was like a giant itch inside that couldn't be scratched. It made him do stupid things, though. Stupid things like what happened yesterday, or was it the day before?

"I'll be back for the tray in a little while. Don't give us any trouble. There's a policeman right outside your door."

Police. Wyman remembered a couple of officers at Safe Harbor. And firemen. And a giant fan that sounded loud as a diesel truck. And the gasoline and how it smelled when it covered him, and getting tackled before he could flick the lighter, and barfing all over somebody's boots. Oh God, it hadn't been a dream.

When the pony-tailed guy left him, Wyman wondered how he was supposed to eat with his right hand locked up. But damn, he was hungry. He fumbled with the top bun on the sandwich and lifted what looked like some kind of chicken thing. He shoved it in his mouth, wishing it wasn't so dry and dull-tasting, but glad to have something going in his belly. Next came the milk, which he sucked down in a few gulps. He didn't bother with a fork to eat the peaches, just popped the chunks into his mouth and let them slide on down. He'd like more food. A lot more.

A pale yellow packet rested on the tray, probably mayonnaise or something. Wyman couldn't see a packet like that without thinking about his friend Stormy. Stormy would steal little ketchup packs from McDonalds and bring them to the tent village where they used to live. He'd squeeze it into a cup of hot water, then brag to everybody it was delicious tomato soup. Stormy was always doing crazy stuff like that. Stuff that made Wyman laugh. And there wasn't anybody as good at dumpster-diving as Stormy was. He was short and skinny as a twig but he could scrabble up the metal side of a restaurant trash bin and gather food enough for the both of them before anyone knew he'd done it.

Wyman tossed the mustard pack back on the tray. Stormy. Just thinking about him made something twist inside. Made him think about the mistakes he'd made, and how mad Stormy got. Made him remember Stormy's blood dripping through his fingers. Carrying Stormy's body to the river because he had to do right by him. His only real friend, Stormy.

Damn him. Hurt and rage filled Wyman like a white hot light. He had to get out of this damn place. He jerked his cuffed wrist hard enough to rattle the bed rail, but it wouldn't give. He tried squeezing his hand out of the contraption, crushing his knuckles as he tried to pull free, but breaking skin, not metal.

"Hey! Stop that!" The policeman who entered had a crew cut and pimple scars on his face. He moved to the foot of Wyman's bed, his hand resting on the butt of his gun.

Wyman gave the rail another rattle just to make his point. The officer came closer. He looked barely old enough to shave. "You better settle down. They got drugs here that will send you to la-la land and make you pee on yourself. I will ask for them if you don't calm yourself."

Drugs. He wondered what they'd give him. Nothing he wanted, because what he wanted wasn't in a hospital. No, what he wanted was miles away. He burrowed down in the bed, closed his eyes, and thought about what he'd do once he escaped.

# Chapter Three

Caleb parked his car in the Safe Harbor parking lot, but didn't even make it out of the car. Lanie Dupree rushed to his Subaru, bending over so that her plump face filled the window like a close-up in a carnival film. "You called them cops on me, didn't you!" she yelled. Her purple lipstick smudged his window.

"Huh?" Caleb climbed out and tried to maneuver around her, but Lanie wasn't budging. She propped a hand on her generous hip, her round five-foot frame a definite encumbrance to his task of getting into the building.

"The cops! They're here! I know you called them!" she yelled.

It was about the hundredth time Lanie Dupree had accused him of something nefarious. Last week, she claimed he reported her to the FBI. The week before, he'd stolen a million dollars from her purse while she slept. Lanie had been living on the streets for ten years because she was too paranoid to live anywhere else. At least she came to Safe Harbor for medications, which, given her mental illness, he considered a miracle.

"No, I didn't call them." Caleb kept his tone affable but firm, the way he dealt with most of her delusions.

"But they're here." She jabbed a finger toward a police car parked by the front door.

Okay, not a delusion this time.

"They said there's a dead guy. They said they found him by the river. I saw the picture. He was all bloated up." Lanie did her best to keep up with Caleb, her short squat legs doing double time as he hurried up the steps.

"Where are the police now?"

"They with the pretty man."

"Pretty man?"

"Mr. Bill," she said, waddling along beside him.

Caleb smiled. Bill Evers did have that perfect hair thing going, but pretty? Not a word he'd use. He reached the battered front door, heard the familiar squeal of rusted hinges as he opened it and stepped inside.

He braved a deep breath. Barely a hint of the gasoline smell, though there was another odor coming from the men in the waiting area, one of whom was snoring. Caleb heard chatter from the food pantry down the hall, like normal. No Wyman. No imminent explosion. Lanie took a seat in the farthest chair and grabbed a magazine. Henry looked up from the reception desk.

"Lanie was explaining that we've had some excitement again today," Caleb said.

"I prefer things to be boring."

"Did you recognize the guy in the photo?"

"Wasn't much there to recognize. Guy had a Safe Harbor meal ticket that somehow survived the river. They'll probably pass the photo around for a few hours, then bury him as a John Doe." He ran a hand over his shaved head. His understanding of the plight of the homeless came from firsthand experience. Eight years ago, he'd been on the streets himself, but Henry was clean now and worked at Safe Harbor as part of his personal recovery plan. "I know them fellas," he once told Caleb. "Makes it harder for them to BS me."

"Where'd they find the body?" Caleb asked.

"Just down the river from Zooville," Henry said.

"Zooville?"

"I didn't name it. It's the tent village on the river just across from the zoo. So some of the people who stay there call it Zooville." He cocked a thumb towards the hall leading to staff offices. "The police'll talk to you when they're done with Bill. Sorry."

"It's okay."

The large appointment book lay spread out on the reception counter. A long list of clients were by his name; he would be in for a busy afternoon if they all showed. But most were like Lanie Dupree and rarely kept a scheduled appointment.

He looked over at Lanie sitting by the window, a pair of cracked sunglasses perched on her nose. She wore them to keep others from reading her thoughts.

"Has Lanie gotten her shot yet?" Caleb asked, loud enough for her to hear.

"Nope," Henry said. "She promised me she wasn't going to give Dr. McAbee no trouble."

"Then I'm sure she won't." Caleb gave the paranoid woman a quiet smile.

"I better not," she said, slapping the magazine shut. "Cause y'all gonna just call the police on me."

"Whatever works," Henry whispered.

Caleb made his way to the small room they called his office. The combination of the wicker desk and chairs, fluffy pink pillows, and plastic flower arrangements protruding from wall sconces made him feel like a Ken doll in Malibu Barbie's dream house. The furnishings had been left by the former clinical director, after she abruptly resigned. The only item that actually looked like office furniture was the dented three-drawer file cabinet in the corner. He tugged open the top drawer and grabbed a file on one of the clients he'd inherited who might or might not show that afternoon.

Bill Evers stopped by his office. "Caleb? You feeling okay? Any problems from the gasoline?"

"I'm fine."

"The police have a photo they want you to see," he said, his voice meek. Nothing about Bill made Caleb view him as guy-in-charge. Bill's tone was always hesitant, every sentence like an apology. Add in the TV-ready hair, the piano-key white teeth, the buttoned-to-the-Adam's-apple shirt, you get a man more suited for insurance work than riding herd on a bustling homeless center.

"Yeah, I figured."

"You should have," another voice—a female voice—boomed. Detective Claudia Briscoe let herself in Caleb's office, scanned the tiny room, and helped herself to a seat by his desk. Bill backed away, looking a bit stunned by her dramatic entrance.

Claudia grinned. "Caleb, Caleb. What are you doing here?"

"I work here."

"You work here." She lifted a plastic-weave covered tissue box. "Really?"

"Mr. Knowles is our part-time therapist." Bill seemed to feel a need to justify Caleb's presence. "Caleb, this is Detective—"

"Briscoe," Caleb interrupted. "It's okay. I know her."

Bill made a hasty exit, leaving Caleb with Claudia. She had been his client years ago, when just starting out as a cop, dealing with the stress of being a black female in a world of white Bubbas in blue. Counseling only took a few months, more for support than treatment. Two years later, she made detective and the police department hired Caleb to consult. It was awkward at first, this change in their relationship, until they'd worked it out and learned to respect—even like—one another. Most of the time.

"Love the new digs." Claudia's crimson-nailed fingers plucked at the yarn covering the tissue box.

"Matthew's idea. Just until Bill hires full-time staff."

"So he rented you out?"

"Let's just say I'm on loan."

"You heard about our corpse?" Claudia asked.

"Oh yeah. Heard all about him. Nice of y'all to flash that picture to the clients."

"I know. But we've turned up nothing but dead ends, so we kind of hoped someone here might be able to identify him." She reached in a portfolio for a manila envelope. "Can you take a look?"

He didn't want to. He'd seen more than his share of dead bodies because of the consulting work he did with the police, but before he could answer, she had the photos spread out in front of him.

They weren't what he expected. The body rested against a rock, his lower legs still dangling in the river. Mottled, streaked flesh could be seen in the tears of a green shirt. The ballooned face was hardly human, the eyes just little dark dents. He slid the photo back to her. "Nobody I know. Not that there's much to recognize."

"I had to ask."

He knew that, knew it was her job. Yet he hated her, at that moment, for it. "How'd he die?"

"Two cuts to the torso." She tucked the pictures away. "We don't have any leads. Just the Safe Harbor meal ticket."

"I don't think showing those pictures are gonna get you any

closer."

"You're probably right." She stood. "If you hear of anyone being missing, or have any other ideas about this guy, give me a call?"

"Sure."

She looked around again. "Is Matthew mad at you or something?"

"Could be. Reckon this is my 'time out' chair?"

"I'm sure you deserve it."


"You really screwed up this time, didn't you?"

Wyman tried to open his eyes. They felt like they were cemented shut.

"Wyman!" the voice snarled. "Look at me. We don't got much time."

Time. What time? He could hear another voice, farther away, like maybe a weather or news report. He liked that weather lady on channel nine. Her blond hair always looked so soft he wanted to touch it.

"The cop outside the door won't give me much time here. So wake your ass up and talk to me!"

Wyman opened his eyes and tried to focus on the fat man standing beside his bed. "Why didn't you call me? You know what you're supposed to do when you get in a fix! Christ, I had to find out you were arrested from the damn ER doctor."

Markham. He hadn't seen Markham in weeks, yet here he was, all red-faced and sweaty. Why'd they have to call him?

"Did you say anything to the police?" Markham asked, his voice urgent.

"P . . . police? When?"

"At the shelter. The place you tried to burn down, you idiot. Did you talk to them?" Markham had a habit of spitting when he spoke, tiny droplets spraying the white sheet covering Wyman.

"No. Didn't." As he tugged at the cotton blanket with his encumbered hand, the handcuff rattled against the bedrail.

"Good. That's good. Keep it that way." Markham slid a chair over to sit by Wyman's bed. "So what the hell were you thinking? Why did you try to burn the place?"

"Don't know. Don't remember."

"It could land your ass in prison. I'm doing everything I can to keep that from happening, but you have to do your part. Don't say a word to the police. I mean it. Play dumb. We both know you do that quite well."

Wyman didn't want to go back to jail. He'd done nine months in juvenile detention seven years ago and hated every second of it. Being locked in a dorm with a bunch of hoodlums. Having to take classes from that fat, acne-faced teacher who looked down on all the boys like they were cockroaches. The counselor who kept trying to get his mother to come in for family sessions, even though Wyman said not to. Even though his mother told the counselor she no longer thought of Wyman as family. People liked to control what Wyman did, who he was.

People like Markham.

"You listening to me?" Markham stood up again, bending over him. He smelled like onions.

"Thirsty." Wyman smacked his parched lips as he looked around for a water jug. Regular hospitals gave you water. The psych ones expected you to get up and get it for yourself. He heard the click and rattle of a cart being rolled down the hall. Maybe they'd bring him something else to eat.

Markham poured a cup of water and handed it to him. Wyman's left hand trembled as he brought it to his lips, water dribbling over his chest. His other arm stung where the IV needle dug into it. He wished he could rip it out and get the hell out of this place.

"The doc's gonna be here in a minute," Markham said. "I need you to let me do the talking. I'm gonna fix it so they give you some of that happy juice that makes you sleep. Should help with the cravings, and keep you from running your mouth off when you shouldn't. Then I'll find a way to get you out of here."

Wyman braved another sip of water. Getting out sounded fine to him.

"I'm hoping I won't have to call your family," Markham said.

"Don't!" He dropped the cup, water splashing his pillow and mattress. "Don't call them!" The thought of them made his insides twist. It had been so long, and he liked it that way. They didn't want him any more than he wanted them.

"You should have thought about that before you did something so stupid. I got a job to do here." Markham shut up when the door opened.

A man with caramel-colored skin came in, holding a chart and pen. He had a stethoscope hanging around his pencil-thin neck. "I see we're awake," he said. "I'm Doctor Whitney."

Wyman hated all doctors. They asked questions he didn't want to answer and poked him places nobody should be poked and pumped poison into his veins. The man reached for his cuffed hand and gave it a shake. A fat ring glimmered on his finger, probably worth a few hundred at the pawn shop.

"My name is Markham Dougherty." Markham moved to the foot of the bed. "I'm Wyman's legal guardian. He stays with me in my boarding home."

"That so? Mr. Carter looks like he's been living on the streets a while."

"He keeps running off from the home. I spend a lot of time hunting him down. Restless spirit, I guess."

"That true, Mr. Carter? You have a restless spirit?" The doctor wasn't looking at Wyman. He started writing something in the chart. Wyman didn't answer.

"Wyman's still a bit confused," Markham said. "I hope he doesn't get too agitated. He can be a real fighter when he gets going."

The doctor wrote something else down. "You feeling upset right now, Mr. Carter?"

Markham gave Wyman a pointed look and nodded.

"Maybe . . . some," Wyman said.

"He was trying to get out of bed just a second ago. I had to remind him he was cuffed to the rail. You didn't hear him rattling it?" Markham said.

Wyman didn't remember trying to move. He squinted at Markham who nodded again.

"You need to stay put, Mr. Carter. We're trying to take good care of you here."

"Can't you give him something for his nerves? Something that will settle him down?"

Wyman looked over at the IV drip. He didn't want more garbage pumped into him. He tried to grab the metal pole to make his point. The doctor jumped back like he thought Wyman might hit him.

"Easy, Wyman!" Markham said. "Let the doctor take a look at you. Maybe he can give you a couple of Valium to settle them jumpy nerves of yours. You do good on that stuff, don't you?"

Wyman nodded. Valium smoothed down his edges and made his head go quiet. Ativan was good, too. He hoped Markham would remember to say that. But some of the other drugs they sometimes gave him turned his brained to oatmeal.

The doctor's stethoscope was cold against Wyman's skin. "Well, your lungs are starting to clear. You're lucky there was no permanent damage from the fumes. And I guess we're all lucky you didn't burn the shelter down."

Wyman wished he had gasoline with him right then. Before it made him sick, it would make him high. If he couldn't get his hands on crack, gasoline would do.

"You in much pain?" the doctor asked.

He looked at Markham who nodded again. "Some burning still when I breathe."

"We'll up the pain killers and add some valium for your nerves. Not sure what they'll give you when you get transferred to the jail though." He did more scribbling in the record, checked the IV, and left them.

Markham reached in his pocket for a crumpled twenty. "Here. I'll stick this in your pillow case. Make sure you grab it when they move you out of here."

A twenty would buy him a few hits. It had been too long, and he ached for it. Twenty would fix him up just fine.

He would find a way out of here. Everything would be okay.


Caleb settled into his leather chair and savored the cup of coffee topped with frothed milk he had every morning at the counseling center. He could smell a faint lemon scent from when the janitor had dusted his office last night. The piles of papers on his desk had been neatened, pink message slips tidied in a stack by his phone. Plants by the window had been watered. And no scratchy old wicker in sight.

The appointment book told him he had four clients that

morning, each of whom was likely to actually come for the appointment. After those sessions, he would have a nice lunch, maybe with Matthew, and head over to Safe Harbor. Where none of his appointments would show yet he'd still see six clients. Where he might help with the unloading of a truck or sort a vegetable donation or hand out hygiene products to men who hadn't showered in weeks. Caleb smiled. Both jobs had their high points.

Matthew greeted him from the hallway, holding a coffee mug and a granola bar.

"That breakfast?" Caleb asked.

"I'm afraid so. Got tied up on the phone this morning. Even missed my run."

"What was it?"

"Bill Evers called, in a panic. He's been summoned to the mayor's office to talk about the future of Safe Harbor."

"Summoned doesn't sound good."

"It's not." Matthew took a seat in Caleb's office. "There are some developers who are eyeing that section of Westville. Of course, they won't touch it with the homeless center there. Bill's afraid the county will try to close Safe Harbor."

"Yikes. Can they do that?"

"Safe Harbor is a non-profit, and a third of its budget is county funding. They cut that and we'll have a big problem." He frowned. "I hadn't realized the financial mess the shelter was already in. Not sure how they can hire anybody. Not even sure how they're making payroll now."

Caleb blew on his cup as he considered this. "Then maybe I should pull out. Don't want them thinking I can stay forever."

"Is that what you want to do?" Matthew was giving him that probing look, ever the psychiatrist.

"Nah. It's interesting work, really. But it isn't fair for you to pay my salary while I'm spending almost half my time down there. Not that I'm volunteering for a pay cut."

"Could you hang on there a few more weeks?"

"Sure. You think they'll have someone by then?"

"Probably not. But I'd like you there while we're dealing with this county stuff. Keep an eye on the staff, make sure their morale isn't negatively affected."

"I don't see much in the way of staff burn-out, except Esther. People work there because they love it."

"Good. Let's hope we can keep it that way."

Janice's voice came through his phone. "You've got Detective Briscoe on line two."

He grabbed the receiver. "Claudia?"

"Got a consult but I'm not sure you should do it. Dr. Rhyker would be a better choice."

"Dr. Rhyker will cost you more." Caleb grinned at his boss. "What's the case?"

"Wyman Carter, your gasoline guy. He's still in the hospital and he's facing multiple charges. But we're not sure how competent he is. Guy looks crazier than a loon to me, but that's more your area."

"What kind of charges?"

"Captain Bentille says there may be federal WMD charges."

"WMD?"

"Weapon of Mass Destruction. That's bad. That could mean a life sentence."

"Good Lord. He's no terrorist, Claudia." Caleb could picture Bentille in front of the TV cameras, distorting the incident with Wyman to make the police—make himself—out to be heroes. It was just the kind of thing he'd exploit.

"I'm not arguing with you. But we need to figure out if his little stunt was based on being crazy or being homicidal. That's where Dr. Rhyker comes in."

"Hold on a second." Caleb pressed hold. "What's your schedule like today? Any time for a consult?"

"Booked solid, I'm afraid. Maybe tomorrow?" He checked his watch and gestured that he had to get going.

Caleb considered seeing Wyman himself. He'd need to be objective. Objective about the facts of the crime, but sympathetic about the symptoms. The last time he'd seen the man, Caleb had almost been killed. Almost. It might be interesting to see Wyman in a safe environment. Maybe Caleb could get answers as to why he'd done such a bizarre thing.

He went back to the line where Claudia waited. "Matthew's busy. I'll do it, but it will have to be this afternoon."

"Caleb," her tone softened. "This guy almost blew you to hell.

Might be better to let your boss handle it."

"I'll give it a shot. If he makes me feel squirrelly I'll pull out."

"You're sure?"

He wasn't sure. And if he discussed it with Matthew, his boss would tell him he was nuts, then give him one of his favorite lectures on having boundaries. Caleb said to Claudia, "I'll be there."

"I'll let the officers watching him know to expect you."


Wyman had his own room on the third floor, not the psych unit. A uniformed officer showed Caleb in, noting that Wyman had been cuffed to the bed frame "as a precaution," but Caleb saw nothing threatening about the man on the bed. He looked both very young and very old. His size made him seem almost boyish, so thin he barely made a bulge under the sheets, yet his face looked tough as an old saddle. How old was he? Where had he come from?

And from the looks of him, Caleb might not get any answers today. Wyman slept, his head tilted to the side, drool trailing from the corner of his mouth.

"Hey, Carter! Wake up!" The officer shook the bed. No response. "Wake up, you got company!" He grabbed the patient's foot, giving it a rough shake.

"Wh . . . at?" Wyman's eyes blinked open. He rubbed his mouth against the pillow case and pulled up a little.

"Want me to stay while y'all chat?" the officer asked Caleb.

"No, that won't be necessary."

"I'll be right out the door then."

Caleb waited for him to exit before easing closer to the patient. Was this the same person from the other afternoon? The man who tried to set himself on fire and burn down the shelter? The memory brought a mental shudder.

"Hey, Wyman. Do you remember me?"

Wyman's gaze drifted around the room until finally fixing on Caleb's face. He let out a loud cough.

"How are you feeling?" Caleb asked.

He coughed again, spit spraying on the sheet. Wyman wasn't exactly in a position to cover his mouth. He peered up at Caleb for a long moment. "I forgot your name."

"I'm Caleb Knowles. Do you remember how we met?"

Wyman's lips moved as though talking, but no sound came. He flinched, his head twisting to the right.

"Wyman?" Caleb came closer. Wyman's lips kept moving in a breathy whisper.

"I can't hear you."

"Huh?" Wyman looked at him, eyes wide like he was surprised to see Caleb.

"Now try to focus. Do you remember me?"

He turned his head away. "You were there at the front desk."

"Yes I was." Caleb's mind flashed back to that evening: Wyman dousing himself, the smell and the lighter and his thoughts of not being alive anymore. Maybe Matthew should have done this visit after all.

"You gonna hurt me?" Wyman's voice sounded strange, like he expected some revenge to be extracted, but didn't really mind it. Learned helplessness?

"No, I don't want to hurt you."

Wyman closed his eyes. The murmuring started again, and Caleb came closer to see if he could make out what Wyman said. "Not hurt, not hurt, not hurt," Wyman repeated.

"That's right, I'm not going to hurt you."

Wyman's voice faded to nothing, but his mouth moved, forming more unspoken words. Responding to internal stimuli, Caleb realized. Voices probably. Drug related? But surely drugs or alcohol would have worked out of his system by now.

"Can you look at me, Wyman?" Caleb asked.

Wyman ran his tongue over his lip and eyed the water pitcher.

"Thirsty?" Caleb reached for the plastic container and the cup beside it. After filling the cup, he adjusted the straw so that Wyman could take a sip. He took a long draw, paused, then slurped up the rest.

"Thanks," he said.

Caleb replaced the cup on the table. "Do you remember what happened?"

"Some of it. Some's a little foggy." Wyman looked to his right, as though some invisible person had just entered the room.

"Did you hear something?" Caleb asked.

Wyman lifted the hand hindered by the handcuff. "S . . . something."

"Do you hear voices?"

Wyman's focus went to Caleb, his eyes wide like he was startled, or maybe afraid.

"It's okay," Caleb said. "Tell me about them."

"N . . . ot supposed to."

"Who told you that?"

"Mr. Markham. N . . . ot supposed to look crazy."

"Who is this Mr. Markham?"

"He takes . . . he takes care of me."

"Takes care of you, huh?" Caleb wondered what kind of care the man offered. Was he Wyman's crack dealer? Pimp?

Wyman nodded, his eyes squeezing shut.

"Wyman? Can you look at me?"

The patient obeyed, eyelids sagging as he tried to focus.

"I need you to answer a few questions then I'll let you sleep, okay?"

"Okay." Wyman slid down, trying to pull the sheet up over him.

Caleb helped with the cover. "Who is Markham?"

"Mr. Markham . . . I stay at . . . the Willows."

That, too, sounded familiar. "Is it a group home?"

He nodded.

"You stay there all the time?" Caleb couldn't imagine what kind of group home would let Wyman get so emaciated and fail to provide enough supervision to keep him from trying to set himself on fire.

"Not all the time. Some of the time."

"When were you last there?"

Wyman started the silent conversation again. It seemed hard to engage him in Caleb's reality, the reality of four walls and a hospital bed, when something firing along Wyman's neurons kept pulling his attention inward.

"Wyman?"

"Huh?"

"Concentrate. I just have a few more questions." Caleb smiled, trying to appear patient.

"Did . . . did my mother send you?" Wyman asked.

"Your mother? No, your mother didn't send me." The question took Caleb by surprise. Wyman had family close by? "What's your mother's name?"

Wyman shook his head, murmuring again. Caleb stepped closer and heard, "A secret, a secret."

"Her name's a secret?"

"No, no." Wyman smiled. His lips contorted, his chin pulled to the side. "I'm the secret. I'm the secret."

And then he laughed. A quiet cackle. "I'm the secret!" he repeated, louder.

"Wyman?"

"I'm the *secret!*" Wyman pulled on the cuffs, rattling the bed frame.

The officer opened the door and came inside. "You okay in here?"

"Uh, fine," Caleb said. "I think I'm done here."

# Chapter Four

Caleb dug in the glove compartment of his car for the police department ID badge that defined him as a "medical consultant." He hated wearing the damn thing, but it would fast-track him through the metal detector and the gate keepers stationed at the front desk. But where had he left it? And why did he have two orange crayons in the glove box, one of which had melted on his car registration? Julia. No doubt his six-year-old didn't want him stranded on some distant highway without an Atomic Tangerine Crayola at his immediate disposal.

There. He spotted the ID badge stuck to a service invoice. After scraping a few bits of orange wax on the photo, he clipped the credential to his pocket and climbed out of the car.

The lobby of the police department was surprisingly quiet. The place usually teemed with activity, every seat holding some impatient customer, but today only a half-dozen people waited, most slouched in chairs like they'd been there a while. As soon as Caleb tapped his ID against the reception window, the desk officer motioned him back without even asking him to sign in. So far, so good.

Caleb heard Claudia's voice echoing down the hall: "You said you'd have it to me yesterday. I can't do my job on this until you finish yours."

As he reached the door to her office, she slammed the receiver into its cradle, grumbling a word he'd never heard come from her mouth. He froze, took a step back, deciding to postpone this conversation until another—calmer—time.

"What?" Her black eyes like lasers on his.

"What?" he answered, meekly stepping into her domain. "Get up on the wrong side of the coffin this morning?"

"I wish I *was* a vampire. I could stay up all night ridding the streets of the scum-sucking douche bags that take up most of my time and energy."

"Am I one of those scum-sucking douche bags?" Caleb asked meekly. "Just trying to get my bearings here."

"Not yet," she said, pointing at a chair. "Sit."

He obeyed. And he did it much better than Cleo, his sheep-dog, ever had when given that order. He looked around the miniscule space: a table holding a dead fern, a second chair with a tear in the seat. Her desk hadn't fared much better. Claudia usually kept things organized. Pristine. But it looked like something had exploded, scattering files and papers, some cluttering the floor. Bad mood, lost control of her workspace—his friend was not doing well.

"So," he said.

Her phone rang. She answered, her replies to the caller a few clipped no's and a yes, then hung up.

"I can see now's not a good time." Caleb started to rise but she pointed to the chair again. Given her mood, he knew better than to argue.

"So you saw Wyman Carter?" she asked.

"Yes. A pretty sick guy."

"Any idea why he tried to set fire to himself?"

"Not really. Except he's having auditory hallucinations pretty bad. If they were command hallucinations, it would explain what happened."

"You've never worked with him before?"

"No. But he should be under somebody's care. He's very psychotic. Hard to imagine he hasn't been hospitalized or seen as an out-patient somewhere. Does he have a police record?" Caleb asked.

"A few nuisance crimes—panhandling and trespass. Of course, if he had charges as a juvenile, the records could be sealed."

"Did they do a drug screen?"

She nodded. "Came up positive for cocaine."

"But that should be out of his system by now. He needs to get into treatment," Caleb said, finally getting around to the purpose of this visit. "I recommend transferring him to the psych ward.

Matthew can do a consult, get him started on some anti-psychotics."

"Or, we can haul his ass down here and put him in jail. He did try to kill you and that other guy—"

"Henry."

"Look, Carter's looking at attempted murder. Plus the terrorist aspect."

Caleb shook his head. "This guy is not a terrorist! He was psychotic, plus strung out on drugs. He had no clue what he was doing."

"No clue, huh?" She lifted her brow at that. Just one brow, like Mr. Spock used to do. "Think about it, Caleb. This was methodical. He got the gas from somewhere. He had a lighter on him. He came to the center because he was mad at that Esther woman who works there. You told me yourself what he said: 'she's gonna pay for what she did.'

"Those aren't the words of someone who wasn't in some possession of his faculties."

She had a point, as much as he hated to admit it. Wyman did come to the shelter with one intent in mind: killing Esther and himself, with no regard for collateral damage.

"But he didn't do it," Caleb said. "He could have triggered the lighter but he didn't."

Claudia opened her desk drawer, her hands fumbling around inside until she pulled out a small manila envelope. She opened the clasp and dumped the contents onto her desk. "This lighter?" she asked, holding up the familiar blue Bic.

"Yes." He wondered what her point was.

She flicked it three times. "He couldn't have gotten a spark out of this thing if he tried all day. Completely empty."

"Wish I'd known that then." He blew out a puff of air. They hadn't been in danger—not really, except for the fumes. "Then he didn't try to kill us. He was guilty of self-endangerment more than anything."

"Is that so?" Someone said from behind him. Caleb recognized the low, bombastic voice, always louder than necessary. A voice about as welcomed as Caleb's ex-wife's.

"I knew I should have left," Caleb whispered.

Claudia stood, smoothing the front of her skirt. "Captain

Bentille."

Caleb remained in his seat, looking up at the man whose hard glare tore into Caleb's personal space. Bentille wore a black suit, white shirt. Polished black shoes that looked like they'd never been outdoors. Hair threaded with silver and cut short, accentuating the knobs of his cheekbones. But it was Bentille's eyebrows that always drew Caleb's gaze. Furry worms huddling together so that they almost touched in the middle. Why didn't Bentille take a hacksaw to them? Caleb would gladly volunteer but probably didn't need to be holding a weapon so close to that particular man. He'd never forget—or forgive—Bentille for once trying to convict his brother of murder.

"You were saying we shouldn't charge Wyman Carter?" Bentille said.

"I'm saying he's psychotic. As in, not competent. As in, needs treatment, not jail."

"Really?" He shook his head. "You're such a bleeding heart, Knowles. I don't see how you're able to do your job with your judgment as clouded as it is. If you had your way, Westville would be a haven for every homeless, drug addicted psychopath in the southeast."

Caleb closed his eyes and mentally counted to ten.

"Any more information on Carter, sir?" Claudia asked.

"SLED didn't pull up anything. But after we get his picture in the paper, maybe someone will recognize him. Man like him probably has a few aliases."

"Excuse me?" Caleb interrupted. "In the paper?"

"Oh yes," said Bentille. "It's needed, after that absurd article that made you out to be some kind of hero. No, this will be the real deal. Front page, I think. The mayor says this is why we have to close Safe Harbor, because it draws in people like Carter. People who bring drugs and other crimes to our town. Wyman Carter is the perfect example of why we need to clean up our streets and send the vagrants and criminals on their way." He was on his soapbox now, gesturing with his boney fingers like he was on stage.

"Don't do this." Caleb spoke through clenched teeth. "Don't politicize what happened."

"I'm not a politician. I'm a police captain. The safety of our citizens is all that I care about. Wish you felt the same way."

"And what about the safety of Safe Harbor's clients? What happens to them if you close the shelter?" Caleb knew better than to argue with Bentille. There would be no getting his point across—the man was too narcissistic to hear an opinion that differed from his own.

Bentille's beeper sounded. He grabbed it with his hairy-knuckled fingers and smiled at the number displayed. "That would be the mayor. Guess I better give him a call, huh?" He spun around and left them.

"Self-important bastard," Caleb grumbled.

Claudia didn't respond.

"This is wrong, Claudia."

"It is what it is. But for the record, I don't agree with the captain. I think Safe Harbor serves a purpose in our community. But some of your clients are a scourge to Westville and I think you know it. Where Carter fits, I'm not so sure."

"Well where he *doesn't* belong is on the front page."

"You got a visitor." Henry stepped back as Sully McNair filled the doorway to Caleb's tiny office. Like Lanie, who'd escaped in a flurry from Safe Harbor after the injection: "Right in my backside!" Sully didn't have an appointment.

"How are you, Sully?" Sully McNair's limp seemed worse than before. He dropped into the wicker chair and stretched his long legs in front of him. His long gray-black hair, gathered in braids, made him look like a Rastafarian grizzly. He wore a frayed denim jacket that offered meager protection from the cold. "Where you staying these days? It's getting cold out."

Sully lowered his head, his braids cascading down so that the shiny hair clips tinkled against each other like wind chimes. "Here and there. This way and that. In and out, in and out," he answered in the unmistakable word salad of the mentally ill.

"At the group home?"

Sully lifted a massive hand to his mouth and didn't answer.

"They say the temperature will go down into the teens tonight. You need to be some place warm." Caleb worked hard to find a private bed for him at a local group home over a month ago, but doubted Sully stayed there more than a couple of nights.

Sully glanced at Caleb and looked away. Eye contact was never easy for him. "I'll be warm. Warm as a bun. Warm as the sun," he said, his deep bass voice sounding like distant thunder.

"Not if you're outside," Caleb persisted. "If you want, I can see if the home still has your bed."

Sully shook his head. The braids clicked.

"Our shelter then."

"People steal your stuff. I lost my sleeping bag and a good wool pea coat last time."

Caleb nodded. Theft was a constant problem in the shelter. Homeless people had so little that a missing cigarette could cause a brawl. And if you were mentally ill like Sully the lack of privacy was a problem. Paranoid people did not do well in dorms.

"How are you fixed for medicine?" Caleb asked.

His client reached in his pocket and pulled out a plastic medicine bottle. "I'm out of the Zee. Need more of the Zee."

"Zee? Zyprexa? When did you run out?"

He heaved a shoulder up in a half shrug. "Out, out. It's all about out."

"Longer than a few days?" Caleb asked, and Sully nodded.

"How are the voices?"

"Gettin' loud. A chorus. A chorus in my head."

"What are they saying to you?" Caleb leaned forward, hoping Sully would answer honestly.

Sully's head shot up. He narrowed his eyes. "Why you want to know?"

The change in Sully surprised him. "Curious, I guess. It's okay if you don't want to tell me."

"Ain't anybody's business but my own." Sully's voice rose. "People always got to be nosey. Prying. Meddling in things don't concern them."

"Okay," Caleb softened his tone, hoping to diffuse the erupting anger. "Sorry if the question upset you."

"I ain't. Ain't upset." He rubbed his knee with the palm of his hand, back and forth, back and forth.

"I shouldn't have pried. You have the right to keep some things to yourself."

"That's right, I do." Sully fixed his glare on Caleb's face. Caleb gave him a soft, apologetic smile, hoping it would do the job of settling down his agitated client, who easily outweighed Caleb by a hundred pounds.

"Anything else you want to talk about?" Caleb asked, letting him take the lead.

Sully reached in his shirt pocket for a medicine bottle and handed it to Caleb. "The doc here? I need some of this here medicine."

Caleb read on the Zyprexa bottle that his last refill had been five weeks ago, which meant he'd missed more than a few days. "How often do you take these?"

"I take them when I can. When I got something for my belly. They mess me up if I don't eat right after."

Caleb wondered how often Sully ate three meals in a day and got three doses in his system. "How about we get you some crackers and stuff to keep with you. That way you can take the pills and keep something in your stomach."

"I like the peanut butter crackers. Barb used to give 'em to me. And oatmeal. That fills me up if I can get hot water."

"So we'll hit the pantry before you see the doc. But back to my other question. Where are you sleeping these days?"

Sully pressed his fingers against his temples as though trying to squeeze out the internal noise. "Jaco's got a trailer. I can go there."

"Does Jaco's trailer have heat?"

"Kerosene. Stinky stuff. But it warms the place. Stay till his drinking buddies come around."

"Is that a temptation for you?" Caleb asked, feeling a knot of tension. He didn't want Sully to think he was prying again.

Sully smiled, his yellow teeth gleaming like candlelight. "I'm clean and sober going on two years. I don't get tempted none from Jaco's friends. Just don't wanna be around it." Sully stood, a dark mountain of man looking down at Caleb. "I see Dr. McAbee now?"

"In a bit. Let's get you some food first." Caleb walked him down the hall to the pantry, a large storage room that held food, toiletries, and second-hand clothes.

Esther Lowell stood in the doorway with a young woman. Esther, pulled taut in her brown bun and gray stretch pants, initialed an inventory sheet before lifting a box from a shelf. Dropping in the standard soup, macaroni and cheese, peanut butter, and soap-shampoo-toothpaste kit, Esther said in her pronounced New York accent, "Try to make this go a little farther this time, Marie."

The young woman lowered her head so that her half-bleached, half-brown hair fell over her face. "Them kids is hungry all the time. Even the baby eats like her brothers."

"But I told you last time, you can't come here every week. I'm giving you this," she handed her the food, "but I don't want to see you again until next month. Do you understand?"

Sully said in a stage whisper, "Esther makes sure we know our place. We gotta be humble when she give us her soda crackers."

Esther's head snapped around to them. "I have to make a little go a long way, Sully. You know that."

"Yes ma'am." Sully saluted her.

"I don't appreciate your sarcasm," she said bitterly.

Sully's massive hands squeezed into fists at his side.

Caleb said, "Why don't you go on down to Dr. McAbee's office. I'll leave some food for you at the front desk."

He didn't move at first, just stared down at Esther who glared right back. "Do what he said, Sully," she said, her voice quieter now.

"And I want to see you in two weeks, okay?" Caleb added.

Sully nodded, extending a fist, thumb up, and Caleb did the same, brushing knuckles with his client. Sully lumbered down the hall towards the psychiatrist's office.

Marie muttered weak thanks as she made a hasty exit. Esther remained.

"Okay if I get some supplies for Sully?" Caleb asked, just to be polite.

Esther held the pantry door open. "Help yourself. But the pickings are slim."

Caleb grabbed a bag and piled packets of instant oatmeal and grits, crackers, peanut butter, cans of diced chicken and Vienna sausages, and the last two decent looking bananas.

Esther lingered in the doorway, watching him. "We don't know when we'll get another shipment. There's just never enough."

"That has to be one of the toughest parts of your job."

"It's all tough." Esther wiped the sweat from her forehead with the heel of her hand. "Dr. Rhyker called this morning. Said you could keep working here a little longer."

"Yep." Caleb wasn't complaining. Safe Harbor paid Matthew's clinic what it could for Caleb's work, but Matthew hadn't altered his salary. It meant long hours for Caleb, but that wasn't too much of a sacrifice. With Shannon away, he had nothing to go home to, except on Wednesdays when he had visitation with his daughter.

Caleb picked up the sack he'd assembled for Sully and took it down the hall to the reception area. "Henry, can you give this to Sully for me?" Caleb asked.

Henry placed the bag on the counter. "Sully hasn't been coming to AA like he used to."

"He's two years into recovery. Guess he thinks he can miss a few groups now."

"Thinking like that gets folks into trouble."

"Maybe you can talk to him when he's done with the doc. Get him to come to your addictions group."

"Maybe. But he knows the drill. It's a decision he has to make." Henry, like many other recovering addicts, believed that attending regular AA groups was the lifeline for anyone in recovery. While Caleb wasn't completely convinced, he did know Sully needed all the help he could get.

# Chapter Five

*Get away, get away, get away.* The voice chanted in Wyman's head, but he didn't need the direction. When the ambulance driver stopped to fill up the tank, and the other man—the big white-jacketed one—decided to go for a piss, he seized his chance. He managed the door with a good strong kick and ran for the woods, ran like the wind, ran like the voice told him to, dodging branches and skirting the underbrush as he disappeared into the trees.

*HURRY!* The voice commanded. He kept moving, ignoring the ache in his right foot. He'd pay later, the foot would give him a fit, but he had to put distance between him and the ambulance. So he zig-zagged through the pines, panting like a dog, until a root tripped him and sent him flying.

Wet leaves scratched his face. The smell of damp earth filled his nostrils. His knuckles stung from where he'd tried to break his fall. He eased himself up, checking himself for other injuries. His ankle throbbed, that old break from several years ago that never healed right. He had been on the streets when it happened so he didn't get to a hospital. That was long after the yellow house, when he had a family and a doctor to go see if he got sick or hurt. He didn't have all that now. He was on his own, and he liked it that way.

*Run.* A full chorus chanted: *Get away, get away.* He grabbed a branch to pull himself up, testing the foot to see if it could bear his weight. It hurt, but it held, so he did his best to keep going. He lasted a good ten minutes before he collapsed against a tree, winded. So tired, but he heard a noise, like a puff of air. Was it the men after him? Were they this close? He looked back and spotted a flash of white. The driver!

He pulled himself up and took off, every step sending fire up his leg. He wove between the trees, hoping they'd give up. There was only so much running he could do.

*Safe.* The voice stopped him. He held his breath, but heard no footsteps, just the wind rustling the leaves. Relieved, he dropped to the ground. He'd rest here for a bit, then go back to the highway and hitch a ride back to town.

Then what? He had twenty dollars in his pocket from when Markham came to see him at the hospital. There had been other visitors, too. The redheaded man who asked a lot of questions. And the silver-haired woman who looked so familiar that it hurt. But it couldn't be her.

Mind fog. He still felt it from the drugs they gave him at the hospital. Then the voices started again, and he couldn't tell what was real and what wasn't. Like one time when he woke up, he thought for sure he heard Stormy talking to him. Stormy always liked to hear his own voice and Wyman never minded listening; and he thought Stormy was there, in the room, laughing and telling stories about his time as a carnie and saying Wyman would make a good carnie, too, because he could convince people to go into the spook house or play a ring toss game that was rigged so only a few people ever won. Stormy said Wyman could make a lot of money. Stormy always was one to make big plans.

But Stormy was gone now. So he couldn't have been there, even though it seemed so real. Just a dream or vision brought on by the stuff they kept shooting into his arm.

Best not to think about it. Wyman needed to focus on what to do next. He groped in the pocket of his jacket to make sure the twenty dollars was there, that it hadn't been imaginary. He pulled out a wadded up bill and smoothed it against his thigh. Real enough. Could get him that fix he needed more than life itself. But first, he had to get back to town.

He zipped up his sweatshirt as much as he could, but it always snagged half-way up. He wore his old Keds but wished they'd given him some socks. His sweatpants felt damp from the fall. Night would come soon, and it would get cold. Best that he found somewhere to stay before that happened.

Where should he go? They wouldn't let him back at Safe Harbor, not after what he did. Markham would want him to stay at the group home but that place smelled like piss and got so loud at night; other residents walked the halls and mumbled like empty-eyed zombies. Sometimes they came into his room and touched his stuff. Plus Markham and Rhetta had so many rules, and told him what time he got to eat or take a shower or when he had to go to bed. Like he couldn't make those decisions for himself.

Wyman wished he could go back to Zooville. He had stayed two weeks last time. He'd brought a girl he'd met, Dawn, because she needed a place to hide out, and he knew she'd fit right in. He got them a tent from the Salvation Army and staked it by the river. He liked feeling the breeze come off the water and sitting around the fire listening to Stormy and the others tell lies. He was happy then, before it all got snatched away.

He'd never forget that night. The guys shared some beer and sandwiches somebody got from Safe Harbor. Stormy and Dawn sat with that guy Johnny, who called himself the mayor, making a big deal about *not* drinking, like they were better than the others for being sober. And that new kid, what was his name? He pulled out a crack pipe right there at the camp fire.

"Don't you dare light that thing," Johnny said.

"Who made you king?" the kid answered. "Hey, anybody got a lighter?"

Wyman did. He tossed it to the guy.

"Wyman!" Dawn said, all haughty like.

The kid lit up and once that burned-plastic smell got into Wyman's nose it pulled him to the pipe. The kid held it for him, tapping the flame to the rock, and Wyman drew in the delicious smoke and felt the wild rush of blood and pleasure flood his head. That drive, that pull, he had no power over that. Never had. Probably never would.

Johnny stomped over to them, grabbing the pipe right out of his hand. "Not here! *Never* here!" he yelled and hurled the pipe into the river. When the kid jumped up and got in his face, Stormy rushed to back Johnny, and soon there was a big fight. He didn't remember who sided with who but when it ended, Wyman was kicked out of Zooville and told never to come back.

No, Zooville was not an option.

And now, all he could think about was the rock. Crack had a way of grabbing his mind and holding on tight as a tick. God, he wanted a hit. Nothing felt as good as it did. Not beer. Not sex. Not the drugs Markham gave him. Nothing.

He had the twenty dollars. If he could find Big John, it would buy him a few hits. And the thought of that made Wyman smile.

A breeze kicked up, cutting through Wyman's cotton sweats. Time to get a move on. He wasn't sure which way to go, but after a few minutes he could hear the sound of traffic. Maybe a trucker would give him a lift back to Westville. Then he could find Big John.

"Nice of you to join us." Esther's thin lips stretched into a sarcastic smile.

"I was detained," Caleb replied, in no mood to offer more of an explanation for his late arrival to the Safe Harbor staff meeting. After an emergency at the private office, squeezed in between four scheduled clients, he was lucky to get to Safe Harbor before dusk. He took the only unoccupied seat, an orange plastic chair split midway up the back and covered with duct tape. The small clinical staff clustered around a folding table in the break room, door closed against the rumble and beeps from a forklift in the donation center.

Esther shot a pointed glance at Gina, who seemed to be doodling in a notebook.

"It's important to be prompt, particularly when we have impressionable interns among us."

"Impressionable?" Caleb turned to Gina. "Have I made an impression on you?"

"Oh, I'm impressed. Actually, impressed doesn't begin to describe it." She flashed a dimpled grin as she kept scribbling.

Esther did not look amused. She lifted a pen, held it like a cigarette between her fingers, and said, "Henry, how's our inventory looking?"

Henry rifled through the pages on his clipboard and cleared his throat. "Same as last week. We're down on grocery donations since the Food Mart up on Wheat Street closed down. Farmer's Market is sending some produce, mostly greens and other fall crops, but it's gonna have a short shelf-life, so we need to get it distributed as quick as we can. Which ain't gonna be easy because

I'm down two men in the distribution center."

"We all have to make do more with less these days, don't we?" Esther inserted the end of the pen in her mouth. Former smoker, Caleb decided. Not long enough in recovery. Maybe that accounted for her sour disposition.

"How's the staff recruitment going?" Caleb asked. "Not that I'm not having a blast here and all."

Esther slapped a stack of papers in front of him. "See for yourself. We've gotten ten applications and I've interviewed half a dozen of them. But nobody looks promising. We can only pay entry level wages but we really need somebody with experience. These people can manipulate the newbies, you know."

Caleb didn't like how she described their clients as "these people" but decided not to comment. With Esther, battle-choosing was a tricky issue.

"I could ask around, see if anybody's looking for a new job."

She turned her stern gaze on him. "I doubt we could afford any of your private practice friends."

Caleb shook his head. What did she think? Even in private agencies, social workers made beans compared to the psychologists and nurses. Caleb did okay but only because he worked for Matthew.

"Any other ideas?" She raised her brows at him, issuing a challenge.

"No, not me. What about you, Henry? Do you know anyone?"

Henry squirmed in his chair like he'd never been asked his opinion before. "I could ask around in the AA community."

"I don't need paraprofessionals, Henry. I need someone with a degree and a license. Someone who can bill for services," Esther said.

"They aren't mutually exclusive, you know," Caleb said. "There are some folks in recovery who go back to school and get the degree." He noticed how Henry was staring at a spot on the table.

"Well I haven't met them." Esther stood her ground. "I understand you're eager to be done here, Caleb. You want to get back to the private office. Back to your cappuccino and leather furniture."

Esther sure knew how to get her digs in, but he couldn't figure out why she did it.

"Don't forget the masseuse on Thursdays," he said. "And the hot tub."

"You have a hot tub?" Gina's eyes widened. "I never saw the hot tub."

Caleb laughed. "No, no, I'm just yanking Esther's chain."

"But she's right about the cappuccino." Gina stared into a Styrofoam cup that probably held shelter coffee the color of dishwater.

"Can we please get back to business?" Esther said. "We need to beef up our food drive if we're going to meet the demand. It's always worse as we start nearing Christmas."

"How do you beef it up?" Caleb asked.

"It's more Bill's department. He solicits businesses about setting up donation boxes. Individual food donations don't make that big of a dent, but it gives us exposure. Food donations often lead to cash donations."

"There's a new Publix up on Rosewood," Henry said. "I don't think Bill's talked to them about meat and produce pick up. Want me to go by there tomorrow?"

She looked at him for a long moment. "Maybe we better let Bill handle that. He's the PR wizard. But you can put together a presentation folder for him to take."

Henry didn't answer. A muscle over his jaw throbbed like he was chewing on unspoken words. He probably wanted to punch a wall. Come to think of it, Caleb did, too.

"Speaking of money, Bill's been with the mayor and county councilmen most of the afternoon. He's concerned they may pull their funding," Esther said.

"Why?" Henry jerked forward in his chair. "How could they do that? Don't they know what it will mean?"

"It'll probably mean closing our doors," Esther said.

"We don't know that," Caleb replied. "Even if they try to pull the funding, we can look for other sources. Can't we get the public involved, see if they'll put pressure on the mayor? Maybe we can get him to leave Safe Harbor alone."

"We? When did you become a part of this place?" Esther said with a smirk. "You're a part-time temp, Caleb. And when you're gone, we'll still be dealing with the same problems. You think the public gives a damn about us? Hell, they'll pat the mayor on the back if he shuts us down. As for other sources, I'd like to hear what you have in mind. You must have a magic wand or something I don't know about."

Caleb sat back in his chair and reminded himself that he had an intern there and he wouldn't be much of a role model if he snipped the bun from Esther's head and used it as a hockey puck. No, he needed to take the high road, even if Esther didn't deserve it.

"Hey, it's worth a try, isn't it? Maybe we could look into grants? See if there's one that fits what we're doing?" Caleb said affably.

"Well then, help yourself. Don't expect me to help. I'm doing the best I can just to keep this place running."

"I can see that. And believe me, we all appreciate how hard you're working." If Caleb Knowles had been Pinnochio, his nose would have extended to the parking lot.


Caleb lumbered down the hall to Gina's office with his hand pressed into the small of his back. Why had he offered to help Henry unload the truck? A half hour spent hauling in boxes of canned turnips and beets left a sizzling burn down his spine. He was eager to get home to Tylenol and a beer, his cure for most anything. As he passed Gina's office he noticed a man there, leaning back in the chair. He looked vaguely familiar; tall, but thick in the middle, with deep set green eyes and a perfectly shaped goatee encircled his thin lips.

Something he said had Gina laughing, a sweet, musical laugh.

"What's so funny?" Caleb asked.

The man straightened like he'd been caught by the principal.

"Todd was just telling me about a couple of the volunteers," Gina said.

Todd stood, extending a hand. "Todd Weathers, sir." He turned back to Gina. "I better get back to work. See you tomorrow."

Caleb watched as Todd disappeared down the hall, traces of Todd's sweat sticking to his palm from when they shook hands. "So he's a volunteer? As in doing community service?"

She nodded.

"You know what that means, right? Community service means he was ordered to work here by a judge. It means he's been in legal trouble."

She shook her head with vehemence, curls bouncing. "It was just child support. He lost his job and got behind in paying his ex-wife. But he's got his own business now and has paid what he owes her. She's very angry about the divorce, even though she's remarried, and that's why she took him to court."

This reeked like a can of catfish bait. Was this guy taking advantage of Gina's naiveté? "So you and this Todd guy are friends? Good friends?"

She let out a laugh. "We're not dating or anything like that."

Caleb narrowed his eyes. Gina was an adult, albeit a very young adult, and entitled to a social life. But still. "It's just when you mix your personal life with your professional one, it can get complicated, and sometimes, it's a disaster. It's best to keep your relationship with co-workers on a professional level."

"Aren't you friends with Dr. Rhyker?"

"Well, yes."

"And your girlfriend used to work at the practice, right?"

"Uhm. Yeah." He scratched his head, wondering how far he wanted to go with this. "Shannon used to work with us. We fell in love, and then working here was very awkward so she moved on to a different job. A job I don't think she likes nearly as much." A job that was too easy to escape when she took the leave of absence.

"Sooo?" Gina looked at him expectantly.

"Just be careful."

Gina smiled. "I am."

"Okay then. You ready to call it a night?"

"You don't have to ask me twice." She wrenched open the battered desk drawer to retrieve a purse. It was a cloth bag with kittens embroidered on the side, about the size of a potato. Shannon didn't own a handbag that wasn't large enough to carry a pony. Whenever she asked him to hold it for her he bent his knees, exaggerating the weight. And Shannon would swat him and say 'you may joke, but if you need anything, it's in there,' and it would be true. An aspirin, a safety pin, hand lotion—all there.

Sudoku book? Yep. Dental floss? You betcha. A fortune cookie? A Yugo sedan? A circus clown? It wouldn't surprise him.

God, he missed her.

"Have you seen Esther?" Gina asked. "I should tell her I'm leaving."

"I think she already left." He'd gone three whole hours without a run-in with Esther. That had to be some kind of record.

They turned off office lights as they walked down the hall; weariness had Caleb moving slowly. He held open the scarred metal door for Gina and they stepped out into the cold Carolina night. A half moon peeked over the silhouette of the bottling company up the road. The abandoned building next door had once been a night club. He could see bats circling overhead that he suspected had made a home there. The odor of spoiled produce from the dumpster filled the air, like it did most nights. He didn't know when the garbage company came to empty it, but it wasn't often enough.

No cars or pedestrians could be seen up the road. The closest streetlight was a half block away and beyond it, a sign that read "Tiny's Bar" flashed in neon pink. He looked back toward the dorm. It had closed its doors for the night, but he could see lights winking from windows. The men hadn't bedded down quite yet.

"Where's your car?"

She pointed to a lone Civic beside the overflowing dumpster. Caleb fought the urge to hold his nose. "It was the only spot I could find," she said apologetically.

"My fridge smelled like this when I was in grad school." He watched as she unlocked her car door and slung her belongings inside. She started to climb in but hesitated.

"What's that?" she asked.

Caleb followed her stare to what appeared to be a pair of shoes on the ground a few yards in front of her car. White sneakers, toes up.

"Stay here," he said. He took a cautious step towards the shoes. Looked around, making sure he was alone. Felt a chill do a spider crawl up his vertebrae.

He spotted a crumpled brown bag close to the left shoe, like the sack lunches they gave out at the shelter. Something blue just beyond. Checked behind him again. He dropped to his knees, touched the blue fabric. A pant leg. His gaze trailed up, saw the sleeve of a cream colored sweater, an arm twisted to the side. The head rested on a squished milk carton. Gray hair in a frayed bun.

Esther Lowell.

"Damn it," he whispered.

He felt her wrist. Nothing. Touched her throat. Cold and still as marble. "You got a cell?" He yelled back to Gina.

"Yes. What—"

He heard her coming towards him. "Stay there! Call the police."

Two hours later, Caleb found Gina sitting on the hood of her car. She stared at the police officers securing the yellow tape that now marked the area as a crime scene, mascara streaks covering her doughy cheeks. Caleb leaned back beside her, nudging her with his elbow. "You okay?"

"I've never seen a dead person before." Her shoulders made a little shuddering motion.

Caleb wished he could say the same. It was never easy. He hoped it never would be.

"What happened to her?" Gina looked confused, like this sort of thing didn't fit in her universe.

"I've got some bad news along that front." Detective Claudia Briscoe walked over, removing a pair of latex gloves. "Caleb, how well did you know Ms. Lowell?"

"Not very. I've only been here a couple of months. Esther was the Director of Operations for the shelter."

"Know anyone who might have a reason to hurt her?"

He looked back over at Gina. "So I take it she didn't die of a heart attack."

Claudia shook her head, frowning. "She was stabbed twice in the chest. Similar to the body we discovered in the river."

"Was it a robbery?"

She shook her head. "Still wearing her jewelry. Nice gold necklace and earrings."

Gina wrapped her arms around her middle and started to tremble again.

"I don't—didn't—know Esther very well," Caleb said. "Don't

know a thing about her personal life, if she had one. She seemed to be here whenever I was."

"She has a sister," Gina said. "I heard her say something about going to see her this Christmas." Her face crumpled as tears emerged, spilling down. "Sorry. It's just so sad."

Caleb rested a hand on her shoulder and scowled again at Claudia. "Okay if she heads home?"

"Sure. Sorry for your loss, Miss Fulton." The sound of crunching gravel startled them and they turned to see Bill Evers' Mini-Cooper pull into the lot. Bill climbed out, looking a bit out of character in sweats and a denim jacket. "You're going to want to talk to him," Caleb said.

"Third time we've been here in a week," Claudia said. "This shelter's sure keeping us busy."

"And keeping us in the news," Caleb said, dismayed. This brutal murder would make the front page. More bad press for Safe Harbor.

Caleb turned back to Gina. "Want me to drive you home?"

"Nah, I'm fine, really." She studied the spot where Esther died. Though the body had been removed, she looked like she could still see it. "You'll make sure someone calls her sister?"

"I promise." He opened the car door for her, then watched as she drove away.

# Chapter Six

The crack of thunder roused Caleb from his sleep. He rolled over, his hand reaching to the other side of the bed, groping for the warm body that should be there. His fingers splayed on cold sheets. His eyes blinked open. Out his window he saw streaks of rain. A flash of lightening revealed a gray, cloud-heavy sky.

Another morning without Shannon. She'd left for Maine on a cool October day, commenting that she'd probably hit snow a few hours before her parents' house.

He'd asked her not to go. Knowing it was selfish, knowing that she had the harder job in leaving than he did in being left. But her father needed her. His rehabilitation would take months, and someone had to manage the family dairy farm.

It said a lot about Shannon that her work granted her a three-month's leave. The managed care company didn't want to lose her. From Shannon's perspective, three month's away from her soul-sucking job was perfect, though she said she hated—really hated—leaving Caleb. He hoped that was so. He hoped she hadn't grown tired of him, of his moodiness, of his tendency to dive head first into trouble.

They talked every day, at first. Then every couple of days. But then they ran out of things to say. Shannon sounded so tired, the dairy farm day starting before dawn, ending after sundown. And her voice had a sad, hopeless edge to it, especially when she told him there may be more surgery for her dad.

So Caleb called in the early afternoon, if work allowed. And he'd taken to writing letters. But the distance seemed to grow with time. Maybe he'd send some flowers next week. Something. Anything. She had to know how much she was missed.

He rolled over to stare at the alarm clock. 7:15. Almost time to—his doorbell rang. Who would be visiting at this hour? "Hold on!" Caleb yelled as he wrestled himself into the T-shirt. Cleo bounded down the stairs and barked at the door as the bell sounded again.

"Move," Caleb commanded, trying to maneuver around the wiggling beast to turn the knob. The bell chimed for the fifth time. "What the hell do you—" he stopped yelling when he opened the door and saw who stood there.

His brother didn't say anything at first, just looked at him. Rain dripped from his jacket and hair, but he didn't seem to mind. He just stood there, staring, like maybe Caleb should have expected him. Finally, Sam said, "Good morning."

"Huh?" Caleb asked, then remembered he'd better sign if he wanted Sam to understand him. Extending a thumb and pinky on his right hand and tapping his chin, he signed, "What's wrong?"

Sam held up his Blackberry. "I've been trying to contact you. You forget to turn on your cell again?"

Caleb wondered what triggered this early morning visit. He pointed both index fingers and motioned them towards the room. "Come out of the rain and tell me what's going on," he signed.

Sam paced by him, removing his wet jacket and slinging it on a brass branch of the hall tree. "You haven't seen the news, have you?" His voice tripped over the "S" in "seen," the way it sometimes did when he talked fast. Normally, Sam's spoken words were as clear as a hearing person's, but not when he was agitated like this.

"I'm not even up yet," Caleb signed.

"Somebody from Safe Harbor was murdered last night. I knew you were working there, but they didn't say who was killed, and then you didn't answer my text message . . ."

"Ah." He understood now, and offered a smile to his very worried looking older brother. "Not me. I'm not dead. Not even a little bit," he signed.

Sam raked a hand through his thick brown curls. "I see that."

"You were worried?"

"No. Not really."

"So you just happened by at this hour?"

"Okay, maybe a little worried."

"Sorry." Caleb placed a fist on his chest, making little circling movements.

"And on top of that, I'll bet you haven't made coffee." Sam moved quickly to the kitchen, pulling the coffee beans from the shelf, grinding them and loading the Krups. Caleb sat at the table and willed his nervous system to wake up. As Sam took the seat across from him, Caleb signed, "I was there last night. I was the one who found the body."

"Of course you did," Sam winced. "Who was it?"

"Esther Lowell. Someone who works at the shelter."

"Do they know who killed her?"

"They didn't last night. I was kind of hoping she was mugged, but it doesn't look like it."

"You think it a client did it?"

"No. Why would you assume that?" Caleb hadn't been too wild about the police asking that question, much less his own brother.

"Because it's logical given where she died. Who else might have hurt her?"

"Are we playing detective now?"

"No, that's usually your job." Sam grabbed two mugs and interrupted the brewing cycle to pour. Caleb breathed in the scent and felt neurons starting to stir.

Sam sipped, and gave Caleb a long stare.

"What?"

"You gonna keep working at Safe Harbor?"

"Sure. At least for the next couple of months. Matthew's got it worked out."

"First a guy tries to torch himself in front of you. Now you stumble on a murdered woman. Maybe you should rethink this plan."

Caleb caught Sam's serious tone. Worrying about his little brother was sometimes a fulltime job for the elder, more handsome, and often smarter Sam Knowles.

"I'm careful. I'm always careful. You don't need to worry."

Sam looked ready to argue but didn't. Caleb decided to change the subject. "So what are you up to today?"

"I've got Isaiah today." A wide smile stretched across his face. "I'm picking him up at daycare and bringing him to my place. I wanted to take him for the weekend but the Mentor Project folks won't let me. It's against the rules. They don't understand how different it is when you're deaf."

Caleb took a swig of coffee and pondered this. When Sam had mentioned that he'd been told about a five-year-old deaf kid in the Mentor Project, Caleb didn't enthusiastically embrace the idea. Not that Sam wouldn't be responsible or dedicated enough. Quite the opposite, which could be a problem. "How's Isaiah doing?"

"Good. Real good. You should bring Julia by. I think he needs to be around other kids who have a chance to understand him. He has an older sister but she can't really communicate with him."

"How about his mother?"

"She's another story all together." Sam frowned.

"What's her name?" Caleb coaxed.

"Diondra. She's twenty-five. Just the two kids, but two different fathers. Neither is involved. I don't think she works. Gets a check though."

"How is she with Isaiah?"

"She loves him, I guess."

"You guess?"

"She's not very demonstrative. I'm sure it's hard trying to communicate when you don't know sign. But Isaiah worships her. He's such a sensitive kid. After all he's been through, he could have walled himself up. We've both seen that happen, haven't we?"

Caleb nodded, remembering Sam after the accident that deafened him. Sam had been the star of the family—athlete, straight-A student. Sixteen years old and riding a motorcycle without a helmet. The crash left him deaf, and he shut down, using the silence around him to prevent anyone from coming inside. Caleb's tenacity, stubbornness, and desperation finally cut through.

So much had happened since then. Sam had a great career and a loyal circle of friends, both deaf and hearing. But when something bothered him, isolation remained his first line of defense.

"Isaiah feels things profoundly," Sam said. "I'm not sure Diondra understands that."

"She probably doesn't understand much if she doesn't sign."

Sam shook his head. "They have a few home signs—signals that only they understand. But when Isaiah started Head Start, they tried teaching him in ASL. He's a bright kid, but he's really struggled. I think he's desperate to communicate, but his mom doesn't follow through on the home front. His teacher tried to get Diondra in an ASL class but she just wasn't interested."

Caleb couldn't imagine why she wouldn't leap at the chance to better communicate with her son. "Where do they live?"

"That's another problem. They're in a one bedroom apartment over on Victor Street. Isaiah sleeps on a mattress on the floor. The place is an absolute pigsty and the neighborhood's gone all to hell. Terrible place to raise kids."

"How's Isaiah doing with you? You see any attachment problems?" Caleb signed.

Sam thought about this for a moment. "I know that's what you'd expect, given the isolation he must have felt. And early on, he was withdrawn. But now he seems like a real normal, energetic kid. We have fun."

"Any temper problems?"

"Well, yeah. He can go off. Sort of like Julia when she's imploding."

Caleb smiled at this, remembering the last Julia-tantrum over her mom's insistence that she wear matching socks.

"The Mentor people said I should have weekly contact with him, but in Isaiah's case, that's not enough. He needs so much that his mom can't—or won't—give him."

Caleb studied his brother for a long moment, feeling a little uneasy about this situation with Isaiah. Sure, the kid had been neglected, possibly abused. But Sam wasn't his parent or even foster parent. Sam's role was volunteer, a part-time mentor. "Maybe Isaiah needs a social services worker."

"Don't get me started on that. He has one, a woman named Amanda Phelps. Know her?"

Caleb shook his head.

"She's nothing like you. I don't think she cares at all about this family."

"You mean she doesn't get overly involved, like you say I do."

"I'm beginning to understand that over-involvement is necessary sometimes." He took a few swallows of his coffee and put the mug on the counter. "So. You have Julia tomorrow. I'm sure Diondra would let me have Isaiah again. Can I bring him over? Maybe after work?"

"Is Isaiah ready for Hurricane Julia?" At six, Caleb's daughter was a year older than Isaiah, but the way Sam described the boy, Caleb suspected he functioned as someone much younger. But Julia communicated fairly well in sign and loved to be around other kids. It would be interesting to see how they get along. And it would be interesting to watch Sam in his mentor role.

"Can anyone really be ready for her?" Sam asked.

"Good point. Come over around six."


At soon as he got to the counseling center, Caleb grabbed the newspaper and took it to his office. Wyman Carter didn't make the front page after all. Or the second. Or the entire Metro section. So maybe Bentille's plan to use the gasoline incident as ammunition against Safe Harbor had failed, or at least been postponed.

Esther's murder comprised only three lines on the crime blotter, probably because the crime happened so late in the day. No doubt it would make headlines tomorrow. They could not spin this tragedy, and fair or unfair, accusation would turn to the Safe Harbor clientele. Caleb thought about the people he'd gotten to know. Lanie Dupree, paranoid every second of the day but doing her best to get by. Sully McNair, a troubled man who fought the voices in his head and his own addiction but sober now, thanks to Safe Harbor.

And Cindy Lowman, Gina's client. A recovering crack addict desperately trying to regain custody of her kids, with the help of the shelter. Each of them lived on the periphery, doing their best against nearly impossible odds. And each counted on Safe Harbor for sanctuary. If the city succeeded in closing the shelter, what would happen to them? Safe Harbor took care of the people no one else would.

Caleb folded up the paper and heard a rap on his door frame. Janice said, "Gina Fulton is here to see you."

"She is?" They had planned to meet at Safe Harbor for clinical supervision at one P.M., when she got out of class. He checked his watch: he had twenty minutes till his first appointment. "Send her back."

Janice paused, tilting her head like something had her perplexed.

"What?" Caleb asked.

Janice came into the office, closing the door behind her. "I noticed that Gina has on a top that isn't really appropriate for this office. I know young girls today think it's okay to wear low cut sweaters. I mean, you watch television and that's all you see. But she's a student, and we're supposed to be teaching her how to be a professional. I think that includes her demeanor, don't you?"

He smiled. Janice had on a pink blouse that concealed most of her neck. A gray skirt that covered her knees. A pink flowered scarf that matched the pink clip in her hair, her pink shoes, and the pink polish on her fingernails. Janice took pride in her appearance. She loved bright colors, but never wore anything revealing. Gina was another matter. Her ample chest tended to bulge out of her low-cut tops. "I'll try to address it with her," Caleb said, though unsure how he would. Janice had a point; Gina needed to learn to dress professionally.

"You're sure?" Janice narrowed her eyes again, looking skeptical. "Or I could do it. You know, girl-to-girl."

"I'll give it a shot," Caleb said. "Send her on back."

Gina came in tentatively, a book bag slung over her right shoulder. She had on jeans and flowery top that fit too snugly and showed more of Gina than Caleb wanted to see. As usual, Janice had been right. Caleb pointed at the chair inviting her to sit. She did, slowly, holding the bag, then putting it beside her, then lifting it back to her lap, clearly flustered.

"Wasn't I supposed to meet you at Safe Harbor?" But now that he thought about it, he liked the idea of meeting with her here. The chairs had comfortable padding. Temperature problems could be solved with the push of a button. And he didn't have to compete with the roar of a forklift.

"Sorry, I probably should have called. Safe Harbor's opening late today, because of what happened to Esther," her voice had a grim tone.

"That makes sense."

"So I thought I'd come here to meet with you. But I should

have called. Sorry."

"No more apologizing." Caleb grinned at her, hoping to coax some life into the conversation. Gina looked a bit lost. "That was pretty awful last night, wasn't it?"

She nodded. "I never saw a dead person before." She sounded like a kid, but then she was barely twenty-five.

"Not easy, is it?"

"Maybe she didn't suffer. I hope she didn't."

"I do too," Caleb said. "Did you sleep okay last night?"

"Not really."

"Were you close to Esther?"

"I don't think anyone was close to her. I don't think she wanted close friends. At least, not at work."

"You may be right."

"But she was a good person. Deep down, I'm sure she was. So why would someone kill her?"

He almost rushed to answer that maybe it was just a wrong time—wrong place kind of crime. But her question ran deeper than that. "I don't know," he said softly.

"She never hurt anyone. I mean, she wasn't the warmest woman in the world, but she gave her heart and soul to the center."

"You're right, she did."

"How many other people would give so much of themselves to work with homeless people? The people everyone else gives up on?"

"Not many." Not me, he almost said. Sure, he'd put in his hours, but he was only there as a temp. He hadn't invested himself in the work like Esther had. He wondered if this accounted for her hostility towards him. Maybe it was partly deserved.

Tears shimmered in Gina's eyes. "She worked sixty, seventy hours a week. Did you know that?"

"No, but I'm not surprised." Caleb couldn't remember a visit to the center when Esther wasn't there. He wasn't sure whether she felt excessively dedicated or simply didn't have life. Probably a little of both.

"It's just so unfair, you know?"

Caleb reached to hand her a tissue, uncomfortable as his hand passed by her exposed cleavage. "A death like this is always hard," he said, mentally kicking himself when he realized how lame that sounded.

Gina nodded, squeezing the tissue into a ball and pressing it against her eye. "Sorry," she whispered.

"Sorry for what? For caring about Esther?"

"I mean about the crying part," she said. "It's not like I knew her that well. I mean, sometimes we didn't even get along."

"I argued with her daily. She could be a bit—retentive." He watched Gina closely over his cup.

Her eyes widened. "That's a perfect word to describe her. It's like she could never let the clients have just a little more, you know? A little more food. A little more time to talk. And she was the same way with the volunteers. She never told them thank you for their work. Never took time to even get to know them, really."

"The volunteers? You mean, like your friend?"

Gina lifted her coffee again, calmer now. "She was over them, you know? Who's going to take that over? They have to have their hours reported to the court or they get in trouble. Will you be handling that?"

"Me?" He started remembering the thousand things Esther did each week. How would the center manage?

"I could help you with it, I don't mind."

"Whoa, back up there. We'll wait to see what Bill or the Board decides."

"Yeah, but in the meantime?" She spoke quickly.

"I promise your friend will be taken care of." Caleb lifted a hand, hoping to end this part of the conversation. So now maybe he could address the issue of her clothing. Yes, now was the perfect opportunity. He'd simply say, "Gina, you need to cover more of your—chest—when you come to work." No, that wouldn't do. "Gina, we don't really have a dress code here, but we don't want you flashing your cleavage at our clients." No, better not.

"Gina?" he said. "Would you stop by Janice's desk on your way out?"

# Chapter Seven

It wasn't a call that came often, but when it did, it made Caleb leap from his chair like a pop tart.

"Julia fell off one of the swings," Mrs. Abry, the kindergarten teacher said. "She wasn't really hurt. Of course we had the nurse check her out. She skinned her left knee and lost that tooth that's been loose."

"Okay." Caleb exhaled, car keys firmly gripped in his hand. No broken bones. No concussion.

"But she's so upset," the teacher continued. "She won't stop crying. It's simply not like her. If you—"

"I'm on my way." Caleb cut in. He blew past Janice, citing a family emergency and that he'd call her soon, and rushed to his car.

He spotted Julia on the vinyl love seat outside the school administrator's office, her head down, bits of grass hanging in her auburn curls. Bouncing her bandaged knee up and down, she clutched a wad of tissues in her left hand. When he said her name she looked up, tears streaking her freckled face, and rushed to fling herself into his arms. He scooped her up, ignoring the pinging along his spine and what it meant about how much his kid had grown. At least a foot and ten pounds since he saw her last week.

"Are you hurt, Julia?"

She shook her head, her nose pressed against his neck. He untangled the knot of tissues from her fingers and saw it was spattered with red drops. Was she bleeding from her nose? Maybe there were internal injuries. Maybe he needed to rush her to the ER.

"From the lost tooth," Mrs. Abry said, coming from behind

him.

"Sweetie? Look at me." Caleb pulled her away and felt her hands clinging to his sweater. "Do you hurt anywhere?"

She shook her head, but the tears kept coming.

Mrs. Abry rested a hand against her cheek. "Your daddy's here. Why don't you tell him what's wrong? Y'all can use my office if you want. I'll be right out here."

He nodded gratefully and carried Julia inside, shutting the door behind him. "I'm sorry, Daddy," Julia said as he lowered her into a chair.

"For what?"

"For making you come." She wiped her eyes with the back of her hand.

"Nothing to be sorry about." He crouched down in front of her and tugged at her T-shirt. "Now, can you tell me what happened?"

"I was swinging on the big swing, not the ones with the wood seat but the one with the curvy one. And I was going real high. And Tamara wanted a turn so I tried to stop and dragged my foot in the dirt but I fell out instead of stopping and bumped my knee and lost . . . lost . . . my tooth!" More sobs huffed out as her eyes overflowed once more.

"It's okay. We knew that was going to happen. You've been wiggling it with your finger for days."

"But I *lost* it, Daddy. I looked everywhere. The dirt under the swing. The grass beside it. The nurse said I may have swallowed it."

Confused and getting a little frustrated, Caleb dropped into the chair with his daughter on his lap. "What's the big deal about finding the tooth?"

Julia took in a deep breath, something he'd taught her to do when she was trying to get control of herself. She rarely had these meltdowns anymore, thank God. "She won't know I lost it. If she looks under my pillow it won't be there!"

Was she talking about her mother, Mariel? That didn't make sense. And then it hit him: her first lost tooth. "So you're afraid that you won't get a visit from the tooth fairy?"

"I don't have a tooth! Don't you see, Daddy?"

"I do," he said, suppressing a smile. "So you think she won't know to leave money under your pillow. But the tooth fairy is way smarter than you're giving her credit for. She's gonna know you lost that tooth."

"But how?"

Think fast, Knowles. "Because you'll write her a note explaining what happened. We'll leave that under the pillow. The tooth fairy will read it and understand."

Julia peered up at him, lip quivering just a little. "Really?"

"Of course. But we'll need to get to work on it soon. Maybe we can finish it before Sam and Isaiah come over."

She nodded, her pale arms reaching around his neck. "Thanks, Daddy."

After making explanations to Mrs. Abry, Caleb dropped her Julia at her aftercare program, where she proudly displayed the gaping hole where her tooth had been that made her look even more adorable, if that was possible. She immediately went to work on her tooth fairy correspondence, choosing pink construction paper and a purple crayon. Caleb wished he could spend the afternoon with her. He dreaded the day when Julia reached the age that a crisis couldn't be fixed with a quick Daddy visit. But for now, she was fine. And he had it on good authority that the tooth fairy would do right by her.

"The plot thickens." Claudia Briscoe looked fierce in her snug black leather jacket. Black shiny boots stretched from her knees to three-inch spike heels. Caleb couldn't imagine how she could chase any criminals wearing them. "We lost Wyman Carter," she said, helping herself to the wicker chair opposite Caleb.

"What do you mean you lost him? Is he okay?"

"It's the weirdest thing. Bentille did a one-hundred-eighty degree turn on him. Went from, 'Let's get him on the front page, make an example out of him!' to 'we're sending him to a private psych hospital for evaluation.' I'm still scratching my head over that when we get a call that Wyman escaped during transport!"

"Where were they taking him?" Caleb asked.

"A facility up in Charlotte. Bridgeton Hall. Heard of it?"

"Oh yeah. Ritzy." Caleb had once visited the exclusive private hospital for a training event. He remembered a beautiful campus with tennis courts, a pool, and a gym. A stay there would cost a fortune. "Who was going to pay for it?"

"I'm not sure. Bentille said it had been taken care of but didn't tell me how. And the more questions I asked, the less he said. Now he wants us to find Carter 'for his own good.' Like I said, a complete turnaround."

"Tell me more about his escape."

"That was odd, too. You'd have expected us to transport him by squad car. But instead, a private ambulance came for him about two P.M. yesterday. We didn't even dispatch an officer to ride with him. When I asked the captain about it he said Carter had been so sedated nobody expected him too flee. The ambulance pulled off the interstate to gas up and Carter jumped out from the back. They tried to catch him but he disappeared in some trees behind the BP station. We sent a search team up but so far, no luck."

"Guess Bentille isn't so eager for the headlines now. 'Attempted arsonist escapes police custody' wouldn't do much for your captain's political ambitions." Caleb smiled, imagining Mr. Unibrow's embarrassment.

Claudia lifted her purse and rummaged inside, finally retrieving a leather-bound notebook and pen. "So do you have any idea where he might go?"

Caleb remembered his discussion with Wyman, when he mentioned the group home. "He stayed at the Willows sometimes. I think it's up in the northeast part of town."

"He had a visit from the guy that runs that place, Markham Dougherty. I've been trying to get in touch with him." She laid a hand on the notebook, the pen in her hand tapping again. "Here's the thing. When Wyman Carter tried to set himself on fire, it was to hurt Esther. He had time to get from the BP station to the shelter. And you said yourself, he was crazy. Do you think he could have stabbed Esther Lowell?"

"I'm not sure his thinking was organized enough for him to get back to the shelter. And you yourself said the lighter he used was empty. We don't know that he really wanted to hurt anyone other than himself."

"But he was openly hostile about Ms. Lowell, so that's motive. I just hope he doesn't hurt anybody else."

"He's psychotic, Claudia. Whenever you find him, he needs treatment."

"There you go with that bleeding heart again." She smirked as she quoted her captain. Irritating.

"Okay, on to other possibilities." She flipped through the notebook until she located the page she was looking for. "I understand there were several Safe Harbor clients who had altercations with Esther before she died."

"Esther was easy to have altercations with. She could be quite gruff. I tangled with her a time or two, myself."

"Anything . . . you need to tell me?" Her lip twitched, fighting a grin.

"No, I didn't kill her," Caleb said, not appreciating her weak attempt at humor. "She was a difficult, unhappy person. She didn't have many friends. But we all knew how hard she worked. How many hours she put in there."

Claudia turned the page in her notebook. "According to some staff, Sully McNair got into it with her. You've worked with this guy, what's your take on him?"

"My take on him? He's a client. I'm not going to break confidentiality, you know that!"

"Ah." She flashed a wide, Cheshire-cat smile and reached in her portfolio for a legal-looking piece of paper. "I got this for you."

Caleb frowned at the court order.

"This entitles me to anything you know about him. So spill."

He scanned the document, wishing he was more fluent in Legalese. "This entitles you to anything in his record. That's not the same thing."

"Semantics, Caleb. You know that."

He wasn't so sure about that point, but knew he could give his client a fairer assessment than a glimpse at a record would offer. "I've only seen Sully four or five times. He's not so great at keeping regular appointments. But that can be said of most clients here."

"How was he at staying on his medication?"

"Same answer. It's hard to stick to a medication schedule when you don't know where your next meal is coming from."

"Is this guy violent?"

"Sully? Nah. I never saw anything like that." Caleb did his best to maintain eye contact, hoping he'd successfully evaded that line of questioning.

"Hmm." Claudia reached for another sheet. "Caleb, Caleb. I'm disappointed in you. How did you miss McNair's criminal history? Simple assault arrests in '98 and '99. A domestic violence charge in '02. Oh, and look—a resisting arrest charge in '05. You're getting slack."

"All of those arrests were back when he was using. He was an addict. He didn't know what he was doing half the time."

"So he's not sounding so harmless now," she said.

"*Was* an addict. He's been in recovery for almost two years. And he's doing great."

"Goes to meetings and all that?"

"Well, no. He's not your meeting kind of guy. He's still somewhat paranoid, even when he's on his medicines."

"You're really selling him here."

Caleb lifted a finger to silence her. "Let me finish. He's mentally ill, you know that. But now that he's off drugs, he's doing pretty well. And Sully has great street smarts—he's a survivor. He had no motive for killing Esther. Just because they squabbled over a box of saltines? Nah. Not his style."

"So that was the argument? Over crackers?"

"Yep. You have to understand Esther. She was very controlling. The kind of manager who counts paperclips to make sure you're not using too many."

Another flip of the page. "One other thing. What's your take on Bill Evers?"

Caleb leaned back and pondered this. Matthew considered Bill one of his best friends, which was why Matthew had been conned to serve on the Safe Harbor board of directors. But Caleb had found the director to be somewhat detached. He never saw Bill in the clinical area. In fact, he'd never even seen him with a single Safe Harbor client. Bill was more of a delegating director, letting Esther do most of the work while he courted businesses and wealthy philanthropists who might donate to the agency. "I don't know him that well, but I'm pretty sure Bill Evers couldn't kill a bug in his bathroom. I doubt he's your guy."

"He didn't seem all that torn up about Esther's death."

"He may not be demonstrative, but he's definitely missing her." Caleb squinted over at the detective. "You talked to anyone in Esther's family?"

"A sister, Margaret Price. She's a schoolteacher up in Charlotte. She'd talked to Esther earlier in the week. Said Esther sounded tired, the way she usually did. No idea who would kill her."

"And you don't think it was a mugging? Maybe the guy got interrupted?"

She frowned. "I'm not liking that theory. The stabbing was more personal. Whoever it was got very close. I'm thinking it was someone she knew."

"Someone she knew" narrowed the search. And would probably keep the spotlight on Safe Harbor. He shook his head, not sure things could get any worse for the shelter.


Isaiah didn't seem to grasp the point of their game. A skinny little mocha-skinned fellow, dressed in jeans and a sweater with gaping holes at the elbows, he stood in the center of Caleb's yard, looking bemused at the others as they tossed the Frisbee. Isaiah was also loud. Caleb had forgotten how much noise a deaf person could make—Sam had always been easy on the ears of the hearing. But this kid, with his guttural attempts at forming words, and his boisterous, almost eerie laugh—made Caleb wish for ear plugs.

Julia didn't seem to mind. She grinned her gap-toothed grin at the boy, her curly red hair bouncing as she gestured for Isaiah to throw the Frisbee. Julia was a little girl now, all trace of the Baby Julia gone, and that made Caleb a little sad. Not that the girl Julia wasn't a wonder in her own right. So smart—brilliant, really—with a wit that continuously surprised him. She had Caleb's eyes, light brown, almost golden. Her delicate white skin, dotted with a constellation of freckles, had definitely come from his ex-wife Mariel.

She would be a gorgeous, he knew. Once puberty hit, off to the convent with her.

Caleb felt the vibration from his cell phone in his pocket and signed to Sam that he had a call.

"Caleb? This is Ron Weston. I wanted to talk to you about Gina Fulton's internship."

"Is there a problem?" Caleb knew Ron from their days in graduate school. He was on faculty at the university now, and had been the one who talked Caleb into taking a student.

"Just touching base. Given the recent incidents at the shelter, I wanted to make sure you thought it was safe for her to keep working there."

"Has she requested to pull out?"

"Quite the contrary. She loves it. And she thinks you walk on water, by the way."

"Funny."

"I'm serious. You should hear her talk about you to the other students. She's got a bit of a crush."

Caleb saw the Frisbee sail by him to land at Isaiah's feet. Isaiah jumped back and pointed at it like it was an attacking alien space craft.

"She's young, Ron. Very young. Remember back when we were in school?"

"A thousand years ago, you mean? Yeah I remember. You had that thing for the statistics professor."

"And five years later, you got to marry her," Caleb commented. "I don't think there's real danger at Safe Harbor. I promise I'll keep an eye on her and I'll let you know if anything changes."

"Sounds good. I trust your judgment, though I can't believe I really said that."

Caleb laughed. "Damn, I wish I was recording this." Caleb clicked off the phone.

"Throw it, Isaiah!" Julia yelled, miming her instructions.

Sam crouched down beside his charge and held up the Frisbee. He let out a deep, coarse laugh and hurled the toy straight up in the air.

"Not the tree again!" Julia mumbled.

But the Frisbee cleared the branches of the oak to land on top of Cleo's dog house. Almost as bad as the tree.

The sheepdog leapt for it. Once she had the disk in her mouth, she darted between all the humans who had invaded her yard, playing her favorite game, "catch me if you can, sucker."

"Dahhhhh!" Isaiah bellowed, rocking up on his toes and flapping his hands.

Cleo, taking this as an invitation, galloped over to the boy and bopped him in the stomach with the Frisbee. "Daaaahhhh!" Isaiah screamed again, tears filling his eyes as he stared, in absolute terror, at the shaggy beast assaulting him.

"It's okay," Sam said, stooping down and wrestling a happy Cleo away from him. "She's friendly," he said, signing with his fingers wiggling in front of his smiling face. But to Isaiah, he may as well have been saying "She bites like a shark." His tears kept coming. Julia and Caleb trotted over, not really knowing how to help.

"Scared you?" Sam signed and said, speaking very slowly.

"Nuhnguh," Isaiah replied, shaking his hands some more. Carefully, Sam lifted the boy. Isaiah's arms went around his neck; he buried his face in Sam's shoulder. Sam gently stroked the child's back.

"How about we go inside? Julia and I made sandwiches," Caleb said.

Julia led the way. Sam followed, with Isaiah entwined around him like ivy. Caleb brought up the rear, arguing with Cleo who seemed to think she'd join their little party.

Sam sat at the kitchen table and peeled the boy from his torso. He lowered Isaiah to the floor, but kept his hands on his shoulders. Julia brought over the tray of sandwiches with grapes and sliced apples while Caleb poured them iced tea.

"Sit!" Caleb exclaimed, patting a chair beside Sam for the boy.

Isaiah looked at him, at the chair, and back at Sam. "Sit!" Sam repeated, signing with the first two fingers of his right hand atop the same fingers on his left. Isaiah lifted his arms, letting Sam place him in the seat.

"He's really taken to you," Caleb observed, sitting across from him.

"Kid's just desperate for contact. He's isolated most of the time."

"He's lucky he has you. Who made the referral to the Mentor program?"

"Amanda Phelps. Which reminds me—I need a favor."

Caleb arched his brows suspiciously as he tapped his third

finger to his chin. "A favor?" the hand asked.

"I need to set up a meeting with her and I need an interpreter. Can I hire you?"

Caleb took a sip of tea as he considered this rare request. While Caleb used to keep himself handy in case Sam needed someone to sign for him, lately his brother had turned to private interpreters. Caleb understood Sam's drive to be more independent, though he kind of missed being needed. "Sure, if you can afford me," Caleb signed.

"Dinner and my undying gratitude?"

Caleb coughed. Julia giggled.

"Can you see if she can do it tomorrow? Maybe over your lunch hour? I hate to push but I have some important things to discuss with her."

"I'll bet." Caleb looked over at the little boy. Julia fed him an apple slice. "I think I can do it then."

"I just want her to do her job, Caleb. She's all Isaiah has."

"What about his mom?" Julia signed. And rather well at that, Caleb thought.

Sam winced. "His mom does the best she can, but she's very young and has another child."

"Do they know how to talk with him?" Julia asked, dropping a grape so she could sign the words.

Sam shook his head, his lips drawn in tight. No guessing how he felt about that. Sam had felt isolated enough as a teen struggling with becoming deaf. That this little boy had been alone his entire life did not set well with him.

Caleb looked over at Isaiah, who made himself busy dissecting the sandwich. He had the table manners of a Hun. Tuna smeared his cheek and chin, a few bits hung from his hair. He chewed the last bite with his mouth wide open, giving them a view that made Caleb want to give up tuna altogether.

"He's so cute," Julia said unexpectedly. "Isn't he cute, Daddy?"

Sam raised his brows at Caleb, waiting for his response. Caleb looked at the boy again, taking in his coffee-colored skin, his eyes that were dark as coal, and the tiny fingers that he'd crammed in his mouth to suck on. Caleb had to smile back. "You know, I think he you're right. Cute as a kitten."

"A rather . . . undomesticated kitten," Sam added, reaching over to squeeze Isaiah's shoulder. The boy looked at him and grinned, traces of tuna protruding between his teeth.

"You may be right about that," Caleb replied.

Wyman dug his hands deep into the pockets of his sweatshirt as he trudged along Highway Nine. The wind had picked up, cutting through the worn cotton and chilling him through to his insides. His breath made a white fog. There never was much traffic out here in the country, so Wyman had little hope of thumbing a ride. The foot still throbbed but not as bad as before. He could tell most of the drugs from the hospital had left his system. The head-voices had started their racket again, like people talking just out of earshot. *Fwushfwush, Fwushhah.* Sometimes they were good company, but more often they were like a private storm tormenting his mind.

The moon was full, a big white eye that could see everyone and everything. He used to imagine it was God's eye. But he didn't believe in God, not anymore. Believing was for people who didn't know the truth about the world they lived in.

*Fwushahhhh.* Louder now, the voice wanted him to hear, even if it made not a lick of sense. Damn it was cold. His foot throbbed with each step. Big John didn't have any crack to sell, which was why Wyman was taking this long, God-forsaken walk out in the middle of nowhere. That Mexican man at the group home sometimes fixed him up, as long as Wyman had cash, which he should have soon.

He finally reached the top of the hill and spotted the Willows. It was a long, ugly building with crappy heat and water that tasted like metal. Wyman would rather sleep under the cold moon than in the lumpy, piss-stained bed Markham saved for him here.

A few lights were on back in the residents' rooms, and the tiny orange glow under one of the trees was somebody who had snuck out to get a smoke. Probably not the Mexican, but that was okay, Wyman could wake him up to get what he came for. But first, he needed to get himself something to eat, and see about getting some money.

Markham kept a key under an empty jar beside the back door

to the office. Markham's house was a big brick place a hundred yards behind the group home. He saw no lights, and figured Markham and his ugly wife Rhetta had gone to bed. Good. Wyman could get what he came for and disappear before Markham even knew he'd come. He twitched the key into the lock and stepped inside.

"Damn," he whispered. He never got used to the odor. Piss and shit as he made his way up the hall, a smell that crawled under his skin. Old grease and garbage when he passed the kitchen. Wyman headed straight for Markham's office, wiggling the locked door knob until the latch slipped out of the catch, a trick an old black guy that used to stay there had showed him. The black guy died a year ago, right in his nasty bed. Markham didn't find the body for two days.

*Watch. Watch.* That voice came in strong. Wyman swatted at his ear, wishing he could make the noise go away. He tiptoed over to the old battered desk where Markham kept his cash. It was locked, too, but a bent paper clip would jimmy it open. Wyman pulled the metal cash box out but there was only thirty-one bucks inside. Not much, but it would take care of his need. He replaced the box in the drawer and slipped out of the room. The kitchen next. He went straight to the pantry, switching on the light and hopping back as the roaches scurried away. At least it wasn't rats this time. He helped himself to a package of saltines, a box of raisins, and two cans of Vienna sausages. That would do until he got back to town. He tore open the raisins and tossed a clump of them onto his tongue.

He remembered that the Mexican stayed right across from Jacob's room. He chomped on the raisins as he headed down the poorly lit hall, ignoring the bugs and a mouse that darted out from one of the rooms. He heard rumbling snores from one room he passed, and muttering from another. The bedrooms were never locked, one of Markham's rules, so he could go in and rouse folks whenever he had a mind to.

When Wyman eased open the Mexican's door, the room was empty. Two beds, stripped of linens, a bureau with drawers hanging out, a lone, stained towel hanging from a nail on the wall.

"He's not here." The voice behind him made Wyman jump.

"Crap. You scared me." He turned around to find his old

roommate Jacob, dressed in a blue sweatshirt with a tear at the neckline.

"Mr. Dougherty kicked him out. I think it was a couple of weeks ago." Jacob looked even scrawnier than he used to. A needle-thin guy with skin as white as a marshmallow.

Wyman smacked a fist against the door. Where the hell would he score now? "Why'd he throw him out?"

"Juan owed some people some money. They came here to collect and started tearing up the place. Mr. Dougherty had to call the cops. So he booted Juan out that same night."

"Anybody else here got stuff to sell?"

Jacob rubbed his nose with the back of his hand. The tips of his fingers were raw from where he'd been chewing on them. "I thought you quit."

"I don't get to quit." Wyman said, not that he owed him an explanation.

"I have some candy if you want. I saved it for you." Jacob waved Wyman across the hall into his room. Jacob grabbed a bag from the crooked bookshelf and tossed Wyman two Snickers bars and a bag of M&Ms.

Wyman tore the wrapper from the Snickers and ate it in three quick bites. "Thanks." He looked up at the Kiss poster that still covered the hole that he kicked in the wall one time when Markham ticked him off. The ratty old bedspread on Wyman's bed looked clean, the pillow up against the headboard like a motel or something. Jacob's doing, he was sure. Between the two beds was the chest of drawers. Jacob crossed to the chest and opened the third drawer. "I washed your T-shirts and put them here. You have the bottom drawer, too. But you can have the top ones if you want. I don't care."

Wyman didn't remember leaving shirts here and wasn't sure why he needed a drawer at all, but it seemed important to Jacob that he have them. He sat on the bed, scrunching up the spread around his shoulders and stretching his achy legs in front of him. He was bone-tired. *Nahz nahz nahz.* Whispers now. Damned annoying. He had to get a hit soon.

"You could stay here tonight," Jacob said. "I'll make sure you're up before Mr. Dougherty comes."

Wyman looked up at him. The guy was so damn lonely.

Markham treated him like dirt. Maybe Jacob had family, but they never visited what Wyman could tell. Who else did he have to talk to? At least the Mexican guy could play a mean game of spades. The rest of the residents here were so bat-crazy it was best not to mess with them.

"Come with me," Wyman said.

"What?" Jacob's eyes went wide.

"Come with me. I got thirty-one bucks. We could hit the road. Maybe go to Charleston." The idea had come all of a sudden but Wyman liked it. He hadn't been to the beach in so long.

"You mean leave here?" Jacob's voice squeaked.

"Hell yeah! Have you even seen the ocean before?"

"Sure I have." Jacob started picking at a loose thread on his sweatshirt. "I can't just up and go."

"Why not?" Wyman smiled. It might be like when he and Stormy traveled around together. Being good company for each other. Watching each other's backs. Or when Wyman brought Dawn down to South Carolina, thumbing rides and sleeping in rest stops. He liked having someone along side of him. Talking to somebody real was much better than listening to the damn voices.

"Because . . . because here's where I'm supposed to be." Jacob sounded so beaten down. The kid always was his own worst enemy.

"What are you so scared of?" Wyman asked.

Jacob's fingers kept tugging at the thread until it unwound from the cuff. "I'm not like you. I can't be out . . . out there."

"Out where? We're not talking about going to the moon. We're talking about two guys going to the beach."

*Leave now leave now leave now.* It sounded faster, more frantic. He needed to get out of here. He needed to get himself fixed up. It didn't quiet the inside noise, not really, but it kept him from caring.

"You don't know what I'm like. How I get. Here is safe for me. I don't have to be scared. If you took me with you, you'd change your mind before we got a mile away."

As screwed up as Wyman was, Jacob was worse. Guy couldn't even leave this hellhole.

"Besides," Jacob said with an unsteady smile. "Somebody needs to spy on Mr. Dougherty for you."

Wyman reached in the chest and pulled out a T-shirt to slip on under his sweats. He had a long walk ahead of him to get back to town. To Victor Street. He had thirty-one bucks, someone would deal to him for that.

# Chapter Eight

Caleb pulled out the business card Sam had given him that read: "Amanda Phelps, Social Services Case Worker" and dialed.

"This is Mandy Phelps." Actually, the young-sounding voice said "Fay-ulps."

"Ms. Phelps, my name is Caleb Knowles. I'm a social worker with Westville Counseling."

"I've heard of you, Mr. Knowles," she said.

He couldn't tell from her tone if that was good or bad. He hoped good. "I'm calling about a child, Isaiah Clayton. My brother is his Mentor."

"Oh, yes. I've met your brother." Her tone tightened. Sam must have made an impression.

"Then you know he's deaf. He's asked me to set up a meeting with you to discuss Isaiah. I'm assuming you have a 'consent to release information' about him?"

"Yes. But that isn't an invitation for him to tell me how to do my job!"

Ouch. Sam *had* made an impression.

"Of course not. He's just new to this Mentor program and worries about Isaiah. Maybe you and I can help him understand your role better."

"He's a very stubborn man, Mr. Knowles," she said. "He seems to think Isaiah is my only client. My agency has limited resources and we all work long hours and never get paid overtime. You gonna help him understand that?"

"Uhmm. We can try?" Caleb almost felt sorry for Mandy Fay-ulps. She did the kind of social working Caleb never could. "Can we come by this afternoon?"

"Can't today, but tomorrow. One o'clock."

"See you then." Caleb sent Sam a text message with the appointment time. That was going to be one interesting meeting. He should sell tickets.

Ten minutes later, Caleb entered Safe Harbor, ready for his afternoon shift. Just a few clients waited in the lobby, but Caleb didn't recognize anyone. Shelter clients, not counseling clients, he decided. Henry stood at the check-in desk, holding a large head of cabbage like Hamlet holding poor Yorick's skull.

"Got a bunch of this stuff in from the Chinese restaurant up the street," Henry explained. "Supplier sent American cabbage instead of some other more expensive kind. So they gave us this."

"You're not going to cook it, are you?"

"Smell this place up but good." He tossed Caleb the cabbage. "Take it home, let your old lady boil it with some fatback."

Caleb smiled at the multiple things wrong with that sentence as he hurled it back. "Let's give this to someone who needs it."

Henry laughed. "We got five hundred pounds of this stuff. I ain't kidding. I called four other agencies and told them to come help themselves. Sent some over to the family shelter. Still have a hundred pounds left."

"Guess you don't get much control of inventory flow here, do you?"

"Feast or famine." He regarded the leafy vegetable again. "Course, ain't many who want to feast on this."

Gina came up to the desk struggling with a large cardboard box, with Todd, the volunteer, carrying two behind her. She laughed at something he said. He rushed to get ahead of her, placing his boxes on the desk and reaching for hers.

"Success!" She wiped perspiration from her eyes. "The kitchen at the Methodist church wants the cabbage. They're going to make soup for tomorrow's lunch with it."

"Because you convinced them," Todd said. "She went on and on about the nutritional value of cabbage. How could they possibly refuse?"

"Whatever it takes," Henry said. "Ain't your shift done?"

"I wanted to stay and help."

"They're coming for the rest of the cabbage now," Gina said.

"I'll get it. You don't need to be lifting something that heavy." Todd grinned at her before disappearing down the hall.

"Todd's almost done with his community service," Gina said. "But he wants to stay on as a volunteer. Is that okay?"

"I'd be a fool to turn down free help," Henry answered.

Gina turned to Caleb. "Did you ask Mr. Evers about tracking the hours? You know, what Esther used to do?"

"I got the time cards," Henry said. "We'll get Todd's hours logged in."

Todd returned, pushing a metal dolly stacked with four cases.

"Soup, huh?" Henry said. "Gonna be one stinky church."

After helping Henry and Todd load the cabbage into the back of the Methodist Church van, Caleb made his way to the room he loosely defined as his office. When he reached in his pocket for his keys, they weren't there.

"Damn it." He muttered, hoping he hadn't locked them inside. He wandered back out to reception, searching the desk, the counter, and even the floor for his missing key ring.

"Getting absent-minded in your old age," Henry comment-ed, tossing Caleb his own set. "The one with the red plastic is the master."

Caleb unlocked his office and searched the desk, his jacket, and even the file cabinet but they weren't there. He'd better find them by the end of his shift or he wouldn't be able to drive home.

The opening strains to "Smoke on the Water" erupted in his pocket and he groped for his cell phone. "Caleb," he answered.

"I think I've stepped into some kind of alternate universe," Claudia Briscoe said.

"Okay . . ."

"I was getting ready to go to the Willows, that place where Wyman Carter stayed. The captain stops me, says not to bother. Says this Markham Dougherty who runs the home had already been into the station. The captain questioned him himself."

"That's curious."

"I mean, I tell Bentille I should go interview some of the other residents to see if they know where he might go, and he says—get this—'that won't be necessary.' It's like my own boss is sab-otaging this investigation."

"He off his meds or something?"

"Like I said, alternate universe." She let out a puff of air. "So you want to do me a favor?"

Caleb stiffened. Claudia asking for a favor was like Lucy telling Charlie Brown she'd be glad to hold the football for him. "What?"

"Maybe you would have a reason to go to the Willows. Maybe you could ask around about Wyman, see if any of the other residents got close to him."

"In other words, do your job because Bentille won't let you do it?" Caleb considered it. Wyman needed help. Caleb hated to think of him living in the woods somewhere, with only the voices in his head for company.

"Something like that," she said. "I'll owe you."

"And I'll add it to the tab."

Caleb clicked off his cell and returned to reception to give Henry his keys. "No luck."

"They'll turn up. My guys are keeping an eye out." Henry was surrounded by files and stacks of progress notes. "I found these old clinical notes. Bill wants me to file them. It ain't pretty."

"I can help you with them later," Caleb said. "After I get back from the Willows."

"Why would you want to go there?"

"Hoping to find Wyman Carter. He stays there sometimes."

"Place is a hell hole."

"Claudia said the guy who runs it is Wyman's legal guardian."

Henry pulled off his glasses and rubbed his eyes. "You sure are chummy with that police woman."

"Not chummy. But I do some consultant work for the PD. Part of my other job." Caleb didn't mean to sound defensive. "Look. We've got two murders with links to Safe Harbor. Believe me, we're lucky it's Claudia who's got the cases."

"Lucky, huh?"

"So can you tell me how to get there? Or better yet, want to take a ride with me?"

"I just don't know what I want to do more. Try to make sense of this mess Barb left. Or go out and talk to Markham Dougherty. If I had a third option of an IRS audit, I might go for it."

Caleb reached for the Safe Harbor van keys from the hook behind the desk as Henry closed the file. "Let me get someone to cover reception," he said. "I'll meet you in the parking lot."

A few moments later, Caleb sat behind the wheel of the creaky blue van, driving north on Highway One. He kept an iron grip on the steering wheel, which shimmied whenever the van reached forty-five MPH. The engine made a strange squealing sound around that speed, too. "When was the last time y'all had this thing serviced?" Caleb asked.

"Me and the guys changed the oil a few months ago. But it ain't had a tune-up in a few years."

"It might be due," Caleb yelled over the rattles and squawks.

They drove past a dozen neighborhoods Caleb hadn't known existed. Windgate Springs, Chimney Ridge, North Pointe. Urban sprawl stretching as far as it could. But Caleb saw a disturbing number of "for sale" signs. Developers gambled there would always be buyers before the housing market tanked. What would happen to all the empty homes? Empty homes here, yet downtown Westville teemed with homeless people: a system out of balance. And now developers were eyeing the Safe Harbor property. Did Westville need another new neighborhood?

They took a right on Hardscrabble Boulevard and Henry directed Caleb to take a left on Depot Drive, an unpaved road with more mud puddles than dry surface. Depot Drive ended at the Willows.

"Look at the place," Caleb grumbled in disgust. It looked like it had been a roadhouse motel fifty years ago. Maybe it was white once, but the paint had faded to a crumbling gray. The front yard was an expanse of sand, weeds, and trash. A broken picnic table stood beside an old pick-up truck that had cinderblocks where wheels should be.

As they climbed out of the van, Caleb noticed a dozen residents in metal folding chairs scattered across the moonscape: an elderly black man in red suspenders who stared at a lizard; a gray-haired woman, dressed in a bathrobe and one fluffy slipper, arguing with someone only she could see; two younger men under a tree drinking generic soda out of cans, a dozen empties crowding their feet.

"And it's worse inside," Henry said. "Prepare yourself. It's gonna get nasty."

When Caleb opened the door, the fetid stench of urine and feces made his eyes water. He wished he had Menthol ointment to dab over his lips, the way crime scene guys did. What must it be like to live here? Did one actually get used to the odor?

It felt almost as chilly as it had been outside. Maybe the heating system was broken. Or maybe the owner saved money by setting the thermostat at fifty degrees.

"These people ain't got family who care about them. Otherwise, they wouldn't be here," Henry said.

"Is this place licensed?"

"Supposed to be," Henry replied.

"What y'all want?" A woman suddenly appeared, her hands propped on ample hips. She had a scrunched up, doughy face, two crooked teeth protruding. She squinted at Caleb's face as if she needed glasses.

"Feel the love," whispered Henry.

"I'm Caleb Knowles, and this is Henry Rudd. We're from Safe Harbor. We're trying to check on Wyman Carter."

"Wyman's become mighty popular all of a sudden, hasn't he?" She wiped her hands on a filthy apron.

"He has?" Caleb asked, but the woman ignored him.

She moved over to a long, dark corridor and bellowed, "Markham? Markham! You best get out here. You got visitors."

He heard the man grunt before he saw him waddling down the hall. "Sorry lump of homo sapien, that one," Henry whispered.

Markham Dougherty lumbered over to them, panting like he'd just run a marathon. He was almost as wide as he was tall, with black hair threaded with silver and Elvis sideburns. "Who are you?" he asked.

Caleb repeated the introductions, but Markham interrupted him when he recognized Henry. "I thought I told you I didn't want you back here! You got some nerve—"

Henry held up his hands in a placating gesture. "I'm just here to find someone. You help us, we're out of here before you can say 'trespassing,' which I know is one of your favorites."

Markham gave his whiskered chin a scratch. "You ain't taking any of my residents!"

"No, no," Caleb said quickly. "We just want to talk with Wyman Carter. We understand he stays here sometimes."

"What do you want with Wyman?"

"We're worried about him. You know he's in a bit of trouble. And he looked pretty psychotic last time I saw him," Caleb said.

"And you care just because you're some kind of good Samaritan, huh?" Markham shook his head. "Sure you are."

"We care because he's our client," Henry said. "So tell us if he's here or where he might be. Since you're his guardian and all."

Markham shuffled over to a battered desk. He opened a drawer, pulled out a thick log of some kind, and dropped it with a thud in front of him. "Wyman isn't staying with me at the moment."

"But have you seen him?"

"I checked on him at the hospital, like I always do. We were trying to get him in a treatment program when he ran. Did you know that? When he comes back, we have a bed for him here. He can stay here whenever he wants."

"That's because you get Wyman's check," Henry clarified. "Markham is Wyman's payee. If he officially discharges Wyman from the Willows, then he's got to send Wyman's disability checks back to Social Security."

"You think I got it easy being Wyman's guardian? You have any idea how much trouble that kid causes me?" He slapped a hand against the book. "You want the job, I'll gladly give it to you. Just say when."

"We just want to find him, that's all," Caleb said.

Dougherty looked at him, dark eyes fixed, assessing. Finally, he opened the tome on his desk and started flipping pages. "Wyman's due to get his allowance tomorrow so I expect he may show up."

"Allowance? What, you think he's a twelve-year-old boy?" Henry said incredulously.

Markham slammed the book shut. "Well maybe that's exactly what he is. You know what happens when Wyman gets more than a few dollars on him? It ends up in his dealer's pocket. And when Wyman runs out of cash, the dealer gets nasty. I've picked that kid up from the emergency room more times than I can say. I've talked the police out of charging him. I've tried to keep him out here, away from the drugs, long enough that he can get over the cravings, but he sneaks away whenever I turn my back for a second." Markham pointed a dirty finger at Henry. "You want to be his payee? Take him!"

Markham did have a point. Because of his drug addiction,

Wyman would be like a sieve with his money. And his mental illness would make him vulnerable to dealers and other users. Being his guardian would require a great deal of patience and understanding. He didn't see those traits in Markham Dougherty. Markham's motives centered on Wyman's check.

A flash of movement caught his eye. A young man, maybe eighteen, with red oily hair, stood just inside the corridor. As he stepped into the light, he saw that Caleb was watching him. He slipped back into the shadows.

"How much 'allowance' do you give him?" Henry asked.

"Thirty a week. Any more than that, he loses to the dealers."

Henry shook his head. "So let me see, you get about eight hundred for him from Social Security. Give him around one-twenty, so you get to pocket six-eighty. Guess that's worth a drive to the ER now and then."

Markham made a sucking sound with his teeth and waddled closer toward Henry. "Just say the word," he challenged.

Caleb stepped between the two men. Markham's eyes narrowed. Hostile. Henry looked amused, like punching Markham would be the most fun he'd had all day. While Caleb understood the sentiment, it wouldn't help them find Wyman.

Markham read something in Henry's face that made him flinch. Finally, he took a step back. "Look, we keep the bed for him whether he uses it or not. We feed him. We buy his meds but he usually don't take them. Plus I got to pay the mortgage, heat and cool this place. And I have licensing and staffing costs. Not that I need to defend myself to the likes of you."

"You know, Esther Lowell understood. She knew how hard it was taking care of Wyman. She knew the kind of mess he liked to get himself into."

"When did you talk to Esther last?" Caleb asked.

"The day before she got killed. She called to tell me what Wyman had done. She was the one that recommended that Bridgeton place up in Charlotte," Markham answered.

Esther never mentioned the conversation to Caleb. He wondered what else they had discussed. Up the hallway, he could see the silhouette of their young eavesdropper.

"How many people stay here?" Henry asked.

"Right now we got thirteen. Two empty beds, if you know

anyone."

Henry cringed at that request. Caleb agreed. He wouldn't place a dog from the pound out here. He turned to Markham and said, "We really need to talk with Wyman as soon as possible. You have any idea where we should look?"

"I know the police are looking for him. He hates the police, and he's good at staying out of jail. Too crazy to be cooped up very long, you know."

Caleb looked at the corridor again. The young man was gone.

"When he's looking for drugs he could be anywhere," Markham went on, "so you're likely to find him where the dealers are."

"Thanks for your time, Markham. If you see him, have him call Safe Harbor." Caleb said, herding Henry out the door.

As soon as they stepped outside, Caleb scanned the residents milling about. He understood now why they sat out in the cold. Inside was no warmer, and outside they were spared the stink. Hell of a place to live.

He saw the psychotic woman mumbling under her tree. The others in metal chairs, smoking and chewing tobacco. And off to himself, close to the dirt road, stood the young man from the hallway.

"Give me a minute, Henry," Caleb said. He zipped up his jacket as he sauntered over to the kid, trying to look as non-threatening as he could.

"Hey there. I was wondering if I could talk to you for a second." Up close, the young man looked pitiful. Long hair held back by grease. Pink skin, with acne eruptions across his nose and chin. Ill-fitting clothes. And he stank—the smell of self-neglect.

The boy wouldn't look at him, keeping his eyes downcast as though his shoes fascinated him.

"My name's Caleb. I work at Safe Harbor. Have you heard of it?"

He nodded, but still no eye contact.

"We're trying to find Wyman Carter. And I'll just bet you know him."

Another nod, followed by a furtive glance towards the home's front door.

"You worried you'll get in trouble for talking to me?" Caleb asked.

No answer. Which was an answer, as far as Caleb was concerned. "How about we walk over there. Behind that tree?" He motioned that the kid should accompany him to the towering live oak tree by the parking area. Once safely hidden, Caleb asked, "What's your name?"

"Jacob."

"Okay, Jacob. Can you tell me anything that would help me find Wyman Carter? I promise, we just want to make sure he's all right."

A brief glimpse at Caleb. "He was my roommate," he said.

"When did you see him last?"

"The other night. Tuesday, I think."

That was the night Esther had been killed. "What time?"

Jacob lifted a finger and ran it across the bark of the tree. "Sometimes he comes here real late. He knows how to get in the kitchen to get some food. Sometimes he stays the night." He continued to trace phantom figures on the tree trunk.

"In your room?"

"He doesn't want Markham to know when he's here so I don't tell him."

"You sound like you're a good friend to him."

"Don't got many friends. Wyman, he's got a sickness, you know? He hears voices and stuff. People don't understand him."

"You mean Markham?"

"Him and Wyman's family." The finger left the tree and went straight into his mouth. Caleb could see black smears under the fingernails.

"Is his family in Westville?"

He nodded.

"Does Wyman ever stay with them?"

"No."

"Why not?"

Jacob looked at him for the first time. "Because they don't want him. Don't claim him as kin."

Something twisted in Caleb's gut. What was it Wyman had said in the hospital room? At the end of Caleb's visit, when Wyman got wild-eyed with psychosis. "I'm the secret," he had said over and over. "I'm the secret."

Caleb reached in his pocket and pulled out a Safe Harbor card, scribbling his name on the back. "Jacob, here's my number. If you see Wyman, maybe you could give me a call?"

When Caleb climbed in the van, Henry was talking on his cell phone. He laughed, clicked off the phone, and turned to Caleb. "We got your keys. You dropped them in one of the cartons of cabbages. Good thing they aren't floating in somebody's soup pot!"

Caleb looked out at the gray sunset, at the skeletal trees pointing bony fingers in the sky. He was ready to call it a day.

# Chapter Nine

The Division of Children's Services was a large cluster of cubicles in the back of the Social Services building. It had once been a plain old Wal-Mart store before Super Wal-Marts invaded the South like Sherman on the march. As Caleb and Sam were led through the cube farm, Caleb wondered if he should have dropped bread crumbs so they could find their way out. His brother had a notebook tucked under his arm and a pensive, determined expression on his face. He hadn't said a word in almost ten minutes. Things might get interesting.

They took three turns, passed two rows of partitions, then another turn, finally stopping at a cube where a woman sat staring at her computer. On the partition above her was a cross-stitch of the name "Mandy," surrounded by elaborate pink flowers.

"I'm Caleb Knowles," he said. "I think you've met my brother, Sam."

She lifted a plump, dimpled hand to shake his but only nodded at Sam. He gave her a tight smile, the kind he might flash at his dentist before getting a root canal.

"Why don't y'all have a seat?" she said slowly so Caleb could sign it.

He had no idea where she expected them to sit. Two stackable chairs had been crammed beside a file cabinet, but each held a tower of files about to topple. They could sit on the floor, he supposed, but he didn't want to get carpet burn from the small fake oriental area rug. He grabbed the charts from one chair and placed them on the rug; Sam did the same with the other seat. Caleb wondered what her rules of confidentiality might say about him handling records of so many clients. Maybe Isaiah's was in that stack.

"What exactly do you want?" she asked Sam, her hand clasping a can of Diet Mountain Dew.

The silent brother finally spoke. "To talk about Isaiah Clayton. And his mother. And that filthy, disgusting apartment where they live."

Probably not the best tactic, Caleb realized.

She pursed her lips at them. A childlike gesture which fit, since she looked all of about twenty-two. She had on a pink sweater that swelled around rolls of fat at her middle and hip-hugger pants that had a lot of hip to hug. "I didn't place her there. She rented the apartment. Diondra moved there on her own."

Caleb signed her comments, arching his eyebrows at Sam, hinting he should soften his tone.

"Why? Why would she want to live there? That neighborhood is full of drugs and gangs. How can you allow her to raise young kids there?" Sam was coiled too tight. Caleb wondered how to calm him down.

"Allow her? Who do you think I am?" Mandy raised her voice. Caleb raised his eyebrows higher as he signed her words.

"I can't tell her where to live. I can monitor the children and try to make sure they're tended to. That's all."

Caleb held up a hand. "Where is their apartment?"

"Off Victor Street," she said. "She gets a rental subsidy from us."

"Victor Street? Sam's right; that area is saturated with drugs."

She propped a pudgy cheek on her pudgy hand. "And what am I supposed to do about that? Get rid of the drugs over there? Or find her a nice three-bedroom house with a picket fence? One that costs less than five hundred a month? Where the landlord won't ask for a criminal background check, or references, or a financial statement because with her history, that would be the end of it."

Sarcasm was hard to sign, but Sam seemed to get the point. It didn't help his tension level.

"There aren't many housing options for people like Diondra," Mandy said. "She grew up near Victor Street. For her, that neighborhood is home."

"What about a Habitat for Humanity house?" Sam asked. "Can't she get one of those?"

"She may be eligible in another year, but she hasn't lived in one place long enough to qualify. And then there's the matter of Habitat's 'sweat equity.' I don't see Diondra wielding a hammer or hauling lumber to a home site." Mandy chuckled like the idea was ludicrous. Caleb signed slowly, watching his brother's reaction. Sam's hand gripped the notebook so tightly that his knuckles paled.

"Plus," Mandy added, "She needs to have a job. Diondra hasn't worked since she got out of rehab."

"She has two kids to take care of. How is she supposed to hold down a job?" Sam got loud, his Ss sounding like "th." Articulation faltered when he got this upset.

"The same way most single parents do. Isaiah has daycare paid for by us. But he only gets there a few days a week because Diondra doesn't get out of bed in time to get him ready for the van. Charmain goes to an after-school program. Things are in place for Diondra to work. She just won't do it."

Caleb heard the frustration in her voice and wished he could sign that. Mandy was too young for a job that was far too demanding. And too important—the lives of children were at stake. "Do you do drug screens on Diondra?"

"I have." She reached for the Mountain Dew.

"How often?"

"I don't have a schedule. We do them randomly. Of course, we ran out of testing strips last month so it's been a while."

"She may be using now?" Sam asked, incredulous. "Diondra could be doing drugs in front of her kids?"

"She went to rehab. She tested clean when she got out." Mandy thunked the can down on her desk with enough force that liquid popped out the opening. "I'll test her again when I can."

Caleb looked at the mountain of records at his feet and signed, "How many cases do you have?"

"I'm the protective services case manager for seventy-two children at last count. And that stack over there," she pointed to about a dozen files on top of the file cabinet, "they're brand new cases. I haven't even met them yet. But I'll bet they'd all like that picket fence house, too. Guess I have my work cut out for me."

That pretty much took the wind out of Caleb. "That's obscene."

"Yes. But that's how it is." Mandy's phone buzzed. She gestured that she needed to take the call. For five minutes she argued with a caller about supervised visitation arrangements. As soon as she hung up, another call came through. Mandy promised to be in family court for a hearing at three P.M. Caleb watched her scrawling the time in an appointment book, scratching out a name already there. He decided he would send Matthew flowers for hiring him and sparing him this kind of job.

Mandy replaced the receiver and turned back to Sam. "I know you think I'm not doing enough for Isaiah. But I'm the reason he has you. I signed him up for a Mentor because I thought he needed some positive attention. I worry about that kid."

"And that's exactly why we're here," Caleb said. "Because Sam worries, too. He worries that Isaiah's language skills are so poor. That he only knows a handful of signs. That Isaiah's mother is hardly able to communicate with him at all."

"But at least he has a mother. Believe me, you don't want Isaiah put into the foster care system. Or sent to an institution."

Sam nearly jumped from the chair; Caleb reached over to grip his arm. "Easy," he signed.

"You cannot let that happen!" Sam boomed. "He'th juth a little boy. And he'th deaf, he'd never make it in an orphanage."

While Caleb hadn't seen that kind of anger from Sam in a very long time, he understood it. Sam remembered life after the accident that deafened him. How very, very alone he was. How he isolated himself from the family, the world—until a desperate Caleb stormed in and demanded that Sam not give up. Caleb learned sign faster than Sam did, and it gave Sam hope for connection, just like Isaiah needed. For any disability, it seemed, isolation was the enemy.

"I don't want that to happen," Mandy said, clearly flustered by the outburst. "But at least Isaiah has a home with Diondra. I have six families who don't even have an address I can put on their record. I do my best to keep them together, but they're living in shelters or rooming houses. So maybe Isaiah's situation isn't great; but believe me, I've got kids worse off than him."

"Isaiah's situation is special," Sam said, quieter now. "He deserves a better life."

Caleb saw a grim determination in Sam's eyes. Sam might feel bad for the homeless families, but Isaiah had his heart.

Caleb signed that they should leave. He could feel the tension emanating from his brother, but Sam would not get his way in this. Caleb knew the system and knew its weaknesses, and maybe he could help Sam understand. Maybe.

Caleb leaned back in the squeaky chair. As much as he hated his stuffy Safe Harbor office, he liked its location, close enough to the reception desk that he could hear what happened in the lobby. For example, even though every chair in the waiting area was occupied, he knew his two appointments, Sully McNair and Lanie Dupree, had not arrived. No matter how hard he stressed the importance of keeping appointments, homeless people did not live in the nine-to-five world. Lanie came to Safe Harbor when her voices told her to. Sully only visited when he needed food or medicine, and he'd just gotten a refill. Caleb was actually glad about that, since the police wanted to question Sully and no way that would go well. Staying away from Safe Harbor might delay a run-in with them.

Henry stuck his head in Caleb's office. "McAbee just called. Running late."

"I'm shocked."

"I'd be shocked if he actually showed up on time. Last time that happened was when Carter was president." Henry eyed the rusty file cabinet by Caleb's desk. "I'm looking for some client records."

"I'll check if you want. What are the names?"

"Cindy Lawton and Nickel."

"Nickel?" Caleb asked.

"That's the only name he ever gave us. It's all I've ever heard him called. He likes to bum a nickel off you."

"Anybody else?"

"Yeah, but see if you can find those first."

As Henry left him, Caleb removed the small key from his desk and tried the file cabinet. It took some tugging to get the top drawer opened because it was so stuffed with records, in no semblance of order. He grabbed as many files as he could and began the arduous task of sorting through them. Just getting them alphabetized, then organizing the clinical notes by date, took over an hour. When he finally found Nickel's chart, it was wedged in the middle of another client's file. Seriously sloppy.

Henry returned, carrying a clipboard and two prescription bottles. "Any luck?"

"Files are a mess." He gave Henry the record and considered the irony of this situation. Back at his day job, it was always *Caleb's* records that needed organizing. Janice constantly reminded him to get his documentation in. Matthew chastised him when late notes delayed billing. But Caleb never failed to keep record of his sessions. He made sure the important clinical info got where it needed to be.

"I doubt Nickel's gonna show anyway," Henry said. "Not with what we got out there in the parking lot."

"What?"

Henry motioned that Caleb should follow him to the lobby, where only three clients waited. "Where'd everybody go?" Caleb asked.

Henry pointed to the window. Caleb could see two police cruisers parked out front. Three uniformed officers stood beside them and chatted with a couple of the clients. "Best way to clear a room around here," Henry said. "They say they're not trying to cause any commotion, just want to talk to folks about Esther's murder. Picked a sucky day to do that."

"No kidding."

"We don't need the police running our folks off. I'm worried about the ones that bolted before Dr. McAbee saw them."

An announcement over the loud speaker interrupted them. "Caleb Knowles, line two."

"I don't think I've ever gotten a call here," he said.

"Guess you're one of us now," Henry replied, heading up the hall.

Caleb reached for the phone. "This is Caleb."

"Hey, it's me. Gina." Gina's voice sounded a little shaky.

Caleb looked at his watch: three-fifteen. Gina's shift started over an hour ago. "Everything okay?"

"Uhm, yeah. I'm just not feeling very well."

"Sorry to hear that."

"I know I don't get sick leave," she said tentatively. "But my stomach's been . . . well, kind of upset."

"Gina, I don't want you here if you're sick. Do you need anything?"

This got a nervous laugh. "No. I just need . . . some time."

"Okay." He fought an impulse to probe deeper. She wasn't his client, he reminded himself once again. "I'll see you tomorrow then. Take care."

As he hung up, Henry tossed him a set of keys. "Want to take a ride? I'm heading to Zooville."

"To Zooville." Caleb was curious about the tent village. Might be interesting to see it for himself.

"Won't take long. Dr. McAbee gave me samples to take to some of our clients. Plus I've got some food and baby stuff in the van we can give them."

"Baby stuff? There's a child living there?" Caleb couldn't imagine how an infant would fare living in a tent, especially when the temperatures dropped below freezing.

"I hear there is one. But don't you go all social worker on me. We ain't reporting this to protective services. They won't ever let us back in if we did."

Caleb didn't answer. He couldn't agree without seeing the child first. If that child looked neglected or abuse, Caleb would have no choice but to report it.


Henry drove the van through downtown, turning right on a road that paralleled the river. Just past the Gervais Street bridge, he made a left onto a narrow unpaved road that looked more suited for ATVs. Even driving as slow as he did, the van bumped over rocks and skirted holes, some as wide as a kiddie pool.

"Nice road," Caleb said.

"Doesn't get used much. Not many Zooville residents have cars," Henry replied.

The sun hung low, barely visible through the leafless trees. As dusk descended, it would summon homeless to return "home," be it a shelter, a bedroll in a graveyard, or here. Zooville.

Henry honked the horn and rolled down the window, waving at a short, dark-haired woman walking ahead of them. "May! Where ya been?"

She took a tentative step towards the van. "What you want?"

"May, it's me. Henry. From Safe Harbor. Brought some stuff for you guys."

She came a little closer to scrutinize them. Stoop-shouldered, she had a face pleated with wrinkles and freckled by the sun. She could have been sixty. Or thirty, ridden hard by life on the streets.

"Who's that?" She pointed at Caleb.

"That's Caleb, he's a new worker with me."

"We don't like visitors down here." She resumed her brisk walk up the road.

"Come on, May." Henry inched the van forward to keep up with her. "Everybody's always been nice to me down here."

"That was before." She gathered her tattered skirt in one hand as she hopped over a puddle.

"What do you mean, before? Has something happened?"

"You want in, you're gonna have to talk to the mayor. He said ain't nobody but family's allowed." She skipped to the left and started towards a path into the trees.

"Wait!" Henry said. "How can we talk to the mayor?"

"Stay here. I'll send him to you." And with that, she disappeared into the woods.

"Mayor?" Caleb asked.

Henry pulled off the gravel road and parked. "Place is like a little community. Has its own laws. You don't follow them, they'll boot you out. I've heard about the mayor but never met him."

"Guess now's your chance." As Caleb climbed out of the van, his foot sunk deep in water. "Crap," he muttered, frowning down at the mud covering his right shoe.

"Zooville's through those pines and over the hill. We could just head there and see what happens. I've never had any trouble getting in before." Henry slipped on a pair of leather gloves. Caleb wished he'd brought some.

"I say we wait. We'll get a friendlier reception if the mayor lets us in."

It took another ten minutes for the mayor to show and when he did, he was in no hurry. Shorter than Caleb, maybe five-ten, he wore a black felt cowboy hat and a red sweatshirt. A gray braid hung over his shoulder and a bent cigarette dangled from his mouth. "May said we had visitors," he said.

"I'm Henry Rudd from Safe Harbor. This here's Caleb Knowles."

Caleb extended a hand, which the mayor ignored.

"What's your business here?" He stepped close to them. A small asterisk-shaped scar sat high on his tanned cheek, like maybe he'd taken a hit of buckshot. He exhaled smoke into Caleb's face. Nice.

"We brought some food we'd like to offer," Henry said. "And there are a few folks I want to check on if that's okay." Henry eyed Caleb, then the van, hinting he should bring out the supplies.

Caleb did his best to avoid the puddle but instead slid right into it, almost landing on his butt. Brown slime now coated both shoes.

The mayor let out a deep, throaty laugh. "You can sure tell he's new. He just ruined himself a nice pair of shoes."

Caleb mumbled curses as he opened the rear door. He grabbed two boxes filled with supplies and carried them over to the mayor.

"Check under the rear seat," Henry said. "Should be a case of baby formula there."

The mayor's eyes widened at that, which Caleb took as a good sign. He found the Similac and added it to the other cases.

"Who you want to check on?" The mayor asked.

"Lanie Dupree and Nickel. You seen them?" Henry asked.

"Maybe." He took a long draw on the cigarette.

"Look, what's going on?" Henry crossed his arms. "I've never had this much trouble getting to the village before."

"We've had some trouble lately. The cops been rousting us. I've lived down here for four years and we never cause a lick of trouble to nobody. But now they say we gotta leave. They say if we don't pack up and move they're going to throw our stuff in the river and lock us up."

"Crap," Henry muttered.

The mayor ground out the cigarette on the sole of his boot and slid the butt into his shirt pocket. "We need to be here. We need to stay together. Some of the family don't do too good on their own. But I think the cops are serious about their threats."

"Just political BS. They're giving the shelter a hard time, too."

The mayor frowned. "What? Everybody who lives in Westville has to have a ranch home and a mini-van? Is that what they think?"

"Well they're full of it." Henry looked over at the path. "So can we check on our folks?"

"Only if you promise to keep your mouth shut about who's here. We don't want to give them any ammunition."

"No problem," Henry said.

Caleb handed a box to Henry and the formula to the mayor, carrying the third box himself. He did his best to keep up with the other men as they climbed the rocks and followed the trail through the woods. A breeze cut through Caleb's jacket. His wet feet stung from the cold. As the path wound through a copse of evergreens, Caleb could hear the rushing water of the Saluda, that grew louder as they got closer, and nearly thunderous when they descended the hill. Caleb caught his first glimpse of Zooville: two wide rows of tents arrayed in an arch, all facing the frothy river. In the center of the village stood a taller tent with plastic plants flanking its entrance. Two Zooville residents sat a few yards away, stoking a campfire as gray ashes twirled overhead.

A brown dog with random spots dashed over to growl at Caleb and Henry. "Mongo, quiet!" The mayor commanded. The dog rushed to him and sat. "He's our lookout."

"Good job, Mongo." Caleb reached out a tentative hand, palm down, so the dog could sniff. Mongo nudged his fingers and wagged his tail.

"He usually doesn't let strangers touch him," the mayor commented.

"Clearly he's a poor judge of character," Henry whispered.

As the mayor led them through the rows of smaller shelters, they passed an older fellow sitting on a stump to lace up a boot. Another man sat under a strange structure suspended from a tree: two beach umbrellas hung from a limb about six feet apart, with a wide sheet of dark netting draped over them. The edges of the net had been staked to the ground. Caleb stepped towards the structure, but a wiry black man rushed at him, glaring like Caleb was Satan incarnate.

"Leave Luther alone. He don't like other people." The mayor gestured that they should keep walking. As they reached the large tent, a few other residents gathered around them. The mayor said, "These men are from Safe Harbor. They brought us food."

"Henry!" A gray-haired man wearing a Columbia Blowfish baseball cap trotted over to them. "I thought that was you!"

"You disappeared on me today, Nickel. Didn't get to see the doctor, did you?"

Nickel flashed Caleb a three-toothed smile. "You work at the Harbor, too?"

"Yep. Henry's been training me."

Henry coughed out a little laugh.

"Henry's the best. The very best. Saved my life last year. Remember that, Henry? Remember when I was so sick and you took me to get some medicine? Remember?" Nickel talked fast, his gaze dancing from one face to the next. Probably manic. Medicine would help.

"You were smart enough to come to Safe Harbor. So you're the one who saved yourself." Henry handed him his pills. "You didn't get these earlier."

Nickel dropped the bottle in the chest pocket of his overalls, not looking the least bit interested in taking them.

"We brought food. You could have yourself something to eat with the pills," Henry said.

Nickel looked into Caleb's box. "I like them Vienna sausages."

Caleb held up a can. "I'll give you this if you take the medicine."

Nickel just smiled.

"Come on, Nick," Henry said. "Don't want you having to go back to the hospital. Folks in Zooville would miss you too much."

The mayor, who had been watching the exchange, spoke. "Henry's right. We don't want you in the hospital. You make the best coffee of anyone around here."

The praise worked. Nickel opened the bottle and popped two pills in his mouth. Caleb tossed him an apple. Nickel took a surprisingly large bite for someone with so few teeth.

"You the man." Henry squeezed Nickel's shoulder.

"Who else are you looking for?" The mayor asked.

"Lanie Dupree," Caleb said. "Does she stay here?"

"We keep a place for her, but she ain't here now." He pointed at a tent set apart from the others, shaded by a loan bottlebrush pine tree. "People like her keep to themselves. It's the only way their minds get quiet."

A quiet mind would be a luxury for someone as paranoid as Lanie. Wherever she was, Caleb hoped she was okay.

Word had spread about Henry and Caleb bringing supplies. As about twenty people clustered around them, Caleb did his best to dispense the food fairly, but in a matter of seconds it turned into a free for all, cans and packages grabbed and tucked in pockets and hats until every item disappeared. Henry held on to the case of formula.

"Who's gonna need this?" Henry whispered to the mayor.

He waved them forward. "Come with me."

They bent to enter the large tent. In the center were two camp-style chairs and a table made of plywood propped on cement blocks. Four plastic crates lined the back wall of the tent and beside them sat a young woman with black hair and a scatter of freckles across her nose. A curly-haired infant cuddled in her arms, holding a small piece of brown cardboard against its mouth.

As the mayor eased down beside the woman, he kissed the top of her head. She had a tattoo of a star on her right arm that looked homemade. The baby reached for the mayor who lifted it to his lap. The young woman kept her dark eyes zeroed in on Caleb and Henry.

"This is Dawn," he said, pointing to the woman. "And this is our little one, Star."

"Who are they? Why are they here?" Dawn asked.

Henry set the box in front of her. "We brought some stuff. Hope this will be useful to you. Got about twenty cans of Similac."

"Did someone send you here?" She persisted.

Henry arched his brows at Caleb. "Nobody but our doc. Why?"

"Like I said, we've had some trouble." The mayor squeezed her hand. "I think they're okay, Dawn. It's okay."

Caleb eased down beside Henry, reaching his hand towards the little girl, who immediately grabbed his thumb and pulled it into her mouth. He laughed. "Teething, I see."

Dawn nodded. "She gets fussy from it."

"I'll bet. My daughter used to howl when hers got bad." He bent over to look at the child, wondering where she'd been born, if she'd had any medical care, but knowing Dawn was too suspicious for him to ask those questions. Besides, she looked pink-cheeked and plump, dark eyes fringed with thick lashes. "Star looks pretty healthy. How old is she?"

"Nine months," Dawn answered. "She had a cold but she's getting over it. Just wish the teeth would come in."

As if in response, Star shoved Caleb's thumb against her gums.

"Orajel can help with that," Caleb said. He wanted to suggest a chilled teething ring but that would be difficult to manage in a home that had no refrigerator. Or electricity. "We have some at Safe Harbor, if you want to come by."

She looked at the mayor. He said, "We can take care of ourselves."

"What about when it gets colder? We can help you get a bed at the family shelter if you want." Caleb could feel Henry's glower without looking at him but he ignored it. He couldn't help but worry about how the child would stay healthy when winter hit full-force.

"We stay warm enough." The mayor opened a can of formula. "Not that it's your business."

Dawn reached in a large sisal bag for a plastic bottle. Caleb wondered how she kept it sterile, but knew he shouldn't ask. As she poured the formula into the bottle, Star smacked her lips, clearly hungry. The mayor took the bottle and slipped the nipple into Star's mouth.

"Y'all know anything about the dead guy?" Dawn asked suddenly. "The one they found?"

"The police came to the shelter. Showed us a picture but we didn't recognize him," Henry replied.

"They found him real near here. Just down river." Dawn pointed out the tent flap. Caleb could hear the rush of water, and see the pines that flanked the riverbank a few dozen yards away.

"But you aren't missing anybody, are you?" Caleb asked. "I mean, from the village."

"Not any of our stay-here people. We got some others who come and go, like Luther. I hope it's not one of them." The mayor and Dawn exchanged a meaningful look.

"Is there someone who . . ." Caleb chose his words carefully. "You're worried about?"

Dawn and the mayor continued a silent conversation. Finally, she spoke. "There's a guy named Stormy. He usually comes here after the weekend but he hasn't shown up. Nobody's seen him, even in town where he usually hangs out. We were wondering if maybe it was him."

"What does Stormy look like?"

"He's white, about Johnny's height." She looked at the mayor.

"I'm Johnny," he clarified.

"Stormy has a tattoo on his shoulder," Dawn added. "It's an eight-ball. You know, like in pool. Do you know if the body had something like that?"

"No, I don't." But Caleb planned to find out. "Do you know Stormy's last name? Anything else about him?"

Another cautious look passed between the couple. Johnny gave Dawn a shrug. She said, "His last name is Bennett, used to travel with the fair."

"Damn. I know Stormy," Henry said. "He comes to my recovery group sometimes. You think he could be the guy?"

"I hope not," she said.

"Does he have family around?" Caleb asked.

"I think he still has family in Sumter, but he doesn't talk to them."

Caleb thought that was probably true of most Zooville residents. Forgotten or detached from relatives for any number of reasons, they had formed a new family with each other.

"If you hear anything, we'd like to know," Johnny said.

"Sure." Henry looked at Caleb and cocked his thumb towards the tent flap that served as the door, signaling they should leave.

But Caleb held up a hand. "One more thing. We're looking for another client, a guy named Wyman Carter. Do you know him?"

"He doesn't stay in Zooville." Johnny's tone chilled.

"But do you know him?"

Johnny looked at Dawn who bit at her bottom lip. "I think we're done here," he said, pointing to the exit.

"Okay, okay, man," Henry said. "Thanks for talking to us. I'll try to get some more formula to you soon, Dawn."

"Thanks," she said, her hand reaching for the black-haired child now sleeping in its father's arms.

As they started the hike to the van, the setting sun hung low on the horizon, a bright orange wafer veiled by a ribbon of purple clouds. The rocky path proved even harder to navigate in the growing darkness, though Henry didn't seem to have much trouble. Caleb wished they'd thought to bring a flashlight. And he wished his feet were warm and dry. But mostly, he wished he knew the loaded history between Wyman Carter and Johnny.

"So Wyman must have been at Zooville," Henry said. "I'd sure like to know what happened."

"Me, too." Caleb answered. He felt in his pocket for his cell phone. On the ride back to Safe Harbor he intended to call Claudia and ask her about Stormy Bennett.

# Chapter Ten

The next afternoon, Caleb was late leaving the practice for Safe Harbor, and decided that having two part-time social work jobs was really like having two full-time social work jobs. He'd spent his morning with three regularly scheduled clients, but a fourth showed up in crisis. Divorce papers had arrived at her house that morning, then her husband called from his office to say he planned to marry their daughter's soccer coach. The client cried throughout the session, but left feeling more in control. She seemed eager to keep the appointment Caleb made for her with Phillip Etheridge, attorney-at-law. Caleb trusted Phillip to go for the soon-to-be-ex-husband's jugular, which might help her more than a year of sessions with Caleb.

Janice had stopped him between clients to tell him Gina hadn't come in that morning and hadn't called in. Odd. Janice offered to call Gina's apartment but Caleb said he'd take care of it if she wasn't at Safe Harbor that afternoon.

Only a half-dozen clients waited in the shelter's lobby when Caleb arrived. He didn't recognize anyone, and he wondered which of the two sleeping men smelled like a distillery. Nobody was allowed to drink at Safe Harbor, but that didn't stop them from imbibing before they arrived. Caleb joined Henry in the reception area where he was pawing through a box of files.

"You seen Gina?" Caleb asked.

"Nope."

"Did she call in?"

"Nope." Henry grabbed a stack of records from the box and placed them on the desk. "We want the interns to be a little more responsible than this."

"Me, too. It's really not like her not to call."

Caleb pulled the slip of paper from his shirt pocket and dialed the number Janice had written down for him.

"Hello?" The woman who answered sounded a little breathless.

"Hi, is Gina Fulton there?" Caleb asked.

"Who's calling please?" Panting, like she just got back from running.

"I'm her internship supervisor, Caleb Knowles."

"Yeah, she talks about you. I'm Robin, her roommate."

Of course Gina had a roommate; part of the whole starving-student routine. "Is she there?"

"No." Robin didn't elaborate.

"Well she was supposed to be at the counseling center this morning, and here at Safe Harbor starting at two. Nobody's heard from her. I was wondering if she was sick or something."

"She was going to see her parents for the weekend. Maybe she left early."

"Did she call and tell you that?"

"No, but it's not like I'm her keeper. She doesn't have to tell me where she is." Now she sounded a bit petulant. "Did you try her cell?"

Of course! Every kid Gina's age had some kind of cellular device. Why hadn't he thought of that? "Can you give me the number?"

She sighed like this was quite an imposition but gave him the number.

"Look," she said. "I'm late for work. I'll tell her to call you when she comes back."

Caleb hung up and immediately dialed the cell number. He got her voice mail, the message saying her mailbox was full. Hopefully, she'd at least see he had called.

He reached for his day timer, flipping to the back where he kept work phone numbers, and dialed Ron Weston, Gina's advisor at the university. When Ron's voicemail answered, Caleb left his cell number and asked that Ron call him back.

Gina was probably okay. Probably just goofing off at her parents' house. When she called back, he'd feel ridiculous for having worried. Probably.

"Got a second?" Claudia Briscoe had a file in one hand and her cell phone in the other when marched into Caleb's office and helped herself to the seat across from him. She handed him a folder.

"I did a check on what you told me about Stormy Bennett. The medical examiner said there was a tattoo on the murder vic's shoulder, though most of it had been torn away. He was able to make out a black sphere and part of the number 8. So mystery solved about the body."

Caleb opened the file. There were four booking reports with badly photocopied pictures of Stormy that relayed arrests for public intoxication, aggressive begging, and an indecent exposure charge for flashing some girls during cheerleader practice. No major time served. A nuisance criminal, not a dangerous one.

"He had family in Sumter, but they'd been out of touch for years. Stormy burned some bridges." She took the file back from him. "So my guess is he was a regular here at Safe Harbor, am I right?"

Caleb reached for his phone. "Let me get Henry in here. He's been at Safe Harbor a lot longer than I have."

A few minutes later, Henry came in carrying a box of Ziploc bags and a giant plastic pail full of white powder. He frowned when he spotted Claudia. "Having police around ain't exactly helping business."

"They identified the body by the river. Stormy Bennett," Caleb said.

"Damn." Henry lowered the bucket and brushed his hands together. He smelled like clean laundry. Caleb leaned forward to look in the pail. Detergent.

"Claudia has some questions."

Henry regarded the plastic bags in his hand. He didn't answer.

"I know you're not wild about this," Caleb said. "But Stormy deserves to have his killer caught. We need to help make that happen."

He handed a baggie to Caleb and to Claudia. "Got another detergent shipment. Y'all can help me divvy it up."

"You're kidding, right?" Claudia asked.

"Two scoops a pop. Makes it go farther. And seal it up good. When it leaks, it's a mess." He set the pail between the three of them.

Caleb grabbed the metal spoon and filled his bag. "Get to

work, woman!"

She frowned, examining her manicured nails, taking her time about removing her gold bracelet. With a sigh, she reached for a scoop. "What can you tell me about Bennett?"

"He stays here now and then. Hadn't been around in a while though. Used to come to some of my groups." Henry eyed Caleb like he wanted to say more but thought better of it. "He's—was— a good guy."

Caleb wondered what Dawn and Johnny would say when they heard of Stormy's death. They probably knew the most about him, but he doubted they'd talk to the police.

Henry took the bag from Claudia and gave it a good shake to check the seal.

"Do you know anyone who might want to hurt Stormy?" Claudia asked.

"Nope." Henry dropped a bag of detergent by the pail and started filling another.

"Maybe another client. Someone he had a conflict with?" she persisted.

"Nope."

"Okay." Claudia's tone cooled. "Maybe not a client? Do you know of anybody who had a fight or argument with him?"

"Like I said, he was a good guy." Henry tilted the pail to shift the detergent to the side, giving them easier access.

"Caleb, what about you?"

"Didn't know him."

She pursed her lips, eyes narrowing. "The man died. You know anything that can help us find his killer, you need to say."

"Don't know anything," Henry said.

"Okay then." She slapped the folder against the arm of her chair. "I guess I could station a patrol car here in your parking lot. Question all the folks who come by."

"Like you did the other day? A dozen people missed getting their medications after that little stunt," Caleb said.

"We do what we can." Her smile was close to conniving.

Henry sealed up another baggie and tossed it to the floor more forcefully than he needed to.

A page came over Caleb's phone: "Henry, you're needed up front."

Henry collected the box of bags, the scoops, and the almost empty pail of detergent. "And I was so enjoying our little talk," he said, leaving them.

Claudia worked at reattaching her bracelet, gold charms of little footballs and Gamecocks glinting. "Okay, Caleb. Tell me what you know. And no BS this time."

"Look, I have a different role here. I can't violate client confidentiality."

"I didn't think Stormy was your client."

"No but . . ." Caleb stammered. Maybe Claudia had a point. "Look. I'll talk to the woman who told me Stormy was missing. If she agrees, I'll give you a call and you can talk to her yourself."

"Somehow, I'm not holding my breath." Claudia pulled out a sheet from the file and held it up. It was the picture he'd seen before: Stormy as the corpse in the river. "You can protect your client if you want. But you're not doing this guy any favors."

"That was low, Claudia."

"You have your clients, I have mine." She replaced the photo and stood. "If I don't hear from you soon, I'm sending a patrol car down this way."

Caleb held up a hand to stop her exit. "Any word on Wyman Carter?"

"No. He's used to the streets. Probably pretty good at hiding himself. You had any chance to check out the Willows?"

"They haven't seen him, either. And that group home is one sorry-ass place, by the way. Nobody should have to stay there. I've been trying to call the licensing people to get them to do an inspection. They should close that dump down."

"Good luck. If we closed down every sorry-ass group home in Westville, Safe Harbor would be busting at the seams."

Wyman knew how to bum a quarter. After all, he'd trained after a master. "Don't look too desperate," Stormy had said. "Just look sad and like you ain't gonna hurt them. Say 'I hate to bother you but can I have a quarter? I need to make a call,' but keep your head down. And if they do or don't give you the quarter say, 'God bless you.' If they didn't give it to you, someone else may be close by who will. Don't hold no grudge against somebody who don't pony up." And Wyman followed that advice. The first man told him to "get a freakin' job." But the elderly couple who overheard fumbled through their change and gave him sixty-three cents. Wyman said, "God bless both of you," and the little white-haired lady gave him a sweet smile.

Finding a payphone was no easy task, now that the whole world had cell phones. But he knew of one beside the courthouse so he headed downtown. He hated having to call Markham, but he needed his allowance, and if it was too soon to ask for it Markham would have to float him a loan. Markham got money from Wyman's family—Wyman didn't know how much—so the least that fat son-of-a-bitch could do was pay Wyman when he needed money for food. Well, to be honest, not just food.

He dialed the number. Unfortunately, Rhetta answered. "Let me talk to Markham," Wyman said.

"Where your manners, boy?" Rhetta said.

"Can I speak to Markham please?" Wyman almost added, "Bitch" because that was what she was, but she'd hang up and he didn't have the money for another call.

"Markham!" she screamed, not bothering to cover the phone. It seemed like an hour later when Markham finally answered.

"I need some money," Wyman said.

"Where are you?"

"Right now I'm by the courthouse, but I can meet you somewhere."

"You know the police are looking for you? They came by, and some guys from Safe Harbor stopped in. You're mighty popular."

Wyman didn't know what to say. He knew taking the gasoline to Safe Harbor had been a damn stupid thing to do. He did not want to go to jail.

"So I'm coming, but I'm bringing you back here. You understand? At least till this legal mess clears up."

"When will you come?"

"Be this afternoon."

Wyman looked around. He wasn't hanging around the courthouse until Markham came. "Come to the lot behind Jumbo's bar."

"Shit, Wyman. Don't you be getting yourself drunk."

"How can I? You've got my money. Can't you come sooner?" Once he had the cash, he'd find Big John and get himself a hit that he wouldn't have to share with a soul.

"You ain't the only person I gotta take care of," Markham said with a long-suffering sigh. "I'll get there when I get there."

Wyman waited behind the bar. He could feel the hollow space in his stomach. He had a sandwich yesterday but nothing today except half a pack of peanut butter crackers that only left him more hungry. Markham better show up soon. He said he would. But Markham didn't always do what he said he was going to do, and that was the problem. Wyman limped over to the corner to check the traffic for Markham's truck but didn't see it. His foot throbbed the way it often did when the weather got cold and misty, and only one thing would take away the ache. The only thing. And it would fill his mind with blue skies and flower garden smells and take away the hurt and the hunger and the feeling that the whole world was better than him. One rock, tiny as an M&M, would give him all of that. And more.

How long had it been? Days and days, but he still hungered for it. At least the voices were quieter than a while ago. He didn't know why. Sometimes they just did that, stopped bothering him or not bothering him as much, like a conversation gone to a different room. Stormy said they would go away if he stopped using because he believed it was the crack that made Wyman crazy. He was wrong though. Getting high kept the voices manageable. Craving made them scream.

He checked the corner again, in case Markham had parked and was looking for him. Wyman zipped up his sweatshirt as far as he could. He used to have a safety pin to close it at his neck but lost it somehow. Had a scarf last year, too, but somebody stole it. He hoped it didn't get too cold today. Of course, once he hooked up with Big John, that wouldn't matter. He could never feel cold when the rock poured that light inside him.

Finally. The giant black truck that rumbled like a hundred Harleys pulled up in a blue parking space even though Markham wasn't any kind of handicapped. He climbed down from the cab of the truck and looked short standing next to it. Short but wide and blubbery because Markham always did like to eat. Of course, Markham never had to eat that crap they served at the home.

"Wyman." He crossed over to where Wyman was waiting. Looking Wyman up and down with a frown. "You doing okay?"

"I need a new jacket," Wyman said, fiddling with the broken zipper. Hoping Markham would give him a little more money this time, which he would not use on a jacket, but on something else to keep him warm. A better kind of warm.

"You're coming home with me," Markham said. "You got a bed and three squares waiting. You got it better than most."

They'd had this argument a thousand times. No, not an argument, more like Markham lecturing and Wyman not saying anything. And if Markham got too red-faced about it Wyman would comply. He'd climb in the truck and let Markham drive him to the Willows but run off the first chance he got. Wyman was good at escaping.

"You realize how much trouble you're in?" Markham said. "You know that Lowell woman got murdered. Police think you did it."

Wyman wasn't sure he heard right. "What did you say?"

"That Lowell woman you tried to burn up. She's dead."

"Esther?" Wyman scratched at his chin. He had been spitting mad at Esther and thought about hurting her but he didn't kill her. At least, he was pretty sure he hadn't. Sometimes crack made the memories slip away from him. But no, he wouldn't have hurt her. "I didn't—"

"We'll get you hooked up with a lawyer," Markham said. "I don't want you talking to nobody till I do that. You understand?"

He nodded. His empty gut roared loud enough for Markham to hear. "So you ready to come home? Let Rhetta feed you?"

Wyman looked away. This was the tricky part—getting money out of Markham without Markham dragging him back to that hell-hole, the Willows. "I have a place to stay. Besides, if I go with you then the police will know where to find me."

"I said I'd get you a lawyer." Markham came closer. He smelled like onions. Markham probably had himself a nice fat lunch while Wyman sat hungry waiting on him.

"They'll still take me to jail." Wyman raised his voice, sounding a little desperate. "No, I'll do better out here where they can't find me. I'll be warm, and once you give me money I'll have food. Just for a few days, until the police find whoever it was that killed Esther."

"Wyman, listen to me. Now is not the time for you to go in

hiding."

"All I need is a little money for food. I won't get in trouble. I'll stay out of sight." He stepped away from Markham, looking towards the road in case he needed to bolt.

Markham stared at him for so long Wyman started getting twitchy. Finally, Markham reached for his wallet. "I'll give you enough for the weekend, but then you got to call me. You understand? I don't hear from you I'll send the police down here. You got that?"

Wyman nodded eagerly. The twenty and two tens Markham gave him were a little damp from Markham's sweaty hand. "Remember I need to get a new jacket."

Markham took his time about opening the wallet again and fishing out another ten. "I want to see that jacket on you, you hear? I mean it. If I find out you spent this money on something else—"

Wyman wondered what Markham *would* do. It wasn't like Markham cared a lick about him. He just liked getting money from Wyman's family. Same with the other guys that stayed at the Willows. Markham pocketed their social security checks but treated them like dogs locked in a pound.

"This ain't enough," Wyman said, studying the cash. "I want a real jacket. It's getting cold out." He kept his eyes on Markham's face, not looking down at the gaping wallet because he couldn't trust his face not to betray him. If Markham figured out how bad he was craving, the wallet would slam shut.

Markham let out a sigh, his pudgy fingers digging into the wad of bills and pulling out another twenty. "One more thing," Markham said. He opened the door to the truck and hefted his fat body up into the cab. "Here."

Wyman caught the black device Markham threw to him. A cell phone.

"Don't use it for anything but calling me, you understand?"

"Okay." Wyman wondered how much he could get for it. Used to be, cell phones pawned for thirty bucks or so. But not anymore.

Markham started the truck. It sounded loud as an eighteen-wheeler. "I'm trusting you boy. Don't let me down."

Wyman smiled. "I won't."

# Chapter Eleven

Caleb fumbled for his ringing cell as he steered his Subaru into traffic. "This is Caleb."

"Hey Caleb, this is Ron. You called about Gina?"

"Yeah. She's missed three days of placement. Called in sick last Wednesday, but didn't come back Thursday or Friday. It's not like her."

"I can check to see if she's made it to classes. But we've got a nasty stomach bug going around campus. Half my students missed seminar yesterday. My guess is she caught it."

"That makes sense." Good. If Gina had the bug, it was best that she stay away from the shelter. Heaven help them if a virus struck one of the dorms.

"Let me know if you don't hear from her in the next day or two," Ron said, clicking off.

Caleb wheeled into the Safe Harbor lot, parking as far from the dumpster as he could. It was still hard to believe that Esther had been brutally murdered so close to where they worked. It was something he wouldn't forget, nor should he. They all needed to be careful until the killer was caught.

Once inside, Henry met him at the door to his office. "You got company."

He scanned the crowded waiting area but didn't see any of his regular clients. "Who?"

"They're in the restroom," Henry clarified.

"Is it Lanie Dupree?"

"Nope."

"Sully?"

"You ain't likely to see him for a while."

"The lieutenant governor? I've been meaning to chat with him about his stance on school lunches for hungry kids." The man had actually compared poor people to stray dogs, saying that you shouldn't feed them because they'd "only breed."

"You and me both, but no it isn't him. It's Dawn, from down in Zooville. Brought her baby with her. I didn't tell her about Stormy. Thought I'd let you do that."

"Thanks," Caleb muttered.

"You the counselor guy," Henry answered.

Dawn jostled the crying infant as she came down the hall. She had on a short cotton dress with black leggings and a pink sweatshirt, the hood pulled up around her head. She carried the large straw sack Caleb remembered from the tent in Zooville. Little Star wore a diaper and cotton sweater with mismatched knit booties on her feet.

"Nice to see you, Dawn," Caleb said.

Dawn struggled to sit, positioning her squirmy child on her knees and bouncing her. Star continued to cry.

"Is she okay?" Caleb slid his chair over closer, nudging Star's chin up to look at her face, bright pink and streaked with tears.

"I don't know. I think it's just the teething but I can't get her to stop crying." She made shh-shh noises, but Star wailed louder.

He touched the child's head with the palm of his hand. "Feels a bit warm, but they can run a fever when they teeth. Any other symptoms?"

"Like what?"

It surprised him that she had to ask. But where else would she get parenting guidance? "Any diarrhea or congestion?"

"Maybe some congestion. And she won't eat so I wonder if her stomach is upset."

Star clutched her mother's hand and pulled it to her mouth. Drool slithered down Dawn's fingers.

"Do you have a pediatrician?" Caleb asked.

"No. We use the ER because they'll take Medicaid. But she's had all her vaccinations."

"And how long does it take for you to get seen?"

"If we get there first thing in the morning, we can be done by noon sometimes. Any later and we're there all day."

Caleb started to caution her about the risks of the ER, how it exposed Star to all kinds of germs, but what options did she have?

"Let's try the Orajel and see if it helps." Caleb left her and made his way to the pantry where two volunteers were stocking shelves with canned goods.

"Hey, anybody know where the baby stuff is?" Caleb asked.

The taller of the volunteers, a dark-haired young man with a pimply face, answered. "You'd better ask Todd. He keeps track of everything."

"Easier to do that than to actually work," the other man grumbled. His sweatshirt read: BEER: PROOF THAT GOD LOVES US AND WANTS US TO BE HAPPY. Funny. Unless, of course, the guy's community service was related to a DUI. So often it was.

"Where's Todd?" Caleb asked.

"Todd!!" The man bellowed as he shoved three cans of stewed tomatoes on a shelf.

"What!" Todd hurried over, carrying a clipboard and looking quite annoyed. But when he spotted Caleb, he flashed a self-conscious smile. "Oh, hey Caleb."

"What's with the clipboard?" Caleb asked.

"Just doing inventory. I've set up a spreadsheet so we can monitor when we get low on different items."

"Or we could just check the shelves," said the man in the beer shirt.

"I can identify trends in donation flow, too. Like we tend to get more canned goods at the beginning of the month. And meats come on Mondays from the local grocery store. The average shelf life is three days, so we're better off freezing what comes in."

"Which is what Henry has us do," the other man said.

Ignoring him, Todd asked, "Something I can help you with?"

"Infant supplies. Where do we keep them?"

Todd pointed to a metal shelf in the back of the pantry. Caleb browsed the supplies until he spotted a tube of Orajel, a pair of plastic baby bottles, and two packages of Pampers that looked about Star's size. Todd handed him a box to put the supplies in.

"When's Gina coming back?" Todd asked.

"Good question."

Todd's head jerked up. "I thought you'd given her time off or something."

"There's a bug going around school. She's probably home recuperating."

"If you hear from her, tell her I hope she gets better soon."

Caleb carried the supplies back to his office. Dawn stood outside his door, Star nestled against her, staring down a short, pudgy man whose back was to Caleb. Dawn shook her head at something the man said, then took a step away from him.

"Excuse me?" Caleb interrupted, not happy about the wide-eyed look of fear on Dawn's face.

When the man spun around, Caleb recognized the black greasy hair and bulbous stomach. Markham Dougherty.

"What's going on?" Caleb asked.

"Nothing," Markham said. "Just catching up with an old client of mine. Didn't realize she'd had a baby and all."

Dawn rested her cheek against Star's curly head. "I was never your client."

"My guest then. After all, you did live at my home. How long was it? A month or two?"

"It was just a couple of weeks."

"Where are you staying now? You got that baby, you need to be somewhere fitting."

She didn't answer at first, just clung to her baby. When she finally spoke, her voice sounded young and defeated. "What do you want from me?"

"Nothing, Dawn. Nothing." He turned to Caleb. "I'm just stopping by for some medicine for one of our clients."

"Henry can help with that."

"Good seeing you, Dawn." Markham reached over to touch the baby but Dawn pulled away.

"Guess I'll be going then."

As Caleb and Dawn returned to his office, Caleb placed the box of supplies beside Dawn's feet. "Hope you can use some of this stuff."

"Thanks."

"So you used to stay at the Willows?" he asked.

She looked at Caleb, then at her daughter. "Can we not talk about that?"

Once again, Caleb was reminded of the mistrustfulness so many homeless people feel. As curious as he was about the tension between Dawn and Markham, he knew better than to pursue it. "Sorry. Didn't mean to pry."

Star wiggled in her arms, drool dripping from her tiny chin. Caleb opened the tube of Orajel and offered to Dawn. "Put a little on your finger," he instructed.

She took care squirting the ointment onto her fingertip and massaging Star's inflamed gum. Little Star looked puzzled by the strange tasting ointment but soon smacked her lips.

"See? Working already," Caleb said.

Dawn grinned, gathering Star close again. Not exactly a Madonna and child, but definitely a loving mother doing her best. "I really appreciate your help."

"You know," Caleb said. "I've got a friend who's a pediatrician. He doesn't advertise that he takes Medicaid, but he does. I'll give you his name. Just tell him I sent you."

He wrote down the information and handed it to her. "Is there anything else you need?" he asked.

"No thanks." She looked down at her daughter, who had burrowed up against her, eyelids at half-mast. Nap time.

"Dawn, there's something else I need to tell you." He paused, unsure how to proceed. "The police made an ID on the body they found by the river. It was Stormy Bennett."

She didn't respond at first, except to hold her baby closer. But then she shook her head, blinking back tears as they welled in her dark eyes.

"Sorry to have to tell you that," Caleb said. "I know you cared about him."

She rubbed her nose against the sleeve of her sweatshirt. Caleb handed her a tissue.

"Do they know who did it? Who killed him?" she asked.

"No." He leaned back, thinking about his conversation with Claudia. "The thing is, Dawn, I talked to the police. I mentioned what you said about Stormy's tattoo. That was how they made the ID."

Dawn stiffened. Star, sensing the change in her mother, sought out her thumb.

"I didn't tell them your name," Caleb added quickly. "I never said anything about Zooville. But they want to find Stormy's killer. And to do that, they're going to have to talk to people who knew him."

"No."

"No what? No you don't want to talk to them?"

"The police won't do anything," she said. "They don't care what happened to Stormy. Not really. Just one less street person they have to bother with."

"I can see how you'd think that." Caleb could imagine what her dealings with law enforcement had been since living in Zooville. And he knew nothing about her before. "But the detective working Stormy's murder is a friend of mine. She takes her job very seriously. Once she figures out Stormy lived in Zooville, she'll be banging on tent flaps until somebody talks with her."

"Nobody will talk to her. Tell her that. Tell her there's no reason for her to come." Dawn pushed the tissue against her eye, wiping away another tear.

"That will just make her more determined. She's very stubborn. It's what makes her a good cop." Caleb could see Dawn wouldn't relent. She seemed ready to out-stubborn Claudia on the issue. So Caleb tried another tactic:

"Dawn, tell me what you know about Stormy."

She narrowed her eyes, all trust gone now. "So you can tell the police?"

"Actually, yes. Unless you tell me not to. I'm just trying to help here. Maybe work as an intermediary."

"An intermediary," she repeated, like she was tasting the word. "I'd have talk to Johnny first."

"Johnny isn't here. By the time you get back to ask him, another day will be gone. Another day with Stormy's killer on the loose." He leaned forward. "Just tell me this. Do you know of anyone who had reason to hurt him?"

She looked away, her gaze cold and distant. Caleb waited, unsure if he'd get another word out of her, but finally she spoke. "Everybody liked Stormy," she said. "He was a sweet, gentle man. He used to drink but he stopped and he helped other people who wanted to quit, too. I mean, he wasn't trained or anything, but Stormy did his best to help people go straight."

"Sounds like a special guy."

"He is—was. He helped me, back when I was pregnant. I never touched another drop or smoked a thing when I was carrying Star. But it was hard and Stormy and Johnny helped me through."

"I'm glad."

Another tear rolled down her cheek but she didn't move to wipe it. A defiant tear. "But there was someone else. Someone he tried to help. Someone he stuck with like glue but it didn't work because the guy liked crack too much."

"Is he someone in Zooville?"

"Johnny and Stormy had to make him leave Zooville. He mouthed off about it. Said some ugly things to Johnny and Storm. But I don't think—" Suddenly she stood, positioning the sleeping Star against her shoulder. "I need to go. I shouldn't have said—"

"Wait, Dawn. Tell me who he was." Caleb stood also, hoping to keep her from bolting.

She hesitated in the doorway and said, "The guy was Wyman Carter."

"You have a free hour," Janice said, greeting him over his morning coffee. She wore a brown sweater with multi-colored leaves on it, a brown skirt and brown shoes. A clip repeating the autumnal motif nested in her bottle-blond hair. "Matthew's tied up at the hospital so he said y'all would have staffing on Friday. I marked out an extra half hour for it on your schedules."

He looked down at the stack of papers in Janice's hand. "So you have a project for me?"

"I thought maybe you could get caught up on some of your notes. I put the charts in your office."

"Yikes."

"It's not too bad. Just four overdue treatment plans and last week's progress notes. Oh, and here's a stack of authorization letters I need you to sign."

"Oh, so that's all." He took the papers from her. Of course he'd gotten behind. A recurring problem, but with the added workload at Safe Harbor, it was even worse. Janice had probably been waiting for this moment for twelve days, and should be commended for her patience.

Caleb drained his coffee cup and drifted back to his office. The first chart had a treatment plan with little sticky arrows pointing to where Caleb should initial. The unwritten progress note had been folded over so it would be easy to find. Janice was like the perfect kindergarten teacher with Caleb as her only student.

He labored through three more records and decided he needed another caffeine injection. As he made his way to the break room, Janice intercepted him.

"Hey, I'm just getting coffee, not making an escape," he said.

"There's a young woman here who wants to see you. She says she's Gina's roommate. She's very upset." Janice looked worried. Brow creased, lips curving into an uncharacteristic frown. He followed her to the waiting area where Gina's roommate stood by the reception desk. She was very thin, with a dancer's delicate physique and lily-pale skin. She wore silver hoops in her ears and left nostril.

"Mr. Knowles? I'm Robin. We talked on the phone."

"Any word from Gina?" he asked.

"No. I told you she was at her parents for the weekend. But they called this morning—she never went there. They didn't even know she planned to go. But maybe she didn't, maybe she just said that, but I don't know where she is and I'm starting to get worried!"

Janice stepped closer, hand outstretched like a concerned mother. Robin wiped her eyes with a shaky hand.

"And nobody's heard from her?" Caleb asked.

"No! I called her sister in Florence but she hasn't talked to her. I went to the school and talked to a couple of her classmates but nobody knew anything. I don't know what else to do. Something could have happened to her!" Her voice trembled.

Janice slipped an arm across her shoulders. "Can I get you anything, dear?"

"I just didn't know what else to do so I came here."

Alarm bells rang in Caleb's brain. This was bad. It could be real bad, given recent events. Nobody had been looking for Gina. After Caleb talked to Ron Weston, he attributed her absence to a virus. He should have been more concerned.

"I'd like to call her parents. Do you have the number?"

She nodded, pulling a pink cell phone from her purse and scrolling through contact numbers until she found it. Caleb read the display and dialed from his desk phone.

A woman answered, her voice thickly southern when she said, "Hello?"

"This is Caleb Knowles from Westville. May I speak with Mr. or Mrs. Fulton?"

"This is Irene Fulton." Irene was pronounced "ah-reen."

"Ma'am, I'm Gina's supervisor." He told her about her missing daughter, speaking softly, gently, imagining what it must be like for her to get this news. If he were in her place, if Julia had disappeared . . . unfathomable.

When he finished telling her, she didn't speak. He could hear ragged breathing coming from her but no questions. No words at all.

"Mrs. Fulton? Are you okay?" He noticed tears shimmering in Robin's eyes.

Another long moment before Irene Fulton asked, "You're her supervisor? The one she always talks about?"

"Yes. Mrs. Fulton, when was the last time you talked with Gina?"

"Last Thursday. She usually calls a few times a week and we hadn't heard from her so we called. She said she had a stomach bug. She—" Her voice trembled. "Has she been missing all weekend?"

"Nobody has seen her since that day."

Another hesitation and then, "Oh God."

Caleb could picture her gripping the phone as the news sunk in, her mind fighting it, wanting desperately for it not to be true.

"Is there somewhere she would go?" Caleb asked. "If she wanted to get away maybe? Does she have a friend she might go see?"

"Uhm. Robin is her best friend. Has been since grade school."

Caleb looked over at the roommate, who rubbed a tissue against her eye. "Anybody else?"

"She has an uncle in Asheville. But she'd tell me if she was going there, or he would."

"Maybe you could call just to make sure?"

"Yes. Yes, I'll do that." The words came out in a rush. She sounded relieved to have something to do.

"Let me give you my phone numbers so we can stay in touch. Also, we're filing a missing person report with the police. They'll be calling you. They'll do everything they can to find your daughter, I promise."

"The police," she repeated somberly, the realization sinking deeper. "My husband just came home. I . . . I need to tell him."

Caleb gave her his phone numbers and hung up.

"I'll give Irene a call later," Robin said, wiping her cheek. "She's probably in shock right now."

"Probably. Next we need to file a missing persons report. If you want, I'll go with you."

Robin looked relieved to have help. Caleb had Janice reschedule his next appointment so he could drive Robin to the police station. When she tried to sign in at the reception desk, her hand shook so hard she dropped the pen. The desk officer told them Claudia was unavailable but asked them a series of questions about Gina's family and friends, places she might go.

"Make sure Detective Briscoe knows about this," Caleb stressed. "It may relate to a case she's involved in."

Robin's eyes widened at that, but he didn't explain further. No need for her to worry more than she already was. When they returned to the counseling center, Caleb walked Robin to her car.

"Anything else I can do?" Robin asked.

"Don't give up hope. And if you believe in prayer . . ."

"I'm starting to. Stay in touch, okay?"

# Chapter Twelve

Caleb eased the Subaru onto Main Street, heading to Safe Harbor for his afternoon shift. Dark, swollen clouds hung over the city, blocking out any trace of the sun, casting the sky a metallic gray. A perfect match to Caleb's mood. The cell phone rested on the passenger seat. He willed it to ring with news about Gina.

She'd been gone for five days now. Five days with nobody looking. He couldn't imagine a scenario where this didn't turn out bad.

He parked behind the shelter, once again trying not to think about the evening of Esther's murder. How upset Gina had been. How such a crime was unthinkable to her. Was Gina a victim now, too? No, don't go there, he told himself. Don't assume the worst.

Nobody sat at the reception desk, but he heard voices coming from the pantry area. He wandered back to where Henry worked with two volunteers. He recognized one guy, once again wearing his beer sweatshirt. The other had brown hair cut mullet-style. McGuyver twenty years later. They sorted through produce heaped in wooden crates.

"What's this here?" asked the beer lover, holding up a purple vegetable.

"Them's beets," Mullet answered.

"Got a shipment from the Farmer's Market." Henry pointed to a vacant spot on a shelf. "Put them with the turnips."

"Is Todd here?" Caleb asked.

"Should be. Should haul his lazy ass back here to help us," Sweatshirt guy said. Mullet snickered.

Henry was studying Caleb like he was a complex math problem. "You okay, man?"

"Yeah, I guess. When you see Todd, send him to my office."

"You got it." Henry reached for another crate of vegetables.

Caleb had just hung his jacket on the coat rack when he noticed someone standing in his door.

"I heard you wanted to see me?" Todd surprised him. He looked pale as a vampire. He wore a crisp button-down shirt tucked into black jeans. Nothing about Todd made one think "manual laborer," especially given that he carried his clipboard like a fashion accessory.

"Have you heard anything from Gina?"

He shook his head. "Why?"

"Her roommate came to see me. Nobody knows where she is. Has she emailed you?"

Todd dropped into a chair, his hand covering his mouth. "Not since—maybe last Thursday evening? She emailed me about getting some supplies Friday morning."

"Supplies for what?" Caleb asked.

"The home visit. She said y'all were going to go check on a client. Though I guess it isn't a home visit if they're homeless, is it? Anyway, I said I'd put together a box for her and leave it at the desk."

"A home visit? Are you sure that's what she said?" Caleb felt something kick in his gut. No way he would have approved her going out on her own.

"Just that you were going to check on a client. I have the email, I think. Want me to check?"

"She said I was going with her?"

"Yes, she emailed me that you were. I asked specifically about that. I didn't think it would be a good idea for her to go alone. I mean, some of those homeless guys can get rough."

"Crap," he whispered, wondering where Gina had gone. And why she hadn't told him anything about it. And how were they supposed to find her? "Do you know where?"

"She said something about the tent village by the river."

"Zooville." He closed his eyes.

"I figured since you were going with her, she'd be okay."

"I didn't know anything about this. I wasn't with her and I have no idea where she went. And now—"

"Now?" Todd repeated. "Oh my God. You think—" he didn't

finish the sentence. He didn't have to.

Caleb called Claudia right after his talk with Todd, and like Caleb, she thought it an important clue to Gina's whereabouts. Not good news. He told her about the email Gina had sent Todd, reading to her from a printout Todd had brought him. "No, Claudia, I didn't know anything about it," Caleb said. "We don't send students out alone. Ever."

"So why did she say you were going?"

"Your guess is as good as mine," Caleb answered.

The rest of the afternoon was a blur. Twelve clients. Three admissions to the shelter dorm. A new shipment from a local grocery store and ten boxes of paper products from a fast food restaurant all sorted and stacked in the pantry. Four pick-up trucks were loaded to take food to rural soup kitchens.

But his phone never rang.

At close to five o'clock, Henry came to his office, looking grim. Without asking, Caleb knew. Claudia followed him, taking a seat across from Caleb. "We found her," she said, her voice uncharacteristically gentle.

"No." Caleb felt the dread filling him, weighing him down.

"By the river. Not far from where the first body was discovered. Just down from the tent village."

Body. Gina's body. Oh God.

"We don't have a time of death yet, but it's been a couple of days at least."

"How did she—"

Claudia watched him very closely. "She was stabbed, Caleb. Just like Esther Lowell. And Stormy Bennett."

He blinked. Tried to take in a breath but his lungs wouldn't inflate. Rubbed his hands along the ridged fabric of his corduroys. Tried not to picture Gina dead.

"You okay?" Claudia asked.

"No he's not okay," Henry said. "How could he be okay? Gina was just a kid."

"I know that," Claudia said sharply, and then more gently, "Caleb?"

"We have to call her parents," Caleb said.

"I've already taken care of that. Captain Bentille is sending a car to bring them down."

"And her roommate, Robin Lyle," Caleb added.

"She knows."

"I could call the school," Caleb continued. Wanting to do it. Wanting to be the one to tell Ron. Just one little thing he could do in a universe where nothing could be done to save Gina.

"That would be good," Claudia said. "I'll need to talk with some of the folks here. Mr. Rudd, can you help with that?"

Henry took a step closer to Caleb. "You okay, man?"

"I'm okay. Can you find a place for Claudia to work? She'll need to talk with Todd Weathers. And you, I suspect. Anyone else?"

"Anyone you think knew her. Interacted with her regularly," she answered, eyeing both of them.

"We all did. She was a very friendly girl. A very likeable girl," Henry said. "Ain't nobody around here that would hurt a hair on her head."

Claudia arched her eyebrows. She didn't like Henry's tone, Caleb could tell, but didn't argue with him. "I hope you're right, Mr. Rudd. I hope you're right about that."


Caleb sat in his car, still parked at Safe Harbor, and dialed Shannon's cell. It was a long shot, of course. If she was at the barn, the cell wouldn't have a signal. If she were home—no, not home, but at her folks' house—she probably turned it off. After four rings, she answered, "Caleb?"

He closed his eyes at the sound of her voice. A rich voice, with so many layers and textures. The way she said his name, Caleb, edged with fatigue and concern. And maybe a little longing. He hoped so.

"Hey," he said, suddenly at a loss for words.

"What's wrong?"

"I just needed to hear your voice."

"It's good to hear yours, too."

"Where are you?"

"I was shoveling the walkway. Up to my ass in snow, by the way."

"Come home." He shouldn't have said it, but the words tumbled out before he could stop himself.

"Caleb—" Now she sounded frustrated. Torn. Guilty?

"I just miss you. I know you can't pick up and leave, I mean, I know your dad needs you."

She didn't speak for a long moment. "What else is going on?"

He told her about Gina. Just a sweet kid with a promising career ahead of her now gone from this earth for no good reason.

"How awful," Shannon said. "I'm so sorry."

"It's okay." He cleared his throat, feeling a strong need to change the subject. "How's your dad's rehab going?"

"Slow. Painful. He's depressed. I think it's starting to sink in that he can't work like he used to."

He fought a burst of panic. Did that mean Shannon would stay? Would her move to Maine be permanent? "What if he can't go back to the dairy?"

"Then I don't know what we'll do."

Those words hit him like a cold dagger. "Your parents can't expect you to—I mean, you have a life to get back to." You have *me* to get back to, he meant.

"I'm coming home, Caleb. I just can't tell you when. I just—" She was measuring her words, he could tell. "I can't be here and there with you. Dad needs me, so I have to be here. Try to understand."

Now her words had an edge. She was normally a patient woman, but he could hear how frayed she was.

"I do," he relented. "I admire you for being such a devoted daughter. I hope Julia feels the same about me one day."

"She'll be taking care of both of us. Visiting the nursing home. Calming down the nurses that you keep harassing." A light laugh. Better now.

"Damn straight. I can race my wheelchair whenever the hell I want."

There was more banter and then a quiet goodbye.

Fifteen minutes later, Caleb pulled into his driveway and climbed out of the car. The feral barking emanating from his back yard surprised him. This was more than Cleo's usual "there's a squirrel running loose" cry. He hoped Cleo hadn't cornered the neighbor's cat because he was in no mood to smooth ruffled feathers next door. Not after his day. After what happened to Gina.

Caleb unlatched the back gate. "Cleo! Come here!"

She didn't come to him, just barked with more fury. He wound his way to the back porch where Cleo paced and pounced against the door. He tugged at her collar. "Easy, girl."

Cleo wriggled out of his grip, snarling as her nose bumped the door knob. What had her so upset? Had someone broken into his house?

Caleb descended the steps to check out the back of his home. The windows looked intact. The door had not been jimmied open. He rounded the yard, exited the gate, and studied the front of the cottage. Windows secure. Front door locked, no new nicks or scratches in the wood. He twitched his key in the lock, inched the door open, and holding his breath, listened for sounds within.

Nothing, accept the noise of the heat pump clicking on. He eased into the living room. TV, DVD player, stereo all where they should be. The equipment was so old who would want it, anyway? The tiny dining room looked undisturbed: piles of junk mail and bills where he'd left them, Shannon's bamboo plant still looked thirsty. No intruder had watered it. He checked the kitchen next: all was as it should be; toaster, microwave, ancient refrigerator where he'd left them.

As soon as Caleb opened the back door, Cleo burst through, an explosion of scrambling paws and rippling fur. She bounded past Caleb, nose sniffing every inch of the kitchen before moving to the living room. When her muzzle touched the knob to the front door, she growled.

Cleo had never been this frantic. A knot of fear worked its way up Caleb's trachea.

"Cleo? What's going on, girl?" Caleb's hand sifted through her fur, trying to calm her, but she slipped from his grasp. When she fled up the stairs, he followed, his staccato pulse pounding in his ears.

The bedroom looked normal; unmade bed, cluttered nightstand, and shoes strewn across the carpet. Bathroom: fine. Julia's room: perfect—canopy bed made, stuffed animals parading across the headboard, curtains open to let in the light. So far, so good, though Caleb noticed his hand was trembling. Cleo moved on to the final room, the room with the door closed. Shannon's home office/guest room.

As soon as he opened the door, Cleo rushed in, nose to floor, to window, to desk. She growled. Caleb's heart hammered against his rib cage. He looked at the dust-covered surface where Shannon kept her laptop when she was home. Dusty, except two spots that looked like they were wiped clean. A shelf over the desk held the router. Why was the device overturned? Had Shannon left it like that? Unlikely. He sat and opened desk drawers. The stack of floppy disks was there, as was the file from last year's taxes and Cleo's veterinary papers. Still, something felt . . . off.

He studied the clean patches on the desktop. Had two arms rested there? Why? It made no sense.

No, probably Julia had snuck in here during her last visit. Maybe she'd come for paper to color on. That made more sense than an intruder who came inside without breaking in and stole nothing from the home. Cleo was just overreacting. And Caleb was, too, which was logical, given the recent murders.

Caleb stood, turned off the light, and hoped to God that he was right.


Five days passed in a blur after Gina's body was discovered. Her death made the headlines: ANOTHER VICIOUS ATTACK: A SERIAL KILLER AMONG THE HOMELESS? Safe Harbor had been under siege by media and community leaders. Bill Evers did his best to fend them off, and Henry had spent most of his time on the streets reassuring Safe Harbor clients that the shelter was still a safe place for them.

Zooville made the papers, too. Letters to the editor speculated that Gina had been assaulted by some homeless drug-seeking fugitive hiding in the tent village. The police had questioned Johnny and a few other residents who all said the same thing: "We're not here to hurt anybody. We just want to live in peace." The city mayor had issued a statement promising to crackdown on "the vagrants and derelicts that make the streets of Westville unsafe," and Caleb vowed to send a thousand dollars to anyone who opposed Mayor Tripp in the next election.

"So don't you ever wonder if it's worth it?" Caleb asked Henry. They had been scouring down the pantry since it was so low on donations. Four hours of back-breaking work.

Henry glared at him like he'd grown a second head. "Why would you say that?"

"Oh, I don't know. The mayor wants to shut us down. We're about to lose most of our funding. We're in the headlines every-day and none of it's good. Oh, and three people have been killed, all with connections to Safe Harbor." Caleb shook his head. He was beyond tired. "Don't you wish you had a job where you didn't have a target on your back?"

Henry gave him a long, assessing stare. Strange for his friend. Unsettling. Finally, he reached for the van keys and said, "You need to take a little trip with me."

The drive took less than twenty minutes, the wipers of the rickety van smearing mist that settled on the windshield. A wind had kicked up, too, and Caleb almost suggested they postpone this field trip, but sensed in Henry's determination that it was something important. Soon, the two of them stood beside an abandoned building off River Drive. It had been a Wal-mart or KMart years ago, but now it was an empty shell fronted by an acre of weed-choked asphalt. It was hard to imagine how the property must have been in its hey-day, with cars crowding the lot and customers bustling in and out. Now it looked as desolate as the moon.

Henry locked the van, pocketed the keys, and pointed to a rocky path that led away from the building. "Just up this way."

Caleb followed. He wished he'd put on a warmer coat and a pair of hiking boots, as the path twisted uphill over craggy rocks and protruding tree roots. When they passed a small grove of pine trees, Henry veered off the trail, moving expertly, as though this was a familiar journey for him. They reached a large rock that jutted out from the hillside and Henry stopped. "This is it," he said.

"This is what?" Caleb peered in the shadows below the boulder, a cave-like space about seven feet across, a few feet tall. Two large pieces of decaying plywood rested on the ground beside it.

"This is where my brother used to live." Henry sat on a smaller rock, gesturing that Caleb should do the same.

"Your brother," Caleb repeated.

There was no house here. No structure at all.

"I don't tell my story to many people outside my NA group, but I thought you should hear it," Henry went on. "Calvin was a year older than me. Always a weird kid. Our mother had a drinking problem and our dad lived up north so to be honest, we sort of raised ourselves. Calvin kept to himself, didn't like being around other people. I shared a room with him but he was pretty much a stranger to me. Very quiet, but easily rattled if I touched any of his stuff.

"Then Mom died when I was seventeen. We'd both dropped out of school by then and we ended up on the streets. I became what you'd consider a thug. I hooked up with a gang, not because I really wanted to but because I needed the protection. The gang gave me what I needed. A place to stay. Money for food. And later—all the pot and heroin I could handle."

Caleb nodded, taking it all in.

"I lost contact with my brother for several years. I was in my own world. Doing stuff I'm still ashamed of. I had no idea what he was going through." Henry lifted a stone and tossed it into some leaves.

"Did Calvin get into drugs?"

"A little. But mostly, Calvin was paranoid. I mean, I didn't know that then, but he had voices screaming in his head. Torturing him. He got so terrified he couldn't be around anyone else, so he moved here. Lived under that rock right there." Henry pointed at the cave-like space with a trembling finger.

Caleb had seen Henry in some tough—and dangerous— situations, but he'd never seen the man shake.

"Know how I found out?" Henry asked. "This guy showed up. Walked right into the crack house where I was staying. A white guy like you. Name was Tucker."

"Where'd he come from?"

"Tucker worked at Safe Harbor. Had Esther's job back then. He'd been working with Calvin, trying to get him help but Calvin wasn't having any part of it. So he came to see me. He said, 'You're his brother. He doesn't have anybody else. Now, are you going to do right by him?'"

"Brave guy."

Henry clucked his tongue. "Brave or stupid, at least that's what

I thought then. But damn if he didn't get me into the car with him. He drove me here and showed me this squat where Calvin stayed."

"Was Calvin here?"

"Not at first. I crawled in—" Henry pointed to the left side of the rock. "He had plywood wedged in on the other side. I couldn't believe how nasty it was. That he had been living that way.

"Then Calvin showed up. He was wearing these God-awful rags, had holes in his shoes and this scraggly beard growing down to his chest. He yelled at us at first but when he got close enough to recognize me his attitude changed. He asked me how I was. Where I was staying. Like it was important to him that I was okay. Here he was, crazed and skittery and skinny as a Feed-the-Children commercial but he was worrying about me."

"Just being a big brother." Caleb thought about all the times it had been the same with Sam. Life dealt him a tough hand, too, but Sam was always there when Caleb needed him.

"After that, Tucker and I took turns checking on him. We'd bring food, blankets, clothes. Tucker even brought the doc out to see him, but Calvin wouldn't take any meds. He thought they came from Satan."

"Was he ever hospitalized?" Caleb asked.

"Tried that, too. They'd keep him a week, maybe a little more, then turn him loose. He'd come right back here, sometimes in worse shape then when he went." Henry ran a hand over his shaved head, his gaze fixed on the shadowy bit of ground under the rock.

Caleb wondered what he was seeing.

"Then one day he wasn't here. I didn't think much of it— sometimes Calvin got so paranoid he wouldn't even let me see him. But Tucker came to the crib later that week, and once I saw the expression on his face, I knew."

As Henry stopped speaking, a heavy silence settled around them. Caleb didn't ask the questions that flooded his mind, not wanting to make his friend any more uncomfortable.

"They found him by the river. He didn't kill himself, though that's what I thought at first. No, he'd gotten a bad case of pneumonia. They told me that he drowned from all the fluid in his lungs. He was only twenty-five years old."

"I'm sorry, Henry."

"The story doesn't end there. Tucker came to see me a week later. I was stoned as hell, had been since I buried Calvin. Tucker asked me to take a ride with him and we ended up at Safe Harbor. It was a Tuesday afternoon. People were lined up to go in. Tucker explained that the people were going into an NA meeting. That if I wanted to honor my brother's memory the best way was to get my shit together. To not let the drugs kill me or turn me into a killer."

"Was that the first time you'd been to Safe Harbor?"

"I'd never even heard of the place till I met Tucker. I knew what it had done to help my brother. I didn't go in that first time, but I did a week later. After that, it's almost like I never left. Safe Harbor helped me let go of that other life. I stayed in the dorm for six months, doing meetings everyday, helping in the food bank. Never fell off the wagon, not even once. I'd like to think I never will but all of us are just one bad decision away from using again."

"I see your point."

"Safe Harbor couldn't save Calvin, but it did save me. And I can tell you dozens of stories that are just like mine. So no, closing Safe Harbor can't happen."


There were a thousand things Caleb would rather do than attend a "viewing." But Caleb couldn't go to Gina's funeral, which had been scheduled for Saturday, when he had visitation with his daughter. So Caleb straightened his tie, buttoned his wool jacket, and opened the heavy doors to McLeavy's Funeral Home. He entered the receiving area, signed a thick book, and glanced around at the other mourners. He saw a few students huddled together, looking nervous. Too young to be dealing with this kind of death. A dozen or so older people stood to the side, perhaps friends of Gina's parents.

"Hey, Caleb."

He turned to find Bill Evers behind him. Bill looked odd. Red-rimmed eyes. Necktie askew. Jacket a little rumpled.

"Bill? You okay?"

"It's just—this is terrible, isn't it? I thought someone from Safe Harbor should be here."

Caleb nodded. A man dressed in a tweed jacket opened a pair of French doors. Beyond those doors would be the viewing area, where Gina lay cold in the coffin. The coffin which was now her home.

"The coroner said she didn't suffer," Bill whispered. Claudia had told Caleb the same thing; a stab wound to Gina's heart had stopped its beating before she could feel pain. He wondered how she knew this, how anyone could know what Gina had felt in those moments when someone stole her life.

"The parents aren't taking this well," Bill said. "But how could they? Their kid just died."

Caleb had nothing to say to that. Their kid might be alive if he hadn't brought her to Safe Harbor.

Bill cleared his throat. "Uhh, I have a meeting to get to. Let me know if there's anything we should do."

Caleb watched him hurry away. Ron Wheaton was next to arrive. His brown hair had turned curly gray. It used to grow lower on his forehead. The goatee hadn't been there when Caleb saw him last.

"It's good you're here," Caleb said, eyeing the distraught students.

"Never had to deal with anything like this before," Ron said. "Our dean's really upset about it."

"We all are."

"He's also worried about liability," Ron whispered. "Losing a kid on a field placement—that's uncharted territory for us."

Caleb couldn't drum up much concern about the legal issues. Gina had died. Her parents had to bury their child. Gina's friend grieved for her. Nothing else mattered.

"It's not like when we were in school. We have so many kids now. I'm advisor to forty students in the masters program, and on fifteen dissertation committees. We're so big, our students must feel like cattle. I'm doing good if I get the names right." He paused, glancing back at the doors. "The police asked if she was having any problems with anybody. And what if she did? Would she have felt like she could come to me? Or anyone on the faculty?"

"Gina was an open kid. I think she would have talked to you if something about school bothered her," Caleb said.

"Did mention anything to you?"

"She was young and naïve. Wanted to save the world like you and I used to. Maybe a little over-involved with her clients."

"The police said she may have gone to see a client. But that you didn't know anything about it." Ron's gaze became more intense.

"I still find it hard to believe that she'd do something like that without telling me. No way I'd let her go out alone."

"Of course not." Ron's expression softened. "You have my numbers, right? If there's anything I can do, let me know."

"I will." They shook hands again and Ron moved on, leaving Caleb to enter the room he'd been dreading.

"An urn," he whispered, suddenly feeling a rush of relief. Gina had been cremated. On a small, draped table rested a brass urn and a photograph. He stepped closer, taking in the image of her face. The open, joyful smile, eyes bright and hopeful. "Gina," he whispered.

He spotted an older couple he took to be her parents. Mrs. Fulton, a soft, pudgy woman with Gina's moon-shaped face. Mr. Fulton had bright white hair and the same hazel eyes as his daughter.

"I'm Caleb Knowles," Caleb said to Mrs. Fulton. "We talked on the phone the other day."

She clutched a lavender handkerchief with both hands. Her eyes were puffy, a streak of mascara striping her cheek. "I remember."

"I'm so sorry about Gina. She was a lovely, talented girl. We all miss her." These words weren't enough, but what could he say that might comfort them?

Mr. Fulton took a step closer to Caleb. "I've been wanting to talk to you."

Caleb tilted his head toward the back of the room and Fulton followed him away—far away—from the urn.

"How can I help you, sir?"

"You probably can't," he answered, and Caleb caught a whiff of alcohol. "I just want to know how this could happen. How she could be off alone like that. The professor said you wouldn't have told her to do it."

"I wouldn't have allowed it, sir. And she knew that." It still made no sense to Caleb. Why would Gina endanger herself like that? Who did she want to see so badly?

"I want to know who did this, Knowles. I want to meet him. I want to look him in the eye and tell him just what he took from us."

This man was speaking from his gut. Caleb fought similar feelings himself. Whoever killed Gina would have a lot of enemies. "Mr. Fulton, I want you to know this. Your daughter was a wonderful student. She was very sensitive and caring. She would have made a great social worker."

"She liked school," he said. Slurring slightly on the "s." "Talked about you a lot. Said you were just what a social worker should be. Said if she could be half as good as you—" he didn't finish, his voice catching.

Caleb shook his head. How could anyone hold him to that kind of standard?

"To be frank, Mr. Knowles, she may have had a crush on you."

"I don't think—"

Mr. Fulton smiled a full throttle grin. "She did! She really liked you. Now here's my question. Did you like her back?" The smile vanished, replaced by a glare like lasers.

Caleb stepped away, stunned. "I like Gina very much. She was a promising student and a delightful young lady. But that's where our relationship ended, Mr. Fulton. I don't know what made you think differently."

The glare softened because of tears brimming in his eyes. "I'm sorry," he said. "I didn't mean—it's just we don't know enough about her life here. And now, we don't know enough about her death. My little girl. She's dead!"

Caleb didn't know how to help, the grief and anger pouring from the man made him uncomfortable. He shouldn't be a witness to something so private.

"I wish I could help you. All I can say is that we have a good police department. They won't give up on this until Gina's killer is behind bars."

Fulton came closer, his breath hot on Caleb's face. "Well,

here's the thing. I don't want the son of a bitch in jail. I want him dead. Dead as my little girl is."

Caleb had no answer for that. He hoped it was the alcohol talking. Or the grief. "Again, I'm sorry for your loss," Caleb said. He turned and left the room.

# Chapter Thirteen

Caleb went home after the viewing. He took Cleo for a walk, let her sniff the neighbor's shrubs and bark at any squirrel that dared cross the street. Watched her greet the boxer fenced in at the end of the block, smiled when Mrs. Whitman from the gray house interrupted her power walk to give Cleo's head a pat. When they returned home, Caleb filled her food dish so she could descend on it like a starved river rat. He wished he had her appetite, but nothing in the freezer looked appealing and he'd already had delivery pizza twice that week. He should have stopped for Chinese take-out, but food wasn't on his mind when he left the funeral home. His stomach wasn't eager for it now.

Where would Shannon be now? She should be here in his house. She should be burning grilled cheese sandwiches and making him laugh and giving him the best reason to come home on days like this.

The ringing phone startled him. He answered, surprised that it was Shannon.

"I was just thinking about you," he said.

"Just checking in. How are you?"

"I went to Gina's viewing."

"That had to be hard. Wish I could have been there with you."

"Me too." He didn't want this conversation to be about guilt. Or about how apart they were. "How are the cows?"

"Fine. They ask about you all the time."

He smiled, glad to hear the humor leaking through her fatigue. "I miss you."

"You wouldn't say that if you could see me right now. Cow dung is not my favorite perfume."

"Quit with the sexy talk. You're making me hot."

A laugh bubbled out of her and faded. The silence that followed felt odd. "You okay?" he asked.

"I'm . . . tired. Really tired. And cold. It's taken me longer to get used to the snow than I thought."

"Maybe you could come south for the weekend? Just to warm yourself up."

"I'd give anything for an escape like that. But I can't leave while Dad's like this." After a pause, she said, "I've been giving some thought to this Safe Harbor gig of yours. When you think about what happened to Gina, and that other woman—"

"Esther."

"Maybe it's time for you to pull out. I'm surprised Matthew's letting you stay, after all that's happened."

"I want to stay. I like it there. Safe Harbor's on shaky ground with all the negative publicity it's getting. But that place is badly needed."

She didn't speak for a moment, and he knew exactly what she was thinking. "I don't want you to get hurt," she finally said.

"I won't. And if I start feeling like it's an unsafe place to be, I will pull out. I promise."

She sighed, and it stirred feelings of guilt again. She didn't need to be worried about him on top of everything else.

"You remember that show, *Murder She Wrote*? Do you think you're getting to be like that Angela Lansbury character? Everywhere she gets invited a body shows up?"

He laughed and heard her chuckle, too. He missed this most of all.

"Look, I need to get back to work," she said. "I've got to get paychecks ready or I'll have a crew on strike."

He closed his eyes, not ready to hang up. "I guess you'd better go then."

"I love you, Caleb. I hope you know that even though I'm a thousand miles away."

A thousand miles. Far enough to be another planet. "I love you too," he said suddenly, surprising himself with how easily those words came.

"Wow," she chuckled. "Are you okay? Didn't lose a body part or anything when you said that?"

"Yeah, yeah. Give my regards to the cows."

• • •

Monday morning Caleb arrived late to the counseling center, which was nothing unusual. Janice generally showed up around eight-thirty, getting the coffee going, collecting messages from the service, and prepping the medical records for the day's sessions. Matthew, an early riser, would have rounds at the hospital before eight so he could start staffing at the center promptly at nine. So Caleb heard morning bustle as soon as he entered, Janice confirming appointments on the phone, Matthew recording his notes into the Dictaphone, and two clients in the waiting room talking about politics. Status quo for the private practice.

Caleb headed straight to the break room and caffeine.

He'd finished half a mug and refilled it when Janice entered, looking upset. "The police are here."

"Claudia?"

"No. Some man. He's got a subpoena!" She clutched at the pink scarf frothing at her neck. "Can you come see what he wants?"

The request surprised him. Janice could talk to anybody. She could make small talk with an IRS auditor or jail detainee or the most withdrawn client. Why was she nervous about this? "You have unpaid parking tickets or something?" Caleb asked.

"Just talk to him, please?"

She was not in the mood for humor. Caleb carried the coffee cup to the front desk where the plain-clothes officer stood waiting. He didn't look familiar, though Caleb had only dealt with a handful of Westville police other than Claudia. This guy had a lumpy, bald head that looked like unbaked bread dough. He held the subpoena at arm's length like it smelled bad.

"I'm Caleb Knowles. Can I help you?" Caleb took the document to see what the man wanted. Usually they came for medical records, but not this time.

"I need access to Gina Fulton's office," he said.

"Office? It's more of a storage room. Well, I mean, we did get a desk in there and some chairs. Janet even donated some pillows." Caleb smiled. The man did not smile back.

"The computer she used. I need to confiscate it."

"Confiscate it? Why?" Caleb asked.

He tapped on the subpoena. "I need access to all her emails

over the past three months. That's when she started here, right?"

"Right." Caleb shot a nervous glance at Janice. "Would she have confidential information on her machine?"

"She typed her own clinical notes. She may have saved them to her hard drive."

"Crap." Caleb wished he had time to get in there and clean the drive. But the detective didn't look like the patient type, and Caleb wouldn't have a clue where to start. "Does Detective Briscoe know about this?"

"Of course. She said you can call her if you want but that it won't change anything."

Double crap. "You understand why we're concerned?"

"You're afraid there is confidential psychiatric information on her computer. But this subpoena gives me access to that, too. Look, I'm not leaving here without that machine. I have permission from a judge. Do you understand that?"

Caleb didn't like the stony glare coming from the lump-headed cop. "Guess we don't have a choice. I'll show you where it is."

In less than five minutes, the detective had the computer tucked under his arm. He left the monitor and keyboard, though he helped himself to the thumb drive Gina had left plugged into the USB port.

As soon as he left, Caleb called Claudia's cell.

"I thought I might hear from you." From the noise coming through on Claudia's end, he suspected she was in the car.

"Why the computer? What's going on, Claudia?"

"Not just the computer there. We're taking her laptop from home and the hard drive from the one she used at Safe Harbor. Our cyber crime guys are going through all her emails. Turning up some interesting stuff, too."

"Interesting? How?"

"I can't go into details but we're finding some correspondence that's raising some red flags."

"Red flags like her killer emailed her?"

"I didn't say that."

"That changes things, doesn't it? I mean, if the same person who killed Stormy and Esther killed Gina, it couldn't be a homeless person. They don't exactly walk around with lap-tops."

"Slow down, you're gonna give yourself an aneurysm. First, I didn't say the killer emailed her. Second, you're wrong about the homeless. Quite a few have email accounts. Especially the younger ones, they can be computer savvy. They go to the library to log on. Your pal Henry Rudd even said that they keep a computer at the dorm for folks to use."

"Are you confiscating that one, too?" Caleb didn't hide his annoyance.

"Not yet. Can you hold on? I got another call."

Leave it to Claudia to have two phone conversations while driving. Pretty poor role-modeling for a cop.

"I'm back. Look, I need you to do a jail consult. Can you fit it in this afternoon?"

He didn't know how. He had three sessions scheduled at the counseling center and planned on a quick lunch en route to Safe Harbor, where med check day meant a frantic afternoon. "Could it wait till tomorrow?"

"I guess. But the guy is seeing things in his cell. We have him in solitary but he's pacing in there like a hungry lion. Pretty damn crazy if you ask me. By the way, you know this guy. It's Sully McNair."

"Sully? How'd he get picked up?"

"Got into a scuffle with another guy. Officers tried to break them up and he got nasty with them. Called them all kind of names and tussled when they tried to subdue him."

"What's he being charged with?"

"Simple assault and resisting arrest, probably."

"I'll come by after my shift at the shelter. If I bring his meds, can the jail nurse make sure he gets them?"

"She can try. He's not exactly being cooperative."

"I'll be there after five."


Caleb finished his session with Lanie Dupree and gave her a warm smile, proud that she had shown up, albeit an hour later than she was supposed to; proud that she brought an empty medicine bottle, which meant she'd been taking the antipsychotic; but proudest because during the entire half-hour they spent together, Lanie hadn't accused him of anything. She hadn't said he'd been following her, or reading her thoughts, or stealing her things when she slept at night. All of which seemed to prove that Lanie's paranoia could be contained when she was properly medicated.

"I hope I'll see you next week, Lanie," Caleb said, handing her an appointment card. "That will be next Wednesday. And you'll see the doctor then, too."

"Hmmm," Lanie said, holding the card very close to her nose as she studied it. "We'll see."

"And here are your pills." Caleb dropped the medicine bottle in the bag that held all of Lanie's favorite snacks. He was not above bribing his clients to get them to return.

"I gotta have that needle in my butt today?" Lanie eyed him over her sunglasses.

"No, not this week." Caleb decided not to remind her of the Resperdal injection she'd get next visit. He'd let that be a surprise.

Lanie looked in the sack. "You don't got any beef jerky? I like me some jerky sometimes."

"I don't think we have any this week. But I promise I'll have some for you next time." Which would be her reward for the needle-in-the-butt part of her visit, even if he had to buy it himself.

He escorted her up to the reception desk. When he returned to his office, Todd Weathers was waiting for him.

"How are you, Todd?"

Todd lingered in the doorway, then inched in, crossed to a chair, and sat. He held an envelope, which he placed in his lap and smoothed with his pale, delicate fingers. He said nothing.

"Todd?"

"Sorry." This was a new side to the spreadsheet geek. Todd stabilized a tremulous lip with his teeth as his hands continued to caress the envelope. "I just—I came to work today and the first thing I wanted to do was go see Gina. And then I remembered. I mean, I hadn't forgotten, how could I forget that she died that horrible death, but I think it's just sinking in now."

"I guess we all kind of feel that way."

"She had this light, you know?" Tears glistened on Todd's lashes. "She had this light that warmed this place. Warmed all of us."

"That's a nice thing to say. And it's a good way to describe her."

"She made me laugh," Todd continued. "At myself. She teased me about my inventory sheets. I mean, some of the volunteers kid around and it's not so friendly. But hers was just sweet. I didn't mind." Todd seemed like a lonely guy. Gina had become his friend and he probably didn't have many of those.

"The police came by again this morning. Did you talk to them?" he asked.

"I wasn't here," Caleb replied.

"They took away the hard drive from her computer." He shook his head like the idea disgusted him. "They're reading all her emails."

"They're looking for her killer."

"But doesn't she deserve some privacy? I mean, she's dead and now they go through her mail and read her stuff. It's a violation."

"That's how it works, I'm afraid."

With her death, Gina stopped being a person and became a crime to solve. Anything that might help the police was fair game. Though "fair" was not the correct word. Nothing about this was fair.

"I sent her emails. Mostly jokes and stuff. Guess they'll read those." He wiped his eyes, still regaining self-control.

"Do you know if she emailed anyone else?"

"Uhm. Her roommate, Robin. A few friends from Sumter."

"The police will want to talk to them," Caleb said. "And you, too."

"Me?" Todd sat straighter in the chair, like some life had poured itself into his spinal column. "Okay, if it will help. That's what matters. That they find her killer."

"Yes," Caleb said.

Todd ran a hand over the manila envelope. Looked at Caleb. Looked away.

"Is there something else, Todd?"

"Yeah. The police—" he paused, rubbing his nose with the palm of his hand. "There was someone who was emailing Gina. And she didn't like it."

"What?" Caleb came forward, stunned by the information.

"It may be nothing," Todd said quickly. "Just some guy that kept emailing her. Some suitor she wasn't interested in, I guess."

"She told you this?"

He nodded. "I think she was flattered at first, but the guy went too far. That's the thing about email, you don't know how what you say is being received. That's what I said to Gina. I said maybe she should talk to the guy face-to-face."

"Did she tell you his name?" Caleb's pulse quickened.

"No. I asked but she said she could handle it. I thought it was another student or something." He fiddled with a thread coming from the button on the cuff of his plaid shirt. He twisted it around his forefinger, turning the tip bright red.

"What else did she tell you about him?" Caleb asked.

"Nothing. The last time we talked about it she got upset so I didn't bring it up again."

"When was that?"

"Right before she got sick. You remember. She missed a couple of days?"

Caleb did remember. Gina called him. That was the last conversation he had with her.

"I better let you get back to work." Todd stood to leave, giving Caleb a self-conscious smile.

"Something else?"

"Just this." He opened the envelope and pulled out a sheet of paper. "This is the report of my hours that's supposed to go to court. Esther used to do it. I didn't want to bother Mr. Evers, he's got some visitors in his office. So would you mind?"

Caleb took the sheet. "Sure. I'll get Henry to give your times and send it in for you."

"Thanks."

# Chapter Fourteen

"Hey Caleb." Bill Evers was Caleb's second surprise visitor that afternoon. His face looked pinched, his nose all scrunched up like he had stepped in something. Bill Evers rarely came into the front section of Safe Harbor, where Caleb and Henry worked. The bustling hub of the place, clients in and out by the dozens.

"I heard you had company," Caleb said.

"Unexpected ones. From United Charities." Bill removed his rimless glasses to rub his eyes.

"About our funding?"

"Yes. They make-up about a third of our budget. They're unhappy about the press we're getting. They may pull the plug."

"I'm sorry to hear that."

"Not as sorry as I am. It's not just the money. United Charities does a bang-up job promoting its causes. And they have the audience we need—businesses, industries. Employees can donate via direct payroll deductions."

Caleb wasn't sure he'd ever heard the phrase "bang-up" used in conversation. "But don't they take a cut? I mean, how much actually comes to Safe Harbor?"

"It's how the game is played, I'm afraid. We get six out of every ten dollars donated through U.C. But that's six we'd never see without them." He slid the glasses back on his small nose. "Do you have a few minutes?"

"Sure." Caleb looked at the large stack of clinical notes he needed to write, hoping this chat would be brief. Bill sat, tossing one of the pink pillows over to the wicker loveseat. "There has been a development related to Wyman Carter I need to discuss with you. It's a sensitive matter."

"Have they found him?"

"Not yet. But I saw Wyman's mother and younger sister earlier. They stopped by."

"No kidding?" Caleb wondered what their story was, why they were so detached from Wyman. If they cared at all.

"Wyman's mother wasn't at all what I expected. Or, perhaps I should say, she wasn't *who* I expected. We had a lengthy chat."

"What did she want? Does she know where Wyman is?"

"She doesn't know. She visited her son when he was in the hospital but before that she hadn't seen him in over three years."

"Does she live in Westville?" Caleb asked.

"Yes. Over in the Whaley Hill area."

"Not too shabby." The average home in Whaley Hill was about five thousand square feet. People who lived there had household staff. He couldn't quite picture Wyman Carter in that area of town.

"Wyman's mother is Margaret Eldridge. Wife of former Senator Ashton Eldridge," Bill said.

"Get out of town!" Caleb remembered Senator Eldridge for his lengthy and annoying "Let's leave the Confederate flag on the state capital" campaign. Eldridge was an arch conservative who stayed in the state senate for twenty plus years.

"But Wyman's last name is Carter," Caleb said.

"Wyman was from her first marriage. The ex-husband was a jerk. Violent, alcoholic. They divorced when Wyman was nine. She worked for Senator Eldridge at the time and married him a year later. Nora—Wyman's sister— is the senator's daughter."

Caleb tried to picture it: Wyman a part of a blue-blood Old South family.

"His story is like many we hear everyday. He burned a lot of bridges." Bill shook his head. "Mrs. Eldridge described Wyman as a troubled child, even as a little boy. Coming from that violence, I suppose it was to be expected. He got into drugs. One of his counselors told her about tough love and the importance of not enabling him."

"So tough love means no contact for three years?"

"Don't be critical of her," Bill scolded. "She did the best she could. Wyman has cost them a small fortune in private schools, rehabilitation programs, and legal fees. The last time he stayed with them he set the Senator's tool house on fire. It almost spread to the house where Mrs. Eldridge and Nora were asleep. Not to mention the potential embarrassment for Senator Eldridge should the media learn the truth about Wyman."

They sounded like a family who had given up. Maybe that explained why they placed Wyman at the Willows. How much did they pay Markham Dougherty? And what exactly were they buying—Wyman's care, such as it was, or Markham's silence?

"So why did Mrs. Eldridge come here?" Caleb asked.

"Two reasons. To apologize to you and Henry for the gasoline incident. Wyman has a strange fascination with fire, so that could have turned out much worse than it did."

"No argument here."

"She wants our help in finding him. She has an attorney who thinks they can get him in drug rehab before he has to deal with the legal charges."

"I'm not sure how much help we can be. I don't know where he is. I doubt he'll come back to Safe Harbor after what he did."

Bill studied his cuticles. They looked like he got a manicure at least once a week. "Margaret mentioned Markham Dougherty. She has retained him to be Wyman's legal guardian, but it's not an easy job."

"Markham Dougherty is a pig. And the Willows isn't fit for the cockroaches that live there. Has she ever set foot in that place?"

Bill raised his brows at Caleb. "You don't know what she's been through. What Wyman's put her through. I think she's afraid of him."

"And the other child, Nora? What's her story?"

"She is a lovely girl. Just out of college and hopes to go to law school in the fall. Margaret thinks she may follow in her father's footsteps." Bill smiled as though he was proud of her. Odd, given they'd just met.

"So she's a lot younger than Wyman. I'm thinking they weren't close," Caleb said.

"She cares about him. I think it was her idea that they come to Safe Harbor. She had a lot of questions about our operation. I even gave her a media kit. She's exactly the kind of donor we need to be targeting. Young, wealthy. And invested in our mission. She could link us to a younger money base. She's very grateful for us because of our efforts to help her brother."

Leave it to Bill to turn the encounter into a PR session. "So let's be on the lookout for Wyman," Bill said. "I've asked Henry to put out some feelers with his contacts. The sooner he's off the streets and in treatment, the better off he'll be."

"Sure," Caleb said. "We'll keep you posted."

As soon as Bill left him, Caleb turned on the computer—something he rarely did at Safe Harbor—and clicked on the Google icon. When he entered "Senator Ashton Eldridge," thirty pages of listings appeared. He scrolled down, looking for news articles about the family. Caleb learned Eldridge was the third in his family to occupy a senate seat. His grandfather served two terms, and his Uncle Portus Eldridge served twice in the fifties. He unearthed a few photos of Eldridge and his new bride, Margaret, but there was no mention of Wyman. The only picture which included the children was taken at an Easter egg hunt when Nora was a toddler. Caleb wouldn't have recognized Wyman, but when he studied the dark haired, sullen child standing apart from the others, he could imagine it to be him.

Eldridge left office four years ago when he chose not to run for re-election. The announcement made the front page of the Westville Chronicle: a full-color photo of Eldridge holding his wife's hand, an attractive teen-aged girl beside them. No sign, nor mention, of Wyman Carter. For his farewell gift from the state senate, Ashton Eldridge received a genuine Confederate Battle flag.

Caleb learned little about Eldridge's later years. He continued to manage the family plantation, seven hundred acres of tobacco and cotton, and lived between the country home and their mansion in downtown Westville. A few generations ago, the family owned a hundred slaves to do that work. More recently, migrant farm workers tilled and planted and harvested for the family. Caleb could scarcely imagine just how much money Eldridge had—old Southern wealth handed down from his grandfather, plus revenue from a successful farming business.

He wondered what growing up had been like for Wyman. Leaving an abusive, alcoholic father to move into South Carolina's version of Tara. Did he ever feel like he belonged? He had been a challenging kid, no doubt about it. But at what point did the family give up on him?

There might be no easy answers to these questions, but Caleb hoped one day to ask them. Yet another reason to find Wyman Carter.

Caleb preferred it when the police brought his jail consults to the private practice. Not just because he hated the jail, which he did—the jail was an odorous, bleak environment—but because it gave the incarcerated client a few minutes of escape. They could come in his office, have their leg irons removed, even sip a cup of coffee while Caleb talked with them, Caleb safe in knowing the cops were right outside his office.

But Sully wouldn't be coming to the clinic, so Caleb waited for him in the detention center interview area. To say the room was Spartan was like saying Marcel Marceau was a little on the quiet side. The ten by ten space held two plastic chairs, bolted to the floor, and a scarred metal table, also immovable. Caleb took the seat closest to the door and waited for the jailer to fetch his troubled client.

Sully made a ruckus coming in. It wasn't just the rattling chains on his arms and legs, it was the flurry of curse words that grew louder with each step. "Leave me the hell alone. Son of a bitch! Not me. Not gonna give it to you."

"Hey Sully," Caleb said quietly.

The man froze and looked at him, yelling even louder. "Not gonna give it to you!"

The jailer shoved him into the empty chair. "Maybe I'd better stay here with him."

Caleb shook his head. "He'll settle down. Won't you, Sully?"

"Go away!" Sully tossed his head, eyes closed in a painful wince.

"Who are you talking to?" Caleb asked.

"Leave me be!" he said, softer now. Caleb looked up at the jailer and nodded. "We'll be okay."

When the door closed behind him, Caleb studied his unhappy client. He saw shadows darkening his eyes and dandruff and fuzz in his scalp. New bruises streaked his massive arms. "How you doing, Sully?"

He shook his head, the Medussa-like braids swaying around

his face.

"I'm sorry they picked you up. Even sorrier that you're locked in here."

Sully opened his eyes, rolling his head to the side as if trying to get a different angle on an abstract painting.

Caleb watched as Sully's face contorted again. "Looks like the voices are pretty bad."

"Got them demons inside," he whispered. "Demons . . . Demons . . ."

"Yeah, I know. I brought some medicine. Will you let the nurse give it to you?"

"Too late. Demons."

"No it isn't too late. But it will take a couple of days to quiet down the demons, okay? You have to be patient and let the medicine work."

Sully didn't answer. He dropped his wrists on the table with a clank.

Caleb inched a little closer, keeping an eye on his client to gauge his response. Sully didn't move. Good. Letting Caleb into his personal space closer was a small act of trust. "They told me you had a fight with someone? Can you tell me what happened?"

"Man I didn't know asked me for money. Man stank of liquor. Ain't got no use for a man like that."

"No, I don't expect you would." Caleb could imagine Sully in his current paranoid state being approached by a stranger. A man as big as Sully could do some damage.

"Demons are winning," Sully said. "They come and they take the best. They're winning, winning, winning . . ." he repeated the last word like a chant, his voice fading.

"Demons take the best?" Caleb asked. "But they haven't taken you."

"Not me, not me. But others."

"Who?"

"They got Stormy. Grabbed him in their claws and carried him away."

"Yes, Stormy is dead," Caleb said. "I'm sorry. How did you know him?"

Sully didn't answer for a long moment. He leaned back, head tilted, eyes partly closed. "Why you ask about Stormy?"

"Because someone killed him and that's a terrible thing."

"Stormy got clean. Living a righteous life. Lending a hand to them who asked for it."

"I heard he was in recovery. And he tried to help others do the same thing."

"It's a rocky road, that one. But Stormy got moving, grooving. The sunny girl, she smiled." Sully lifted his head to stare at the ceiling. "She smiled like all sunshine."

"Sunny girl?" Caleb struggled to tease fact from Sully's word salad.

"She say she proud, proud to know him. And he stood tall, man. Stood tall."

"Who stood tall? Stormy?"

"She warm like sunshine. All smiles. So the demon took her, too."

"Are you talking about Gina?" Caleb's pulse quickened. Did this mean Gina had seen Stormy? But Caleb knew all her clients and Stormy wasn't one of them. Maybe this was just Sully's psychosis speaking.

"Sully, look at me. I'm trying to understand what you're saying. Did you see Gina and Stormy together?"

He rocked back, turning his head—towards the voices?

"Sully?"

"She smiled. Made Stormy stand tall. Sunshine. Demons come take her away. I got nothing else to say. Nothing else to say."

Abruptly, Sully stood and took faltering steps to the door, the chain rattling in his wake. The jailor appeared and said, "Y'all done in here?"

"It seems we are," Caleb said, standing. "Make sure he gets his medicine, okay?"


Claudia was waiting for him at the reception desk. "Well?"

"He needs to get out of there."

"His hearing is tomorrow. But he's not likely to get a PR bond. You think he has money to bail himself out?"

Caleb shook his head. He wished Safe Harbor could help, but its financial problems made that unlikely. "Could we get him transferred to a hospital?"

"Last I heard the state gave up all its psychiatric beds."

"You're right about that. Another reason to love our governor." Caleb looked back at the closed door leading to the cells. "Just make sure he gets his medication. I'll try to get by tomorrow to check on him. One other thing—any luck finding Wyman Carter?"

She shook her head. "Captain's got every officer keeping a lookout. But no luck so far."

Caleb suspected Bentille knew about Carter's family. It certainly explained Carter's being transferred from the jail to a private rehab facility when he made his escape. Bentille would want to suck-up to the senator to foster his own delusional political ambitions. It would have been nice if the police had shared that info with Caleb before.

"One more thing," Claudia lowered her voice. "I need to ask you something. It's about Gina Fulton."

The change in her tone took him by surprise. "What?"

"Exactly how well did you know her?"

"I told you. She was my intern. I worked with her three days a week, at both the counseling center and Safe Harbor."

"Yeah, that's what you said. What about after hours?" Claudia fixed a steely gaze on him. He'd seen the look before when she questioned suspects.

"Why the hell are you asking me that? There were no after-hours with Gina. She was just a kid. And I'm not exactly single." Caleb backed away from her, not liking where this was going.

"That doesn't stop a lot of men," she said.

"Where is this coming from?" Annoyance rang in his voice. "You know me, Claudia. You know me a lot better than to ask me that."

She didn't flinch, her coal black eyes tracking his.

"Something's happened," he said, trying to ignore the fluttering in his chest. "What is it?"

"I can't tell you," she said. "But Caleb, if there was anything— and I mean anything—going on between you and this girl you better tell me right now."

He stood there, stunned, for almost a minute.

"I already answered that," he said through clenched teeth. "You want me to take lie detector test?"

She shook her head, but not with much conviction. "I doubt it will come to that. Let's just say that this investigation is taking some twists and turns we didn't expect."

"I agree. One of them is having my friend Claudia question me like I'm a suspect. That's a pretty damn confusing turn."

"Caleb," she cautioned. "I am your friend, but I'm investigating three murders. And like it or not, you're smack in the middle of it. And if my doing my job ticks you off, you need to just deal with it."

He had nothing to say to that. He turned and walked out the door.


Caleb drove. Dusk had come and gone, night laying thick over Westville. He drove out to the country, past the state park, his car CD player belting out blues that only Billie Holiday can do justice to. He drove back to town, spotting a man with a with a grocery cart that he'd seen at Safe Harbor before. He didn't stop, just kept driving.

Claudia had treated him like a suspect. Like he had some-thing to hide. She was his friend and he didn't have a lot of those. He felt betrayed. Furious. And more than a little scared.

He didn't want to go home to an empty house. A Shannon-less house. Cleo was probably hungry but she would have to wait a little longer because he needed to drive.

The moon hung like a bright coin overhead, not quite full. Waxing or waning? He didn't remember. He let the window down a little, the air like icy fingers against his skin. November had been a chilly month and that didn't bode well for winter. They had to find some way to keep Safe Harbor open or homeless people would have no refuge from the cold.

But Safe Harbor's future was more vulnerable than ever. Three murders with ties to the shelter. Money problems with no solution in sight. A mayor who wanted it closed down and greedy developers hungry for the real estate. And nothing but bad publicity for the past five weeks. And what had Caleb done to help? He'd brought a kid intern there to learn how to be a social worker. And now she was dead.

Yeah, Caleb had been a terrific addition to the Safe Harbor

staff.

This was not a healthy line of thinking. He turned up Billie and pointed his car down Lake Drive.

A half hour later he stood on Sam's front porch, wondering if he should push the door signal. Wondering why he was even here. He turned around. Time to go home.

Or not. Sam's van pulled into the drive. Sam climbed out and slammed the door shut. Caleb checked his watch, close to ten P.M.

"Hey," Caleb signed.

Sam took the steps two at a time to join him on the porch. "Everything okay?"

"Everything sucks," Caleb said. Sucks was one of his favorite signs because it was so graphic. Lips puckered, one hand simulated a Hoover sweeping the palm of the other. "How are things with you?"

"Ditto. Come on inside." Sam unlocked the door. Caleb followed him into the living room and dropped on a leather sofa that was as supple as a glove. He was still chilled, but slowly thawing. He gathered a fleece throw around his shoulders.

"Where were you?" Caleb asked.

"I was supposed to pick up Isaiah at six P.M. Went to the apartment but nobody was home. So I went looking for him."

"Looking for him? How? Where did you go?" Caleb's mind flashed on a scary picture of his brother knocking down doors along crack alley.

"Nowhere useful. Kept going back to the apartment. They still aren't there."

"So it may not mean anything. Diondra probably forgot."

"I hope that's what it is. She lives life on the edge. She could be in trouble."

"And that's not your problem," Caleb signed.

Sam gave him a tight, unconvincing smile. "Figured you say that. But I do have some responsibility to Isaiah. I want him to know he can count on me. Don't want him thinking I stood him up."

"Did you leave a note or anything?"

"Left two, one for her, one for Isaiah. Not that he can read." Sam tossed his keys on the table with enough force that they slid to the edge.

"Hey, careful with the furniture. I know the guy who made it," Caleb said. The coffee table had been one of Sam's earlier works, Brazilian rosewood in a curved "S" design. How Sam could let books and newspapers pile on something so beautiful made no sense to his brother.

"So what's up with you?" Sam asked.

And Caleb told him all of it. About Gina and her father's questions about his relationship with her. About the surreal conversation with Claudia.

"So she wanted to know if you were in a relationship with your student?" he asked incredulously.

"Yeah."

"Were you?"

The question hit in the solar plexus. "*No!*" he yelled, two fingers snapping against his thumb.

Sam smiled. "Got ya."

"Sam!"

"Hey, no way you'd mess around with a student. You're too afraid of Shannon to try something like that."

"Damn right."

"But it's weird Claudia would take that tactic with you."

"She used to be a friend."

"She still is your friend. But right now, you have to let her do her job." Sam stood, holding up a hand. "Wait here a second. I have an idea."

Caleb needed to get home, he had a hungry sheepdog waiting. It was too late to call Shannon, but maybe he could do that before work in the morning. Sometimes just hearing her voice helped.

Where had Sam gone? Caleb wandered to the back of the house to find his brother in his office clicking away at the computer. "You're reading emails?" he signed, annoyed.

"Nope." He pressed print.

The inkjet started rumbling and a document popped out of it. Sam checked it over before handing it to Caleb.

"A plane ticket?" Caleb asked.

"You leave tomorrow at four. Arrive in Maine at nine. Come back Sunday night. You'll just miss a few hours of work, hope that's okay." Sam was grinning, clearly quite proud of himself.

"You're sending me to Maine?"

"I'm sending you to Shannon. Let her listen to your griping for a while." Sam grabbed his shoulders and turned him around. "Now go on home and start packing. I'll be by to collect Cleo in the afternoon."

Caleb clutched the ticket like he'd won the lottery as he rushed out the door.

# Chapter Fifteen

The plane made its descent. Lights lay spattered across the landscape, the small city awake to greet the night. The captain announced the weather for Portland, ten degrees, four with the wind chill, as the plane bumped onto the runway. Caleb had barely cleared the gate when his cell phone rang.

"You're here? You're really here?" Shannon said.

"Where else should I be?" He trotted down the nearly empty corridor. Portland wasn't exactly an airline "hub," and apparently, his was the only plane due in after nine P.M. "Where are you?"

"Baggage claim. Wait, I see you!"

He picked up the pace, spotting the woman waving at him. The beautiful, amazing woman. "I'm hanging up now," he said.

"Me too. Because I'll need both arms—" she didn't get to finish her sentence. He grabbed her, lifted her, pulled her close. She pressed her face against his neck, then her lips into his.

He held on tight, breathing her in. Shannon. Finally.

"Okay, maybe I missed you a little," he said.

"Hmm. Not me. I've been keeping company with the cows." She gave him another kiss.

"I hear they're udderly entertaining."

"You're going to milk that for all its worth, aren't you?"

"I butter not." He loved the sound of her laugh, especially when she tossed her head back and let it roar. He'd do almost anything to hear it, save pursuing this line of bad puns any farther.

"You have luggage?"

"Just this." Caleb pointed at the Pullman carry-on. "Shall we go?"

"Bundle up. It's a bit cool outside."

Cool, she said. Leave it to a Mainer to describe four degrees as "a bit cool." He zipped the parka, tightened the scarf, and slipped on gloves before stepping out into the bone-chilling night. "How do people live here?"

"I ask you the same question in July, don't I?"

She had a point. Between the Arctic clime of Maine, and the Hades temps of a South Carolina summer, they covered the whole gamut.

Caleb hurled his suitcase into the bed of the pick-up and they climbed into the cab. "Heat!" Caleb begged.

"Wimp." She cranked the ignition and aimed vents towards him.

As she maneuvered around large banks of dirty snow from the plowed entrance he asked, "What is that stuff?"

"It's snow, remember? We had two flakes in Westville last winter and you ran out to buy bread."

"Snow. Right. You have bread at your folks' place?"

"Better than that, we have beer."

It was an hour drive northwest once they'd left Portland, down narrow rural roads where the sparse traffic obeyed speed limits of forty-five. Caleb leaned against the window, watching Shannon. She looked beautiful, but tired. He suspected she'd lost ten pounds, but if he said anything she'd make a smart comment like "good riddance." He could see the strain of the past weeks etched in the lines around her mouth and eyes.

"How's your dad doing?" he asked.

"It's slow going. Bones don't heal as fast when you're his age."

"You take him to physical therapy every day?"

"Just twice a week. But it's an hour each way, and it's a hard trip for him."

"No home health around?"

"Not that I can find." She turned on the radio and Caleb settled into post-flight fatigue. He must have dozed a little because the next thing he knew she was turning onto her parents' road.

"So. Where am I sleeping?" Caleb knew how old fashion Shannon's mother was.

"In the guest room of course." She flashed him a wicked smile. "Which happens to be beside my room, on the other end of the house from Mom."

"So we're sneaking around? Even though she knows we live together?"

"Hey, you want to broach that topic with her, go right ahead!"

"No, no. Status quo is fine. Besides, it might be fun to sneak into your room. Maybe I'll wear a disguise. Play up to your milkman fantasies."

"One more milk comment and I'm taking you back to the airport."

Myrtis, Shannon's mother, had gone to bed, which was a lucky break. They stole up the creaking steps of the old farm-house, tossed Caleb's suitcase in the guestroom, and slipped through the door leading to Shannon's bed. She had his shirt off before the door latch clicked. Her sweater landed on the antique dresser, followed quickly by her jeans and his khakis. He fumbled with the clasp to her bra, which made her smile, and to expedite matters she deftly unhooked and slung the contraption out of the way.

They fell in a tumble on the bed, hungry bodies seeking, holding, merging. It felt like he couldn't get enough of her, couldn't get close enough, and he had a wild thought that the friction from their lovemaking might make them both combust. He could imagine the newspaper coverage: Death by delayed gratification.

When they finished, they lay sweat-drenched, tangled in each other's arms.

"Still cold?" she asked.

"Uh, no. Seems like a warm front's coming through."

"And I'm very glad it is." She snuggled into him, her head on his pillow, his arm going around her, and they drifted off to sleep.

Caleb awoke the next morning at the crack of nine to an empty bed. He slipped on yesterday's clothes and tiptoed into the guestroom. On the bed, the covers had been pulled back, pillows awry. Smart girl, that Shannon.

"Well good morning, Caleb." Myrtis McPherson was a tiny woman with twinkling blue eyes and wavy white hair cut short. "Shannon said to let you sleep in because you don't get the concept of farmer's hours."

He liked her New England accent, skipping over Rs: farmers pronounced fah-muhz.

"She's right. You have any coffee around here?"

"Brewed a pot just for you." She poured him a cup from an honest-to-God percolator. It tasted so weak he wasn't sure it held caffeine. "Thanks. Where is that daughter of yours, by the way?"

"Out at the barn." Pronounced "bahn." "Should be back pretty soon. Said something about you buying lunch for her."

"Where's Luke?"

"He's napping in the den. Still gets up at four, like he thinks he can work. But he wears himself out so fast."

"Guess recovering from something like that just takes time."

"Guess it does." She pulled out a bag of bagels from the fridge and handed them to him. "Shannon said this is all you eat for breakfast."

"She's right about that." He pulled out a raisin cinnamon bagel, his favorite. Bless you, Shannon.

Myrtis sat across from him at the table, eyeing him carefully. "I need your help with something."

"Sure." He tried to disguise his reluctance.

"Luke's fall has messed him up pretty bad."

"I'm sorry. For all of you."

"Thank God we have Molly. She's worked for Luke going on nine years. She's helping Shannon manage things. Don't know what we'd do without her."

Shannon had told him about Molly, a strong-backed, earthy Mainer who actually loved it when the temps sunk into the teens. "A bit balmy out," she'd tell Shannon.

"Luke has osteoporosis," Myrtis continued. "That means his bones are as brittle as finger nails. He may not like it, but he can't keep working the farm." She pressed her lips together like she had more to say but was censoring herself.

"From what Shannon says, it's very demanding work."

"He should have given it up years ago, but he's got that McPherson stubborn streak. What am I saying—you probably know all about that."

Caleb thought it best not to take that bait. "So you think he should give up the farm?"

"Yes I do. I've thought it for years. But Luke is a proud man. And the farm's been in the family for three generations. McPhersons have lived in this house for almost a hundred years."

"It's an amazing place." He liked the huge kitchen. Shannon

had paid to renovate it, installing a new stove, side-by-side refrigerator and the kitchen's first dishwasher.

"It's a lot of work is what it is. But I don't mind. What else would I do?"

"Maybe that's how Luke feels."

"Luke isn't the kind of man who's going to retire to Florida. Work is too much a part of who he is. But the farm is more than he can manage. He can't handle the workload. And I'm not going to let it kill him."

"Have you talked to him about selling?"

She sipped her coffee without answering, her arthritic, knobby knuckles gripping the cup. Finally, she said, "Luke and Shannon are the same. He can't let go of the farm because of her, because it's all he has to give her. And she can't help him let go because she's afraid of what it will do to him. She says he lives for that farm. But that's only partly true. He lives for his family."

He felt her eyes probing him, but kept his gaze steady. "And so does she," he said. "Only now, her family includes me and Julia."

"So you see my point. We have to help two very stubborn people do what's in their own best interest. Think you can handle it?"

He wasn't wild about stepping into this McPherson family drama on his first day here. "You've talked to Shannon about this?"

"I've tried. She just says 'It's up to Dad.' But she's wrong. Her dad needs for her to let go before he will."

"I'll talk with her. But like you said, she's stubborn."

Myrtis carried her cup and saucer to the sink. "There's nothing I'd like more than for my daughter to move back here. We miss her terribly, and South Carolina is so far away. But even more than I want that, I want for her to be happy. She has a life with you she needs to get back to, doesn't she?"

"Yes she does." And he'd do anything to get her back to it.

Caleb climbed the stairs for a shower and as soon as he finished, Shannon appeared. He gave her a long "good morning" kiss despite her objections that she hadn't showered and smelled like a Guernsey.

"Always been a big fan of the cow," he muttered, tugging at

her blouse as she swatted his hand away.

"Caleb! Stop that. Mom will have a stroke. Look, I'm going to get myself cleaned up then you and I are going into town for lunch. Then I'm yours for the afternoon until milking time." She slipped out of his grasp, Caleb returning to the guest room, where he took his time about unpacking. He liked the feel of the room. The panes of wavy glass in the tall windows. The lacy curtains filtering the sunlight. The cold touch of the marble-topped dressing table. The four-poster bed with its plump flowered comforter. The corner closet, added years after the farmhouse was constructed, with just enough room for a few hanging garments and a dozen shoes. This room, like this house, was like stepping back into the forties.

But this wasn't the forties. As much as Shannon and her dad wanted to hold onto the past, it might be time to let it go. Of course, it wasn't his decision to make. He'd talk to Shannon, but support her in what she decided. After all, wasn't that why he was here?

Shannon drove them into Warwick, a quaint, old New England village closest to the farm. They ate lobster rolls at a table by the blazing fireplace in a rustic local restaurant. After, they held hands as they explored a few shops nearby. A bookstore. A pottery place. A few antique dealers. Shannon's cell phone rang and Caleb worried she'd have to return to the dairy farm. But instead, she said, "That was Molly. She said she'd handle the afternoon shift. It feels weird to have this much time without rushing back."

"I like that Molly!" Caleb nudged her into a small coffee shop at the end of Main Street. "I need a fix. And I need to be somewhere that's warmer than sub-zero temperatures," he explained.

"This is a warm snap! It's twenty-eight toasty degrees."

"I think my eyeballs are freezing over." He ordered coffee for them both and they sat at a café table by the picture window. In the distance, Caleb could see snow-covered mountains. Strange, it was only four P.M. but the sun hung low on the horizon. Life on planet Maine.

When the waiter handed him the coffee, Caleb wrapped his hands around it to absorb the heat. What did homeless people do up here? How could they survive on the streets?

"This is heaven," Shannon said, inhaling the steam from her cup. "Free time. Warm coffee. And I even got to have sex."

"Could you say that a little louder?" Caleb looked around, but the other customers didn't seem to be listening in.

"Sorry." She gave him an impish smile. "So fill me in. Any other developments in the Safe Harbor murders?"

"Not really." He knew he was being evasive, but wasn't sure what to say about the strange conversation with Claudia.

"I don't need to be worrying about you from way up here."

He stifled the urge to say, "Come home then." Instead, he reached for her hand. "You don't need to worry. Claudia's gonna have this resolved soon. She's got that pit-bull focus thing going." It sucked that her focus seemed to be on him.

"The student intern who was killed. Gina. Tell me about her."

"She was a sweet kid. Had lots of promise. Died way too young." He took a sip of coffee to quell the chill he felt inside. Gina. "But I think she was involved in something at the shelter I didn't know about. One of my clients mentioned her in connection with Stormy, the body they found by the river. I knew all her clients and she wasn't working with Stormy."

"Maybe she knew him outside of the shelter."

"How do you mean?"

"I mean she had a life before social work school. Maybe she knew Stormy's family. Or met him at the laundromat. Do you know where Stormy was from?"

"Crap." He remembered Gina telling him she'd encountered someone she knew in high school. And Claudia said Stormy was from Sumter—where Gina's parents lived. Why hadn't he put that together before? He explained the link to Shannon.

"Maybe you should call Claudia and tell her."

"I'm surprised Claudia hasn't already figured it out." Maybe she would have if she wasn't wasting her time implying Caleb had been having an affair with Gina. He squeezed his cup, fury still way too close to the surface.

"Did I ever tell you that I used to work with Bill Evers?" Shannon said.

"No. When?"

"My first job out of graduate school—at the Children's Home."

"I remember you worked there. You told me you liked the kids and wanted to adopt twenty of them. But that the hours sucked you dry."

"Damn right they did. Not as bad as the dairy farm, but pretty long. A ten hour day was the norm, and I was on call every other week. I'd get called in when there was a crisis, sometimes in the middle of the night. Those kids could be a handful."

"What was Bill's role?"

"That's a good question. He was the clinical director, so technically he was my boss. There were two other social workers besides me, so that made four clinical staff total. But only two of us were ever on call, me and a woman named Fiona. Bill really liked the other social worker, Suzanne something. Lyons maybe. Anyway, he made her his assistant so she didn't have to cover weekends or evenings."

"Did Bill ever handle on-call?"

"Nope. Not one time. I remember I had the flu and I called Suzanne but she said it wasn't her job. So I tried Bill. He was very apologetic but had weekend plans, so I had to come in and do my best not to breathe on the kids."

"Sounds like he wasn't a very good manager," Caleb commented.

"I never knew what he did. He rarely saw a client. Fiona had been there longer than me and called him "Teflon Bill" because nothing ever stuck to him. He didn't carry the responsibility we did or work the hours we did, but he sure would take the credit when something went right. Fiona thought maybe Bill and Suzanne were sleeping together."

"What did you think?"

"I didn't think it was my business. But it would explain the preferential treatment." Shannon ran a hand through her thick hair. "I know he and Matthew are friends. Matthew's usually a pretty good judge of character. So maybe Bill's changed."

"Maybe, maybe not. Safe Harbor is a complex machine. There's something going on all the time. Trucks to unload, clients to serve, donations to collect. But Bill's always in his office. We need a director who will roll up his sleeves and help with all of it. Then there's this guy, Henry Rudd. He's the recovery director, but he's the guy that takes care of everything. Not Bill."

"So which kind of guy are you? A Bill or a Henry?"

He let out a little laugh. "I'd be a Bill if I could get away with it. But Henry keeps me working my butt off. And I have to say it's a nice change of pace from sitting in the private practice office all day."

"Getting back to your social worker roots, are you?"

"God help me," he answered.

Shannon sipped her coffee and lowered the cup. "Changing the subject, how was breakfast with Mom this morning?"

"She didn't figure out our sleeping arrangements, if that's what you're asking. Probably a 'don't ask, don't tell' kind of thing." He looked at her, remembering how it felt to wake up in her bed. "She did talk about your dad and the farm."

"She wants Dad to sell."

"She's worried about what this job does to his health. Just seeing how exhausted you are, I have to agree with her."

"Well that's great. Teaming up on me."

He reached over and squeezed her hand. "No. Definitely not teaming up. I am on your side, and will always be on your side."

"Doesn't sound like it to me." She pulled away.

He sighed. "Tell me what you want. What you think is best for your dad."

Her eyes filled with tears.

"You're in a tough spot, aren't you?" he whispered, reaching up to stroke her hair.

"Mom's right. It is too much. But Dad's right, too. The farm is in his blood. I think he may die if he has to give it up."

"Myrtis says he wants to keep it for you. Does Luke think you'll stay here to run it?" He kept his hand on her, softly caressing her neck.

"He wants me to."

"And what do you want?" He felt a knot twisting in his stomach at the weight of this question.

"Do you really have to ask?"

"You know me. Mr. Self-Confident."

"Yes, I do know." She leaned in closer, linking her arm under his. "What do I want? To get back to my life."

"With me," he added, needing the clarity.

"No, with Cleo. She's the only one who really understands."

He laughed into her hair and heard her giggle back, a private giggle. "So maybe there's another option."

"Door number three?"

"Maybe. What if you kept the farm, but hired someone else to run it? Luke could still be a part of things, but in more of an oversight position. And if you hired the right person, Luke would only be as involved as be could handle."

"That would be wonderful. But our cash flow isn't all that great. I don't think we could afford someone of that caliber."

"You've talked about Molly. You say you can count on her, right?"

"She's priceless. But she has to work at a bookstore on weekends because we don't pay her enough. We do the best we can, but the money isn't there. It's really a shame, too, because she loves the farm as much as we do."

Caleb studied her for a long moment, thinking. "Okay, you and I both know that I understand squat about business. But think about this: What if you offered Molly the job of manager, but paid her in shares? She could become part owner of this place, in partnership with your dad and you. She wouldn't have to invest money, but she'd invest her time and energy. You could work out some kind of system so that in a few years' time, she legitimately owns half of the farm."

She stared at his face, her mouth opening, then closing. He waited, watching her process this. Finally, she spoke. "You know, that might actually work. She's got the skills, no doubt about it. And Dad loves her like a daughter. And we both trust her. She's mentioned that we could expand, maybe build onto the barn for more cattle, and sell to another distributor over in Vermont. I couldn't fathom doing more than we're doing but she could pick up that ball and run with it!"

He smiled, loving the enthusiasm he heard in her voice. "And she understands Luke. She'd give him room to do whatever he needs to."

"I may need to put some money into it, especially if she expands. But we could maybe get a loan. Why the hell not?"

"Why the hell not," he repeated, feeling oddly proud of himself for coming up with this solution.

"I'll talk with Dad. If he's okay with it, I'll talk to Molly tomorrow." She reached her arm around his neck, giving him a sloppy, loud kiss. "I love you, Caleb Knowles."

"I love you, too, oh Mistress of the Cows."

# Chapter Sixteen

"Nora?" Wyman held the cell phone against his ear. He wasn't sure he'd dialed the right number. The woman's voice could have been hers but it was hard to hear over the piercing yaps from a dog.

"Who is this please?"

"It's me. Wyman." He hoped she wouldn't hang up on him, though it was what he deserved.

"Wyman? My God. Are you all right?" She didn't sound mad. The dog barked louder, like it was on the phone with her.

"Quiet Edgar," she said. "My dog. He's a pain sometimes."

He remembered her dog. That hairy gray thing looked like something you'd dust with.

"Can I see you? Can we meet somewhere?"

"Okay, I guess." His heart pounded. How long had it been? Did she even know the kind of trouble he was in?

"Tell me where."

Somewhere safe. "How about Finlay Park? By the fountain?"

"Sure. I can be there in an hour."

"Okay." This next part was going to be harder than he thought. He said, "Uhmmm. Could you lend me a little money? I'll pay it back I promise. Just . . . just thirty or so."

"Sure, sure," she said, like she'd been expecting it. "I'll see you in a little while."

"Thanks."

Wyman waited by the fountain. Nora had said she'd come in an hour, but Wyman didn't have a watch and he didn't have Stormy's ability to guess the time and get it right nine out of ten tries. So as soon as he turned off the cell he hiked up to the park and took a seat at a shaded picnic table.

He had regrets about his sister. He could have been a better brother, but he couldn't be a part of that family, not really. He wasn't like his mother, he couldn't just pretend they didn't have a life before. He couldn't forget his real dad, a bulky man with big beefy hands who taught Wyman to throw a football and broke two of Wyman's ribs after Wyman failed a math test. His mom stayed scared of that man till the day they left him.

It wasn't much better without him. During the year before the Senator, Mom had been with a couple of men. Wyman would never forget one guy, Barry. How excited she was when she put on make-up as she got ready for her date. The way she told Wyman to be quiet when they came back from the bar. He didn't mind being alone, though he was probably too young, but he did mind it when Barry and Mom came through the apartment door giggling and tearing at each other's clothes. He heard them in her bedroom, the squeals and gasps and banging sounds. After, the apartment got real silent, then he heard a door open. He felt the bed shift as Barry sat. Barry tugging at his pajamas, saying "shhhhh or I'll beat your mama!" No, he shouldn't remember that.

He tried to tell her. She said she was tired of all his lies. Then she met the Senator. "It's all going to be different now, Wyman. You'll see."

She was sure right about that. Not that the Senator hit him— he did just that one time when Wyman burned the tool shed. But Wyman wasn't like his mother. She could put on the expensive suit, the shiny heels, the pink nail polish, and turn herself into a rich lady. She knew when to smile and how to chat with strangers. She could walk arm-in-arm with the Senator like she always belonged there.

Wyman tried to belong but never could. When Nora came along, the perfect daughter, the child the Senator always wanted, it was as if Wyman vanished behind a curtain. But that was the past, best forgotten.

A couple of kids walked by. The boy's hand snaked under the girl's sweater. It looked like they might do it right there in front of Wyman! Live porn in the park.

They moved to a bench and sat, the girl sucking on the boy's face. As he wrapped an arm around her, she snuggled close, saying something about being cold. The day had a gray tint to it, clouds hanging low, rain probably on its way. At least it wasn't as cold as yesterday. When Nora brought him the cash, he'd be high before dusk, and rain and cold wouldn't matter a lick.

A policeman came down the steps on the other side of the fountain. Wyman limped behind the tree to watch. The last thing he needed was to get hauled in to jail. The officer circled around to speak to the kids. The boy said, "Hello officer."

"Shouldn't you two be in school?"

"Teacher's work day." The girl looked down at her feet, which meant she was lying.

The cop stood beside them like he had no intention of leaving, so the couple finally got up and walked away. Wyman wished the cop had left with them. He pressed himself against the tree, trying not to breathe too loud. Someone else came down the steps: Nora. She had the damn little dog on a leash, and it went to the policeman and started sniffing his leg.

"Edgar!" Nora said. "Sorry officer. He's just very curious."

"It's okay, ma'am." He bent down to scratch the dog's head. They were acting so friendly that Wyman started wondering if Nora had called him. Had she told the police where to find him?

*Don't trust her.*

He rested his forehead against the trunk of the tree, unsure what to do.

*Don't trust her!* The voice screamed. *She wants to kill you. They all want you dead.*

He should make a run for it. But how? His damn foot was so sore he couldn't move very fast. Besides, he'd have to get to the steps, which meant going right by the cop.

*She wants you dead!*

The voice got louder, drowning out other sounds, other thoughts. Damn it. This was a trap. That cop was going to handcuff him and lock him in a cell. Damn himself for being so stupid. For thinking he could trust her.

"Well, have a good day, ma'am." The policeman patted the dog again and climbed the steps, soon disappearing. Wyman watched Nora sit on the bench and check her watch.

*Don't trust her.*

He wanted to ignore the voice, but that was never easy. Should he take off? If he did, he'd miss out on getting the cash Nora promised him. And the money would get him the one thing, the only thing, that would make him feel better.

The small dog yapped again, straining at the end of the leash. Wyman stepped out from behind the tree. "Hey, Nora."

She clutched at her chest. "Oh, you scared me."

The dog barked some more, its tiny teeth nipping at Wyman's shoe.

"Shhhh, Edgar." Nora scooped it up. "How are you, Wyman?"

He couldn't meet her gaze. Nora was so beautiful. A tiny thing, with dark hair like her father, but freckles like their mother. Her fingernails were bright red and shiny. She wore a fur-collared jacket and black pants. A bright gold bracelet glimmered on her wrist. She was always nice to him, even when she was little. Even when her father—his step-father—kicked Wyman out, first to boarding school, then to the streets.

"Mom's been worried," Nora said.

He looked up, wanting to believe her. Nora fussed with the dog's collar. "She went to see you in the hospital. Did you know that?"

"I thought that was a dream." Or even a vision. His mother had stood over his bed, her blue eyes peering down. She wore her silver hair chin-length now. Had more wrinkles around her eyes and mouth, but still beautiful, like she could be on TV.

"She says she'll get you a lawyer. She and Mr. Dougherty have been working on it."

"Does she know I called you?" He took a step back. *Don't trust her.*

"No, Wyman," Nora said quickly. "She doesn't know I'm here. I swear."

*Don't trust her.*

He eyed the steps to see if the cop had come back.

"This is just me and you. They'll never know I saw you if you don't want them to."

He nodded, wanting to believe.

"I have money for you." She set the beast on the ground and opened a little red purse. "Here. Sixty dollars."

He took the money, crisp, clean bills that looked like they'd just been printed. He stuffed them in the pocket of his sweats. He

wished she brought more. A hundred. Two hundred. Enough to
keep him high for days, floating and free.

"One more thing," she said. "I know you're not staying at Mr.
Dougherty's place. Mom doesn't understand why you don't. She
says his house is very nice."

He almost laughed. So this is what Markham told them—that
Wyman stayed in the fancy brick house behind the group home.
That he actually lived with Markham and Rhetta.

"But I think I know why you don't stay with him. You like to
be by yourself. And you don't like people telling you what to do.
You've always been that way, haven't you?" She looked up at his
face, her eyes soft.

"I worry about you, you know. Mom does too," she added.

He wished she'd quit talking about their mother. It brought up
a tangle of feelings and made him so hungry for crack he could
hardly stand it. Nora's eyes moistened, like she might cry right
there. He could never stand to see it, even when she was just a
baby. She was too sweet to ever have to cry about anything, and
here he was, causing those tears.

"I need to get going," he said.

"Okay. Take care of yourself. Please."


Caleb's flight home landed three hours late. Stormy weather in
DC, where he changed planes, meant sitting on the tarmac for
over an hour, his jet in a growing cue of postponed take-offs.
When they finally reached the runway, a flash of lightening caused
a longer delay.

It was close to midnight when they landed in Columbia, and
the small airport looked like it had already gone to bed. No
personnel greeted them at the gate, and beyond the security
checkpoint Caleb saw only a few cleaning people. And Claudia
Briscoe, wearing jeans, a sweatshirt, and a pronounced frown.

"Claudia?" Caleb greeted her warily, his stomach doing some
interesting gymnastics. Had something happened to Sam?
Matthew?

"You left town." She crossed her arms. She looked mad.

"Went to see Shannon. What's wrong?"

"You might have mentioned that last week. Might have said,

'by the way, Claudia, I'll be in Maine over the weekend.'"

"Last minute thing. Oh, and by the way, I don't report to you. You're not my boss. And I'm pretty sure you're not my mother."

"I'm a friend, I thought."

"So did I, but last week that sort of changed, didn't it?" The anxious churning of his insides turned to anger. Claudia's visit wasn't about bad news, it was an exercise in chain-yanking. He adjusted the handle on his Pullman and started walking to the exit.

But Claudia stepped in front of him. "Don't you think I have a good reason for coming out here at this God-forsaken hour?"

"I'm not sure I care," Caleb answered, and realized it wasn't just rage he felt. It was hurt.

"You better care." She nudged him to a pair of incongruous rocking chairs near the main entrance to the airport, but he didn't sit, determined to keep this interaction as brief as possible. Sam had dropped Cleo at his house, so he had a hungry dog and a bed waiting twenty miles away. A dog and an empty bed, he remembered.

"Caleb, I came here because you are my friend and I need to give you a heads-up. This investigation has turned up some . . . information," she paused, glancing around like she was looking for spies who might overhear her.

"What kind of information?"

"We found hundreds of emails on Fulton's computer. Not just the computer from the counseling center, but the one she had at home. She regularly posted on Facebook and Myspace. Our tech guys have been sorting through pages and pages of contacts."

"That's how it is with kids today."

"What about you? You pretty keen on emailing?"

He let out a half-laugh. "Not exactly. I email Sam sometimes, but usually we text-message."

"Really." She was watching him with narrowed cop eyes, like she had the other day.

"Yes really! What is up with you?"

She twisted her mouth into a tight, unfriendly smile. "Did you know Fulton was in a relationship?"

"Gina. Call her Gina, she was just a kid. She was in a romantic relationship? No, I had no idea."

"She never mentioned it to you."

"No. But why would she? I was just her placement supervisor. Do you tell Bentille who you date?"

"From what we can tell from the emails, it was a young relationship. Just a couple of months. But the kid was in love. Sappy, romantic crap you wouldn't believe."

"Who was the guy?" Caleb asked.

"The guy is worse than Fulton. Goes on and on about how just seeing her takes his breath away, how they'll be together forever, etc., etc."

"You didn't answer my question." He had an idea where she was going with this. Most murders were committed by someone known by the victim. Had Gina's death been a crime of passion?

"I didn't answer because we're not sure who the guy is. Though we're getting close."

"What, he didn't use his name?"

"Signed everything YAF. Weird initials, don't you think?"

"I guess. Can't your tech wizards trace the emails to their source?"

"That's not as easy as you'd think, but yes. We've managed to find the computer that sent about half of the messages."

"Okay," Caleb said tentatively. Why was she trickling out the information instead of just telling him? And why was she looking at him like that? His last trace of patience evaporated. "What the hell is going on?"

The intensity of her glare was almost painful. He lifted his hands, palms out, saying *what?*

"I can't tell you. But I need you at my office first thing tomorrow."

"First thing? I have three clients scheduled."

"Not anymore you don't. Be there at eight." She reached in her jeans pocket for her keys.

Rage, gone. Patience, gone. Fear welled like a tsunami. Not fear for someone he cared about, but for himself, and it felt strange and unsettling. "Claudia?" he yelled, because she was almost out the exit.

"What?" She stopped at the glass door.

"Do I need a lawyer or something?"

She turned back to face him. "Might not be a bad idea." And

with that, she left him.

Caleb slapped at the alarm buzzer trying to silence its piercing shriek. Missed it. Swatted again, the sound burrowing into his brain like a rabid bloodworm. Third strike met its target, the noise blessedly stopped. He cracked open an eye. The clock read six-fifteen.

He rolled over, attempting to send commands through his nervous system to get his limbs moving. He had to get showered and dressed so he could meet Claudia at the police station. For his interrogation, it seemed.

But the legs weren't cooperating. Not fully, anyway, probably related to the alcohol still working through his system. The first beer he had when he got home had not done its job of calming him down enough to hit the sack. He felt Shannon's absence like a physical ache, and the conversation with Claudia wouldn't stop ping-ponging through his brain. The second beer almost did it, but it took number three to get him horizontal and relaxed enough to sleep. Not passed out, mind you. He never drank that much, not since his grad school days. But if the truth be told, he had overdone it last night. Which in hindsight wasn't very smart, given what was facing him. He needed to be sharp.

Shower then. He stepped over a snoring sheepdog and made his way to the bathroom.

At least he didn't have to worry about saving hot water for anyone. The cottage's plumbing was at least sixty years old and needed to be upgraded. He should get one of those tankless water heaters, too. Maybe before Shannon came back. Wouldn't that be the perfect gift: thirty minutes of steaming hot water anytime she wanted. Thirty minutes in the shower with Shannon . . . no, better not let his mind—or body—go there.

He toweled off, feeling marginally better, except for the marshmallows wedged in the back of his throat. Cleo led him to the back door so that she could do her business. After filling her food dish, Caleb poured himself a cup of coffee. The clock read six thirty A.M.

Was it too early to call Phillip Etheridge? Caleb's friend and attorney didn't have the personality of an early riser, but Caleb had to make sure Phillip could meet him at the police station. And how weird was that? Caleb needing representation in a murder investigation?

He dialed. No answer, and, figuring Phillip might be screening his calls, Caleb didn't leave a message. He wasn't sure how he would measure up against whoever was sleeping on the other side of Phillip's bed. He dialed again. No answer so he hung up again. He'd learned this technique from a client who somehow got Caleb's home number. Keep dialing so the phone keeps ringing and annoys the hell out of the person you're trying to reach.

Through the window he could see that the newspaper had arrived. He fetched it from the front walkway, noting the others Sam had collected on the table by the front door. He unfolded the *Westville Chronicle* as he made his way back to the kitchen and the telephone. When he dialed again he got a grumpy, "What the hell do you want, Caleb?"

"You have caller ID?"

"I'm a freakin' lawyer. Of course I have caller ID. Now what's the emergency? And there sure as hell better be one for you to call me at this hour."

"It is." Caleb told him all of it. Phillip didn't interrupt, and Caleb hoped he was processing what Caleb was saying. He probably hadn't had his first cup of coffee yet.

"So you don't really know why they want to question you?" Phillip asked.

"Not really. Claudia was being evasive as hell. But this has me good and nervous."

"Yeah I'll bet. Hold on a sec."

Caleb stretched the limit of his phone cord to reach the refrigerator door. Not much looked promising for breakfast, but he grabbed the milk, sniffed it, and decided it would do for one more day.

"I have to rearrange some stuff but I can meet you there at eight-thirty. Don't say a word till I get there."

"Okay."

"I mean it, not one word. I know Claudia's your friend, but she isn't right now."

"You got that right," Caleb answered softly. "See you there."

After hanging up, he grabbed a box of Shannon's cereal, some twigs and fiber mixture that didn't seem too stale. He choked down half a bowl and checked the clock again. Seven o'clock. He knew someone who was definitely up. Matthew answered on the second ring.

"Caleb?" Was he the only person on earth without caller ID?

"I'm gonna be late this morning," he said, relaying the saga to his boss and friend.

"They came back to the center on Friday," Matthew said. "Had a court order for your office PC and for the medical records of Gina's clients."

"Crap."

"We didn't have much choice in the matter. And we've had to tell the clients about Gina and the potential breach in their confidentiality."

Caleb fell back against the counter, suddenly feeling winded. "I don't know what's going on, Matthew. But I'm getting creeped out."

"Have you called Phillip?"

"Yeah, he's coming."

"Anything I can do?"

"Can you let Henry at Safe Harbor know I'll likely be late there, too?" Caleb wondered how much this was going to disrupt his life, and the lives of the clients who counted on him.

"It's going to be okay, Caleb." Matthew spoke in the concerned therapist voice he used to calm down upset clients. "You did nothing wrong and they're going to see that."

Caleb thanked him and hoped like hell that he was right.

# Chapter Seventeen

He felt a bit ridiculous in the necktie but wasn't sure what the dress code was for this shindig. Phillip would be his usual Armani self, Claudia probably in a power suit. Caleb needed to be on equal ground. So he grabbed the tie Shannon had bought for him, even pressing out a wrinkle, and wore a button-down Oxford shirt that made him feel like an accountant.

The officer at reception didn't wave him back, despite the Westville PD identification card, but had him sit in the waiting area. He took a seat between an Elvis-wannabe in a motorcycle jacket and a young woman holding a crying toddler. He wondered what their stories were. And wondered if they had the same thought about him.

Claudia marched over to him, heels clicking on the linoleum, and motioned for him to follow. She didn't speak a single word. He did his best to keep up, but Claudia seemed to have a head of steam going, and blew past her office and Bentille's. She led him into the large interrogation room he'd been to before, though in previous visits, he'd been on the other side of the table. He didn't have to give his "I'm not speaking without my attorney here" speech because Phillip showed up seconds later, looking fierce and frighteningly un-caffeinated. Not a good combination.

"Thanks," Caleb said, when Phillip took the seat beside him.

"Here." Phillip placed two Starbucks cups on the table. He turned to Claudia and said, "Sorry, detective, I suppose I should have brought you one, too."

"That's quite all right. Can we get down to business?"

"Sure, but I'd like a word with my client first."

She cocked her head, regarding them like they were elementary school boys caught rough-housing on the play ground. "I'll give you five minutes."

When she left, Caleb pointed to a wall and whispered, "That's a one-way mirror, by the way."

"Hell, I know that, but they know they're not supposed to eavesdrop when you talk to me. I wanted to mention two things to you. One, don't answer any question without looking at me first. If I raise my eyebrows, keep your mouth shut."

"Why do I feel like I'm working for U.N.C.L.E.?"

"Two," Phillip said, ignoring him. "We need to ask questions ourselves to figure out what they have on you. The best way to do that is to keep your answers vague, yet insist that they be specific. I'll help with that. But you need to keep your cool through all of this, okay?"

Caleb nodded, though he wasn't sure how he'd do it. He felt strange. Out of place. The necktie tightened around his throat. Gina was dead and they were questioning him? Why weren't they out there finding the real killer?

"Can we get started now?" Claudia returned, holding a thick file and a notebook. Phillip slurped his coffee.

Claudia's questions were the same she had asked last night, though her tone was different. Steely. Poised. All business. Caleb's answers were no different, and Phillip only interrupted a few times with questions of his own.

And then Claudia opened the file. She handed him a stack of printouts about an inch thick, and gestured that he should read them.

"What are we looking at here, Detective?" Phillip asked.

"These were emails sent to the victim from September seventh through November twelfth, the day before she died."

Curious, Caleb read the first page:

I know we've just met but I feel this connection with you. Do you feel it too? I think it was the way you laughed, that glorious smile you wear. The warmth I see in your eyes. Just wanted you to know. YAF.

She pointed at the letters. "This is how he identifies himself."

Caleb read through other emails. Several came each day, the message growing more intense, more intimate as time passed. It felt strange and voyeuristic to read them, Gina's most private correspondence.

Claudia flipped through a half inch of sheets. "Note the change in tone. Starting here—" She pointed to a sheet dated October twentieth.

"Why won't you see me this weekend? I know you have school work to do but you have to eat sometime. I'll cook for you. I'll bring the food to your house. Anything, just to be with you a few hours. Please?"

Caleb shook his head. Gina seemed to be distancing herself from the friend and he sounded desperate to keep the connection. Desperation could lead to dangerous measures.

"I waited for you after your class. I waited two hours and twenty minutes but you never came, never called. Don't you think I deserve more respect than that?"

"Uh oh," Caleb said.

"Exactly," Claudia answered, pulling the sheets from his grasp and returning them to the folder.

Phillip eyed the exchange with interest. "So you think this YAF turned out to be some kind of stalker?"

Claudia didn't answer. She turned back to Caleb. "So tell me, Caleb, why did you send these emails to Gina Fulton?"

Air left his lungs. Suddenly, the room became hotter than a kiln. "Wh . . at?" he could barely squeeze out the word.

"Detective, what is your point?" Phillip's voice rose.

"Each of these emails was sent from your computer, Caleb."

"That's . . . not possible." Caleb started to feel dizzy. He forced himself to draw in a long, slow breath, mentally rehearsing the word, *Calm, be calm* . . .

She patted the file. "Oh but it is. The emails started one week after you and Ms. Fulton—Gina—started working at Safe Harbor. All the contacts happened over the shelter's server. You sent them, Caleb, to that young student."

*Calm . . . Calm.* He was aware that two sets of eyes had fixed on him. Two friends, Phillip and Claudia, but Claudia wasn't a friend anymore. Right now, Claudia was the enemy.

"Caleb? You okay, buddy?" Phillip asked, his hand touching Caleb arm.

*Calm, calm.* His fear slowly evaporated. Rage replaced it. How dare Claudia accuse him of this? How could she think—

"I'm fine." He glared at the detective.

The detective evaded his stare, suddenly not as composed as before.

"So you think I killed Gina? Is that it?" Caleb pressed into her personal space. "And Esther? I stabbed her, too? And Stormy? I killed a man I'd never even met?"

"Caleb!" Phillip cautioned.

"If you didn't send these emails, then who did?" Claudia asked.

"I don't know. Her killer maybe?" he answered, teeth clenched.

"I think we're done here," Phillip said, standing. "Unless you plan on charging him with something?"

"No, he's not being charged at this point. But we may have questions later."

Phillip plucked a business card from his shirt pocket and tossed it on the table. "You have more questions, you go through me. Come on, Caleb. Let's get the hell out of here."

Caleb offered a terse farewell to his attorney as he left the station. He could tell Phillip wanted to talk, probably to strategize, but he was in no mood. He climbed into his Subaru, pulling the necktie loose and over his head. What now? Go to work? Not until he could calm down. He stopped by the house to change shirts. Checked the answering machine to see if Shannon had called. Wondered if he should call her, but decided she didn't need to hear this news. Not yet.

His hand trembled on the steering wheel, anger and fear competing for control. Someone had sent the emails from the computer in his office at Safe Harbor, but who? Security was marginal at the shelter, but Caleb kept his office locked because of the clinical records. Who had a key?

Henry did, but Henry would never do something like this. Esther had a key to every office. Did she have them with her when she died? Did anyone think to ask about that?

Okay, look at it from the other direction. Who knew her at Safe Harbor? Henry. Esther. Her clients. The volunteers. Todd.

What about Todd? He used a computer in his work. But he didn't have access to Caleb's office. And he couldn't imagine Todd having much of a motive. Bill Evers? Caleb didn't really have a handle on the guy, but trusted Matthew's judgment. But then, Bill had seemed upset at the viewing. Maybe he knew Gina better than Caleb thought.

More questions filled his mind but few came with answers. Maybe he'd ask around when he got to Safe Harbor that afternoon. If they wanted him to return, given that he'd become a "person of interest." That realization stung, but Caleb knew better than to dwell on it. He needed to keep busy. He needed to go to work.

When he walked into the counseling center half an hour later, Matthew and Phillip were waiting outside his office. Phillip tapped his watch, looking impatient. "Y'all having a meeting?" Caleb asked.

"Your attorney has very little to say. Something about lawyer-client privilege," Matthew replied.

Caleb slipped a key into the lock to open the door. He said to Phillip, "Tell him everything. This affects him, too, since Gina worked here." Caleb half-listened as Phillip filled him in. Caleb passed between them to turn on his office lamps, find his appointment book, check to see who was scheduled. Janice had canceled the first two clients, leaving his eleven and noon sessions still pending. Caleb wasn't sure he was fit to see them.

"This is completely absurd," Matthew said.

"Caleb, any idea who might have sent those emails?" Phillip asked.

"No. But I plan to do some snooping when I get to the shelter this afternoon." He looked at Matthew. "That is, if you think I should go back there. If the media finds out I was questioned, it's gonna be bad for Safe Harbor."

"We'll burn that bridge when we come to it," Matthew said, letting out a sardonic laugh. "But I'm not so wild about the idea of you snooping. We're talking about a cold blooded killer."

"That was going to be my line," Phillip said.

Caleb fiddled with a stack of unfinished progress summaries because he needed to have something to do with his hands. "Phillip, this looks bad, doesn't it?"

The attorney and his boss exchanged a strange look. "We'll get to the bottom of this, I promise. Just have a little faith," he said.

"Okay." Unfortunately, that was something he had never been good at.

Caleb had just arrived at Safe Harbor when the text message arrived: **Need help**. Beethoven's fifth announced it was Sam.

**So what else is new?** Caleb typed, wondering what his brother needed help in lifting, hauling, or installing.

**HELP. 225 B Victor St. 9-1-1.**

Crap. That got his attention. Times like this Caleb really hated Sam being deaf. A thousand questions stormed Caleb's mind but couldn't be answered in short text messaging bursts. He typed **coming** before dashing out to his car.

Caleb wheeled into traffic, his foot pushing hard on the accelerator. Victor Street was where Isaiah lived, a drug-infested hell-hole neighborhood. What had happened? How bad was it?

He took the turn onto Victor, a narrow road riddled with pot holes, and lined with a row of duplexes that looked like they should be condemned. He passed 215, 217, and 219, then a small empty lot. There. Sam's van, beside a larger brick structure with 225 in rusty numbers over a porch.

Caleb practically leapt from the car. As he hurried to the building, he saw a couple of teenage girls standing by a car up the block. An old Ford pick-up with pounding bass stereo eased up the street.

He stepped through the gaping doorway leading to a poorly lit hall. The stink made his eyes water. Garbage with dirty diapers, probably in one of the black plastic bags cluttering the corridor. He could see two doors on each side. The last one on the right was opened just a crack.

"You Caleb?" A young voice asked.

He spun around to find a girl, about ten years old, staring up at him. She wore a pink sweatshirt, her hair a mass plump frayed pigtails. She had dark chocolate skin and wide-set dark eyes that somehow seemed familiar.

"Yeah, I'm Caleb," he whispered. "You know where my brother is?"

"You better come fast. He got hurt."

Hurt. Hurt could mean lots of things, Caleb told himself, fighting off the terrifying images crowding his brain. Sam shot. Sam knocked out. Sam . . .

The girl grabbed his hand and tugged, and he was grateful for the guidance, because panic seemed to have taken away his ability to put one foot in front of the other.

"He in here. Jo-Jo done busted him up." She pushed open the door. Sam. Sitting on the floor, his back to the wall, looking dazed and dreadful and holding a rag against the side of his head. But alive, Caleb told himself. Hurt but alive.

He stooped down beside Sam and nudged his chin up with a shaky hand. "Hey."

Weary brown eyes met his. Sam pulled back the rag to reveal a bloody gash just over his ear. A pinkish knot doubled the size of his left cheekbone and his upper lip had a bulge like a marble. "Damn it, Sam," Caleb signed, slashing the air with his finger.

Sam tossed the rag onto the floor.

"You should have called an ambulance." Caleb lifted the cloth, found a section that hadn't made contact with the filthy floor, and held it against the oozing cut. He needed stitches. "Where else are you hurt?" He asked, signing with one hand.

"Where doesn't hurt? Chest is on fire, by the way."

"Who did this to you? What happened?" Panic gave way to rage in Caleb.

Sam looked over at the girl and waved her over. "Charmain, can you go back over to Mrs. Farley's? She said you can stay there till Diondra comes home."

Diondra, Isaiah's mom. "This is where Isaiah lives?" Caleb signed.

"Yep. Run along, Charmain. I'll be okay."

After the girl left, Caleb gave him a closer look. Sam cradled his arm close to his chest and winced with each little movement. Caleb almost called the EMTs but thought it smart to get out of the apartment before the assailants returned. "We need to get you out of here. Can you stand?"

Sam nodded, grimacing as he struggled to get his legs under him. Caleb hooked an arm around Sam's elbow and hoisted, frowning at the string of muttered curses.

The drive to the hospital, hindered by traffic snarls, took longer than Caleb would have liked. He kept one eye on the road and the other on his silent brother—silent except for groans and sighs that told Caleb he was in pain. What if there were internal injuries? What if he lost consciousness on the way? What if . . . no, best think positive. And drive faster.

He wheeled into the emergency lane of the Westville Memorial ER and laid his hand on the horn.

"Is that necessary?" Sam asked.

Caleb turned on the car's dome light and signed, "Like you can hear it?"

"Like I don't want to annoy the people who are going to take care of me. Now come on." Sam opened his door, leaning on the handle to pull himself into the standing position. Caleb raced around the car to help, but Sam waved him off, suggesting he park somewhere that wouldn't get him towed.

"After you're settled I'll move the car."

It was a miracle that Sam got sent to the treatment bay quickly. Dr. Watts, a tiny woman with dark eyes and a husky northern voice, whisked Sam off for x-rays and other tests to make sure there was no damage to Sam's brains or innards. "A precaution," she said in her baritone voice.

Caleb used the time to move the car and put in a reluctant call to Claudia Briscoe. After his morning encounter, he wasn't sure if she was friend or foe, and her terse "What is it, Caleb?" didn't help.

But as soon as she heard what happened to Sam, she softened. "Victor Street? That's like the intersection of Crimespree Avenue and Gangbanger Drive. What the hell was Sam doing over there?"

"He was worried about a little boy who lives there."

"Sam hasn't reported this?"

"He hasn't been in any shape to. But I am. Whoever did this to him needs to be locked up. Actually, I'm thinking the death penalty would be too lenient." A fresh burst of rage bloomed inside him. Someone had attacked his brother. His deaf brother.

"I'll send officers to the hospital for a statement. Give them as much detail as you can. And tell Sam I hope he's okay."

"I will," he said, grateful for the brief reappearance of his friend in the detective's voice. "Thanks."

Dr. Watts motioned him into one of the ER cubicles. "Can you interpret for me?"

"Sure. But he reads lips pretty well. How is he?"

The curtain was pulled back. Sam looked even more haggard, his head shaved around the cut which had been stitched and bandaged. The V of his green hospital gown revealed a crimson streak around his neck.

"He's pretty lucky," Dr. Watts said slowly, Caleb signing for Sam. "The head CT didn't show any internal bleeding or other cause for concern. He has a cracked rib that we've stabilized. Nine sutures in the head. A sprained wrist. And what's going to become a spectacular black eye in a few days."

"Does he need to be admitted?" Caleb asked.

"I'm right here, guys. Could you maybe talk to me?" Sam said irritably.

Caleb circled his chest with a fist, signing, "Sorry." He hated it when people did to Sam what he'd just done: talked around him.

"I'm sorry, too," Dr. Watts said. "You can go home, but you need rest. We need to keep the rib from moving, so no heavy lifting or exercise of any kind. Plus I'm giving you some pain killers that should knock you out, so no driving of course.

"But I expect you'll make a full recovery," she added.

"Thank God." Caleb let out the breath he'd been holding since Sam's call to him. "I knew that hard head would be good for something."

"Can I go home now?"

"Not yet," Caleb answered. "There's an officer coming who wants to hear what happened. As a matter of fact, so do I."

"You called the police? Did I say I wanted the police involved?" Sam's voice escalated.

"I didn't ask. Didn't think I needed to," Caleb signed crisply. "Someone assaulted you. I want that someone caught. So I'm bringing the officer in here and you're telling both of us what happened. This isn't negotiable."

Sam wasn't happy about the arrangement, Caleb could tell from the choice curses being whispered as he brought in Officer Gordon to take a statement. But after a bit more coaxing, Sam relented. "Diondra was supposed to bring Isaiah for lunch. I'm Isaiah's mentor and I try to see him at least twice a week, sometimes more. I waited till about two, but they didn't show. So I got worried. I went to her apartment."

"Where?" the officer asked.

"Victor Street. She wasn't there. Her daughter answered the door. Charmain was home alone. Said Diondra had gone off with a friend. She just left the girl there by herself! She's only nine years old."

"Where was Isaiah?"

"She took him with her."

"So what happened? Who hurt you?"

"I thought I'd wait for Diondra to get back, because I didn't want the kid to be alone. She was watching some crappy cartoon on a fuzzy television. Hadn't eaten anything, so I tried to make her a sandwich. Peanut butter was all I could find—the kitchen was disgusting. Roaches everywhere." Sam shuddered.

"That's life on Victor Street," Caleb signed.

"Diondra never showed. There must have been a knock on the door because Charmain answered it. Two guys came inside. The kid was terrified. They were asking for Diondra. Said she owed them money."

"Terrific," Caleb muttered.

"I don't know what happened next. I couldn't follow all that they were saying, but they got animated, Charmain was crying and hiding behind me. The next thing I knew, one of them took a swing at me. I shoved him back, got Charmain to lock herself in the bedroom. The other guy grabbed a bat from beside the door and hit me. Things are foggy after that. Next thing I know, they were gone, and I managed to dial your number. I kept thinking Diondra would show but she didn't."

"You're lucky you aren't dead. Are you supposed to show up at Isaiah's house unannounced like that? Because it's a seriously bad idea," Caleb signed.

"Can you describe the men?" the officer asked.

"One was African American. Tall, light-skinned. Freckles on his nose. The other was white, young. Tattoos on his arm. Chains hanging from his jeans."

"Did either of them use a name?"

"Remember my brother is deaf, officer, so he didn't hear a name. But Charmain told me one of them was named Jo-Jo. I didn't ask for a last name," Caleb said.

"I'll see if I can talk with her at the neighbor's house." The officer pulled out a business card and handed it to him. "If you think of anything else, give me a call."

# Chapter Eighteen

Wyman stood beside a tree and looked out at the river. The water was gray and hurried; white froth bubbled around the rocks. This was where he had brought Stormy's body. His favorite spot. It was close enough to Zooville that he could hear folks talking, but not so close that he'd be seen. He didn't know why he'd come back. Maybe the river had called him.

He pulled out the pipe. He liked to be alone when he used because he didn't have to share his stash. Besides, sometimes crazy stuff happened in his head and he didn't need an audience. The only person he didn't mind sharing with had been Dawn. He liked how she got so happy. How her eyes sparked, how soft she felt up against him.

Not that it mattered. She was just over there, in the village, but he wasn't going to be sharing crack or anything with her again. Not after Johnny tossed his ass out of Zooville and told him to never come back.

Shouldn't think about that. He loaded the pipe, made from a glass tube, pushing the rock against a wad of tinfoil. As he lit the match, his teeth gripped the open end of the tube and sucked. The rock was just a pee-wee, he only had ten bucks, but it would do. He drew in the smoke, warm on his tongue. He felt his mind spring open. Felt his nerves sizzle and smile. He hardly noticed when the flame burned his fingers.

He tapped the pipe and lit another match. Harder to draw this time. A spark flew up, bright orange against the night. One last puff, pulling in, in, in. Love flowed through him. Filled him. He leaned back against the tree, no longer cold, letting the cocaine lift him, carry him, hugging the stars, the night, the universe. Nothing rivaled this. Nothing ever could. He felt complete.

The matchbook in his hand called to him. He struck the last match and held it close, the yellow flame dancing in the breeze, a coy and beautiful thing. He couldn't tear his eyes away. He held on as long as he could, until the tiny fire kissed his fingers. It made him sad to blow it out, like he'd lost another friend.

Too soon the high left him, too. The pipe felt cold in his hand. The icy air crept through his clothes, his skin, his bones. The crash left him empty and longing, a desperate hunger down to his toes and he wanted to weep, to beg, to steal or kill to make it go away.

*I'll kill you. Kill you!* The voices preyed on him in these moments after.

*Kill kill kill.* He shook his head, trying to shut up the screams.

*I'll kill you, you son of a bitch. Kill.* Should he run? Were the police after him? Would they shoot him?

"Stop!" he yelled. He tried to stand but it hurt too much. It all hurt, and nothing took away the pain except more crack and he didn't have more. He looked out at the river, a giant black snake weaving through the rocks and trees. He wanted to ride the snake, to let it carry him away. Why not? What the hell did he have to live for?

*It'll be all right.* He knew that voice.

*Stay still, it'll be all right.*

"Stormy?" He savored the reassuring words, the voice he missed more than he'd ever missed anything. Not here though. Stormy was gone. Dead, like Wyman should be.

"Twinkle, twinkle little star." A new voice. Singing. In his head? Or was it real?

"How I wonder . . ."

A girl. Another voice he knew. But it sounded outside of him, not inside. He shook his head, sometimes the haze after he used muddled his brain.

"See up there? That bright star beside the moon?" She was real. Wyman moved behind a tree as he heard footsteps coming towards him. It was Dawn, carrying the baby.

"Now you can see better. The brightest star up there is Polaris." She pointed to the sky. The baby tugged at her sleeve. "The North Star. It's very powerful. It will help you get your bearings if you ever get lost. You'll always be able to find your way home. That's why we named you Star."

The baby made a gurgling sound. Dawn laughed.

How old was the kid? Not even a year. He'd only seen it once before, when he spotted Dawn carrying it away from the Emergency Room. She wouldn't talk to him. Told him to stay away.

"Up above the world so high. Like a diamond in the sky." Dawn swayed, rocking the baby. She looked like she really loved it. Dawn was smart: she would take good care of the child. He wanted to walk over to her. To say how sorry he was, to talk about how bad he missed Stormy and how screwed up his life was and ask could she ever forgive him.

"There you are." Another voice he knew, but not one he welcomed. Johnny had on his cowboy hat, that long rope of hair hanging down his back. He stepped so close to Wyman's tree that Wyman froze. If Johnny spotted him, he might toss Wyman in the river.

"She's not sleepy yet," Dawn said.

"Little night owl," Johnny held out his arms for the baby. He kissed her little curly head and tucked her under his chin. The three of them looked up at the stars.

Wyman felt sadder than he'd ever felt in his life.


"This isn't the way to my house," Sam said from the passenger seat of Caleb's wagon.

Caleb waited till he stopped for a light and signed: "My place. I plan to keep an eye on you."

"Do you have anything that resembles food?" Sam watched him carefully, and, getting no response, said, "I thought not. Take me home. You can feed me there."

Caleb reluctantly agreed. It wasn't so cold that Cleo couldn't spend the night in her doghouse, and Sam would be more comfortable in his own bed. He parked close to the back door and rushed around the car to help Sam.

"This treating me like an invalid is getting old."

Caleb backed away, letting Sam climb the porch steps on his own, noticing how he frowned when his hip brushed the top rail. Once inside, Caleb opened the prescription bottle Dr. Watt had given him and thumped out two pills. Sam took them without complaint; a sign of how bad he felt. He pointed to his freezer. "There's some soup in there. I'm going to go wash up."

Caleb fought the impulse to escort his brother to the bathroom. Sam seemed to be moving okay on his own, but that would change as the drugs took hold.

He removed a large plastic container marked "Veg. Soup" from the freezer and stuck it in the microwave. Fifteen minutes later, Sam reappeared. When Caleb placed the soup in front of him, Sam stared at it like there were worms floating on the surface.

"Eat," Caleb said, pouring a glass of water for him.

Sam trolled his spoon through the broth. Caleb made himself a cheese sandwich, suddenly starved.

"I need to go back," Sam said.

"Back to the hospital? You feeling okay?" Caleb signed, panic resurfacing.

"No. Back to Diondra's."

"What? Have you lost your mind?" Caleb circled his index fingers on both sides of his head with exaggerated vehemence.

"I have to make sure they're okay. What if those men came back? What if they hurt Charmain? Or worse, Isaiah? I have to check on them."

"No," Caleb signed crisply. "You're supposed to take it easy. Hell, you could have been killed, Sam. No way I'm letting you go back."

Sam watched him, his expression softening. "I scared you. Sorry about that."

"Just . . . just don't do it again." He took a bite of the sandwich and wished he had a beer. Alcohol wasn't something Sam kept around.

"But I have to go. I won't be able to rest until I check on them. I'll take a cab if you won't drive me. Besides, I can't leave my van there overnight. My tools would be gone by sun-up."

He had a point about the van. Neighborhood thugs may have already stripped it like a de-boned fish. "You're not going anywhere," Caleb signed. "I just gave you painkillers. You're already stoned."

"I have a fortune of equipment in the van. My new drill. Paid a

lot of money . . ." Sam's eyes were at half-mast. Sweet pharma-
ceutical surrender.

"Where are your van keys?" Caleb signed.

Sam fumbled with his jacket, searching the sleeve, the hem,
and finally, the right pocket. He handed the keys to Caleb. "Going
somewhere?"

"To get your van."

"I go too," Sam slurred. He stood, grabbing the ladder-back of
the chair when he listed right.

"You go to bed," Caleb signed. He took Sam's arm to guide
him up the hall and into the bedroom. Sam looked like he wanted
to protest but the drugs had high-jacked his tongue. Caleb helped
him to the bed, ignoring Sam's slow, quiet groan.

"I'll be back soon," Caleb said, not bothering to sign since his
brother's eyes were closed. He switched off the light and went to
call a cab.

Dusk cast a gritty orange light over the streets of south
Westville. The cab driver asked again for the address, and Caleb
wondered if he hadn't heard or just questioned Caleb's good
sense in going to Victor Street after dark. He checked his pocket
for the third time to make sure he had Sam's van keys.

The plan was to hop in the van and drive away. They could
check on Diondra and the kids tomorrow. In the daylight. Maybe
by then the police would have captured Sam's assailants.

As the cab turned into the neighborhood, the driver clicked
the automatic door locks. "Can't be too careful in these here
parts." His voice sounded gruff, like maybe he'd smoked too
many of the Camel unfiltereds protruding from the cab's visor.

"You got that right."

"You said 225 was the address?" The guy eyed Caleb from his
rearview mirror.

"The lot beside it."

There weren't many cars on the street, but he spotted two
young men coming out the front door of Diondra's building.
There wasn't enough light for Caleb to see if they matched Sam's
description. The men took no notice of Caleb as he climbed out
of the cab.

"Word of advice," the driver said. "Don't hang around too
long."

Caleb handed him the fare plus ten for hazard pay. He checked the streets again before trotting over to the van, which at least still had its tires. So far, so good.

He tried to unlock the door, dropped the keys, rushed to find them in the dirt. When he climbed into the van, he heard a voice.

"Hey, mister." Charmain appeared on the sidewalk. "Is Mr. Sam with you?"

She wasn't alone: a lanky black woman walked beside her. She wore jeans and a sweatshirt. Diondra? Then Isaiah appeared, standing behind the woman, holding on to her pant leg. Reluctantly, Caleb stepped out of the van.

"Hi, Charmain," he said, signing. "And Isaiah! Hi!"

The woman came towards him. "You know Mr. Sam?" she asked.

Up close she looked like a kid herself. So skinny he wondered when she'd eaten last. Face speckled with acne. Fearful wide-set eyes that looked older than the rest of her. "I'm his brother," Caleb said, signing slowly. Isaiah peered at him from behind Diondra, thumb inserted in his mouth.

"Tell him I'm sorry about earlier. I didn't know he was coming to the house, then Jo-Jo showed up and—" She paused, looking down at Charmain.

"Sam was worried about Isaiah."

"I had him with me. Charmain was at a friend's house and wasn't supposed to come home till later." She cast a critical look at her older child.

"Where were you?" Caleb asked.

She released Charmain's hand and started fiddling with a visible bra strap. "Don't think that's any of your business. Is Mr. Sam okay?"

Caleb decided not to sign this part of the conversation. "He's pretty busted up. What's the deal with this Jo-Jo and his friend?"

She moved on to the other bra strap, bright white against her dark chocolate skin.

"Not your business, either."

He came closer. "They attacked my brother. They could have killed him. The police are looking for them, Diondra. They'll want to talk to you."

She stiffened. Isaiah, sensing the change, moved behind her

again. "You called the cops?"

"Look, I don't know what kind of trouble you're in but understand this: I won't let my brother get hurt again." He didn't mean for anger to seep out in those words, but he was running on adrenalin, still scared from the what-ifs parading through his mind.

"He's been good to my boy," she said, speaking softer now. "Isaiah don't have anybody but me and Charmain till Mr. Sam. Please don't make him quit coming. Please." As she looked at her son, tears filled her eyes. Isaiah made a guttural noise, deep in the back of his throat.

"It's okay." Diondra patted his head.

Caleb stooped down in front of the boy. "Okay," he signed.

"You do that hand talking too," Charmain said. "Like Mr. Sam."

Caleb took her hand and closed the finger tips against the thumb. "That's the 'o' part, and here's the 'k.'" He lifted two fingers, pushing her thumb against the meat of the middle. "Okay!"

"Okay!" she signed, smiling.

"Isaiah don't know all that yet," Diondra said.

"No, but he can learn. Sam wants to teach him." When Caleb stood, he spotted the men from before. Diondra saw them, too, and pulled her children close.

"Is one of them Jo-Jo?" Caleb whispered.

"No. Jo-Jo don't live around here. Them's just a coupla punks. Gang wannabees."

The men stopped at Diondra's building and turned to face them. Diondra stood tall, hands on hips, as though daring them to come closer. The men moved on.

"Do you owe Jo-Jo money?"

Diondra kept her eyes on the men until they rounded the corner out of sight. "He thinks I do, but I don't."

"Is Jo-Jo a dealer?"

Diondra squeezed her daughter's hand. "Charmain, you got your key?"

She nodded.

"Then take Isaiah inside. I'll be right there."

The girl, who had been busy practicing the "okay" sign, took her little brother's hand and led him to the building.

"I don't use anymore. I been clean for six months," Diondra said.

"That's good. But is that why Jo-Jo came here? Is that why he beat up my brother?"

"I don't gotta answer to you, you know." Her mouth twisted to the side. "But I figure I owe Mr. Sam. So here's the deal: I used to work for Jo-Jo but I don't anymore. He thinks I kept some of his money but I didn't. Somebody took the stuff and stiffed me. Jo-Jo keeps coming here, like he thinks I got the money stashed somewhere but I don't."

"So it's dangerous for you here. For you and your kids." He wondered if her social worker, Mandy Phelps, could be coerced into doing something about it.

"I can handle Jo-Jo."

Caleb wondered if she could, especially if Jo-Jo returned with his friends.

"I best go see to my kids," Diondra said. "Tell Mr. Sam I'm sorry, and I hope he feels better soon."

Caleb watched her till she reached the front door before turning back to the van, eager to leave the area and get back to Sam's. A flash of movement caught his eye. He didn't move, not wanting to draw attention to himself in case it was Jo-Jo and his friends. A lone figure passed under the street light. It was a wafer-thin man limping at a pretty good pace, face down, a baseball cap on his head.

"Wyman?" Caleb called out.

Wyman took off at a run.

"Wyman! I'm Caleb, remember? I just want to talk with you!"

Wyman swatted at his ear like Caleb's voice was a pesky insect and kept moving, Caleb trotting behind him. "Come on, Wyman. I'm not going to hurt you."

Wyman hobbled past the last duplex on the block, looked over at Caleb with a pained, anguished expression, and turned down a narrow alley.

"Crap." Caleb questioned his own sanity for going after Wyman in a neighborhood like this. Wyman stopped, hunching over, like he was too tired to keep running. Caleb inched closer. A single streetlight shed too little light; reeking dumpsters lined the alley.

"Easy," Caleb said. "Let's just talk for a minute. Your mother is looking for you. Did you know that? She wants to get you some help."

Wyman coughed. Hands on his thighs, head bowed, hacking like he was about to eject a lung, then wiping his mouth with the back of a dirty hand. Caleb heard the rumble of a vehicle, low-pitched and loud. Headlights swept them and a horn sounded as a truck appeared at the opposite end of the alley. A gas-guzzler, like a Dodge Ram or Silverado or some other macho vehicle.

"Leave him alone!" a man yelled as he climbed out of the vehicle. Wyman's head shot up.

Caleb tried to get a look at the figure standing in front of the dieseling pick-up. Short and wide like a bulldog. "Get your ass over here, Wyman," the man snarled.

Caleb recognized the voice. "Markham?"

"Knowles you leave him alone. This ain't none of your business." He turned to Wyman. "Get over here. Now!"

Wyman obeyed, taking a few faltering steps before breaking into a jerky run. Markham grabbed his arm.

Caleb followed but Markham held up a hand. "No closer," he said. "You think you're something, don't you? You called the licensing people on me. Think you're gonna shut me down? Never happen."

"I just want to talk to Wyman."

"Too damn bad. Best thing for you to do is get away from here and forget you ever saw him."

The threat sounded cold and real, like Markham had a weapon he was prepared to use. Caleb watched him push Wyman into the pick-up and climb in on the other side. The truck crunched over a plastic trash container as he backed out of the alley. A second later, it disappeared. Caleb jogged back to his brother's van. It was getting late, and he needed to get out of here.

He needed to check on his brother.

Wyman sat in Markham's office. The jitters had his knees bobbing up and down, up and down, like the time he was in that rehab place and got caught toking it up with another guy. He'd had to sit in the director's office, first for the lecture and the threats of jail, then for his mother and stepfather to come for him. His mom had rushed in, all teary-eyed and hand-wringing, "How could you do this to us?" And the Senator, tanned the color of bread crust, saying, "You've been a tremendous disappointment to your mother." But he had that secret smile, too, like he was really glad Wyman had blown it. They turned him loose after that, told him to make his own way. "Tough love," the director had called it. Wyman got the tough part, but never saw the love.

He eyed Markham's desk, wishing he had time to jimmy open the money drawer, take some cash and vanish. But Markham was too close and already fuming about something. Wyman couldn't risk being caught.

Wyman knew his mother paid Markham to keep him, but he didn't know how much Markham got. Why didn't she just give the money to Wyman so he could take care of himself? No, she wouldn't do that. She had to have an intermediary so she wouldn't have to see Wyman or talk to him. None of them talked to Wyman anymore, except Nora.

*Close the door.* The voice sounded urgent. *Close the door.* He checked to make sure it wasn't someone outside of him but knew it was inside.

He did his best to keep the part of his mind that did the remembering closed off. He didn't need to think about the yellow house, the big kitchen with its biscuit smells, the little girl with the dark eyes who said "Wyman" before she could walk. And his mother, shiny hair and high heels and red lips that never smiled. Hating him. Embarrassed by him.

Probably wishing he'd never been born.

*Close the door.* Louder this time. Had his mother always felt that way? Even when they left his father, when it was just the two of them living in the apartment. She had loved him then, hadn't she?

*Close the door.* He had to turn off these thoughts, but he needed a fix to do that. But first, he had to get away from the Willows and Markham and his nasty wife.

Finally, the door slung open and Markham waddled over to the desk. Wyman sat up, pressing his hands against his knees to still them. His stomach rumbled.

"Rhetta will get you some breakfast when we're done."

Markham dropped his fat butt into a chair. "I'll be calling your mother later to let her know we found you. She wants you to meet with a lawyer. With these other murders, well, things ain't looking good for you."

"I didn't kill anybody," Wyman said, not expecting to be believed. Not even caring if he was.

"Yeah, yeah. Figured that's what you'd say. Hell, you could have done it and not remembered. You get so screwed up when you're high."

Wyman looked down at the desk, at the left side, where Markham kept his money.

"But that's not why I wanted to talk to you. Nope. You been keeping a secret from me. A huge secret, and I ain't too pleased about it."

Wyman had lots of secrets and Markham never cared, as long as Wyman stayed out of jail and out of the hospital. He noticed Markham's eyes getting squinty, like raisins stuck in batter.

"I ran into someone you know," Markham said. "That skanked out crack witch you brought here from Charlotte. Dawn."

Something clenched in Wyman's stomach at the name. Markham met her right when they first came to Westville, when Wyman's pockets were empty and Markham owed him a month's worth of allowance. The money would have filled their pipes for a whole weekend but instead it went to pay the doctor.

"Don't you think you should have told me, Wyman? Don't you think I had a right to know?" Markham spewed out the words like they tasted nasty in his mouth. Wyman closed his eyes, feeling the trap doors slamming shut.

"Now you look at me. Look me dead in the eye. Esther Lowell told me about the baby. Said it was probably yours. But I didn't know Dawn was still around until I saw her at Safe Harbor."

*Close the door. Clang, clang.* The bars closed down around him.

"The baby's a cute little thing, too. I figured about nine months old, and you showed up here with her close to a year and a half ago. Timing's just right."

"It's not my kid," Wyman said. It was the truth. Little Star was not Wyman's child, not since they kicked him out of Zooville. Maybe it was him that made the baby grow inside Dawn, but she'd made it clear that he'd lost all rights to it. He had thought she would get an abortion. She said she would, and he was trying to scrape together the money, but then Dawn hooked up with Johnny and everything turned upside down. She said she wanted to change, that the baby was a fresh start for her. She said Wyman wouldn't be a good father and she was right about that. What kind of life could he offer Dawn and the kid? As much as he hated Johnny, Dawn had made herself a home with him. She had quit the crack, and maybe she would stay clean this time. And Star had a father. Johnny seemed to love her like she was his. Maybe he didn't even know she wasn't.

"I don't believe you," Markham said. "I don't believe hardly a word you ever tell me, so why would I believe this?" He groped in his shirt pocket for a Salem and lit it. Wyman looked at the lighter, his eyes widening. Light—flicker—flame. Light, flicker, flame. If he had a rock. If he had the money to get a rock . . .

"So I have to tell your mother. That's her grandchild, she's got a right to know." Markham spoke out smoke. "What's she gonna think when she finds out it's living in a damn tent? Has it had medical care at all? She may want to get custody. I wouldn't blame her if she did."

Wyman's knees started bouncing again. What was Markham's angle in this? He sure wasn't interested in the kid. Maybe he thought Wyman's mother would give him money for telling her about the child. Why would she? Why would she even care that little Star had been born at all?

"You bring shame to that good family, you know that, Wyman? The senator has a powerful name in this state." Markham gestured with the cigarette, the orange ash glowing like a tiny sun.

"What's he gonna think when he learns his wife's grand-child is being raised by a whore living in Zooville? Make a damn good story for the papers, won't it?"

The pieces clicked into place. Markham's plan was to get Wyman's mother to buy his silence. It would probably work, too, if Wyman didn't find a way to stop Markham. Markham's fat, stubby fingers ground the cigarette out in a chipped ashtray. "So you got anything to say for yourself, you sorry piece of shit?"

"It's not my kid. You can't prove that it is."

"I can't, but a bit of genetic testing will. You run on, get you some breakfast. I got a few calls to make."

# Chapter Nineteen

Caleb carried the coffee down the long hallway to Sam's bedroom and pushed open the door. His brother was a sleeping lump in the middle of the four-poster bed he had built himself. Caleb placed the mug on the night stand—burled oak, another Sam Knowles creation—and tapped his brother's shoulder.

"Huh?" Sam stirred.

"Wake up!" Caleb's forefingers sprung open from his thumbs.

"Huh?" Sam repeated.

Caleb sat on the edge of the mattress to survey the damage done to his brother. His right eye was a plump purple and red collage. His shaved hair and stitches gave him just the hint of a Frankenstein look. The way Sam was clutching his right wrist told him it was hurting, and he suspected the broken ribs throbbed, too. Caleb felt a fresh surge of anger at the hoods that had done this to his brother.

"Do you feel as good as you look?" Caleb asked.

"Probably." Sam winced as he pulled himself up. Caleb handed him the coffee.

"Any dizziness?" Caleb's hand circled his own head as he signed and Sam shook his head.

"Not dizzy. But not so happy about being conscious. Thanks for the coffee."

"So you need to eat something, then you can take more painkillers and crash again." Caleb wondered if he should hang around today. He had a ton of work to do at the office but felt a stronger pull to stay with Sam. He could stop by the house to feed Cleo, then grab some paperwork from the office and bring it here to work on. That way, if Sam needed anything . . .

"Quit it."

"Quit what?" Caleb asked.

"Quit worrying. I'm going to eat some breakfast, then see if I can get some work done."

"But the doctor said—"

"To take it easy, which I will. If my wrist won't let me use my tools then I'll tackle some paperwork that's piled up. You can go to work."

"You're sure?" Caleb wasn't, but Sam was getting that stubborn glint that told him to be careful where he trod.

Sam looked at the window. "I need to go get the van."

"Taken care of, but don't drive anywhere until the drugs are out of your system. I'll be back to check on you around lunchtime."


Caleb was glad for the busy schedule at the counseling center. Four clients back-to-back meant little time to think. Mr. Castleman's crisis over his wife's affair and Mrs. Thomas's worries about her son in Iraq helped Caleb put his own problems in perspective. Things were bad, but could be a whole lot worse.

After he finished the session, he decided to call the Willows. The strange encounter with Wyman and Markham Dougherty last night had him worried. Maybe he and Henry could ride out there that afternoon to check on Wyman, maybe even get him admitted into a treatment program.

"Hello?" A woman answered, probably Markham's wife, Rhetta.

"Is Wyman Carter there?"

"Who wants to know?"

Caleb reluctantly gave her his name.

"What do you want him for?"

"I just want to make sure he's okay."

"Well he was last I saw him. He ain't here now. I fixed him a nice lunch, went to get him, and he was gone. Par for the course for Wyman. He'd rather live on the streets then sleep in a nice bed."

Caleb bit his tongue. He'd could only imagine the nice bed Rhetta had for Wyman.

"Any idea where he went?"

"You think he'd tell us? We won't hear a word from him till he needs more money. I don't know why my husband puts up with it like he does."

"If you do hear from him, can you let us know?" Caleb asked.

"I'll tell Markham you're looking for him."

Caleb had a good idea how that conversation would go. He hung up the phone.

At noon, he bought sandwiches from his favorite deli and took them to Sam's house. Sam griped about not being able to work because of his wrist, griped that it might mean delaying his gallery opening, and you'd think he could at least get some stuff done one-handed, and . . . Caleb decided that if his brother felt well enough to complain that much, he was well enough to be left alone for a while.

His afternoon at Safe Harbor was a strange contrast to his morning. He had five walk-in clients, one of whom failed a drug screen ("It was just pot. Give me a break!") and was referred to the drug rehab group. Two clients needed food. One asked if he could call his mother in Virginia and burst into tears when he heard her voice. Caleb used his speakerphone to do an impromptu family session that ended with a promised bus ticket for the homesick young man. As soon as Caleb finished, one of the volunteers met him outside his office and said, "Can you come up front? There's some woman here. Asking a bunch of questions. She got Cindy all upset."

"Cindy?" Caleb wondered if he meant Cindy Lowman, Gina's client. He followed the man to the reception area where a petite woman in black pants and a yellow sweater sat beside a sobbing Cindy.

"I'm sorry," the woman said, clearly flustered. "I didn't mean—"

Caleb rushed to them. "What's going on?"

Cindy rubbed at her face with quivering hand. "She said . . . she told me that Gina's dead. Why would she say something like that?"

The woman stood, clutching a notepad against her chest. "I'm sorry. I thought you knew."

Caleb stooped down in front of Cindy. "Cindy, look at me."

"I'm supposed to see her today. At two o'clock. Gina gave me this so I could remember." Cindy held up a wrist encircled by a bright blue plastic watch.

"She would be proud of you for coming today," Caleb said.

"She told you about me?" Cindy asked.

"I was Gina's supervisor, so yes, she told me about how hard you've been working to get your kids back. She really admired you."

"What happened to her? Is what she said true?" Cindy pointed an accusing finger at the woman.

Caleb looked over at the visitor, wondering who she was and what the hell she was doing at Safe Harbor. He turned back to the client.

"I'm afraid so. Somebody killed Gina. But the police are working hard to find her killer."

Tears filled Cindy's eyes. "Who would do that? Gina was so nice and sweet. She didn't care where you came from. What you were. She treated you like you were somebody special."

What a wonderful description of his student, who would never know what she meant to clients like Cindy.

"What do I do now?" Cindy asked. "Gina was helping me with social services. She told them about my clean drug screens. She fussed at them till they let me have visitation."

"She did huh?" Caleb gave her a weak smile. "Well don't worry about that. I'll follow-up on what Gina started. Are you seeing the doctor today?"

Cindy nodded.

"Well when you finish with him, come by my office. We'll give social services a call then."

The other woman fished a tissue from her purse to give to Cindy. Caleb returned to the reception desk and told the volunteer to make sure Cindy was the first client Dr. McAbee saw. Then he turned back to the stranger.

"What exactly is your business here?" he asked.

"I'm with the *Westville Chronicle*. My name is Jasmine Saul."

"And you thought you'd stop by and upset our clients? This is what you call journalism?"

"I thought everyone knew about the murders. It's been on the front page for three days."

"And we really appreciate the negative publicity, by the way.

Nothing like perpetuating stigma to keep the citizens happy. How was Cindy supposed to read the articles? It's not so easy to keep a newspaper subscription when you don't have an address. Hard to catch the evening news when you're sleeping under a bridge."

"I get your point, Mr.—"

"Knowles. Caleb Knowles." He looked away, hoping his name wouldn't be familiar to her. Hoping she didn't know about the police questioning him.

"Hey." She lifted a hand. "I want to be fair here. Not everyone agrees with the mayor that Safe Harbor should close. I want to do a balanced piece. Let people see what the shelter does to help people."

Caleb studied her face, wanting to believe her. She looked young, not even thirty, with straight brown hair angled along her jaw line. She wore two sets of earrings and a gold hoop in her eyebrow. A small flush of acne spread across her nose, covered with powdery makeup. She reminded him of Gina.

"Here's the thing," Caleb said. "Cindy and our other clients come to Safe Harbor for sanctuary. She gets food if she needs it, medicine, and counseling. We have dorm beds in the back and she can sleep here if she wants. But her coming here is a private matter. We work very hard to protect our clients' confidentiality. Winning their trust is not always easy. Do you understand?"

"So what you're saying is you don't want me interviewing your clients. Even if it helps keep Safe Harbor open?" She eyed him carefully, measuring his response. The aggressive reporter; Carl Bernstein in the making.

"I'm saying you don't just show up here unannounced. I'm saying you let us talk to the clients first, see if they want to be interviewed."

"Who said I just showed up here? Mr. Evers told me to come by. I'm supposed to meet him."

Caleb called over to the volunteer, "Is Bill here?"

"Not yet. Supposed to be, though."

"So while I was waiting I started chatting with Cindy. I didn't mean for this to turn into a big drama." She rolled her eyes, looking petulant.

The front door opened and two more clients entered, a white-haired man and a woman. The woman helped the man sign in at reception. Caleb didn't want Jasmine questioning them, too.

"Okay," Caleb said. "How about I show you around the place while we wait for Bill?"

Jasmine eyed the couple.

"Come on," he said. "Let me show you the food pantry. And our ginormous freezer."

Reluctantly she followed. He led her through the various shelter work areas, steering her away from clients and rattling off some of the statistics Henry had taught him about how many people they served and the greatest needs of the homeless in Westville.

"What made you want to work here?" Jasmine asked.

"Actually, I'm on loan. At first I liked the work because it was different. But the longer I'm here, the more I love this place. The clients—they are not easy to engage. They live a tough life. They don't trust anything or anyone but they do trust Henry and the staff here. They have so little, but they don't ask for much. Maybe food to get them through the week. Some donated clothes to keep them warm. Maybe they want to make a phone call to talk to family they're afraid have forgotten them. Or maybe they need to see a doctor because they haven't had a physical in years. Safe Harbor tries to do all that and more. If we have to shut our doors, it would be a devastating loss to so many people." Caleb paused, surprised by his own rant. He'd gotten loud, his hands gesturing. Caleb Knowles sermonizing. Jasmine was writing feverishly in her notepad. Caleb didn't want his words in the newspaper.

"This is the kind of angle I need." Jasmine stepped closer. "And if I could put some faces to the issue—show a client getting food. Talk to a client who's finally getting healthcare—that's the kind of story that may sway some readers."

"Uhhh, I'm not sure that's a good idea. Like I said, trust is an issue for many of our clients."

"But not all." Bill Evers finally arrived, looking warily at Caleb. "Sorry I'm late Ms. Saul. I see Caleb's giving you the tour."

Caleb stepped back, relieved. "I was just about to show her the freezer. You can park a bus in there, I'm not kidding."

He slipped between them, more than ready to make his escape, but Jasmine had other plans. "Don't go just yet. I'd like to continue our conversation. Mr. Evers, maybe the three of us could sit down somewhere?"

Bill frowned. Caleb got the hint. "No, I think Bill has the story you need. I have some work I need to get to."

"Just a few minutes then," Jasmine said. She turned to Bill. "I'm very interested in Mr. Knowles' perspective about the shelter."

"Okay." Bill gave her a taut smile and relented. "How about we all go to my office."

Caleb didn't want to follow them. He wanted to hide in his office or dash back to the pantry. He'd even offer to help Todd with his freaking spreadsheets if it spared him this opportunity to make a complete ass of himself on the front page of the *Westville Chronicle*.

Bill brewed some coffee and offered each of them a cup. Caleb almost declined but the smell summoned primal urges he could not suppress. His first sip surprised him. This was not the dishwater served to the clients and staff at Safe Harbor. Bill had himself a private stash, probably Costa Rican or Hawaiian. Caleb needed to become a more frequent visitor to this little nook of Safe Harbor.

"So tell me about the people who died," Jasmine began. "Stormy Bennett was a regular client?"

"Yes. We've known Stormy for five years. He was a typical Safe Harbor client, a man who worked very hard to turn his life around." Bill tapped the rim of his pottery mug with neatly trimmed fingernails.

"But he did have a police record," Jasmine said.

"From his life before. But he'd become a leader in the recovery community. Stormy always did his best to help others. They feel his loss profoundly."

Caleb noticed the poise with which Bill responded. He used a soft voice, speaking slowly, articulately. Not at all defensive. Bill was clearly quite at home with the press.

"What about Esther Lowell and Gina Fulton?"

Bill closed his eyes, pulling his lips in tight. "Forgive me," he whispered, like he needed to collect himself. He cleared his throat and continued. "It's still hard for me to accept. Esther and I worked together for ten years. She was my right hand."

Caleb sipped his coffee and studied Bill, amazed at the change.

Still very much in control, but with tears glistening in his eyes. He couldn't help but wonder if they'd been manufactured.

"And Gina Fulton?"

"What a remarkable young woman," Bill said. "A kind, gentle spirit. She wanted to come to work here when she finished school. We had a long talk about it. I told her we'd be honored to have her."

Another surprise. Gina never mentioned that conversation to Caleb.

"Gina was so good with the clients. But she was also someone who would roll her sleeves up and load supplies, or help in the pantry, or do whatever we asked her to. She once told me that getting to know our clients was making her a better person. She said they had taught her more than school ever had. Yes, that was our Gina." Bill's voice trembled just a little. He shook his head as though embarrassed.

Caleb tried not to gape at him. Had he actually spent time with Gina? What he said might have come from her. But still, Caleb doubted his sincerity. The lines sounded rehearsed, just for the interview.

Jasmine turned to Caleb. "Who do you think killed them?"

Well it sure as hell wasn't me, Caleb wanted to yell. Instead, he forced calm into his voice. "I don't know who did it. Someone who is very angry. Maybe someone who doesn't like Safe Harbor for whatever reason. But we need that person to be caught."

"The mayor is using these crimes as ammunition against Safe Harbor, which, we all know, he wants to close. What do you think about that?"

"I think the mayor is lucky he's never been homeless. He's lucky he hasn't had to eat his meals in a soup kitchen or sleep under a bridge or beg for medicines when he was sick. Maybe if he had—"

"We understand the mayor's position," Bill hurried to say, interrupting Caleb. "But Safe Harbor does a great deal for this community. We hope to come to some agreement with city council to keep our shelter open."

"Mr. Knowles, if you could talk to the mayor, what would you say to him?"

Caleb fought a wave of panic. Bill had a horrified look on his face as though he expected Caleb to use the f-word or something. Jasmine had her pen poised, ready to record every word.

Out the door, he could see Henry with Lanie Dupree standing beside the food pantry. Lanie had her sunglasses on. Henry handed her a new pack of beef jerky. Behind them, Cindy Lawson was getting a prescription from Dr. McAbee, her mouth bending into a nervous smile.

Caleb said, "I'd invite the mayor to come meet some of the Westville citizens we serve here. I'd invite him to have lunch at the soup kitchen and maybe suggest he stay the night in our dorm. Understand, I don't mean this to be a dare or challenge. I just want him to get to know some of the amazing people I've met here. It might help him see how important Safe Harbor really is."

Bill let out a sigh. Maybe relief, maybe exasperation, but Caleb wouldn't have taken the words back if he could.


The rumble of a tractor-trailer backing into the lot behind Safe Harbor was almost deafening. Henry climbed out the passenger door of the cab, slamming it shut. When he saw Caleb, he yelled, "What the hell is going on?"

Suddenly, Caleb wished he'd called in sick.

"They took you to the police station? They actually questioned you about the murders? That's BS man. Complete and total BS."

"You'll get no argument from me," Caleb replied.

"Took the computer from your office. Did you know that?"

"Yeah. I think I've turned that thing on like twice."

Henry removed his wraparound sunglasses and tucked them into the V-neck of his sweater, giving Caleb a thorough study. "Thought maybe you'd bail on us after that."

"I wondered if I should. Safe Harbor doesn't need any more bad press."

The truck driver honked the horn and Caleb nearly leapt out of his skin. Henry hopped onto the back bumper to open the rear door. "Got a donation from the Piggly Wiggly distribution center. Truck got stalled so it's a few hours late. We have to unload it right away because it's all perishables."

Terrific. Most of the staff had already gone home, and Caleb wished he'd made it out of the lot before Henry spotted him. For the next hour they sorted, stocked and inventoried meats and produce. Caleb preferred vegetables to meats. Lettuce, cabbage and potatoes were stored in the main warehouse area, but the meat had to be shelved in the massive freezer. Caleb donned work gloves and the sweater he kept in his office, but the cold air entering his lungs chilled him to his bone marrow. He had new respect for Henry and the other guys who worked in these conditions every day.

"How many have you brought in? Why wasn't I notified? I have to log in each case!" Todd marched over to them, holding a clipboard and looking peeved.

"Driver's on the clock. Couldn't wait on you," Henry said.

"Wait on me? I was in the office! You just needed to page me!" His voice rose in pitch.

"Don't see how you missed us." Henry heaved a box up to the top shelf like it weighed mere ounces. "An eighteen-wheeler backs up to the building and you don't hear it? Now we gotta mess of crap to unload. Take off that tie and roll up your sleeves."

Todd glowered at him. "You're kidding, right? I mean, I have to log all this in."

"Seems to me you can count them when we got them on the shelves. Now get out to the truck and give us a hand."

Caleb could see Todd stiffening and eyeing the hall like he was ready to bolt. "This'll go a lot faster if we have an extra set of hands," Caleb said. "Please?"

Todd looked over at Henry and another worker struggling to stack cartons on a dolly. "Okay, I'll help."

"Thanks."

At the driver's insistence, they finished unloading the truck by stacking the crates just inside the building; it was slow, grueling work. The truck drove away, but the men still had to get the food in the freezer before it thawed. Henry recruited another helper: Alec, one of the homeless clients who stayed in the Safe Harbor dorm. Caleb handed gloves to Alec and Todd. "Why don't you two bring in the chicken stacked over there," he pointed at a dozen stacks of frozen poultry boxes. "Henry and I will handle the rest."

Todd frowned. "I'd rather work with you."

"Okay." Caleb didn't appreciate the glare Todd was sending Alec. Choose your battles, he reminded himself, as he helped Todd heave five cartons of frozen chicken onto a dolly and then into the freezer. The cold air bit through his gloves and stung his hands. Todd seemed to manage it better than Caleb, which was a surprise. When Alec passed them, Todd frowned and turned away.

"What's the deal, Todd? Alec doesn't have to help us but he is."

"He smells," Todd whispered. "The least he could do is take a shower."

Caleb wondered if there was any use in pointing out that showers weren't always accessible for homeless people. Instead, he busied himself with the task at hand, eager to be done with it. At Henry's insistence they took frequent breaks, for which Caleb was very grateful. As immense as the freezer room was, something about it felt claustrophobic. Claustrophobic and so damn cold.

It was after six P.M. when they made their way back to the break room. Weary. Teeth chattering. Shaking their heads at the last stacks of boxes yet to be hauled into the freezer.

"I need to cancel my group," Henry said.

"Tonight?" Caleb asked.

"In a half hour. Up at the Salvation Army."

"You can't. You bail on an AA meeting and it sends the wrong message. You know that."

Todd backed against a counter. "I can't stay, either, Caleb. I'm supposed to meet my counselor in a half hour. It's too late to cancel."

Would have been nice to know about that little conflict sooner.

"That's okay. It's just a few more boxes. I'll take care of it." Caleb tried to offer a smile, but it probably looked more like a scowl. He was supposed to take Sam out to dinner at seven but there was no way he'd make that. By himself, hauling, sorting and stocking the remaining meat would probably take over an hour. And Sam had promised to pick up the tab, too, as a thank you for the Victor Street rescue. Maybe if he hurried.

Hurrying didn't work. There was no rushing when handling

frozen rump roasts and butterballs, and when a rack of ribs slipped through his icy fingers and almost crushed his toes, he decided to take another break from the Safe Harbor's version of Antarctica.

As soon as he exited the freezer, he checked the clock. Ten till seven, no way he'd get there on time. He should have called Sam. He slid the cell phone from its holster and dialed his brother's number. He texted: **Sorry. Going to be la—**

A sudden noise interrupted him. It sounded like the back door, which was supposed to be locked. Footsteps echoed. Someone was here. Caleb carried the phone back into the warehouse, trying to chose between stealth mode or the loud "I'm really not all alone here, really" strategy.

Something thudded in the rear.

"Hey! Who's there?" Stealth mode abandoned.

He heard a scraping sound, like something being dragged on the floor. Not good. He turned, deciding the better course of action was to get the hell out of there and call the police. But after two steps, the room went dark.

"Crap!" He whispered, squinting into absolute blackness. The door was where? To his left, another fifteen feet?

Quick footsteps echoed. He looked down at the cell, still lit from his incomplete call to Sam. He punched 9-1—something plowed into him, toppling him to the concrete. He landed hard on his elbow and hip, whipped around, reaching for whoever had attacked, clawing at hairy flesh. Strong hands rolled him so Caleb's face hit the cement. "Acch," he gasped. He fumbled with the cell, his thumb seeking the "Send" button as something hard pounded against the back of his head.

And then. Nothing.

Cold. So cold. He opened his eyes, trying focus through the white blobs on his eye lashes. What the hell?

His face had attached itself to the floor. But not the same floor as before. This one colder. So much colder.

The chattering of his teeth was the only sound he heard. He looked up at the light. He could see tall shelves but he wasn't in the warehouse anymore. He was in the freezer. He tried to pull himself up, but his arms and legs didn't want to respond. He sucked in the frigid air, pressed a palm against the icy concrete, and heaved his torso off the floor. Bad idea. Dizzy. He closed his eyes, fighting off the nausea and at the same time perversely wondering what happened when puke landed on a sub-zero surface.

Get a grip, he said to himself. Get the hell out of here. Which will require movement. If only he could get his body to comply.

He hoisted himself unsteadily to his feet. The feet weren't pleased, numbed and tingling by the cold and now called upon to perform. His shaking hands grabbed for the corner of the metal shelving, and he tilted precariously, his brain all muddled and unfocused. Hold on. For now, just hold on.

He couldn't quit shaking. He could see traces of blue in the beds of his fingernails yet his fingers themselves were on fire. Why were they burning when it was so cold? That rattling from his teeth was damned annoying, too. The freezer door was just a few steps to his right. He moved his foot, not entirely sure that the message to "move" made it from his brain to his foot until he actually saw it slide over a few inches. Good. He released the shelf and stumbled to the right, grabbing the metal handle on the door. Okay, you're here.

He yanked the handle down and shoved. Nothing happened. Huh? He knew there was no lock on the door, that would be too dangerous, that might mean someone could get trapped inside. He pushed again but it didn't give. Someone had blocked the door.

"Crap," he whispered.

His limbs ached. How long had he been in here? He tried to focus on his watch, peering through the condensation on its crystal. Seven thirty-five. He'd been locked in here for over half an hour.

His phone! He grabbed for the holster to find it empty. He must have dropped it when the guy attacked. Of course, it probably wouldn't work in the freezer anyway.

Did the message get through to his brother? Unlikely. His last attempt to hit "send" had been a blind mashing of buttons. He'd probably dialed his favorite Chinese take-out place instead of Sam. 9-1-1. Emergency Moo Shu pork needed.

He laughed, knowing full well there was no reason to laugh and realizing he was getting a little hysterical. With good reason.

He fell forward against the door, tugging down on the handle as hard as he could with hands that felt like flaming timbers. No give. Nothing. He slid down the door, landing hard on the icy floor.

He was so screwed.

He scrunched himself into the smallest ball he could, pressing his cumbersome hands between his knees, tightening the sweater across his middle. He could survive here all night, if he had to. He'd just make sure to stay awake. To move his hands and feet now and then before his blood forgot the pathways to them. It was probably how cold? Not even zero degrees. Piece of cake. Northerners withstood temps like that all the time. Shannon did, routinely. He could, too. He would not turn into a pop sickle.

Someone would come. Just not for a while. He just had to stay awake. For Julia. For Shannon. For Sam.

Dozing. No, not supposed to do that. He jerked up, blinking white-crusted eyelashes. Still in the freezer. His hands no longer burned, more like icy pinpricks from his fingertips to elbows. Not the feet though. Come to think of it, his feet didn't feel much of anything.

He thought about Shannon. Probably driving back to her parents' place after finishing up at the farm. He could see her, snug in her down jacket and wool hat. Maybe she was thinking about him, wishing he was there, beside her. In her arms.

"Shannon," he whispered. Stay awake for Shannon. Stay . . . he couldn't fight it any longer. His eyes closed, his head fell back. The darkness closed over him.

# Chapter Twenty

A scraping sound woke Caleb. Where the hell was he? He tried to move but his body wouldn't comply. In fact, his body didn't feel like it belonged to him at all.

Another noise, like a grunt. Then a voice. "Caleb!"

The door opened and Sam burst through. "Christ, Caleb," he whispered, dropping to his knees.

"Sss . . ." That was as much of his brother's name he could get out. Signing wasn't even a remote possibility with hands like wooden blocks.

Sam rested a hand against Caleb's face, grimacing. "Hey. You in there?"

He nodded. At least, he thought he did. Another face came into view. Henry.

"Help me get him out of here," Sam ordered. He came behind Caleb, his good hand looping one arm while Henry grabbed him from the other side.

This was ridiculous. Caleb should be walking out of there, not being carried like an invalid. He tried to pull free of all the hands and felt Sam tighten his grip. "Easy! You're two hundred pounds of frozen meat. Don't make this harder for us."

"Nowhere near . . . two hundred," Caleb said, as they carried him out of the freezer.

A few minutes later, Caleb was bundled on the small sofa in his office, a hot cup of tea in his hands and Sam fussing with a blanket tucked around him. When he started to feel his toes he wished he couldn't. His fingers curled around the mug but didn't absorb the heat. Every few seconds, Sam guided the cup to Caleb's lips. "Drink. The ambulance will be here soon."

"Don't . . . need . . . ambulance." His teeth chattered with such force that he wondered if he'd chip them. His hands still weren't up to signing, so he said slowly, "How . . . you get here?"

Sam slipped Caleb's shoes off and wrapped part of the blanket around his feet. As he touched Caleb's ankle, he scowled.

"How?" Caleb repeated. He started to shake, Sam grabbing his hands before the tea sloshed out.

"You called me. Sort of. I got a strange page from you with 9-1 at the end. Figured I'd better come find you."

"Wasn't sure I'd sent it." He closed his eyes, the cup of tea pressed against his chin. He breathed in the steam. Breathed in the relief. One last sip and he let Sam take the tea.

"I finished with the police," Henry said, coming in with more blankets.

"Police?" Caleb curved his stiff fingers into a C and bounced it against his chest for Sam. Good, he could sign. Almost back to normal.

"Hey, I didn't know who he was! I see a big white guy with that Frankenstein haircut throwing a cinderblock through a window, what am I suppose to do?" Henry handed the packing quilt to Sam who piled it on top of the other blanket. Caleb was beginning to feel buried.

"Are they still here?" Caleb asked.

"They sent for Detective Briscoe. She said she'd catch you here or at the hospital."

Caleb wanted to sign, "Hospital? Why?" but his fingers had lost their hinges.

"You're still freezing," Sam said.

Yes, he was freezing. And sleepy. The kind of sleepy he felt when he took that prescription cough medicine Shannon gave him, when he didn't wake up for fourteen hours.

". . . much longer. Is he still with us?" Henry was speaking, probably to him.

"Caleb?" Sam pressed harder on his fingers and Caleb pulled away, not liking the stinging pain shooting through his nerve endings.

Henry tapped Sam then pointed toward the door. "Ambulance."

These weren't EMTs that Caleb knew and the realization almost made him laugh. He'd had way too many experiences with

Westville's first responders: The fire at the clinic three years ago. Being held hostage a few weeks later. A car crash the next year that turned his pick-up into a mangled knot of metal . . .

Oh, the EMTs had questions for him. And from Sam's bulging-eyes look of horror, Caleb wasn't answering them. Concentrate, he told himself. His teeth chattered as they inserted the digital thermometer but he didn't break it. So why were they all frowning at the device? "What?" he asked.

"Ninety four degrees. Still too low. We need to get you to the hospital."

All in all, it was the strangest trip to the hospital he'd ever taken. The ER doc was also new to him, but he liked her efficiency and the way she introduced herself as "Amy Stroud" instead of "Doctor Stroud." She had the nurse assistant wheel him down to the Physical Therapy Department, which wasn't even open, and pour a whirlpool bath for him. It felt strange, stripping down to his jockeys and climbing into the lukewarm tub. Sam stayed in the room, pretending not to understand when a nursing tech instructed him to wait outside, and hovered like Caleb might drown in the four feet of water. Amy joined them later, examining the skin on his arms and legs, and adjusting the water temperature.

"You're pinking up nicely. We have to be careful to raise your body temperature very gradually so it doesn't shock your organs. Wiggle your toes for me."

"Ow!" Wiggling his toes seemed to catch them on fire.

"Sorry," she said. "Your nerves are waking up."

"What's wrong?" Sam inserted himself between Caleb and the doctor.

"It's okay," Amy said, letter signing "OK."

"Caleb?" Sam seemed to need verification.

Amy waved to get his attention and signed, "His hands and feet are going to sting—" She pinched her thumb and middle finger together and poked her arm with it, then made the same gesture over Caleb's hands and feet. "It means they are getting warm. Don't worry. He'll be fine." She signed "Fine" like "Heal," pulling both hands from her chest and closing them.

Sam's face softened. "Good."

"Good? It's great!" Caleb said. "I have a doctor who signs!

Where'd you learn that?"

"Had to take a foreign language in college, so I picked sign. Don't get to practice it much, though." She jotted down something in a file. "A little while longer in the water, then I'll send you home with some painkillers. If you have any blistering, call me right away. I see from your record that you had a tetanus shot last year. Oh, and quite a record, I might add."

"Thanks."

"And you're a social worker? Didn't know that was such a risky field."

A half-hour later, he was back in his clothes and sitting across from Claudia Briscoe. Sam and Henry stood behind them. Caleb could see Matthew in the hall, cell phone pressed to his ear. Claudia kept asking questions about Caleb's attacker that he couldn't answer. "I remember his hand. And a big hairy arm. But I didn't see even that. Felt it though. The guy was strong."

"Must have hit the lights before attacking you," Claudia summarized. "Did he say anything?"

"Not a word." Caleb had a hard time looking at the detective's face. She used to be his friend, but not anymore.

"You remember anything else? Did anything feel familiar about the guy?" Claudia scratched at her chin. Her nails were long and crimson-tipped, like they'd recently drawn blood. His, he realized.

Caleb shook his head. It could have been anybody.

"How about size. You mentioned a big arm."

Caleb's head hurt. His hands and feet burned. He just wanted to get away from her and go home. "I said I don't know, okay? He knocked me down. Maybe my size or a little bigger. Or at least heavier, that much I do remember." He studied his fingers. "I think I scratched him."

Claudia grabbed for his hands. "We need to scrape under your nails."

"I've been in a tub for an hour, I've never been this clean."

"What about that spot on your shirt?" She pointed to a tiny brown dot on the sleeve.

"I don't think it's my blood." Without waiting to be asked, he unbuttoned his shirt and handed it over. Sam removed his jacket and gave it to Caleb.

Matthew entered the room. "I can't get in touch with Bill Evers."

Henry shrugged like it was no big surprise to him. "I'll tell him in the morning."

"Well, he should be here right now." Matthew made a fist around the cell phone and turned to Henry. "How did that guy lock him in the freezer? Surely there are safety precautions."

"There are," Henry said. "But he stacked six crates of potatoes against the door, each about seventy-five pounds. Caleb could have pushed that door all night and never gotten out."

Matthew shook his head. "We've got to shut down. I can't have people risking their lives there."

"No." Caleb spoke sharply. "We can't just give up."

"This is my fault," Henry said. "I was running late for my meeting. I always check all the doors before I leave but I didn't tonight. I'm sorry. I didn't do my job, and that's why he got hurt. You can have my resignation this minute, if you want it, but please don't close Safe Harbor."

Caleb heard an edge of desperation in Henry's voice he'd never heard before. "Not his fault," Caleb said. "I was still there, I was the one who should have checked the doors." He really should have, he realized. In that part of town, anything could happen.

"Insuring you already costs me a fortune," Matthew commented. "And if Sam hadn't come to the center tonight . . ."

"Hey, don't remind me." His mind flashed on those hours in the freezer. "I'll be more careful next time."

"You want to keep working there?" Matthew sounded incredulous.

"It really isn't about me. The work Henry and the others are doing—it's too important." He felt a new wave of anger at Claudia. She had done nothing to find the real killer. If she had, maybe this wouldn't have happened. And maybe they wouldn't be talking about closing Safe Harbor.

Claudia must have felt his stare. She asked, "You doing okay, Caleb?"

"I'm just dandy."

"Sure you are."

"Okay, you want the truth? I don't understand why you

dragged me downtown the other day. I don't like being a 'person of interest' in your murder investigation. I can't just overlook the allegations that I stalked and killed my social work intern." His voice got loud, his rage raw and bubbling over. "You know me, Claudia. And if you would do your damn job and find the real killer, maybe nobody else will get hurt. But you seem to have other priorities."

Matthew faced the detective. "Caleb's right. We've had three murders, and now another attempt. Are you any closer to finding out who's behind it? Unless you think Caleb locked himself in the freezer."

Claudia narrowed her eyes. Ticked, but Caleb couldn't care less. "The captain's put me and two other lead detectives on this. If this is trace blood evidence on Caleb's shirt, we may be further along than before. You mentioned the exits, but we don't know that this isn't someone on the inside. Can you think of anyone who works at Safe Harbor who might have done this?"

Caleb thought about all the familiar faces from the shelter. Staff, like Henry, who had helped save Caleb's life. The volunteers, like Alec and Todd. There was Bill Evers. Caleb didn't really like the director but couldn't imagine him as a murderer. "I can't see it being someone on the inside."

"Someone sent those emails from your computer, Caleb."

Yes, someone had. He looked over at Henry. "When did Safe Harbor get the computers?"

"They were all donated by a software company. About five years ago, I think."

"And are they all the same?"

"Exactly the same."

"So what if someone got in my office and switched their computer with mine?"

"Wouldn't you have noticed?" Claudia asked. "I mean, your files and stuff would be gone."

"I've only used the thing for looking stuff up on the Net. I haven't stored anything on the hard drive."

"But you keep your office locked," Henry said.

Caleb nodded, he was careful about locking the door since he kept client records in Wicker World. He turned to Henry. "Remember a few weeks ago, when I couldn't find my keys?"

"Damn."

"How long were they missing?" Claudia asked.

"A few hours. They turned up in a carton of cabbages."

"Plenty of time for someone to make copies." Claudia flipped through her pad and jotted something down.

She looked at Henry. "How many computers do you have at the shelter?"

"I think we got twenty-five in all," Henry answered. "Got them in every office. Four are set up in the back for the volunteers. And we keep about seven in the dorms for the clients to use."

"So your suspect could be any number of people connected with Safe Harbor." Matthew said. "I'm assuming Caleb's off the radar screen now?"

"I can't really discuss that with you," she answered.

"There's one more thing." Caleb went on to tell them about the afternoon after Gina's body had been discovered, when Cleo had alerted him about an intruder.

"You should have called me," Claudia said. "We could have checked for fingerprints, even if nothing was taken."

"If we stay open, we need to make sure the staff is safe. Can the police help?" Matthew asked.

"I'll have a uniform there at eight and we'll keep him there as long as it takes."

"No uniforms," Caleb said. "It scares off the clients."

"Plainclothes then," she answered.

"I can increase my staffing, too," Henry said. "Make sure we have at least two in the warehouse all shifts. Nobody works alone."

Matthew turned back to Caleb. "So? You can back out. I'd almost prefer that you would."

"I'm not leaving. I'm getting good at this manual labor stuff."

"Heaven help us," Matthew said.


The next morning, Caleb downed another three Tylenol. Hypothermia had some strange aftereffects. Pinprick-stinging in his fingers and toes. Muscle tenderness like he'd lifted fifty pounds too many at the gym. And a soft banging against his skull, his own pulse loud enough to hear, reminding him he was still very much alive.

The phone rang. "You're up!" Shannon's voice sounded wonderful.

"And you've been up since four."

"Damn right. I'd say it was the best part of the day but we both know I'd be lying. How are you?"

"Cold."

"Yeah, right. Must be almost fifty degrees down there. Brrrr." His laugh sounded forced even to him.

"Okay, what aren't you telling me?" she asked.

"A little freezer mishap yesterday, but I'm fine."

"A what?"

"Nothing really. How are you? And the cows?"

"We're good. Actually, we're great. Molly, Dad and I met with a lawyer and drew up the papers that give her shares in the company. Dad is so relieved about this, Caleb. It's amazing. He gets to be a part of the farm without it breaking his back."

"I'm happy to hear that." He stifled the urge to say, "So when are you coming home?"

"It's a relief for me, too. I can finally see the light at the end of the tunnel. Maybe another three weeks and I can come back to South Carolina."

"Really?" His voice caught in his throat.

"Yes," she said with a laugh. "How's the detective work going?"

He filled her in on most of it. "I have a favor to ask. You mentioned when you worked for Bill Evers—there was a woman, Suzanne Lyons. Would you mind getting in touch with her?"

"Why?"

"Bill said something strange about Gina. It made me think maybe there was more to their relationship than I realized. Maybe that's a pattern with him."

"You think he killed her?"

"Hard to believe that, I know. But I'm grasping at any straw I can find."

"Okay. I'll look her up on the Internet. If she's still licensed, I'll find her and give her a call."

"Love you," he whispered.

"Damn. Distance does make the heart grow fonder."

Caleb hung up and reluctantly stepped out into the cold Carolina morning. He stared up at the sun, wanting it to pour through his many-layers of clothes, wanting to be washed by it. He'd never been so grateful for the Subaru's seat warmer.

He managed a busy morning at the counseling center, answered hourly text messages from Sam checking on him, and felt marginally better when he got to Safe Harbor. His muscles still ached, and for some reason, his jaw throbbed like he'd done a round with Mike Tyson, but once he got busy he could forget these discomforts. Of course, he planned to steer clear of the freezer area. He wasn't prepared for the inevitable flashbacks.

"Where's Henry?" Caleb asked the volunteer manning the reception desk.

"He's getting into it with the director."

"Excuse me?"

"All I knows is Mr. Evers come in late and asked for Henry. Henry went into his office. Things got a little loud and they closed the door. Ain't neither one of them come out."

"Any idea what they were arguing about?"

"Ain't none of my business, really." The guy looked around as if making sure nobody could overhear this juicy bit of gossip. "But I did hear Henry say something about a meeting and Mr. Evers said he didn't go like he was supposed to."

Caleb wondered what meeting they were discussing. A board meeting? Matthew hadn't mentioned it. A meeting with the city? Bill was unlikely to forget something like that.

As Caleb wandered back to his office, he could see the door to Bill's office was closed. He had a fleeting thought of pressing his ear against it but knew it wasn't his place to meddle. A few minutes later, he heard Henry come out. Caleb grabbed a file and hurried to the reception area, hoping to intercept him. Henry beat him to the desk, dropping into the chair and closing the log book with a slap.

"I'm surprised to see you," Henry said.

"I'm okay. Have a new appreciation for central heating though." He looked down at the jacket he'd been wearing all day. He should take it off. Really, it wasn't cold inside the building. Just couldn't bring himself to do it.

"So you've been meeting with Bill?" Caleb asked.

"Yep."

"What about?"

"Nothing." There was a set to Henry's jaw.

"Nothing?" Caleb persisted.

Henry's head shot up. "What is with you? Why is it any of your business? Me and Bill were talking about something personal. That's allowed, isn't it?"

Caleb deserved the chastisement. He had no right to be intrusive, though it surprised him that Henry and Bill would confide in one another.

"You're right. Sorry."

Henry waved a hand at him. "It's okay. The center is damn soap opera these days, ain't it?"

Caleb almost commented that horror movie seemed more fitting.

"By the way, I got some news for you," Henry said. "Sully's out of jail. Guess the bond magistrate decided to be lenient. Or maybe the jail was tired of dealing with Sully and his voices."

"Great. Where did he go?"

"I took him to the emergency room. Of course there ain't no psych beds for people like Sully anymore. People that don't have insurance, I mean. But they said they'd keep him a day or two, see if they can get him quieted down."

"There's still the one public hospital in Columbia. I'll have Matthew do a consult," Caleb said. The emergency department at Westville General was like any other: chaotic, loud, and often busting at the seams. Not a place where one's mental health could easily be restored. But with so few public psychiatric beds, EDs all across the state had morphed into inadequate, understaffed mental health facilities. Psychotic patients could remain for weeks, doctors doing their best with medications but there was no real treatment. ED staff resented the task, non-psychiatric emergencies complained of the noise, and the mental health patients were left to recover in a place that could scarcely manage them. Matthew could beg for a hospital placement for Sully, but more likely, Sully would return to the streets, the voices still raging in his head.

"I don't know how you do this work," Caleb said to Henry.

"What do you mean?"

"Knowing there is so little out there to help our clients. Knowing for most of them, we're it. And now that the city wants to close us down—" Caleb shook his head. Sometimes it was too much. Sometimes it felt beyond hopeless.

"They can't close down Safe Harbor. If they do, I'll find a way to open another shelter. If not here, maybe across the river. It will take more than a camera-loving mayor and a bunch of greedy business-types to run me out of Dodge."

Caleb thought about Henry's brother Calvin. How his death brought Henry to Safe Harbor and into recovery. What would have happened if Safe Harbor didn't exist?

"I like your spirit, Henry, but you've got to have money to get another program going. Just like it'll take money to keep Safe Harbor afloat."

Henry smiled. "Sometimes, Caleb, you just gotta have a little faith."

"One day at a time, right?"

"Damn straight."

Caleb jumped when he felt the vibration of the cell phone in his pocket. He flipped it open.

"Mr. Knowles? You need to do something about your brother. He's really off the chain this time. Sticking in his nose in things he shouldn't be messing with. Telling me how I'm supposed to do my job. I'm sick and tired of it!"

He recognized the voice: Mandy Phelps (Fay-ulps), Isaiah's beleaguered caseworker. How she got his cell number, he had no clue. "Mandy, slow down. I don't know what you're talking about."

"He just showed up at my office. Didn't even bother to bring an interpreter because he didn't give a lick about listening to what I had to say!" The pitch of her voice climbed higher and higher, well into the soprano range.

"Did Sam tell you what happened to him? About Jo-Jo and the other man who attacked him at Diondra's apartment?"

"What was he doing over there anyway? Isaiah wasn't even home. Boundaries, Mr. Knowles. We're talking about a serious lack of boundaries. It's becoming quite clear to me that he is not an appropriate Mentor for little Isaiah."

"Hold on there. He's just trying to help."

"Do you even know what he has in mind? That he wants to pay off the man Diondra owes money to? That he's buying a house for Diondra and the kids? How he plans to move the family?"

Caleb closed his eyes. He should have seen this coming.

"Do you have any idea how this will look? What does he expect in return for this generosity, Mr. Knowles? What kind of exploitation are we looking at here?" Her rant reached the highest end of the keyboard.

"Okay, calm down. You're over-reacting. Sam has a special interest in Isaiah's welfare but that is all. I didn't know his plans but I promise I will talk to him."

"I have to call the Mentor people. They need to know what he's done."

"Don't call them until I have a chance to look into this. I promise I'll call you back tomorrow. Just don't do anything until then."

She hesitated. He imagined a can of Diet Mountain Dew squeezed in her hand. "You have till tomorrow. After that, I'm calling Mentor."

Caleb hung up, wondering if that damn brother of his was home. Why hadn't he told Caleb his plans?

"Not to be eavesdropping, but I heard you mention Jo-Jo. Did you mean Jo-Jo Kyle?" Henry asked.

"I have no idea what his last name is, but he's a sorry SOB." Caleb told Henry the Isaiah saga and about his stubborn brother's over-involvement.

"That sounds like Jo-Jo Kyle. He can be bad news. A street punk who'd kill you for a quarter. Last I heard he'd joined the UBN gang. If Diondra owes him money he's going to get it one way or the other. Sam could get himself killed messing with them."

Caleb thought about the evening he'd found Sam after the beating. If Sam was determined to stay involved with that family, he could still be in danger. This was not acceptable.

"I need to talk sense into him." He checked his watch. Almost seven. "You want to do me a favor? I'll buy you supper in return."

"What?" Henry looked appropriately suspicious.

"Come with me over to Sam's. Tell him what you know about Jo-Jo. Maybe he'll listen to you."

"Maybe. But my experience with you Knowles boys—you're a bit on the stubborn side."

# Chapter Twenty-One

Twenty minutes later, they pulled behind Sam's van in the driveway of his lake house. Caleb watched as Henry climbed out of his car, his eyes widening as he took in the large A-frame house, the ground-to-roof windows, the garden and lawn leading to the rippling blue water of the lake.

"Damn," Henry said. "Looks like he's done all right for himself. I should have tried that art stuff."

"Don't think I haven't thought the same thing. Sam's really talented. But if you asked him, he'd say he was really lucky. Maybe it's a bit of both."

"Damn," Henry repeated.

"Well, here goes." Caleb trotted up the front steps and hit the door signal. When Sam opened the door, Caleb wasted no time getting to the point: "Are you out of your freaking mind?" Caleb's hands snapped the gestures.

"Hello," Sam replied. "How are you feeling?"

"You told Mandy Phelps you're going to pay off Diondra's dealer?" Caleb continued, his hands flying as he signed. "And buy her a house? What else do you plan to do? Give her a brand new Lexus?"

"Nice to see you, too, Henry," Sam replied, ignoring Caleb.

"Uh, hey." Henry eyed them both warily.

"How have you been?" Sam asked him.

"I'm not so great, myself," Caleb waved his hands to interrupt him. "I have a brother that's gone completely nuts."

"I didn't think you social workers were supposed to use words like that. Do you want to stop ranting and come inside?"

They followed Sam into the living room. With a frustrated sigh, Caleb dropped onto the sofa. A fire blazed in the fireplace.

A stack of papers rested on the curved table beside Sam's flashing Blackberry.

"Do you want something to drink?" Sam asked.

"Why didn't you tell me your insane plan?" Caleb asked.

"I was pretty sure what your advice would be." He turned to Henry. "Coffee? Soda?"

"I'm good." Henry took in the impressive room.

"Henry's here for back-up, by the way," Caleb continued. "I was worried this would happen. This whole Mentor thing—I knew you'd get over-involved. Isaiah's a great kid, don't get me wrong, but he isn't *your* kid. And Diondra. That woman's a mess. Do you have any idea what kind of precedent you'll be setting with her? Once she figures out how much money you have she'll suck you dry."

"You're judging her too harshly. And worse, you're under-estimating me. I know what I'm doing." Sam crossed to a chair and sat. A mug rested on the table beside him. He lifted it.

"Do you know Mandy thinks you're some kind of pedophile? What you're planning is so over-the-top, she can't help but suspect your motives."

"Mandy Phelps is an idiot. I'm through dealing with her."

"You won't be if she has you removed as Isaiah's Mentor."

Sam stared into his cup. He said nothing.

Caleb tossed a pillow at him to get his attention.

"Hey!" Sam looked affronted. "What exactly do you expect me to do, Caleb? Walk away? Leave Isaiah, Diondra and Charmain for Jo-Jo to find? Is that what you want?"

"Yes. I have lots of clients who live in bad situations. I do what I can for them but I accept my limitations."

"Do you? Really?" Sam shook his head, eyes narrowed. "Because I'm remembering a fifteen-year-old kid named Kevin who had a gang gunning for him. You had to stick your neck out to help him and came pretty damn close to getting yourself killed in the process."

"That was different," Caleb signed, though he knew it wasn't. Kevin Lumford had been Caleb's client several years ago, the teenage son of a murderer, living on the fringe of gang-life. Caleb knew he was Kevin's last chance. Rescuing Kevin from the pursuing gang members cost Caleb his truck and ten days in the hospital. He had scars on his leg, chest and hairline as reminders. But Kevin survived. It was worth it.

"Look," Sam said. "I'm not Isaiah's social worker. I don't even know how to define how I feel about him. Yes, I am over-involved but I intend to stay that way until I know he's safe and happy." He looked at Caleb, his expression softening. "You're too protective of me. Not just because I'm your brother, but because I'm deaf. Annoys the hell out of me, but I understand. So try to imagine what life for Isaiah is like. Try to imagine how vulnerable he is. How incredibly isolated he feels. Then try to imagine what it would take for me to walk away from him."

Caleb felt Sam's words as clearly as he heard them. There would be no changing his mind. He would do whatever it took to help Isaiah and his family, even if it put himself at risk. But he wasn't doing it by himself. He looked over at Henry. "Tell him what you know about this Jo-Jo creep."

Sam turned to Henry. "Really? You know him?"

"Yeah. Not well, but I know him. Jo-Jo Kyle is a gang-banger with the UBN gang. A big player. Not someone to mess with." Henry spoke slowly, watching Caleb as he signed Henry's words.

"UBN?" Caleb asked.

"United Blood Nation. You've heard of the Bloods, right? They're connected. Anyway, if Diondra owes him money, he's going to get it one way or the other. He'll lose his street cred if he don't."

"How much does she owe him?" Caleb asked Sam. "Do you know?"

He nodded. "Just over seven thousand."

Henry said, "If Sam takes care of Diondra's debt, it might get Jo-Jo out of your hair. That way he saves face. From his perspective, he can't go around letting some drug mule keep his money. Bad for business."

"But say Sam pays it," Caleb said. "What would keep Jo-Jo from coming after him for more cash?"

"I'll find another way to get him the money," Sam said.

Henry lifted a hand. "Look. Only one way this can go down. If you want to pay off Jo-Jo, you need to let me be your emissary. Y'all don't need to be anywhere in the picture."

"What do you mean?" Sam asked.

"I mean this is a street transaction. And you slices of college-educated white bread don't know squat about that world. Sam wants to pay off Jo-Jo, me and some of my buddies will handle the transaction."

Caleb pondered the offer. It was more than generous, and he didn't feel right about accepting, but he didn't see another option. "You sure you want to do that?"

"I'm sure it's the only thing that will work. But that only solves one thing. You got the other issue of where Isaiah lives. Jo-Jo's just one of many problems in that hood."

"That's why I'm buying Diondra a house," Sam said.

"Damn it, Sam—" Caleb interrupted.

"No, listen. There's no way he's living in that rat trap any longer. It's too dangerous and you know it." Sam reached for the stack of papers on the table. "I've been researching neighborhoods and schools in Westville. The best kindergarten and elementary school for special needs kids is in the north side of town. I found this—" He handed a sheet to Caleb. "It's a small home in a safe neighborhood that I can easily afford. I'll rent it to Diondra. I tried to talk to Mandy about what would be a fair amount. Diondra needs to get a job, and needs to feel like she's providing for those kids."

Henry looked at the listing. "Nice. I know the area. Used to be rough but it's turned around. Good families live there now."

Caleb studied the photos on the flyer. Yellow siding. Green shutters. Brick walkway with flowers on either side. Three small bedrooms, a galley kitchen. But it would probably feel like a palace to that little family. "You sure you want to do this?"

"I'm sure I'm *going* do this." Sam turned to Henry. "Tell me when you want the money. But I'm going, too. I want to make sure nobody gets hurt during this."

"I'll be in touch. Probably best if you ain't there. This has to go down soon, so expect to hear from in the next day or two."


Wyman sat on the big tan boulder that protruded out over the river and tried to summon his courage. In the summer, he'd lie on this rock, let the sun beat down on him as he listened to the rushing water. He and Dawn spent hours here, getting hot until they glistened with sweat, then hiking down to wade in the river. No matter how hot the air was, the river water stayed cool, and they would splash each other and laugh and sometimes sit right down in the current. "This is one way to wash our clothes," he remembered Dawn saying.

Dawn was the reason he was here. He had to talk to her alone, and getting her away from Johnny wasn't easy since the guy stuck to her like a kudzu vine. Wyman had private things he had to say to Dawn and she wasn't going to be happy to hear them.

All because of that damn Markham. He had to go and stick his nose where it didn't belong. Had he already told Wyman's mother about the baby? What would she do if she knew? How much cash would Markham weasel out of her to buy his silence? Or worse, what if she decided to take little Star away from Dawn?

These were troubling thoughts. Part of him wanted to hit the highway and never look back. But he couldn't do that without warning Dawn first. She was too easy to find in Zooville, and he sure didn't want Markham to get his hands on her and the kid.

He looked over the river, at the current ripping by as fast as a freight train. People in Zooville knew that when the river raged you'd better stay away. "Don't let the river snag you and pull you down," Stormy used to say. Always one for advice, Stormy was.

The river wasn't the only thing that was mad. Wyman could hear voices in the tent village getting loud. He could hear Johnny yelling and another man saying something about "Clean up this trash." Wyman wondered who he was and why he was there, so he decided to sneak up closer for a look. The wall of pine trees that separated Zooville from the river gave him good cover. He moved carefully, hiding behind the foliage, being careful of where he stepped. Pine needles made less noise than leaves.

The man talking to Johnny had on a fancy business suit. Another man, dressed in camouflage pants, stood by him, arms crossed and mean-looking like he was a bouncer in a bar.

"Tourists come to the river to enjoy the scenery." The man pointed across the river. A tall fence enclosed the zoo but sometimes you could hear the animals, especially the elephants, if they got frisky. "Children come here. And what do they get to see? Your trash piled up on the rocks. The mound of beer cans on the shore. One kid told me saw some tramp taking a piss into the river like it's his toilet!" The guy was all in Johnny's face, finger jabbing at him like a hammer on a nail.

"You can't blame all that on us," Johnny said. "We live here. We take pride in our home."

"You call this pride? Pride is having a damn job! Pride is having a real place to live, not squatting on land that isn't yours!"

Wyman noticed Dawn behind Johnny, easing back from him. The baby in her arms made little whimpering sounds. They shouldn't fight like that in front of the kid.

"I think you'd better leave." Johnny's voice snarled. Three other Zooville men stood behind him like his very own posse. The camouflage guy moved in front of the man.

"Look, I'm doing you a favor here." The man's tone changed. "You need to understand, we're closing down this village. One day soon, and I mean real soon, the police will show up here with bulldozers and mow down every tent and every shelter y'all have built. Don't you think it would be better to move on your own? Or do you want to see all this destroyed?"

Dawn had a stricken look on her face, a look Wyman had seen only one time before, when he got caught with that crack pipe and got kicked out of Zooville. Dawn looked like something had broken inside her.

"They can't do that." Johnny spoke to Dawn, not the man, who didn't seem to notice.

"They can and they will. You have no legal right to be here." He turned to the camouflage guy. "Let's get out of here. They don't want to leave, let the police take care of them."

As the two men disappeared down the path, Johnny turned back to Dawn.

"They can't do that, can they?" She rocked the baby, moving side to side.

"Police can do whatever the hell they want, you know that." Johnny turned to his companions. One cocked a thumb towards Johnny's tent and the three of them stooped to enter the canvas doorway. Dawn didn't. She jostled little Star and walked towards where Wyman was standing. Had she spotted him? No, she moved on to the path, going down to the water's edge.

He followed until she stopped. The baby rested its head against her chest, eyes closing, like the sound of the rushing river was a lullaby to her. Dawn stared out over the water, a pinched expression still on her face. She loved Zooville, and the life she was living with Johnny. All that was about to change.

"I just want to talk." Wyman eased over to her, hand outstretched. "Just for a minute."

She looked all around him like she expected others to show up but nobody did.

"It's just me. I'm not high, if that's what you're worried about."

"What do you want?" She heaved the baby up a little, her hand coming up to the back of its head.

"She's a cute little thing."

"What do you want?" she repeated.

"You have to leave here, Dawn. You can't keep staying in Zooville." There, he'd said it. Maybe he could leave before she got mad or tearful or demanding. He wished he hadn't mentioned getting high, now crack was all he could think about.

"Are you talking about the police? Did you hear what that man was saying?"

"I heard, but that's not what I'm talking about." He looked back over the river. Whispers were starting in his head. Craving made them come.

"Maybe you should just mind your own business."

"It's Markham. He knows about Star." Wyman told her the rest of it, his words rushing out like the current beside them. She didn't say a word, just listened. She nodded when he mentioned his mother; they had talked about his family before, back when they were on the road together. Both of them had pasts they needed to escape.

"So what will your mother do?" Dawn's voice sounded so young.

"I don't know." He knew his mother wouldn't want Star. Not really. But she wouldn't want people to know her grandchild was living in a tent. What would the neighbors think? The senator's family? "Markham will take advantage, no doubt about it. He smells money to be made. He'll probably want you and the baby to move into the Willows so he can trick my mother into paying for it."

"I hated that place."

She'd only stayed a few days with Wyman at the Willows. She said the place grossed her out and she thought a rat got in her bed. Wyman looked at the child sleeping in her arms. Living in a tent or on the streets wasn't great but it was better than the Willows.

"Leave Westville," he said urgently, knowing it was the only right answer. "You and Johnny take Star far away from here. Head south, and stay gone. Markham will try to find you but he's not smart enough to track you on the road."

Dawn turned towards Zooville. They could hear the thuds of firewood being stacked, the clang of pots readying for supper. "This is the only real home I've ever had."

Wyman nodded. Zooville had been a home for him, too, up until he got himself tossed out. Somehow he'd become very good at losing the things that mattered.

He needed to stop thinking about that. Now the crack pipe filled his mind and he craved, craved from the ends of his toenails to the ends of his hair.

Dawn shifted the baby who blinked awake. "Guess I better go tell Johnny. If the police are going to destroy Zooville anyway, we might as well move on."

As she took a step towards the path, Wyman felt something catch in his throat. The little girl looked up at him. She had Dawn's dark hair, but maybe those were his green eyes. Did she like cheese and peanut butter? Did she love animals like him? Would she grow up to make something of herself, or would she get into drugs and have them screw up her life? He prayed she'd be spared that.

Wyman reached out a tentative hand. Dawn didn't pull away, but let him touch the child. Her hair was so soft, little ringlets curling around his finger. "Sweet little girl," he said.

"Our Star," Dawn replied. "Goodbye, Wyman. Hope you can get yourself straight."

He watched them leave, an ache filling his chest, his lungs, his heart. And then the craving swept through him. A torrent. He was damn sure he'd get himself some crack, even if he had to steal it.

# Chapter Twenty-Two

"I wasn't planning on you being a part of this little shindig," Henry said, arms folded as he leaned against the Safe Harbor van.

"Hey, I didn't want to be here. But Sam got real insistent that he was going. And Jo-Jo's already had one run-in with him," Caleb answered.

"So you volunteered? Didn't I say this was best handled by me and my guys?"

"Yep, you did. And yep, I believed you. But Sam's got another perspective on this thing. He doesn't think it's fair for you to handle this for him. But don't worry, I have no intention of interfering. In fact, I'm happy to wait in the van while this goes down. But I'll be near enough that if you need help I can get it for you. Get it as in I'll have a cell phone in hand." Caleb waved the phone to make his point.

"Suit yourself, but you're gonna have to do what I tell you. My guys will be here in a minute. They don't know you and they ain't likely to trust you. So you sit in the back of the van and keep your mouth shut. We want to get in and out as quick as can."

"Okay." Caleb held up the duffle bag that Sam had given him; seven thousand three hundred dollars in tidy bundles were inside.

"Let's hope this pacifies Jo-Jo."

Henry's friends met them in the parking lot. They were an interesting duo. Ike had tattoos covering every inch of exposed flesh. His shaved head gleamed like a shiny doorknob. He stood beside Henry, his bulldog shoulders bulging, wearing all the expression of a lump of coal.

Rush was thin as a flagpole and all movement. Hands flailing, feet shifting, nostrils flaring. When Henry introduced him, Rush gave Caleb's hand a quick shake but wouldn't look him in the eye.

"We know where to find Jo-Jo?" Henry asked them.

"I been asking around," Ike said. "UBNs took over that neighborhood south of Lafayette. Jo-Jo and some bangers been slanging out of a empty house."

"What are they packing?" Henry asked.

"Trey Eights and a gauge all I saw. But I hear Jo-Jo's got him a AK." Ike looked over at Caleb, assessing.

"Guns?" Caleb asked.

"Thirty-eight calibers, shotgun, assault rifle," Henry translated.

"Crap," Caleb uttered.

"Ain't no Sunday in the park, white man," Rush said.

"Last chance. You can stay here," Henry said.

Caleb shook his head before he realized he'd done it. Why was he going with these guys? Because they were risking their lives for his brother, that was why.

Ike pulled a wool cap from his pocket and slid it over his head. "Need to go before it gets too dark."

"We'll pick up Diondra on the way." Henry unlocked the van and they climbed inside, Caleb working his way to the very back seat. The drive to Victor Street took twenty minutes; not a word was spoken by the three men. "Which apartment?" Henry asked Caleb.

"That quadriplex. Right side."

Diondra waited for them in the open doorway. She had on black jeans and a hooded jacket. She pulled herself into the van, sitting opposite Rush. Caleb could see she was shivering. Caleb introduced her, but she said nothing to the men. Her eyes were wide black pools of fear.

"This thing will be done soon." Henry turned in his seat so she could see him. "And we'll get you on to your new life."

"That's what I want to believe," she answered.

Caleb looked out the back window as they drove back to Main Street and then turned onto Lafayette. Sparse traffic, but plenty of action on the cracked sidewalk. An older man walking a dog. A couple of prostitutes in heated debate. Two men in black do-rags slowly lumbering up the road.

The van jarred when Henry made the last turn, and Ike and Rush lowered their windows.

"Two blocks up," Ike said.

"Already got some action." Rush twisted around to look at Caleb.

"What do you mean?"

"Couple of bangers there." He pointed at an old Impala moving slowly towards them. Black, with bright orange graphics of fire around the wheels. A beast of a car. It slowed as it passed, two sets of eyes giving them a cold, hard stare.

"You know them?" Caleb whispered to Diondra.

"Nah."

The car sped up, a cloud of smoke puffing out from its exhaust.

Henry eyed them from the rearview mirror. "They ain't turning around."

"Let's do our business before they do." Ike pointed to a small dilapidated house surrounded by a chain-link fence. Two men stood on the porch. Diondra sucked in an audible breath.

"You've been here before," Caleb realized.

"I been most everywhere this side of town," she answered.

Henry parked the van and switched off the ignition. Ike bent down to fiddle with the leg of his jeans and when he straightened, he had a revolver in his hand.

"Hope we don't need that," Henry said.

"I don't go to my mama's without this."

They climbed out of the van, lingering in front of the open door. Diondra zipped her jacket, hands tucked deep in pockets. Caleb moved to the second bench seat for a closer view. He felt as out of place as he had among Shannon's cows—completely out of his element. A knot of fear worked its way up his throat as he thought about Jo-Jo and his gang and Ike's revolver.

"Here's what you're going to do." Henry spoke to Diondra, his gaze direct but gentle. "You're going to give him the cash. You're going to tell him this settles your debt. You're going to tell him you're leaving Westville, that you're starting over with your kids, but you don't want any bad blood between you."

"Okay."

"Be strong, Diondra. Be tough. We're right behind you so nobody is going to do anything to you."

She stiffened, her head coming up ramrod straight, mouth twisting. She looked more scared than Caleb felt.

Rush nudged her with his arm. "Jo-Jo ain't nothing but a punk. He's gonna be glad to be done with this."

Diondra reached for the duffle from Henry. He gave her a tight smile, but it vanished when he spotted something behind her. Diondra turned and Caleb strained to see around the door frame.

"That's him," she said.

Jo-Jo was as wide as Ike. His arms were covered with random tattoos, like he'd fallen asleep near a toddler armed with a sharpie. His two companions walked a few paces behind him. Mirror-image hoods, in black do-rags and sweats—gray and red.

"Good," Rush said. "Best we do this outside."

Suddenly Diondra pushed past them, bag in hand, and yelled, "Jo-Jo! Hey!"

Jo-Jo turned to face her. She swung the duffle as she walked towards him, hips swaying. Henry, Ike and Rush exchanged surprised looks but followed close behind.

"I got something for you." Diondra put some sass in her voice.

Jo-Jo's companions moved as one, positioning themselves in front of him to block her.

"I ain't here to hurt him," Diondra said with a forced laugh. "I'm here to give him the money he thinks I owe him."

"'Bout damn time," Jo-Jo said. He motioned for his colleagues to back off and crossed to Henry. "Ain't seen you in a while. Brought some back-up, I see."

She shot a panicked look back at the three of them, but they didn't speak, simply stared at Jo-Jo, looking fierce as Rottweilers.

"Them? Them are my movers," Diondra said. "I pay you, I'm getting the hell out of Westville."

Jo-Jo let out an ugly laugh. "Westville's a damn hard place to escape, ain't it Henry?"

"But you can rise above the streets." Henry's voice was low and icy.

Jo-Jo's smile faded. "People think they can. But my experience is the streets take 'em back."

Henry didn't say anything in response, just gave Jo-Jo a steely stare like he could see through skin. Caleb had never seen this version of Henry. He'd hate to have those eyes directed at him.

"Let's do this, Jo-Jo." Diondra held up the backpack. "Here's your cash. Seventy-three hundred."

Jo-Jo nodded to one of his thugs who took the bag, opened it, and counted the bills.

"We was a good team once," Jo-Jo said to Diondra.

"Not anymore." Diondra said. "I got responsibilities. I got kids that need me."

"How's that deaf mute boy of yours?" Jo-Jo's smile was back, a Cheshire white flash of teeth.

"He ain't none of your business!" She pointed a finger, close enough to poke him in the chest. "You come near him and I swear—"

Sensing a threat, Jo-Jo's cohorts shifted towards her. Henry pulled her back.

"He ain't coming near your children again," Ike said. "Cause if he crosses that line . . ."

Jo-Jo cocked his head as if noticing Ike for the first time. His gaze fixed on a tattoo that covered Ike's knuckles: MS-13 in crimson red. A rival gang. Jo-Jo backed up a step. "No, we're cool." He turned to Diondra. "Good luck with your 'new life.' Guess I'll see you when you crawl on back here."

"Don't count on it," she said, head held high.


Caleb searched the shelves in the Safe Harbor break room for a clean mug. Usually the crew did a decent job of tidying up after themselves but today the sink overflowed with dirty dishes. The coffee in the carafe was the color of mud, so Caleb decided to hit the vending machine instead.

"There's a lady wants to see you." Henry intercepted him. "One of them other-side-of-the-tracks people. I think her purse cost more than my car."

"Okay," Caleb said, curious. "She give you a name?"

"She gave me this. Said it was her calling card. I thought she meant one of those long distance things we give our clients but it wasn't." He held out a white business card with elaborate script printing that read: *Mrs. Margaret R. Eldridge.*

"Wyman's mother," Caleb said. "Guess I better see what she wants."

Mrs. Eldridge stood by the window, far from the waiting area's other occupants. She extended a hand to him.

"I'm Caleb Knowles," he said. He felt soft, kid leather when she squeezed his fingers. Her gloves matched the gray purse and the wool skirt she wore. She wasn't a tall woman, just chin-high to Caleb, with silver hair. The lack of wrinkles around her piercing blue eyes made him wonder if she'd had plastic surgery.

"I won't take much of your time," she said. "Is there somewhere private we could talk?"

He led her back to his office. She eased into the wicker chair like she thought it might break on contact.

"As you probably know, my husband is former Senator Eldridge." She spoke with pride, a low-country lilt to her voice. "When I called Bill Evers he suggested that I talk to you. He said you were a counselor but I swear, Wyman has been through so many therapists, psychiatrists, addictions counselors. Sometimes I think my son is beyond help." Her tone was detached, like she was talking about the weather rather than her own child.

"I hope he isn't. I'd like to understand him better. Would you mind answering some questions?"

She removed her gloves slowly, deliberately, folding them in her lap. "Really? Must we dredge up ancient history? What would be the point?"

"Wyman hasn't been able to tell much. And nobody knows him better than you." Caleb smiled. She didn't.

"Oh, I know how this works. I tell you about what our life was like, and you decide if I toilet trained him too early or separated from his father when he was at an impressionable age and that's why he's addicted to cocaine. Isn't it always the mother's fault?"

"No, actually." Caleb wondered why she was so hostile. He tried a change in tactics. "You mentioned Wyman's father. Can you tell me more about him?"

"What do you want to know?"

"How long were you married to him?"

"Too long. It was a mistake from the beginning." Her hand gripped the gloves. "We got married because I was pregnant with Wyman. Divorced nine years later. Nine very long years."

"Was he abusive?"

She nodded. "It wasn't too bad at first, but it worsened as time went on. He couldn't keep a job longer than ten minutes. We had horrific money problems, so I worked two jobs just to keep our apartment. I kept hoping Danny would change. That he would see what his drinking was doing to us." She looked away.

"That's often how it works," Caleb said, his voice gentle. "It makes it hard on families. Was he ever violent to Wyman?"

"He hit me a few times, but when I found bruises on my son, that was the last straw. I moved us out. I had twenty-five dollars, two suitcases and a confused child. I had nowhere to go. This was not the life I had planned for myself."

"You did the hard thing." In an instant, Caleb's own father's face filled his mind. The red-rimmed, unfocused eyes when his anger sparked. The sour smell of bourbon. But Caleb's mother didn't leave. Didn't protect him. That job fell to his older brother, Sam.

Caleb swallowed, wanting to submerge these memories. Sometimes they came like this—unbidden. Not often, but powerful.

"I lived a hard life then," Mrs. Eldridge said. "I was working temp jobs as a secretary and barely scraping by. Then I got hired to work on Ashton's campaign. When Ashton and I met, it was like a car crash. We fell in love. My life changed in that instant."

What if Caleb's mother had taken Sam and Caleb away? What might their lives have been like? Maybe Sam wouldn't have grown to be so reckless. Maybe he wouldn't have been on that motorcycle without a helmet. Maybe Sam wouldn't be deaf.

Where were these thoughts coming from? He had to push the memories away. He needed to be here, in this room, with his client's mother.

Mrs. Eldridge looked down at the ring on her fourth finger. A dime-size sapphire encircled by diamonds.

"And Wyman?" Caleb asked. "How did he adjust?"

"He was such an angry boy. He had such rages. He got in fights at school. His grades were terrible. And at home, he got more and more . . . destructive."

"Destructive how?"

"Many ways. For example, my husband gave him a telescope. A nice one. Ashton always loved astronomy and thought that was something he and Wyman could share. But a week later, it was nothing but a pile of glass and metal. Wyman demolished it with his baseball bat."

"I understand he burned a tool shed?"

"He loved to play with fire. First the shed. Then we sent him to a special school and he set the dock on fire."

"Why did he do it? Did he say?"

"Why? Who knows? He was probably mad because someone said no to him. Or one of the other kids dared him to do it. Or he just wanted to see what the flames would look like. He never said. Never showed an ounce of remorse, either. We spent fifteen thousand on tuition then another twelve to rebuild what he destroyed." Her tone took on a bitter edge.

"By the time he was sixteen, he was in the juvenile justice system. My husband was still in office and Wyman was locked up in a detention program. Somehow, it never made the papers, thank God."

Caleb wondered if this was when Margaret Eldridge gave up on her son. He had been a trying child and worse as an adolescent. Still, she was his mother. Had Wyman sensed her choosing her husband over him? Did he feel abandoned?

Caleb's mother made a similar choice, staying with his father, despite the drinking and the violence. Despite what it did to her sons. And it had hurt in ways Caleb still tried to understand.

"I suppose I should get to why I'm here," she said. "Bill said you can help me with my problem. I hope you can. I used to talk to Esther Lowell. Well, not often, but a few times. She was the one who first told me about it. Then Markham Dougherty got in touch with me last week. Quite frankly, I didn't know what to do."

Esther? She had talked to Esther about Wyman? "Mrs. Eldridge, I'm not sure I understand."

"No, I suppose not." Her hand traced the ridges of the wicker armrest. "This is difficult for me. But I don't want anything bad to happen. That's why I'm here."

"Okay." Caleb kept his voice soft, listening.

"Wyman has a child. A little girl. Esther told me about her because she was worried that it might not be getting good care. At least, I think that's why she told me. Markham—well, Markham had different motives, I think. But all of that is neither here nor there. The point is the baby exists. And it needs to be taken care of."

A child? Good lord. Where was it? Somewhere safe, he hoped.

"You know the mother, Mr. Knowles, though you might not realize you do. It's a homeless girl. Dawn is her name. Markham said she was a cocaine addict." Mrs. Eldridge's nose wrinkled like she smelled something foul.

"Dawn? Yes, I know her." So Wyman was Star's father.

"Wyman met her when he was on one of his road trips. That's what we call them. He just picks up and leaves town. Markham doesn't hear from him in weeks, then he'll come stumbling back. Last year, he brought Dawn with him. They didn't stay, though. Dawn ended up in that horrible tent village they've talked about in the papers."

"Zooville."

"Yes. What a ridiculous name. Anyway, the truth is that child is my grandchild. So I have to be concerned about its welfare. I'm sure you understand."

"Have you met the little girl?"

"No. Is it healthy? I mean, its mother has serious problems. It's been living in a tent. Is it . . . normal? Does it look retarded or have other problems like that?"

Caleb didn't like the way she phrased the questions. Or the way she kept calling Star "It." Mrs. Eldridge's hand kept stroking the wicker, cupping around the end of the armrest.

"Your granddaughter is perfect. A lovely little girl."

"Good. That's good. I'm relieved to hear it."

"You said Mr. Dougherty had discussed her with you?"

"He's offered to take in Dawn and the child. A generous offer, I suppose. He'd give the girl a room, food, other essentials." She fiddled with the sapphire. "Esther had asked me about taking custody, myself. But I couldn't. You have to understand—I just can't fix all of Wyman's problems."

"So you'd rather let Markham Dougherty take care of your grandchild?" He didn't hide his incredulity.

"You probably think we should involve social services. But I have my husband's family to think of. I can't let this unfortunate situation call undo attention to us. I have to protect the Eldridge name."

"The situation, as you call it, is a living, breathing child." He felt his teeth clenching.

"I understand that, Mr. Knowles," she said tightly. "She is why I am here. Do you know what the police are going to do to that tent village? They are going to raze it. Every shelter there will be completely destroyed. All the people living there will be escorted off the property with the threat of arrest should they return."

"They can't do that!"

"Of course they can." She gave him a little sideways look that irritated him even more. "My husband is a close friend of the police chief. He's been kept informed."

"When?"

"Soon. Today. Tomorrow. That's why I'm here. I want to make sure Dawn and the child are safe. If you could get a message to them, tell them about Markham's offer. Tell them I will pay for their room and board and medical care, but they have to agree to follow Markham's rules."

"Have you been to the Willows?"

"Of course I have. But Markham assured me that Dawn and the child would stay in the house with him and Rhetta, which is where Wyman stays when he decides he wants a roof over his head."

The pieces clicked into place. Mrs. Eldridge could console herself that she hadn't abandoned her son nor granddaughter— she just had to believe Markham's line of crap about where they stayed. Caleb looked at the tiny woman, purse tightly gripped on her lap now. Diamond ring shimmering. He could tell her the truth about where Markham housed Wyman, but doubted that she'd care.

"I'll relay the message." He stood, eager for this encounter to end. "I'll tell Bill Evers what she decides. That is, if Zooville isn't already smashed to bits."

"Thank you then," she said. She stood, brushing off the back of her skirt as though she'd been sitting in potting soil, and left him.


Caleb hurried down the hall to Bill's office. The door was ajar, lights on, a wide swath of papers covering the desk. Two file cabinet drawers gaped open, files protruding out like manila tongues. The clutter was a sharp contrast to the other day, when Caleb and Jasmine had sipped lattes and talked city politics with Bill.

"He's gone home." Henry slipped by Caleb. He closed the drawers, straightened the papers, and turned off the lights.

"Home? It's the middle of the afternoon."

"He's going to take a little time off. Has some things he needs to take care of."

"You're kidding."

"Man deserves to take a break."

Caleb scrutinized his cryptic friend. He had a hundred questions about Bill's sudden disappearance but remembered the last time he attempted to pry.

"Well I need to ask him something," Caleb said. "Would you mind giving me his home number?"

"You won't find him there." Henry closed the door, turning to face Caleb in the hallway. "I know you think I'm being evasive, but trust me. There ain't a thing Bill can help you with right now."

Caleb looked at the brass nameplate: William Evers, Executive Director. "He sure picked a strange time to disappear on us. Christ, Henry. There's a killer loose. We're doing our best just to keep our doors open. And Bill decides to take a personal day? Could have picked a better time."

"I think he'll be gone more than a day. Whatever you need from him, you'll just have to handle on your own."

"Henry!" someone yelled from down the hall. "Henry! Come here quick!"

They both ran to reception to find a very agitated Lanie pointing to the door.

"What's wrong?"

"You gotta come, Henry!" Lanie implored. "They're tearing up the place! They took down Luther's tent. He tried to fight them and they put him in handcuffs. You gotta come *now!*" Lanie's hands flew in the air as she talked. Behind her was a thin, waif of a woman Caleb remembered from his visit to Zooville. Henry had called her May.

"Damn it," Caleb uttered.

"They're burning our stuff." May folded her arms against her chest. Tears streamed down her dirty face. "My clothes is all gone. My food. They say we gotta leave Zooville or go to jail. They can't do that, can they?"

"No they can't." Henry's voice shook with rage. He turned to Caleb. "I'm heading to Zooville. Coming?"

Caleb followed Henry to the parking lot. He climbed into the passenger seat and listened to Henry rant as the van squealed into traffic.

"They showed up there like the damn Gestapo," Henry said. "You see that knot on May's arm from where one of them grabbed her?"

Caleb was livid. "How can they get away with that?"

"You're still living under the delusion that homeless people matter. That they got rights like the rest of us. Well, not according to the mayor or the cops!"

"I hope Dawn and Star are okay." Caleb filled Henry in on his conversation with Mrs. Eldridge. Interesting that Esther had told her about Wyman being Star's father. Esther was dead. Were the two events related? Markham knew, too, and planned to take advantage of the situation. That man was capable of anything. Had he killed Esther to protect his own interests?

If so, how did Gina and Stormy fit in? Stormy had been Wyman's friend—Dawn told Caleb that. But there was a falling out because Wyman wouldn't stop using. Could Wyman have killed Stormy and Esther to keep them from telling anyone about Star? But Gina barely knew Wyman. What would be his motive for killing her?

The van jarred as Henry pressed on the accelerator.

"I didn't know this thing could go over fifty." Caleb held onto the door handle to steady himself.

"I'm worried about my folks getting themselves in worse trouble if they try to fight the cops."

"I wonder who else knows what they're doing." Caleb gave it about a second's thought before he pulled out his cell and the card Jasmine Saul had given him. "You want to see how this city treats our homeless? Come see what the police are up to." He gave her directions to Zooville and told her she'd better hurry.

"Not bad, white man," Henry commented.

Ten minutes later they stood among the scattered remains of

Zooville. A rope was attached to the pole of the one remaining tent. The other end was connected to an ATV that revved as the driver took off, ripping the structure from the ground. About twelve law enforcement personnel poked through the other downed shelters.

"Sweet Jesus," Henry said.

The strange structure that had housed Luther had vanished. In its place was a huge bonfire that crackled as officers tossed in bundles of clothes and other belongings. One of them laughed when a blue kerchief caught fire and rose up like a flaming ghost.

Caleb walked over to one of the officers, a young man with a bristly crew cut and a complexion like lumpy oatmeal. "Is Detective Briscoe here?"

"Nope." He threw a paper sack that probably held someone's lunch into the flames. It burst into a blue and yellow blaze.

"Is this legal, what you're doing?" Caleb persisted.

"Don't see how that's your business." He moved on to another destroyed homestead.

"Nickel!" Henry yelled out from the other side of the fire. "Hey! Over here!"

Nickel limped over to him, one shoe on, one off. He was red-faced and shaky. Eyes skittering around, taking in the chaos.

"You okay, man?" Henry asked him.

"They burning everything." Nickel's voice trembled. "They took my medicine from me. The stuff you brought me. They was samples, remember? They said I couldn't have them."

"Who said that?" Henry glared at the officers.

"One of them men," Nickel said. "They running us off, Henry. How can they do that? We wasn't hurting nobody."

"Where's Johnny? Where's Dawn?" Caleb saw that the central tent had been torn down, poles like bones protruding from the canvas carcass.

"Gone. They left last night sometime. Maybe they knew what was coming because they up and left without a goodbye or nothing!" This seemed to disturb Nickel as much as the destruction by the police.

"Take it easy, man. You're coming with us. You can stay at Safe Harbor for a few days, till we can figure out what to do next."

Nickel nodded, clearly relieved to have somewhere to go.

"Gather up your buddies," Henry said. "We'll take as many as will fit in the van."

They wandered around the wreckage, studying the burned remains of someone's nest, someone's clothes, someone's food. The fire had an acrid smell, like burned plastic. Gray ashes flew skyward then drifted down like dirty snow.

Caleb wondered about Dawn and Star. He hoped they were safely away from Westville. Away from this devastation. Away from Markham Dougherty and Margaret Eldridge. Little Star didn't have a home, but at least she had two people who loved her.

A policeman held up a tattered cowboy hat that could have been Johnny's. He flung it in the air. The fire reached for it like a bright orange hand.

"I'd feel better if I could punch somebody," Henry said.

"Me too." Caleb noticed two new faces in the chaos, a petite woman and larger man—Jasmine Saul had brought a colleague. Jasmine walked right up to the buzz-cut officer and fired off a question. Her companion had a camera and clicked several photos before the policeman waved him away.

"Remind me never to piss you off," Henry whispered to Caleb.

Caleb watched as a police official tried to field questions from a persistent Jasmine. The photographer went to work getting shots of the fire, the crushed tents, and the distraught faces of the people who had lost their home.

"This better make the front page," Caleb said.

# Chapter Twenty-Three

An hour later, they had Nickel and six others in the lobby of Safe Harbor. They looked like refugees from war. Nickel sat closest to the reception desk, telling the story of what had happened to anyone who passed by in a manic explosion of words. Two of his friends sat near the door, warily eyeing the exit. The others just looked lost, and Caleb felt a renewed rage every time he looked at them. Henry was looking for something in the reception area, cursing as he fumbled through drawers and cabinets.

"Can I help?" Caleb asked.

"Need to do bed assignments. Can't find the log."

"Todd had it the other day," one of the volunteers said.

"Where is Todd?" Caleb wondered.

"He's missed his past three shifts. I'm telling the court, too. Man is so full of it. Acted like he cared about this place but disappears when we need his help." Henry kicked shut a cabinet door.

"I can check out his office if you want."

"Be my guest." Henry tossed him his keys.

Caleb unlocked the door to the tiny room that Todd had staked out as his office. A folding table for a desk, a wooden chair, a filing cabinet. And a computer, of course—just like the one in Caleb's office.

He didn't find the dormitory log. It wasn't in the filing cabinet and or under a stack of files on the table. He lifted Todd's ever-present clipboard and beneath it spotted a small set of keys.

Three very shiny keys, bunched together beside a small brown sack. Attached to the sack was a receipt: Moore's Hardware, dated two weeks ago. One key looked a lot like Henry's master key to the internal doors. Caleb compared it to the key that he'd just used—not quite a match. He tried it in Todd's door but it didn't fit there, either. Curious, Caleb wandered down the hall to his own office and slid the key into the lock. His door clicked open.

"Damn." Caleb pulled out his own key ring. He splayed it out on the desk, Todd's keys beside them. A brass one with a rectangular end caught his eye. He pressed it against the key to the front door of his home. A perfect duplicate.

"Damn," he repeated, dropping into the chair. Why would Todd want keys to his house? Caleb thought about that evening when he stepped out of his car and heard Cleo going ballistic in the back yard. Had Todd been the intruder?

Caleb looked at the empty place on the wicker desk where the computer had been. The computer that looked just like Todd's. What if Todd broke into his office and switched computers? What if it had been Todd who saved the emails to Gina, then planted his computer in Caleb's office?

Maybe he'd gone to Caleb's house for the same reason. Maybe he thought Caleb had a computer at home and wanted to plant evidence on the hard drive. He certainly had the skills to do just that. Of course, the only computer they had was Shannon's laptop—and it was in Maine.

Had Todd killed Gina? It was hard to imagine the geeky guy doing something so aggressive. But if he sent her the emails, he had to be worried about getting questioned. Given his legal troubles, he couldn't afford that kind of attention from the police. One thing was certain, Caleb would find Todd and demand some answers.

When he returned to the reception area, Henry was gone.

"He done got the log. Said he had to make another run to Zooville to see if anybody else needed a place to stay. I'm supposed to get them settled in the dorm." The volunteer pointed to Nickel and his friends. He tucked the green book under his arm and motioned that they should follow him.

Caleb eyed the rolodex on the desk and started flipping through cards, looking for contact info for Todd Weathers. After writing down the address, he left a note for Henry telling him where he'd gone.

He'd get answers from Todd, one way or the other.

● ● ●

Todd Weathers lived at 11012 South Pryor Drive in Carolton, a town-turned-suburb between Westville and Columbia. Caleb wrote the information on a piece of paper and stuck it in his pocket.

The drive to Carolton took twenty minutes, not due to distance but due to traffic. The swelling in Columbia's population over the past ten years had spilled over to the tiny towns around it, but the infrastructure hadn't caught up. County highways evolved into major arteries to feed the city, but hadn't been widened to accommodate the quadrupling of traffic. Caleb thought of all the people who had this drive for a commute. It gave him new appreciation for Westville and his seven-minute drive to work. But if Columbia continued to expand, his hometown might be the next victim.

When his cell phone rang, he pulled over to take the call.

"Detective Shannon McPherson reporting in."

"Hey there." Just hearing her voice warmed him. "You okay?"

"I'm good. I finally reached Suzanne Lyons. She was surprisingly chatty. She stays in touch with Bill Evers, though she insists there was no affair."

"What else did she say?"

"I don't think he's your killer. Suzanne said Bill is a recovering alcoholic. That was what they had in common—they went to AA meetings together. Then he fell off the wagon and lost his job. Got sober again a few years ago."

Caleb remembered Henry and Bill arguing about a meeting he didn't attend. Was Henry his AA sponsor? And then came Bill's unexplained absences. Maybe he started drinking again. The stress of recent events could have been the catalyst.

"Sorry if this doesn't help you," Shannon said.

"It does. I'm relieved Bill isn't the killer. And hopefully, this is going to get resolved soon."

"Just don't get yourself in any trouble," she cautioned. "I'm coming home, and I want you in one piece when I get there."

"Can't be soon enough for me. Love you." Caleb clicked off and pulled back into traffic. He remembered Pryor Drive intersected with Highway One on the east edge of town, near the river. He took a right and read the first mailbox: 2-0-4. He had a long way to go.

After about thirty blocks, the road transformed from smooth asphalt to gravelly, pot-hole ridden pavement. Cute suburb houses morphed into cement block duplexes and singlewides. Another half mile and Pryor turned into a clay dirt lane and Caleb half expected to hear dueling banjo music. Welcome to rural South Carolina.

He finally spotted Todd's address. A white house with black shutters and manicured azalea bushes. Purple ornamental cabbage lined the walkway leading to the front steps. Bright green rye grass glowed in the November sun. Neat, attractive. Out of place at the end of this God-forsaken road.

Nobody answered the doorbell, so he knocked on the door hard enough for it to rattle. Again, no response. He circled around the tiny home to try the back door and spotted a pick-up truck in the carport. When he banged a fist against the door frame, the door inched open.

"Todd? Are you in here?" Caleb said through the crack. He could see a pristine, very white kitchen. Stainless steel sink with a dish rack beside it holding two plates and a cup. Gleaming countertops from the eighties, white streaked with gold, held a lone coffee maker.

"Todd?" Caleb eased inside. He approached an avocado green refrigerator with three photo magnets attached: two of redheaded boys and the third, a picture of a smiling woman with curly brown hair. She looked very familiar: Gina. So maybe their relationship was more than Todd or Gina let on.

He moved into what looked like a living area, repeating, "Todd?" but getting no response. It was a small room, black leather sofa with tape along the back, two pale green upholstered chairs, a narrow table with three framed photos displayed on its top. Caleb lifted one of them: not a flattering photo, taken at too great a distance, but it was Gina, standing by her car. The others were also shots of her. Gina opening the door to Safe Harbor. Gina with Safe Harbor clients behind the building. Caleb studied her face in that shot, and realized it matched the expression in the photo on the fridge. Todd had cropped and enlarged her image for the close-up. But why? Did she even know he had taken these photos?

Someone was sending her emails, Todd had said. *Someone who wouldn't leave her alone.*

"Todd!" He yelled, ready for some answers.

Caleb started down a dark hall and stopped at an open door. A small room that held a desk, chair, and bookshelf. A cursor flickered on a flat-screen monitor on the desk. Curious, Caleb punched a key on the keyboard. Light filled the screen. In the center was a colorful icon with Todd's name beside it. Caleb jiggled the mouse to position the cursor and clicked.

"Holy–" He dropped into the chair. A collage appeared, layer upon layer of photos cascading into view. Gina. A thousand shots of Gina. In the parking lot. Coming from class. At the front door of Safe Harbor. How did Todd get them? Why were they on his computer?

So clearly Todd was obsessed with Gina. Had Todd loved her? Maybe. But too many of the photos looked like surveillance shots—the subject, Gina, unaware her picture was being taken. Had Todd stalked Gina? *Someone who wouldn't leave her alone.*

Caleb clicked the "Start" icon and tried to open the Internet access. He needed to get to Todd's emails. If Todd saved them on his hard drive, maybe they would match what had been sent from Caleb's computer.

"What do you think you're doing?" Todd's voice bellowed behind him. Instinctively, Caleb clicked off the monitor.

"You break into my house and help yourself to my computer?" He stomped over to Caleb, looming over him.

"I knocked, you didn't answer. So I came around the back. The door was unlocked," Caleb said in a rush. He tried to slide the chair back to stand but Todd's grabbed the armrest.

"You were in my personal files! You had no right! This is a gross invasion of my privacy!"

The quivering in Todd's chin could be from rage or fright. The knot coiling in Caleb's stomach was unadulterated fear. He had no idea what the cornered man might do.

"You're right, I shouldn't have looked. I apologize."

"Why are you here?"

"You haven't been back to Safe Harbor. I had some questions I wanted to ask you." Caleb wished he could snatch the words back as soon as he spoke them.

"Questions about what?" Todd leaned over Caleb, pushing

into his personal space.

"About Gina."

Todd's reaction surprised him. His face contorted, eyes squinching shut. "How dare you."

Caleb eyed the door. Maybe he could slip away while Todd tried to collect himself. But Todd grabbed Caleb by the back of his jacket collar and yanked him up. Caleb twisted, trying to free himself of Todd's grasp. Todd punched him square in the face.

"Hey!" Caleb grabbed his nose, feeling the blood drip from a nostril.

"Yell all you want. Nobody's going to hear you." Todd shoved him against the wall. Caleb tried to steady himself but Todd pushed him into the hallway and threw open another door. Before Caleb could resist, Todd hurled him inside. Caleb crashed to the floor.

The room was completely dark. He felt Todd's hands patting him down, finding his cell phone and tossing it out into the hallway. A second later, the door slammed shut. Caleb pulled himself up. Plastic crackled under him. He pinched it to determine thickness. Some kind of heavy-gauge plastic sheeting. But why?

He spotted a tiny stripe of light on one of the walls, not enough that he could actually see where he was or where furniture might be. He crawled towards it. He felt more plastic, pulled taut across what felt like a window. The four-inch tear offered the only illumination, and Caleb slid his fingers through it, trying to lengthen the cut.

"Damn." The plastic was tougher than he expected. He could barely touch glass. He felt for a window latch. There, he could just reach it when he angled his arm. He shoved it with his thumb, but the lock didn't budge. He shifted for better leverage, the plastic's crackling louder now, and gave another push. No luck. Maybe he could break the glass? But Todd would hear him.

Caleb moved along the wall, his hands chest high as they swiped the plastic, feeling for a light switch. He reached a corner, turned, continued his search. Reached the door. Stopped, the switch should be beside it. There! A bulge in the sheeting. He pushed until the bulge moved up, but no light came on.

He spent another ten minutes feeling the edges of the room,

hoping to find a tear or a small bit of loosened plastic. No luck. Discouraged, he sat on the floor and considered his options. Surely Henry would notice when he didn't return to Safe Harbor. But how long would it take for him to get concerned? Would he call the police?

The sensory deprivation in the black cave was already affecting him. Patience had never been his strong suit.

"Todd? Are you out there?!" he yelled.

He heard footsteps, and wondered if there was a way to position himself to overpower Todd. Before he could act, Todd slung the door open.

"What?"

"I have to use the bathroom."

"Too—" Todd seemed to have a change in heart. "Okay, I'll take you to the can." He grabbed Caleb's arm, his grip pinching Caleb's flesh. Caleb eyed the hallway to get his bearings. A quick stomp on Todd's foot and he'd be out the door.

"I wouldn't try it." Todd punctuated his comment with the cold barrel of a gun.

Caleb felt the weapon pressed against his ribs as Todd pushed him down the hall and into the bathroom. "Here you go. I'm right outside, in case you think you're going to climb out through the heating duct or something."

Caleb closed the door. The small tiled room had one window that Julia might fit through, not a six foot man. He turned on the faucet in case Todd was listening. The medicine cabinet had little to offer: an unopened box of Advil, bandages, and a small prescription bottle. Caleb read the label: Prozac .25 mg. prescribed six months prior, still full. Maybe if Todd had taken the anti-depressants, things wouldn't have spun out of control.

He flushed the toilet and pretended to wash his hands. He couldn't bear the idea of getting locked in the cave again. He needed to get Todd talking. Sympathize. Find out what had happened to Gina and why. He opened the door and Todd lifted the gun.

"You don't need that," Caleb said. "I'm not going to fight you."

"We'll see." Todd gestured with the weapon.

"Can we just talk for a little bit? I promise I won't put up a fight when it's time for me to go back in there but can't we just talk first?" Caleb averted his eyes, trying to appear as non-threatening as he could.

"Talk about what?"

"About Gina. I mean, I know you loved her. I just want to understand what happened." Caleb kept his voice gentle.

"I did," Todd answered. "I loved her."

"So can we just sit down and talk?"

Todd considered, his gun held steadily in his hand. Caleb couldn't quite read the intensity in his gaze. Anger? Hatred? He kept his own expression soft, even letting a little fear show. Finally Todd nodded. Caleb walked slowly to the living room and sat on the sofa.

"Don't move." Todd hurried to the kitchen and reappeared with a plastic cup. He placed it in front of Caleb. "Water. I figured you might be thirsty."

"Thanks." Caleb wasn't sure what to think about the offer. Was it an olive branch of sorts? Caleb lifted the cup, wondering if it was safe to drink.

"No poison, I promise." Todd sat down, the butt of his gun resting on his knee as he pointed it at Caleb.

Maybe if he took a sip, Todd would see it as an act of trust. He braved a few drops, relieved that tasted like water, no hint of drugs or anything else. Another taste felt so soothing to his dry throat that he drank half of it.

"So what do you want to know?" Todd asked.

"Did you know Gina before Safe Harbor?"

"No. I met her when you brought her to us."

If only Caleb hadn't, if he'd let her work all of her internship hours at Matthew's practice.

"Gina told me you were friends," Caleb said. "I didn't realize—"

"We didn't want anyone to know. Gina said there were rules she had to follow. And we didn't break them. We kept our relationship pure," Todd said. "And it would have stayed that way. But the others—the others tried to ruin it. Ruin us."

"Others?"

"You know." He gestured with the gun, his lips drawn in tight.

"Actually, I don't. But I want to understand, Todd." Caleb

noticed a few details he'd missed before. The gray stubble across Todd's chin. How unkempt his hair was. The red, raw cuticles on his fingers. And a sour smell—Todd hadn't showered. He was a compulsive man. What would it take to cause this kind of deterioration? And what did it mean?

"I hated Esther," Todd whispered. "Even before. She was such a mean-spirited person. Always so critical of everyone. So judgmental."

"Yes, she was." Caleb felt a hint of guilt talking about her this way, but colluding with Todd was too important.

Todd wiped his nose. "She saw me talking to Gina. That was all. We were just having a sandwich and laughing together. But that evening as I was leaving the shelter, Esther followed me out to my car. You wouldn't believe the things she said. She talked to me like I was some lesser life form, like I didn't deserve to be in the same room with someone like Gina. She said if she saw me with her again, she'd call my probation officer and have me hauled off to jail."

"That must have really upset you." Caleb used his therapist voice.

"How dare she treat me like that? After all I've done for Safe Harbor? How dare she?"

"Like you said, she was judgmental."

Two quick nods. "She liked belittling others. Maybe it made her feel big or something."

"She didn't appreciate the sacrifices you'd made."

"Exactly!" Todd bobbed up a little in his chair. "I tried to walk away from her. She was still jabbering at me but I ignored her and got in my truck. I was going to drive away but she just kept talking and talking. She said I wouldn't be finishing my time at Safe Harbor. She'd see to it that I never set foot in there again."

"She went too far." Caleb attempted to sound sympathetic.

"She didn't notice when I opened my glove compartment. Didn't see me reaching for—" He stopped speaking. Blinked, like he was coming out of a trance. Looked at Caleb like he'd forgotten he was there.

"It must have felt like you were trapped, Todd. Like you didn't have many options. It was unfair that she put you in that situation." Caleb met his stare, straining to keep his face neutral.

"I gripped the knife so the blade was hidden by my sleeve. I told her okay, maybe we should go talk to Bill Evers. I climbed out, walking beside her toward the building. And when we passed the dumpster, I knew that was the perfect place. And I knew what I had to do. I don't think she felt much," he rushed to say. "I was careful, I knew where I had to put the blade. The details are so important."

"Yes, they are," Caleb replied, his mouth gone dry again. He reached for the water and drank. "It's good that you were careful like that. How did you know exactly what to do?"

Todd moved the gun to his other hand and stretched his fingers. "I knew because she wasn't my first."

Oh God. It was like the oxygen had been sucked from the room. Two murders, at least. It seemed to get easier for Todd with experience. Caleb didn't want to be added to the list. His hand quivered as he returned the cup to the table.

"Was Stormy the first?" he asked, his voice more tenuous than he meant.

"Stormy," Todd parroted, shaking his head. "Did you ever meet him?"

Caleb shook his head.

"Stormy was a filthy man. Had disgusting black spots in his teeth. Gunk under his fingernails. His clothes didn't fit and had probably never seen a washing machine. He smelled like he hadn't bathed in years. Like some beast."

Caleb wondered what it said about Todd's state of mind that *he* hadn't bathed or washed his hair. Things falling apart for him.

"And he had the nerve to talk with my Gina," Todd went on. "Gina was an angel. She would talk to anyone. How dare he take advantage like that!

"You and Henry think Safe Harbor serves a purpose, but don't you realize how it is just perpetuating the problem? All the men like Stormy—they come, they bring their stink, their dark lives of drugs and drink. And Gina, my angel, she thought she could save everyone of them. But they don't want to be saved."

Caleb heard venom in Todd's tone, the fracture in his normal self-control.

"Stormy talked to her outside the shelter," Todd continued. "Brought her a flower he'd picked because she had been nice to him the day before. Talked to her about their hometown, about how Gina knew his brother. And then . . . Then he kissed her! She tried to pull away but he held on. I grabbed him by his filthy hair and wanted to beat the crap out of him but Gina said no, that Stormy didn't mean anything, and Stormy ran off before I could finish with him. She said she just wanted to forget it but I could see in her eyes how it had hurt her."

Todd's hand shook as he gestured with the gun. Escalating. "And you wanted to protect her," Caleb said.

"But Stormy came back. It was starting to rain and thunder, and there was Stormy asking for Gina. Thank God she'd gone home for the day." Todd paused, looking down at the table. "Do you want more water?"

"No thanks." The niceties felt perverse in this discussion about murder.

"Why did he come back?" Todd asked. "What kind of stupid retard would think he could have someone like Gina? Did he think I'd let him touch her again?"

"Of course not." Caleb leaned back against the sofa, his body relaxing into the cushions. Not really a bad couch. Comfortable. He felt curiously calm—all the panic from before had evaporated.

"She needed protection." Todd eased back, too, as though mimicking Caleb's composed posture. "I would never let someone like Stormy near her again."

"So what did you do?" Caleb realized he wasn't scared anymore, and Todd seemed more trusting. That had to be a good thing.

"Why don't you finish your drink?" Todd said.

"Okay." Caleb guzzled the last of the water, licking his lips like Cleo when he was done.

"Want more?" Todd asked.

"Sure."

Todd tucked the gun under his arm and reached for Caleb's cup. Caleb closed his eyes, listening as Todd clomped into the kitchen. A moment later, the cup was in Caleb's hand again.

"So we were talking about Stormy. You want to hear the rest of it?"

"Sure." Caleb sipped, getting almost sleepy.

"I went out back where Stormy was. He stood there, looking

like a filthy drowned rat. I got to my truck first—I had to get the knife. Then I called Stormy over. I apologized for being so hard on him before. He said he understood, but that he was turning his life around and he hoped I could see that he'd never hurt someone as wonderful as Gina. How could he even say her name."

"You hated it. Really hated it." Caleb thought about the word "hate." How it rhymed with "late" and "ate" and even "eight." Weight. Wait?

"Yeah." Todd smiled him. "Most of the staff had gone home so we were by ourselves out there. I even put my hand on his shoulder and guided him over to the alley. He was yammering about how he had a twelve-step meeting that night and I spun him around and said, 'I don't think so.' He looked perplexed. That was the expression frozen on his face when I sunk the knife into his chest. The funny thing is, I planned to move Stormy's body. I had to go back into to Safe Harbor to get a tarp to put him in but when I returned, he was gone. Vanished. Freaked me out at first, I thought maybe I hadn't really killed him. I got rid of any signs that he'd been there, just a few spots of blood already getting washed away by the rain. I was sure the police would come after me. But then I learned someone had dragged his body all the way to the river."

"Wow." Caleb wondered why that word seemed to fill his entire being. It echoed inside him, bouncing off his ribs and intestines and streaming through his arteries. Wowness felt exhilarating so he pantomimed the word again, opening his mouth wide as a chasm to let all the letters out.

"You feel pretty good, don't you Caleb?" Todd placed the gun on the floor beside him.

Caleb realized he should reach for it. He should pick it up and point it at Todd and get out of here. But his limbs wouldn't comply. He felt wobbly and disconnected. He felt . . . drugged.

"What . . . what did you give me?" Caleb fought a flutter of panic, like he could almost slide outside himself and look down at his paralyzed body. He had tasted nothing in the water. Why had he drunk all of it? What had he done to himself?

"Funny thing about doing community service at Safe Harbor. You meet all kinds of interesting people. Got this stuff from a kid for about twenty bucks. Pretty good deal, I thought." Todd's voice had a strange echo to it. His smile seemed to twist his entire face.

"What stuff?" Oh God. Caleb felt smushy, his brain stretching and contracting and distorting everything he saw.

"Stuff to make you feel very good. Stuff to keep you from fighting me." Todd lifted the gun, checked the clip, and laid it in his lap. His movement left a trail of colors in the air. Caleb thought again about the gun, wishing he could take it from Todd but it wasn't possible in his present state.

"What . . . it is?"

"It's nothing to worry about. It's called GHB. It makes you happy. And very pliable." Todd laughed, and Caleb could see vibrations in the air current around him.

GHB sounded familiar. Something Matthew had talked about. A dangerous new drug that kids used at parties and clubs. The phrase "date rape" came to mind.

"You . . . gave it to Gina?"

Todd's expression hardened, lips pulled taut, eyes averting his. "Not at first. But later, when she was upset. I wanted to see her happy again. I wanted her to smile and know that I would take care of her. That she had nothing to worry about. Don't you see? All I wanted to do was protect her."

Caleb tried to focus. This was how Todd's squirrelly brain justified what he had done, all to protect Gina and his fantasy of their relationship. But Gina was dead. Dead. The air around him rippled as he exhaled. He wanted to laugh, to see if the tiny waves would undulate, as his mind struggled to stay focused on his situation.

"But what happened with Gina?" Caleb fought to keep his gaze on Todd's face and not on the shift in air currents.

Todd lifted a hand, his index finger extended. "Maybe I pushed a little too hard. I mean, that was the error. I knew what she and I could have, *knew* it. But she was young and it scared her. I didn't recognize the mistake at first, perhaps if I had, I would have understood why she took a step back from me. Why she needed time and space to process. Because here's the thing: there was a kind of power in our connection. It had to overwhelm someone as young as Gina and I didn't realize that."

Caleb watched how he gestured with the finger. Professorial.

"Are you following what I'm saying?" Todd asked.

"I am. Uhmm. I'm trying to," Caleb conceded. "She took a step back."

"Good, Caleb. Very good. Now why don't you finish your drink?"

Caleb lifted the drink like he had no choice but to comply. But he did have a choice. And there was no way he was imbibing any more of that poison. He pressed the cup to his lips and pretended to drink, feeling curiously proud of this act of rebellion. He placed the cup on the floor, his hands trailing up to the narrow table where the framed photos of Gina rested. "Gina was an amazing woman," Caleb prompted.

"She was my angel. I've never loved anyone the way I loved her. Not my wife. Not my sons. Nobody. Have you ever loved someone like that? Like there is nothing you wouldn't do for them?"

"Yes," Caleb answered. Shannon's face filled his thoughts, radiant and smiling. Shannon would be coming home soon, so he had to stay alive for her to come home to. He had to get away from Todd.

"She came for dinner one night. I'm not much of a cook," Todd gave him a sheepish smile. "But I grilled steaks. She insisted on bringing dessert. Brownies she made herself."

"An official date," Caleb said.

"Yes. It started out great. We sipped wine and she talked about what it would be like to be a social worker. About her career plans." Todd paused. He seemed to be measuring his words carefully. "And she talked about you."

"Me?"

"Don't act surprised. I know what was going on, even if she didn't. She adored you, Caleb. But what she didn't realize was how you were manipulating her. Toying with her feelings."

"No!" Caleb said, louder than he meant to. "I didn't. She was my student, I would never—"

"Please, Caleb. You're a man. Having a beautiful woman like Gina practically worshipping you, of course you took advantage. I'm not saying you slept with her—it hadn't gone that far yet. But I knew what you had planned."

"You're w-wrong." Caleb's effort at self-defense was feeble at best. He could still understand what Todd said, just couldn't answer back with any substance.

"She lit up when she talked about you. Did you even realize that?" Todd's face contorted into an expression of disgust. "I tried to tell her she was wrong, that you would only hurt her in the end, but she didn't listen. She always saw the good in everybody. Even you."

"It wasn't—"

Todd lifted his finger again, this time to silence Caleb. "Our first fight was about you. Bet you didn't know that. But I couldn't stand for her to be upset so I changed the subject. We ate her brownies and sipped more wine, but I could feel her pulling away. She kept glancing at the clock. I wondered if maybe she planned to meet you somewhere."

Caleb shook his head. He was like a marionette with cut strings. Snip, snip, snip. How long would it take for the GHB to work its way out of his system?

"And here's where I made my mistake. She spotted the photo of her on the fridge. I wanted her to know how important she was to me. How much I loved her. So I showed her the other pictures. The ones in my office. And those—" Todd pointed to the coffee table. "She said they made her uncomfortable. That she didn't know I'd been photographing her. She said it was a violation of her privacy."

"Wasn't it?" Caleb asked.

"Maybe. But I had no malicious intent. That's what I tried to explain to her. But she couldn't seem to hear it. She had made up her mind and—" Todd closed his eyes.

"She thought you were stalking her, didn't she?" Caleb tried to imagine what it had been like for her to glimpse this side of Todd: his obsession. How terrifying it must have been.

"No! She misunderstood. I tried to tell her that. I couldn't hurt her, not ever. She was my angel."

"But you did hurt her." Caleb's words came out more clearly. At least he'd stopped hallucinating air currents. That had to be a good sign.

"I thought she would understand if I gave her enough time. But I needed her here, with me, so that I could show her how I felt. So that I could protect her."

"So you put her in that room," Caleb said, suppressing a shudder. "How long did you keep her in there?"

"Just a couple of days."

Caleb tried not to imagine the horror Gina lived in that black cave of a room. The tiny slit in the thick plastic—had that been her attempt at escape? "And what happened?"

Todd's gaze flicked away to stare at her picture. "I thought she would come to understand how much I loved her. How I adored her—the way she adored you."

"She didn't. You have that wrong." Caleb wasn't stumbling over his words, and he relished that bit of control. Maybe soon he'd be able to control his muscles. Then he could escape.

"And so I put the GHB in her tea. Just to help her relax. To make her happy. That was all I wanted to do."

"What happened to Gina?"

"I gave her too much. I didn't mean to. I didn't know. I would have never—" His voice broke. Tears spilled from his eyes. "She fell asleep and I couldn't wake her up. I tried everything. I shook her. Put her in the shower and ran cold water on her. Nothing worked. Nothing. So I held her, felt her pulse slow to almost nothing. Felt her breath become just tiny wisps. Felt her slipping away."

Todd wiped his face.

"But that wasn't how she died," Caleb said.

"When I realized that she wasn't coming back to me, I knew I had to take her to the river. I figured if the police found her body near where they found Stormy, they'd think some homeless tramp had killed her. I had to stab her, so her death would match Stormy's and Esther's, but she didn't feel it. She was almost gone by then. I just helped it end more quickly."

"Pretty damn noble of you," Caleb said, before he could stop himself.

Todd's head shot up. He glared at Caleb and grabbed the gun. "Did you finish the drink? Did you?"

"Uhmm. Sure." Stupid. Caleb should have pretended to be stoned.

Todd leapt from his seat and seized the cup from the floor. "You liar! Do you think you can trick me? Do you think I'm a fool?"

Caleb struggled to stand but Todd shoved him back into the sofa, pressing the barrel of the gun against his head.

He pushed the cup against Caleb's lips. "This is your fault you know. I had a more humane death in mind for you when I locked you in the freezer. Just go to sleep and not wake up. But you blew that chance. So now you have two choices: You drink this now—all of it—or I shoot you right here. Makes no difference to me."

Caleb saw icy determination in Todd's glare. Caleb's choice was to die now or maybe die later. He opened his mouth and let the poison come in.

Todd sat on the coffee table, the gun angled toward Caleb, and waited.

"What now?" Caleb asked.

"I'll give you a little time. Want you nice and relaxed. Then we're going to take a little ride."

That didn't sound good. He wondered if there was any way to fight the effects of the drug. But so soon, he felt it, the slackening of his resolve, his muscles turning to over-stretched elastic, the strange calm that sucked away any impulse to fight or resist. He didn't even move when Todd left the room, or when he returned, carrying the fat roll of duct tape. He held out his arms when instructed to, watching as Todd wound the tape around his wrists. Noticed the strange, bitter taste of the tape when Todd slapped it across his mouth.

# Chapter Twenty-Four

"I think you're ready now," Todd said affably. "Time for a trip."

"Wrrr . . ." Caleb choked out.

"Where else? To the river. Your body will be discovered close to where the others were. Horrible thing, that crime spree. Some drug addict tramp probably killing them. Good reason to close the shelter and get rid of the scum trying to take over our city."

Caleb wondered how Captain Bentille's words managed to come out of Todd's mouth and feared he might be hallucinating again. He felt a tug on his wrists as Todd yanked him up and out the back door. Caleb nearly tripped down the narrow steps leading to the carport.

"Easy, Cowboy," Todd said jovially, like they were drunken friends. Caleb squinted into the setting sun, willing his body to resist but having no way to govern it. He sent the message "Run!" to his legs but all they managed was an uncertain step away from his captor that had him teetering and almost crashing to the ground. Todd slammed him against the truck before unlocking the camper shell and tailgate. When Todd tossed him inside, Caleb landed hard, like gravity had been turned up a notch. The ridged floor of the bed felt cold against his hip and vibrated when Todd started the engine.

Caleb tried to sit up. If he could get his hands free, he could stabilize himself. If he could get his hands free, maybe there'd be a chance for escape.

He wiggled his index fingers and managed to poke through the tape. As the truck hit another bump he fell over, his ribs smashing against the wheel well. He righted himself and tried to think through the wooziness in his brain. *Duct tape off.*

With a fingertip he scratched at the tape over his mouth,

tugged off a corner of it, and jerked. *Yes!* He took in a mouthful of delicious air. Next step, hands. He studied the duct tape, but the shadowed light made it difficult to see. He brought his hands to his lips and felt for a loose edge, but a turn had him tottering sideways, his head banging against the camper shell latch.

The truck took a hard curve the left and Caleb fell over and decided to stay that way. Pointless to sit up, only to be knocked back down. And futile to keep chomping at the duct tape. What were his chances against Todd anyway? His head hurt, he still felt half-drunk, and Todd had the gun.

With the next turn they were off pavement. He peered out the streaked window to see trees. A tall pale green water tower. A rocky hill that seemed familiar.

Caleb needed a plan. Giving up couldn't be an option, nor could going willingly with Todd. He had to run, no matter how dizzy he felt. The truck squealed to a stop. Caleb bent his knees and waited.

He heard Todd rounding the truck. Heard the squeak of the camper shell latch and the thud as Todd lifted it open. Caleb lay perfectly still as though unconscious and waited for his chance.

"Wake up, Caleb," Todd said jovially as he dropped the tailgate.

*Now!* Caleb kicked Todd in the chest with all the force he could muster. As Todd toppled over to land on his butt, Caleb jumped from the truck bed, a little unsteady but able to get his legs moving, and ran.

The hill . . . he did remember it. Henry parked near this spot earlier when they visited Zooville. Maybe Henry and the others were still there.

He slid on a wide rock, also familiar, and his bound hands grabbed a branch for balance. He clambered up the rocky slope. He could hear Todd running behind him but didn't dare look to see how close. He kept moving.

Wyman squatted in the woods and watched. There was hardly anything left of Zooville. No sign of Dawn or Johnny. May and Lanie and that crazy guy Nickel had all gone, run off by the police just like that man in the suit had predicted. It made Wyman sick to see it.

The river roared along like nothing had happened. The setting sun flashed orange streaks in the water. He needed to find something to eat. He still had five bucks left from his allowance tucked in his shoe so if he could find Big John, he could have a little something else before he bedded down for the night. He stood, his knee creaking like a door hinge. He wove through the trees until he reached the path leading back to the road. A brisk wind blew up the hill so he stopped to pin his jacket.

"Help! Somebody! *Help!*"

Wyman jumped at the man's shout, his gaze skittering about looking for the source. He spotted a flash of red, heard the crunch of footsteps from someone running up the path.

Then he heard the gun shot.

"Help!" Louder this time. The man must have fallen because Wyman heard a thud, then a groan. Not something he would get in the middle of. Not with a gun involved. He turned, ready to run the other way, when he saw the man scrambling to his feet. The redheaded man, Caleb, the one who came to the hospital and talked to him in the alley.

"Wyman?" Caleb lifted his hands and Wyman saw how they'd been tied together with silver tape. Then came another shot.

Wyman grabbed him and shoved him behind a tree. He could see the other guy coming. Glasses. Mean.

It was Todd. The man from Safe Harbor, the son of a bitch who killed Wyman's only friend. He had talked to Stormy like they were buddies then shoved a knife into his chest. Tossed Stormy's body to the ground like he was garbage. Left him bleeding to death in the dirt.

Wyman looked over at the redheaded man, then back at the killer and knew what he had to do. He kept perfectly still. All he could hear was the panting breath of the man beside him. He spotted a pinecone by his foot. The gunman cocked his head, listening. Wyman hurled the cone as far as he could up the path; leaves crunched where it landed. Todd hurried towards the noise, but lost his balance. Wyman lunged.

They crashed to the ground, Wyman grinding his fist into the man's chest, his other hand reaching for the gun.

"Wyman!"

From the corner of his eye Wyman saw Caleb coming, sliding on his butt down the path to where they struggled. His foot hit Todd in the knee and that just made him madder. Todd spun around fast as a rattler, trying to bring his gun down but Wyman blocked his arm. Caleb got to his knees and groped for the weapon with his taped hands.

The echoing thunder of a gunshot froze all three of them.

"Caleb! Get back!" A woman's voice. Wyman rolled to his side as two others rushed up the path. A black woman and Henry, his friend from Safe Harbor.

"Wyman!" Caleb yelled. "Come here! Get away from Todd!"

Wyman didn't know what to do. He liked the man, Caleb. He liked Henry. But he was pretty sure the woman was police and the man under him still had the gun. The man who killed his friend.

"Wyman!" Caleb insisted. "Move!"

Another shot, beneath him. The shot went wild, Todd trying to aim the gun at Caleb but Wyman gripping his arm.

"Wyman!" Henry's voice. "Back off! Trust me, okay?"

Moving wasn't really an option. Not with that gun still held by Stormy's killer. He saw Caleb scrambling to his feet and Henry helping him to safety. The woman came closer, her pistol held steady.

Todd tensed beneath him. Wyman understood. Todd wouldn't give up. Couldn't. Had to keep pushing, had to get his way even when it was impossible. It was why he killed Stormy, so he could have the girl. But Todd wasn't going to kill anybody else.

"Wyman, back away. Please." Caleb's voice shook. "Claudia will lock him away in jail and he will never, ever get out. I promise you that."

Wyman looked at the policewoman, who held the gun as steady as stone. "Let him up. He won't hurt anybody else." She spoke with tough confidence.

And for some reason, he believed her.

Wyman tried to remember the last time he'd ridden in a cab. Once when Markham paid the driver to pick him up from a gas station and bring him back to the Willows. Funny, he was heading to the Willows now. Only this time, it was Wyman's idea.

The cabbie didn't want to give him a ride until Wyman showed him the cash. Then he did exactly what Wyman asked: called three other cabs to meet them at the Willows. Wyman promised him a fifty dollar tip for his trouble, but that was okay. He had money to spare.

It was hard to believe what had happened. After arresting Todd, they took Wyman to the police station and Wyman thought he'd be put in jail, too. But instead, they just asked a bunch of questions. Markham showed up, acting all nice like he really gave a shit, and all Wyman could think about was how Markham had screwed up too many people's lives. Markham deserved to be locked up just like Todd.

When the door opened again, it was his mother. The police left him alone with her which was maybe worse than being arrested. She sat across from him, looking small and caved in on herself, and wouldn't look him in the eye. She asked how he was and he said, "Fine," and she said she'd heard he'd help the police catch a killer. He wanted to hear pride in her voice, but it wasn't there.

She placed her shiny black purse in the chair beside her. He asked how Nora was and she told him Nora was close to being engaged and the Senator's heart trouble seemed to be better on his new medication. Wyman hadn't asked about the Senator.

His voices started then. *She hates you!* He thought they were probably right.

His mother asked where the restroom was. He pointed across the hall. When she left the bag there, he wasted no time opening it, picking through the wallet, and fingering the cash she kept inside—all the bills in order, facing the same direction, just like when he was a kid. He snagged four hundred and sixty, clicked the purse shut, and before she came back he was out the door. Markham could chat with his mother and the police as long as he wanted—Wyman had something important he had to do.

*Do it!*

The cab turned into the dusty driveway leading up to the Willows. Soon the other taxis arrived, and Wyman told them all to park out front and wait for him. He figured Rhetta had served the residents a crappy supper a couple of hours ago, then gone to the big house. But it wasn't so late that they'd all be in bed. He trotted up to the front stoop and passed four familiar faces sitting in folding chairs under a tree. He waved and went inside.

Lord, the stink. Markham was the sorriest son of a bitch that ever lived for making people have to smell that all the time. Wyman went up the hall, pounding on doors, telling everyone, "You got to go outside! There's a surprise!"

Jacob emerged from his room, barefoot, hair all shaggy. "Wyman? What's going on?"

"Grab your shoes and your jacket and go outside. I have a big surprise for all of you." Wyman gave him a genuine smile, adrenalin pushing him on. He couldn't wait. In just minutes, he would do what he'd waited ten years to do.

Jacob shuffled out of the room, wearing untied canvas shoes and a sweatshirt. He took a step towards Wyman but Wyman shook his head and pointed to the door. Jacob nodded and obeyed.

Getting the old lady two doors down to budge took a lot of effort. Her roommate, a bony black woman Wyman hadn't met before, hooked an arm under hers and helped Wyman guide her out to the porch. He looked in the yard. Thirteen people were gathered under the tree. That should be everybody, but he checked all the doors again just to be sure. Last stop: Markham's office. He jimmied open the desk drawer and grabbed another two hundred dollars. Perfect.

He ran outside. He felt energy in every inch of his being, flowing, surging, carrying him. So soon, it would all be as it should be.

He went to Jacob first. His friend Jacob. Jacob the lonely. Jacob the scared. "I need your help, Jacob. You're not going to want to do what I tell you but you've gotta do it. I need you to trust me."

Jacob's eyes widened. "Uhmmm. Okay."

Wyman pulled out the wad of bills, catching the eye of all the other Willows residents. "I need you to get in one of those cabs. You're all going to Safe Harbor."

"What?"

Wyman flipped through the cash, grabbed a fifty, and folded it in Jacob's hand. "Go. You'll understand later."

Jacob chewed at his lip as he looked over at the cab. The other people moved closer, hands outstretched. They looked like ghosts. They probably hadn't held real cash dollars in a long time.

"Go!" Wyman prodded Jacob towards one of the cars. He looked scared but he did what Wyman said.

"Now the rest of you, listen!" Wyman held up the money. "Y'all get in the cabs, and I'll give you some money too. But not till you do as I say."

There was a mad rush for the cars. Four residents tried to squeeze in one back seat and it reminded Wyman of playing musical chairs back in kindergarten. Jacob helped the old lady into one cab and told the others to spread out among the waiting taxis.

*Do it! Do it!* The voice screamed in Wyman's head.

Yes, yes he would. He went to each driver and gave him fifty, instructing them to drive straight to Safe Harbor. Each resident received a twenty dollar bill, and arguing commenced about who owed what to who, bills being snatched from one hand to another.

"Hey! Everybody keeps their own. I mean it!" Wyman sounded fierce, sort of like Johnny.

It worked. The cash was handed back, stuck into pockets, sleeves, and brassieres. "Now go."

As the taxis drove away, Wyman saw Jacob watching him from the back window. He waved goodbye.

*Do it!* Yes, he would now.

The door to the shed was locked, but he used a brick to bust through the rotten wood. He found the gas can. He twisted open the cap from the nozzle and breathed in the scent. His nerves tingled, wanting more. Not yet.

*Do it! Do what you're here to do.*

Ten minutes later, Wyman stood in the kitchen of the Willows, mesmerized by the flames that licked the walls and chewed away at the wooden tables. Brilliant yellow light, climbing the molding, bending and shifting as it danced across the floor, as graceful as a ballet. He lowered the gas can. He felt the rush of heat as the flame inched closer. Delicious.

Was there anything so beautiful? The fire crackled as it touched the billowing curtains and bloomed into larger life. Yes.

Yellow and orange and green swirling in the blaze. He imagined a woman, reaching out, reaching for him.

"Dance with me," she said.

*Dance*, said the voice.

And so he did.

# Chapter Twenty-Five

Caleb loosened the tie that Shannon insisted he put on for the gala. She wore a simple black dress with a sea-blue scarf that made her eyes look like pale sapphires. He would never grow tired of looking into them, not in a hundred million years.

Bill Evers came over, noticed they were empty handed, and waved to a waiter. Caleb reached for two glasses of champagne. Bill looked better. Two months out of rehab, now back to working part-time at Safe Harbor.

"Good turn out," Bill said.

"An interesting mix of folks." Caleb looked over at Mayor Cramfield, all decked out in gray tweed and a smile that looked as fake as a toothpaste commercial. On the other side of the room, Nickel with Cindy Lawton, dressed in the best dress-clothes Goodwill had to offer, hovered close to Henry as though afraid some of the other guests might bite. Jasmine Saul stood beside Matthew while her photographer friend snapped shots of the Westville elite making their entrances. Caleb led Shannon over to them.

"Shannon!" Matthew grabbed her and kissed her cheek. "Damn, it's good to see you."

"Great to be here. Great to be warm." She turned and introduced herself to Jasmine.

"This boyfriend of yours got me the best story of the year." Jasmine flashed Caleb a wicked grin. "The paper's entering it in the South Carolina Media awards contest."

Jasmine had done a great job on the story. Front page shots of the decimation of Zooville, police officers tossing the meager belongings of a resident into the bonfire. Close-ups of the displaced homeless, some with tears, some covered with soot from the fire. A picture of little Star's stuffed bear buried under trash. Letters of protest filled the editorial page for over a week. The mayor, desperate to calm down his citizenry, awarded Safe Harbor a twenty-thousand dollar increase in city funding—not much, but a start. Squawks from developers that had been interested in the Safe Harbor property were quickly silenced by all the attention. And then came the idea of this gala/art auction. Sam Knowles, esteemed sculptor, challenged his colleagues in the art world to develop a piece of art around the theme "Finding Home." Each donated piece was then auctioned off, profits going directly to Safe Harbor. Sam's work, two ten-foot hands with fingers folded like corners, the stylized sign for "hope," now stood as a permanent installation at the entrance. The mayor would not be foolish enough to touch Safe Harbor now that it housed a Sam Knowles original.

Caleb scanned the crowded room for his brother, spotting him with an interpreter talking to two county councilmen. He had on a new gray suit that probably cost more than Caleb's monthly salary and a braided thread bracelet on his right hand—a gift from Isaiah. When Sam saw Caleb, he crossed to him, motioning to Henry to join them. "Jackpot," Sam said.

"Huh?" Henry asked.

"We made sixty thousand on the auction. But get this—an anonymous donor just sent a check for a hundred thousand!"

Henry stared at Sam as if he'd started speaking Swahili.

"Henry?" Caleb nudged him. As new Operations Director for Safe Harbor, Henry had his hands full. Now, at least, he could hire more staff. Of course, Caleb wouldn't mind if that took a while. Matthew had agreed he could continue at Safe Harbor, at least a few hours a week, until all the vacancies had been filled. After that, well, Caleb would find a way to stay involved.

"An anonymous donor?" Henry looked at Caleb. They both knew Margaret Eldridge had probably sent the money out of guilt about her son and grandchild.

Caleb often thought about Wyman. It made him sad to think that Wyman never broke free of his addictions, to crack, to fire. To self-destruction. Destroying the Willows put Markham Dougherty out of business. The clients stayed at Safe Harbor until Henry and Caleb located new group homes for them. The experience had badly shaken up Jacob, but at least he was coming for therapy now. Maybe Jacob's story would have a happier ending than Wyman's. Caleb hoped so.

They never found Wyman's body. The fire burned hotter than a kiln. Caleb liked to imagine that Wyman survived. And that one day, Wyman Carter would walk through the front door of Safe Harbor again—and find himself a temporary home.

## About the Author

Carla Damron draws on her experiences as both a southerner and a clinical social worker in her short stories and mysteries, including KEEPING SILENT (2001), and SPIDER BLUE, (2005). Her interest in exploring social issues through the vehicle of fiction led Damron back to school; she hopes to complete her MFA in Creative Writing in 2011. She continues to work in the field of mental health.

Damron resides outside Columbia, SC, where she enjoys life with her husband, their small herd of animals, and a garden that grows despite her neglect.

CPSIA information can be obtained at www.ICGtesting.com
Printed in the USA
241534LV00001B/56/P

9 781933 523897